NEWS FROM THE NAIL BAR

Christy Powell

News from the Nail Bar

Christy Powell

ISBN: 978-0-9569993-0-6

This book is published by Christy Powell in conjunction with Writersworld Limited and is available to order from most book shops and Internet book retailers throughout the United Kingdom.

Copy edited by Sue Croft

Cover design by Jag Lall

Printed and bound by www.printondemand-worldwide.com

www.writersworld.co.uk

WRITERSWORLD
2 Bear Close
Woodstock
Oxfordshire
OX20 1JX
England

The text pages of this book are produced via an independent certification process that ensures the trees from which the paper is produced come from well managed sources that exclude the risk of using illegally logged timber while leaving options to use post-consumer recycled paper as well.

Acknowledgements

Thank you so much to all the team at Writersworld who have done a great job putting this book together: Graham Cook, my editor Sue Croft, and Jag Lall for his creative brilliance. Thank you also to my agent Simon Trewin, who gave me the confidence to get my book published.

I owe a ton of gratitude to Claire Gill for taking the time to read my book and getting it through the door of United Artists. Also to Clare Keswick and her inspirational team at Flamingo Productions.

Thank you to all my family who have been unwavering in their support. To my mum who created the caricatures for each chapter, allowing those who are not so inclined to read, the option to just look at the pictures - her artistic talent knows no bounds. A special mention to my three-year-old, Carla, who has had to suffer me working on the same manuscript for her entire life. I would also like to thank my sister Suze, who has the same warped sense of humour as me and laughed out loud while reading each new draft.

To my wonderful husband Nick, for supporting me when I decided to leave my perfectly good day job to go into the nail business, something I knew nothing about. Also for taking it well when I told him I wouldn't be using a pen name for this book.

Thank you to my great friend Bumble Sparrow, who suffered five years of hysterical highs and crashing lows while running our nail bar company. I could not and would not have wanted to do it without her.

A huge thank you to all my friends who have helped this book get published and been so enthusiastic about the idea from the start. I could never have imagined or asked for more. A special mention to Will Turner, Adam Keswick, Jimeale Jorgensen, Blake and Leini Ireland, Annabel Byng, Maddy Green, Yana Peel, Luli Orchard and Jade Yan. Thank you.

Dedication

For Lara

Contents

Monday 19th September 2011

From: Rebecca Harris rebeccaharris@thenailbar.co.uk **19.09.11 12:09**
To: Joe Doyle jdoyle@doylebrothers.com
Subject: Kensington Building Works

Joe,

WHAT THE HELL IS GOING ON? The Kensington Nail Bar is a complete shambles. I went there this morning and only one of your guys was on site. Where is the rest of the team?

As you know, we are planning a huge launch party at the beginning of next month. Invitations have already been sent out and Ms Foreman is flying in from America for it. The place looks like a tornado went through. I can't see how you can possibly be finished on time? I'm heading back there in an hour so please make sure you're there.

Rebecca

From: Rebecca Harris **19.09.11 12:14**
To: Phoebe Combes phoebe@thenailbar.co.uk
Subject: nail files

Did any of the glass nail files survive or were they all smashed in transit? If we can salvage enough for the goodie bags, that would be something. Could you send an email to the Nail Corp distribution office? I think the new woman there is called Margarite – see if they can get us a new stock before the opening. You might want to mention the word "bubblewrap" to them while you're at it.

Thanks

Bex

From: Rebecca Harris **19.09.11 12:19**
To: Barbara Foreman barbaraforeman@nailcorp.com
Subject: news re Kensington

Barbara,

How was the trip to Chicago?

I had a site visit this morning at Kensington and all is looking good. Everything is going according to plan for opening at the beginning of October. Joe is on schedule and I'm confident that he'll be finished in 10 days, which allows us plenty of time to get the place ready for business and the opening party.

I've made a few staff changes recently, which seem to be working well. Do you remember Phoebe Combes from Accounts? She was

1

only part-time but she approached Felicity when she heard we were going to outsource most of the accounting. She was keen to be part of our new PR department. Her résumé was so impressive that Felicity has put her in charge of the department, and it's been flourishing. She's been onto both Tara Palmer-Tomkinson's and Laura Bailey's agents already about coming to the opening party, and both agents are sounding positive, which should guarantee lots of press coverage. We have two others in her team and they're all doing a great job. I have asked her to photocopy all press clippings and have them sent over to you on a regular basis.

Unfortunately, Rick Van Shear cannot do the flowers for the party. He's been booked for months to do a celebrity birthday that day which he absolutely cannot cancel. However, I have several other top florists who are very keen, so I don't anticipate any problem finding a substitute.

Pink Mango is doing the catering and I have a friend called Tom at Goedhuis & Company who has given us an excellent deal on the champagne and wine.

We have the goodie bags all ready with Nail Corp's new French Manicure range and pink glass nail files, which look fantastic.

I understand from Nancy that you are taking the "Red Eye" on the 29th – would you like me to pick you up from Heathrow?

Rebecca

From:	**Joe Doyle 19.09.11 12:26**
To:	Rebecca Harris
Subject:	Re: Kensington Building Works

Automated response: Joe Doyle is out of the office until next week.

From:	**Rebecca Harris 19.09.11 12:28**
To:	Tania Cutter Taniacutter@th`enailbar.co.uk
Subject:	re-schedule

Tania,

I'm off to Kensington, can you re-schedule my meeting with Phoebe from 1.30 to 2pm this afternoon.

Thanks, Bex

From:	**Barbara Foreman 19.09.11 124:6**
To:	Rebecca Harris
Subject:	??

Rebecca,

Where are you?

Being on the right side of the Atlantic is meant to be an advantage as I should always be able to get hold of you first thing. I don't remember having this problem with your predecessor? As it is, I spoke to Tania, who seems to be single-handedly running the office and who informed me that you were still out to lunch . . . Disappointing.

Barbara

From: **Rebecca Harris 19.09.11 14:30**
To: Barbara Foreman
Subject: Re: ??

Hi Barbara,

Sorry to have missed you, I was in the meeting room with Phoebe, working on some new promotional ideas for boosting retail sales. We put some of these into play last month, and as I am sure you have noticed, the August figures are looking great.

Rebecca

From: **Barbara Foreman 19.09.11 14:34**
To: Rebecca Harris
Subject: finances

Rebecca,

I don't really know whether to laugh, cry or fire you when I get your emails.

The very reason I have been trying to get hold of you is because I don't have the August figures. This, as you can imagine, makes it a little difficult for me to comment on them, not to mention my meeting with Vice President Jim Knight yesterday evening, which was a little awkward.

We are half way through September and I have no idea of the financial situation of the company. How do you expect me to be in control of this company if I am not kept informed? You may have taken on a slightly more senior role, Rebecca, but don't fool yourself about who is ultimately in charge. I need to be aware of whether we are making a killing (miracles have happened) or haemorrhaging cash (a far more likely scenario) so I can make the kind of executive decisions that just might make this business survive. Please remember your job is to keep me informed at all times.

Need I remind you that the nail bar business now makes up 45% of Nail Corp's entire portfolio, and that is thanks to me. I built up this business and it was my idea to take it international, and I'll be damned if I'm made to regret that decision, Rebecca.

Nail Corp now owns one hundred and seven nail bars across America, with the additional three in the UK. All 110 are under my supervision and yet I seem to have to spend a good 30% of my time on problems in the UK. Even by your calculations you must see that this is a disproportionate amount of time? So, as exciting as it may be that Tara Palmer-whatsit may be gracing us with her presence at the opening party, what you should really be focussing on is whether or not we can actually afford a goddam party, let alone the financing of a fourth nail bar.

The rate of expansion for UK is way off what I had envisaged, and indeed promised, Nail Corp. I know that is almost entirely down to the complete ineptitude of Charlotte Harcourt, and in part myself for allowing the woman to operate under a free rein. I won't make that mistake again, Rebecca. You may have triumphed with the Marylebone launch but don't think you can ride on that success for ever. I'm watching you like a hawk.

Barbara

From:	**Rebecca Harris 19.09.11 14:36**
To:	Tania Cutter
Subject:	August's figures!!

Tania, I have just had an email from Barbara saying she hasn't received the takings sheets for August????????????? They were meant to have gone last week, what the hell happened? When Phoebe moved to the marketing department, you assured me that there was no need to outsource any more of the accounting work because you had plenty of spare time and wanted to flex your "highly proficient, numeric skills", but it seems this is not in fact the case. Please tell me there is a very legitimate reason for this because Barbara is looking for blood and I am in danger of becoming anaemic.

Rebecca

PS Next time Barbara calls and I am in the toilet, please do not tell her that I'm out to lunch when you know perfectly well that I'm not.

From: **Tania Cutter 19.09.11 14:39**
To: Rebecca Harris
Subject: Re: August's figures!!
Attach: Minutes of Meeting 7.7.07

The takings sheets were Fed-Exed this morning. The delay was a result of the paperwork at the Marylebone nail bar being locked in a cupboard, the sole key bearer being Suki, who was meant to have come back from holiday after two weeks but hasn't. This problem won't be repeated as I have personally been to Marylebone (in my lunch break) and had an extra copy made to keep in the office. I would also like to add that I put forward a suggestion at the last group meeting that we should keep a copy of all salon keys in the office (please see attached minutes of 7th July meeting at which both you and Felicity were present), but my proposal was obviously ignored.

Tania Cutter, PA

The Nail Bar Ltd

PS I believe it is impolite to say when someone is in the loo.

From: **Rebecca Harris 19.09.11 14:44**
To: Tania Cutter
Subject: !!!!

WHAT DO YOU MEAN SUKI IS STILL ON HOLIDAY – WHO'S RUNNING THE MARYLEBONE NAIL BAR????????????

From: **Tania Cutter 19.09.11 14:45**
To: Rebecca Harris
Subject: Re: !!!!!

I'm afraid I have no idea. I would have thought that would be Felicity's department. As Head of Personnel, presumably she should be keeping you informed of the whereabouts of your staff?

Tania Cutter PA

The Nail Bar Ltd

From: **Rebecca Harris 19.09.11 14:47**
To: Felicity Jones felicityjones@thenailbar.co.uk
Subject: Suki

Fi, I've just heard from Tania that Suki is still not back from holiday?

5

From: **Felicity Jones 19.09.11 14:50**
To: Rebecca Harris
Subject: Re: Suki

Shit, sorry Bex. I thought she might have shown up by now, but no one is answering the phones at Marylebone so I haven't been able to find out.

From: **Rebecca Harris 19.09.11 14:52**
To: Felicity Jones
Subject: Re: Suki

Then don't you think that's probably an indication she's not back? It must be mayhem over there. Why didn't you mention it before? We need to start pre-empting disasters instead of existing in an almost permanent state of crisis management. In the meantime, does anyone know where she might be?

From: **Felicity Jones 19.09.11 14:54**
To: Rebecca Harris
Subject: Re: Suki

According to Suki's cousin Coco (junior manicurist we employed last month), she missed her flight from Shanghai but was meant to be in by this morning. Don't know if that's true or not, but more likely Coco is just covering for her. I didn't mention it before because I figured you were pretty strung out as it was and could do without the added stress. I was hoping to be able to tell you the problem was solved by now.

From: **Rebecca Harris 19.09.11 14:56**
To: Felicity Jones
Subject: Re: Suki

Fi, this consistently seems to be the case with Marylebone. Everyone covers for everyone else and I never know who is doing what or where the hell anybody is. We'd better put someone in to sub for Suki for the next few days and hope to god she is back by Friday. We can't have Marylebone without a manager for the weekend.
Do I really look strung out? I thought I was being all Cool Hand Luke, considering the crap I've been up against.

From: **Felicity Jones 19.09.011 14:57**
To: Rebecca Harris
Subject: ??

Who's Cool Hand Luke when he's at home?

From: **Rebecca Harris 19.09.11 14:58**
To: Felicity Jones
Subject: Cool Hand Luke

Are you kidding?

Cool Hand Luke was one of the coolest dudes ever. Possibly the best role Paul Newman ever played. I know it's an old movie but it's a classic. Are you joking? You must have heard of him!

From: **Felicity Jones 19.09.11 15:01**
To: Rebecca Harris
Subject: Re: Cool Hand Luke

Are we talking about the salad dressing guy?

From: **Rebecca Harris 19.09.11 15:02**
To: Felicity Jones
Subject: Marylebone

Yes, exactly, but he was slightly cooler as Luke. Anyway, let's get back to Marylebone. If we put someone in to sub for Suki will there be an outcry? I know they're all very particular about who is in charge up there. Would it be better to let Kai Yin manage and put a beauty therapist from one of the other nail bars to replace her?

From: **Felicity Jones 19.09.11 15:04**
To: Rebecca Harris
Subject: Re: Marylebone

Difficult to say. The whole thing is warped as shit. Suki's running the Marylebone nail bar like a totally separate company. She has way too much power and we're paralyzed from making any changes. All the staff are related to her so their loyalty is to their family rather than us. We need to swap some of the Aussie staff from Westbourne with her staff, mix it up a little. If she ever decides to leave (something she frequently threatens) she'll definitely take her whole team with her and we'll be completely buggered.

From: **Rebecca Harris 19.09.011 15:05**
To: Felicity Jones
Subject: Suki

Hmmm not a pleasant thought.

From: **Phoebe Combes 19.09.11 15:06**
To: Rebecca Harris
Subject: Pink nail files

Hi Rebecca,

I have just been counting and I think approximately one in twenty of the glass nail files survived, so we should be ok with getting two hundred for the goodie bags – what a relief! I gave one a go and they don't work very well at all, but I don't think it really matters. I know I would buy one anyway just because they look so nice. I will get an email off to Margarite. Are you going to mention the files to Barbara?

From: **Rebecca Harris 19.09.11 15:07**
To: Phoebe Combes
Subject: Re: Pink nail files

Barbara doesn't get too involved with promotional items so I think it's better if you just deal directly with Margarite.

From: **Rebecca Harris 19.09.11 15:10**
To: Felicity Jones
Subject: staffing

Fi, I'll leave the mixing up of the Marylebone staff to you, but remember, Marylebone has only been open for six months. It is already way and above our most profitable nail bar and we have Suki to thank for that, so I don't want her getting upset. I know we are all pretty petrified of her but it is a small price to pay for her productivity.

On that note, I can't stress how important it is to get our figures up this year. We are over budget on Kensington, the takings at Westbourne are down for no apparent reason, and Mayfair fluctuates like a hormonal teenager. I know this is my problem, not yours, but so much depends on the manager of the shop, so I'm relying on you to find a really great one for Kensington.

Track down Suki and move some of her staff to Westbourne as quickly and smoothly as possible.

From: **Felicity Jones 19.09.11 15:11**
To: Rebecca Harris
Subject: Re: staffing

Don't worry, I'll handle it. I'll sort the staff change without so much as a squeak from Suki, let alone her going completely Kung Fu fucking crazy.

From: **Rebecca Harris 19.09.11 15:12**
To: Felicity Jones
Subject: Re: staffing

I'm sure you can and that would be great, but it's when you use phrases like" Kung Fu fucking crazy" that I get a little nervous.
I really need you to get this right, Fi.

From: **Rebecca Harris 19.09.11 15:20**
To: Katherine Lease katherinelease@hotmail.com
Subject: Aeron

Kat, I'm having a horrible day. I know I'm always saying that but today is in a league of its own – a letter came from Aeron . . . he's getting married.

From: **Katherine Lease 19.09.11 15:24**
To: Rebecca Harris
Subject: Re: Aeron

Really?? I can't believe that. I didn't think people wrote letters any more. Just kidding, darling, but listen this isn't a biggy. If you really think about it, does it bother you that much? You're absolutely not in love with the guy anymore, in fact I have doubts that you ever were and it's been nearly two years since you split. I know he told you that he wasn't into marrying, but he obviously just grew up a bit.

From: **Rebecca Harris 19.09.11 15:25**
To: Katherine Lease
Subject: Re: Aeron

I haven't told you everything yet. The witch-to-be is pregnant with twins.

From: **Katherine Lease 19.09.11 15:26**
To: Rebecca Harris
Subject: No!

THAT IS TOTALLY UNACCEPTABLE. What a thoughtless bastard. What a low-life, son of a bitch, self-centered bastard. I'm really mad now. You poor darling, are you alright?

From: Rebecca Harris   19.09.11   15:33
To: Katherine Lease
Subject: Re: No!

Not really.

I've scanned the letter, take a look.

Dear Beccy,

I hope this letter finds you well?

I have some news that I feel is important to share with you even though I am aware that it may cause you some upset. Miranda is pregnant with twins and we have decided to get married over Thanksgiving this year. We are planning a very private wedding with family and close friends, so I don't think it would be appropriate for you to attend, but I am sure you understand that.

With the twins' arrival in the New Year, Miranda has felt the need to be away from the hustle and bustle of London and so we find ourselves almost full-time in Sussex. I commute three times a week and work from home Mondays and Fridays which allows me to help Miranda with preparing the nursery for the boys — did I mention that we're having boys?!!

Miranda is remarkable and really only looks about four months pregnant even though she is seven. She remains incredibly active and we still play tennis every Saturday morning, although I now insist she serves underarm!!!

I get news of you from time to time from Caris who presumably gets it from Oliver. I believe those two are once again thick as thieves, which may in part have contributed to the distance that has grown between my sister and me. When you and I were an item I tolerated Oliver for both yours and Caris's sake, as you both seemed so inexplicably fond of him, but now that phase of my life is over, I have to say I am somewhat relieved to be rid of the man. He always struck me as rather idiotic and insincere. I could never understand how you and C couldn't see through the immaturity and lack of sophistication. I'll never forget that ghastly time he insisted that we take our dinner plates onto the front lawn and make Sunday lunch a picnic! Poor mother didn't know whether to carve the lamb indoors or out. She was in such a fluster and all because Barker thought it was too nice a day to eat indoors. I know father still hasn't forgiven him for driving the tractor into the ha ha and Mrs. Carmichael was mortified at being forced to play strip croquet — another ridiculously juvenile invention of his.

Perhaps I am too judgmental. Now that I have discovered the joy of creating one's own family I cannot understand why others don't take to it. Yes, Beccy, this archetypal Peter Pan has finally grown up and is blissfully happy!

Anyway, I digress...

I hope your little company is thriving but not keeping you too busy to have some fun — you always were over-conscientious — you need to live a little.

Please send my regards to your mother.

All the best

Aeron

Ps Of course Miranda knows about Poppy but we have our own family now and I wouldn't want anyone getting confused. I'm sure you understand.

CAN YOU BELIEVE THAT?

What the hell does he mean "I'm sure you understand". I don't understand AT ALL. Aeron made it crystal clear from the beginning that he was happy to help out with Poppy financially, but being a father just wasn't part of his "genetic makeup", and now suddenly its all yippee doo, I'm having two!

After all this time of absolutely nothing, not a squeak, and now this, it's just such a shock. Kat, he said he NEVER intended to have children and that marriage is "an unrealistic alliance" with "unnaturally high expectations" and "impossible commitments", and now he's professing about it as if he invented the institution and he's throwing twins in to boot. TWINS!

I may not love him anymore but I did love him when I got pregnant with Poppy and I would have married him at the drop of a hat. Who the hell is Miranda anyway and what significance is Thanksgiving, for Christ's sake? He's Welsh.

I don't know how he does it, but Aeron still has the ability to crush me and make me feel utterly worthless. It's not that I want him back either, because I don't, it's just the rejection drop-kicks my self-esteem into space and leaves me feeling less than crap. But all of that pales in comparison to how devastated I feel for Poppy and how completely incapacitated I am to do anything about it. Why is he willing to be a dad to kids that haven't even been born yet when he's not to his own child that is living and breathing? Do you realize he has never even seen Poppy apart from in photos? I used to send him pictures of her every week until he called and told me not to. You know, I always thought if he just saw her once it would change everything, he wouldn't be able to help himself falling in love with her.

I wonder whether he plans to leave Miranda in the final hour too?

I have always told Poppy that her father didn't think he was capable of fulfilling his role; that he wasn't the "dad type" and some people

are just like that. What if she finds out later that he's spawned the Von Trap family and they all go on bike rides at weekends wearing curtains and singing about tea with jam and bread?
Bex

From: **Katherine Lease 19.09.11 15:37**
To: Rebecca Harris
Subject: Re: No!

Bex, my angel, we've always known the man is pond scum. He doesn't deserve any form of happiness and he certainly doesn't deserve your tears. More importantly, as Poppy's godmother, I would never allow her to wear curtains in public.

You have every right to feel angry. In fact it has always blown my mind that you let Aeron get away with so much. After all, his so-called adversity to children only became apparent once you were pregnant.

Sweetie, Poppy doesn't need a father like that in her life and you are doing a brilliant job bringing her up on your own. I know the financial support isn't what you're after and you would love Poppy to have a father figure in her life, but that just isn't going to happen with someone like Aeron. The most important thing is that Poppy has one fantastic parent and a huge support team in your Mum, Clara and all of us who love her like our own. When she's older, if she wants to meet her dad, then we can address that situation at the time, no point agonizing about it now.

Burn that letter immediately and do not spare another thought for the prick.

PS Quite like the sound of a bit of strip croquet with Oliver Barker, who I like even more now I know Aeron doesn't. Was it just a character clash or something more sinister? Give details, bored at work.

From: **Rebecca Harris 19.09.11 15:39**
To: Katherine Lease
Subject: Aeron

Aeron took a dislike to Olly from the start, but he had to tolerate him because he was a friend of Caris's. It was such a relief the first time Caris brought him down to Aeron's parents' house for the weekend. I was thrilled not to be the only non-family member. I had come to dread the trips to Wales, driving for miles through the Friday night traffic with Aeron insisting on listening to his CDs or The Archers. Then two days of unbelievably stiff family meals with Gale (Aeron's mother) tutting every time I picked up the wrong knife or, horror of all horrors, cut the nose off the Brie. I remember one time Olly started eating the salmon mousse appetizer using his dessert spoon. I really thought Gale was having some kind of stroke. Her face drained of all colour, jaw dropped open, she couldn't speak but just pointed at Olly and her eyes kept blinking like she was trying to communicate in Morse code. Aeron's father, Bob, came to the rescue and suggested that Olly might want to try a different piece of silverware. As soon as Olly had located the correct one and was eating his mousse again, Gale miraculously metamorphosed back into a functioning human being.

Bob thought Olly was terrific. The two of them got on like a house on fire and use to spend almost all the weekend together in the woodshed making go-carts and bows and arrows and stuff. That story about the tractor is true but what Aeron didn't mention is that Bob was on the tractor with Olly at the time and both of them were drunk as skunks when they went into the ditch.

Do you really think I shouldn't acknowledge Aeron's letter in any way at all?

From: **Katherine Lease 19.09.11 15:41**
To: Rebecca Harris
Subject: Re: Aeron

Absolutely not!! Anyway, it would be a bore to have to go and buy writing paper and he's certainly not worth the price of a stamp.

What happened to Caris? I never hear you talk about her. I like to pride myself that I blind-sided her and stole you for my best friend when she wasn't looking.

From: **Rebecca Harris 19.09.11 15:43**
To: Katherine Lease
Subject: Caris

She's living in Ireland, just out of rehab and singing in a folk rock band. She has the most wonderful voice but was heavily messed up with drugs for several years so hasn't done as well as she could. She was never my best friend. She ended up marrying this total loser called Keith who was the drummer in her band, although I think they may have separated now. Olly was pretty cut up when Caris ran off with Keith. He'd been in love with her for years. Shortly after that Olly flew off to America to do an architectural degree of some sort and we lost contact. I was hurt that he didn't keep in touch as I always thought we had a friendship outside of him and Caris, but I think it was just too hard for him to have any contact with any of us. I tried calling and emailing but when he didn't reply I just stopped trying. The next time I heard from him was on Poppy's 2nd birthday. He called out of the blue to say he was back and would love to meet Poppy.

From: **Katherine Lease 19.09.11 15:44**
To: Rebecca Harris
Subject: looking on the bright side

Poor bastard, he's such a nice bloke as well. Anyway, back to you. Focus on what's good in your life. You're currently dating Charles 007 Balford, much to the envy of many a Chelsea slut. You have recently been promoted to managing director of a very successful chain of nail bars and you're doing a mighty fine job of running them. You have a very happy three-year-old who is terrorizing the hell out of her kindergarten, which shows great character and potential, and the stress of your recent life has resulted in you shedding a good two kilos in as many months which, let's face it, you needed to. So who, quite frankly my dear, gives a damn about Aeron and his lousy witch-to-be Miranda?
Oh and you should probably chuck out your copy of The Sound of Music.

From: **Rebecca Harris 19.09.11 15:47**
To: Katherine Lease
Subject: Ok

The 'needed to lose two kilos' bit was a little unnecessary, but I will try and focus on the good stuff.
Thanks x

From: **Rebecca Harris 19.09.11 15:55**
To: Barbara Foreman
Subject: August figures

Barbara,

The takings sheets were emailed to you last night and the hard copies should be with you first thing tomorrow. The delay was caused by a minor incident at Marylebone, but we have already instigated measures to ensure that this doesn't happen again.

Rebecca

From: **Barbara Foreman 19.09.11 16:01**
To: Rebecca Harris
Subject: Please note

Good. I would also like an update on the staff recruitment for Kensington, another obviously crucial issue, ranking slightly higher than goodie bags and glass nail files. I expect you to make sure that Felicity is on top of this as I do not want a repeat of the disastrous Mayfair Nail Bar launch.

Tell that lazy SOB Joe that if Kensington isn't finished on time he can whistle for his final payment, and remind him that I am American and we sue in this country for breach of contract.

On the subject of the party, which I know you are itching to get on to . . . I am extremely disappointed about the flowers; did you tell Rick that they were for me? If not, go back to him and do so. I am solely responsible for the launch of that man's career in America and he owes me big time.

I have never heard of Pink Mango; they sound like a hip-hop band? Please assure me that you have researched this and not just got them out of your High School yearbook.

I am also slightly surprised that Miss Combes is doing the PR for the party. Since when does a part-time accountant moonlight as a public relations guru? Could this possibly be why I have not received the end of month figures yet?

No, I don't want you to pick me up off the Red Eye, much as I enjoy being squashed in amongst the potato chip and candy bar wrappers of your Mini Cooper. I think I might be persuaded towards Mandarin Oriental's offer of a limo.

Barbara

From: **Rebecca Harris 19.09.11 16:04**
To: Barbara Foreman
Subject: Recruitment

Fi, Babs the Bitch is far from calm about staff recruitment for Kensington. What's the situation on that?

From: **Barbara Foreman 19.09.11 16:11**
To: Rebecca Harris
Subject: re your email to Felicity Jones

Rebecca, am I right to assume that the "Babs the bitch" you refer to in your email to Felicity Jones, is in fact myself? If so, I would consider your position as Director of The UK Nail Bar on shaky ground, wouldn't you?
Try not to let your emails go to the wrong people, Rebecca, especially ones in which you refer to your boss as a female dog.
Barbara

From: **Rebecca Harris 19.09.11 16:13**
To: Felicity Jones
Subject: BIIIIIG mistake!!!

FUUUUUUUXXXXXXXXKKKKKK. I just tried to forward you Barbara's last email and by mistake I pressed reply and the email went to her instead of you.

From: **Felicity Jones 19.09.11 16:15**
To: Rebecca Harris
Subject: Re: BIIIIIG mistake!!!

How bad was it?

From: **Rebecca Harris 19.09.11 16:16**
To: Felicity Jones
Subject: Re: BIIIIIG mistake!!!

It contained the words "Babs the Bitch".

From: **Felicity Jones 19.09.11 16:17**
To: Rebecca Harris
Subject: Re: BIIIIIG mistake!!!

You're toast.

From: **Rebecca Harris 19.09.11 16:18**
To: Felicity Jones
Subject: shit

I know, I know. Shit, shit, shit.
Before I go back to her you have to give me some good news. Is there anything at all about recruitment that might soften the blow?

From: **Felicity Jones 19.09.11 16:21**
To: Rebecca Harris
Subject: Recruitment

Not really, the staff situation is a bit bollocks, I'm afraid. To be honest, there is about a gnat's fart of a chance of us having a full team for the opening. Trying to find someone who can do a reasonable manicure and actually string a sentence together in the English language seems to be a tough order. I have a pile of curriculum vitaes in which the average age is 17 years old, number of GCSEs is two, and most common language is Czechoslovakian – but I'm working on it.

From: **Rebecca Harris 19.09.11 16:24**
To: Felicity Jones
Subject: Re: Recruitment

Oh god, is that really it??

From: **Felicity Jones 19.09.11 16:29**
To: Rebecca Harris
Subject: Re: Recruitment

We do have two great girls ready to go and I have a couple of interviews lined up, one for this afternoon and the other for tomorrow. The one for tomorrow is Czechoslovakian. She's had five years experience back home as a manicurist in her mother's nail salon, but speaks no known language (something had to give). She arrived in England a month ago and is here on a two-year visa. I actually need a favour? She's arriving at South Kensington tube station (it's the only place she knows in London). Could you meet her there and put her in a taxi to the office? You mentioned that you're going to be at the Kensington nail bar most afternoons so I thought it might be easy for you? I think the chances of her getting on the right bus in this rain are slim.

The one for today is a woman called Sylvia in her late forties. She sounds very experienced, used to work at Clarins, LOVES our concept and is from Basingstoke, so no problems on the language front. There is a small issue however . . . she has a pacemaker; do you think this is a problem? I mean, I know she has worked in other salons but things can get pretty medieval in our nail bars, especially on weekends. Of course I will make sure that the contract exempts us from any emergency medical care, but let me know what you think.

From: **Rebecca Harris 19.09.11 16:32**
To: Felicity Jones
Subject: Re: Recruitment

Fi, are you telling me only TWO staff for Kensington and TWO weeks to go? If Barbara gets wind of this she is going to implode.

I can pick up your girl from the tube. What's her name and what does she look like? Hopefully she'll be another Bianca – remember the Polish ex-manager at Mayfair? She didn't speak a word of English but was a brilliant manager.

If this Sylvia woman is good, then hire her. I don't care if she's got no arms, and manicures with a file between her teeth, we need all the help we can get.

Is that it on the good news?

From: **Felicity Jones 19.09.11 16:35**
To: Rebecca Harris
Subject: Re: Recruitment

'fraid so, and if you don't want Barbara to know about the staff situation then don't tell Tania, she's our resident mole.

The interviewee is called Katya and she says you will recognize her because she is wearing a hat like Jay Kay from Jamiraquai.

From: **Rebecca Harris 19.09.11 16:37**
To: Felicity Jones
Subject: mole

I didn't know we had a mole. No wonder Barbara is always onto me. How d'you know it's Tania?

From: **Felicity Jones 19.09.11 16:39**
To: Rebecca Harris
Subject: Re: mole

Because I was the one who trained her before she went all Jason Bourne on me. When money went missing from the Westbourne till last year I sent Tania in undercover to find out what was happening. I told her how to act and what to look for, and within a week she'd sniffed out the culprit. Problem is, she's now gone rogue and there's no controlling her. If information is sailing across the Atlantic, then you can bet money that Ms Cutter is at the helm.

From: **Rebecca Harris 19.09.11 16:42**
To: Felicity Jones
Subject: Re: mole

Wow that's good to know. How come you're so up on spy tactics?

From: **Felicity Jones 19.09.11 16:44**
To: Rebecca Harris
Subject: I spy . . .

Brian is a huge Robert Ludlam fan so every Sunday night it's either "Identity", "Supremacy", or "Ultimatum". I must have watched each one ten times. They tell you all you need to know about how to become a one-man, undercover fighting machine.

From: **Rebecca Harris 19.09.11 16:45**
To: Felicity Jones
Subject: Re: I spy . . .

Are you finding these skills useful in London?

From: **Felicity Jones 19.09.11 16:46**
To: Rebecca Harris
Subject: Re: I spy . . .

You'd be surprised, my friend.

From: **Rebecca Harris 19.09.11 16:47**
To: Felicity Jones
Subject: Re: I spy . . .

Not as surprised as I am to hear we only have two staff lined up for Kensington.

From: **Rebecca Harris 19.09.11 16:55**
To: Barbara Foreman
Subject: Pink Mango canapés
Attach: Pink Mango canapé list

Barbara, I'm terribly sorry about the mis-sent email. Of course you know I have the deepest respect for you, and the terminology I used in my email was only to scare other members of staff into action. I also want to point out that in England we use the "b" word much more loosely than you do in America. It is almost a term of affection for someone with a strong personality, a bit like saying "tough cookie". In fact, a lot of the younger generation in England use the word "bitching" to describe something that is great – sort of ghetto-speak for "cool".

Anyway, some good news . . . staffing for Kensington is all very much on track with lots of really great potentials. Felicity has a pile of CVs and is interviewing non-stop, so we should have a strong team of 10 in place for the opening.

Pink Mango did the catering for the opening of the new Tate Modern museum and I think they might have done Elton John's wedding as well. I have attached their canapé list and marked the ones I thought sounded good.

Rebecca

From: **Barbara Foreman 19.09.11 16:58**
To: Rebecca Harris
Subject: Re: Pink Mango canapés

Don't be moronic, Rebecca – I hardly think that you are into "ghetto" speak.

Pull off the Kensington opening successfully and I may revise your status from dire to precarious – and get some IT lessons, for Christ's sake.

From: **Rebecca Harris 19.09.11 17:16**
To: Phoebe Combes
Subject: Purple Rain

Phoebe, I want to run that nail polish promotion for Purple Rain right away. We need to up retail sales as Barbara is "watching the figures like a hawk" – direct quote. Nail Corp have estimated that we should be placing orders from them for around 40,000 bottles of nail polish a year for both retail and salon use, and we are well off this figure. If you can get some posters designed and in the windows of each of the nail bars as soon as possible, that would be great.

Thanks. Bex

From: **Phoebe Combes 19.09.11 17:20**
To: Rebecca Harris
Subject: Re: Purple Rain

Gosh it's all quite hectic today, isn't it? No worries, I will get onto it right away. I like the top you're wearing by the way. Is it Chloe?

From: **Rebecca Harris 19.09.11 17:22**
To: Phoebe Combes
Subject: Zara

Thanks, um no it's Zara

From: **Phoebe Combes 19.09.11 17:25**
To: Rebecca Harris
Subject: Re: Zara

Oh, I love Zara, although I find it so frustrating the way the collections change so regularly – it means you can never copy anybody. It's terribly annoying, especially as I always prefer what other people are wearing, but by the time I get around to going there, the item is already out of stock – do you find that? What am I talking about? You always look so lovely. I'm sure everyone is trying to copy you rather than the other way around.

From: **Rebecca Harris 19.09.11 17:28**
To: Phoebe Combes
Subject: Re: Zara

Phoebe, that's very nice of you to say, but I'm a bit busy. Can we have this discussion another time?

From: **Phoebe Combes 19.09.11 17:30**
To: Rebecca Harris
Subject: Re: Zara

Absolutely. Sorry to rabbit on. I will get on with the posters right away.

From: **Oliver Barker 19.09.11 17:32**
To: Rebecca Harris
Subject: hi

Hi Bex, I'm sorry I missed your call. I'm actually in a meeting but I just stepped out. You didn't sound very happy. Are you alright?
Olly
Message sent via BlackBerry ®

From: **Rebecca Harris 19.09.11 17:35**
To: Oliver Barker
Subject: Re: hi

Hi, Ols, so sorry to get you out of a meeting, it's just work is going really badly and I need someone to talk to. It seems to be a constant stream of disasters. Every time I manage to sort out one problem another one jumps up and replaces it.

Also, Aeron's having twins, which is fine but it shook me up a bit when I heard about it. You probably know about this from Caris, but I've only just heard. Love, Bex

From: **Oliver Barker 19.09.11 17:37**
To: Rebecca Harris
Subject: Re: hi

I know you well enough to know that when you say you're fine you are far from it, and I'm not surprised, you poor thing. Aeron having twins must be a huge shock. I spoke to Caris last week but she didn't mention it. Mind you, she's going through such a messy divorce with Keith I don't think she can focus on anything else. I'm so sorry you couldn't reach me earlier.

This meeting is pretty much over so I'll come and pick you up from work. We'll go for a drink and talk about this, or if you need to go home to Poppy we can just talk in the car.

Message sent via BlackBerry ®

From: **Rebecca Harris 19.09.11 17:40**
To: Oliver Barker
Subject: thanks but no

Ols, you're so kind, but please don't end your meeting for me. I really am fine and I'm perfectly ok to take the bus. But thank you all the same. Sorry to hear about Caris. Poor her. X

From: **Oliver Barker 19.09.11 17:43**
To: Rebecca Harris
Subject: Re: thanks but no

I'll be there by 6pm X

Message sent via BlackBerry ®

From: **Rebecca Harris 19.09.11 17:45**
To: Oliver Barker
Subject: Re: thanks but no

Yay X

From: **Rebecca Harris 19.09.11 17:49**
To: Felicity Jones
Subject: internal meeting tomorrow

Fi, I'm going to Kensington tomorrow morning but I'll be back in time for the internal meeting, so will you make sure everyone is well prepared? Maybe we could get people to come to the meetings better prepared so that we have a more productive outcome? It would be great to get a bit of input from the others rather than it always being me telling everyone what I think. I don't mean to sound pedantic, but it might even be an idea if everyone wrote down a few constructive thoughts on paper beforehand and brought them to the meeting?

From:	**Felicity Jones 19.09.11 17:50**
To:	Rebecca Harris
Subject:	IM tomorrow

Shit. Forgot about IM, will have to cancel T'ai chi class – remind me what meeting is about?

From:	**Rebecca Harris 19.09.11 17:51**
To:	Felicity Jones
Subject:	Re: IM tomorrow

Fi, we discussed it on Friday – Staff Incentivizing – I was hoping you might have been working on something?
I thought you were learning kick-boxing?

From:	**Felicity Jones 19.09.11 17:53**
To:	Rebecca Harris
Subject:	Re: IM tomorrow

I was until Brian threw me a surprise party at the beginning of the year – he jumped out from behind the curtain as I walked in the door. Poor guy didn't even get the "surprise" out before I'd kicked his balls into his mouth and had him in a neck lock.

From:	**Rebecca Harris 19.09.11 17:55**
To:	Felicity Jones
Subject:	Re: IM tomorrow

Ouch.

From:	**Felicity Jones 19.09.11 17:57**
To:	Rebecca Harris
Subject:	no worries

Tell me about it. Anyway, don't worry about the IM. I know we have all been completely crap about contributing ideas in previous meetings but I'll sort it out and I'll get a motivational speech ready. Actually I have had some quite good results following the butt-kicking seminar I gave the managers last week. Some of the girls have made radical improvements. A couple more follow-up sessions and we'll have everyone so incentivized they'll be handcuffing themselves to their manicure stations and begging not to take lunch breaks.

Ciao

From: **Rebecca Harris 19.09.11 18:00**
To: Felicity Jones
Subject: Re: no worries

Well, if we could start with getting them to turn up on time in the morning, that would help. Then feel free to work on the handcuffing.

See you tomorrow.

Bex

Tuesday 20th September 2011

From: **Rebecca Harris 20.09.11 8:42**
To: Katherine Lease
Subject: what to do?

Hi Kat,

Olly drove me home from work last night and I showed him Aeron's letter. He thinks I should write back and suggest to him that we try and keep communications open for Poppy's sake. He said that I should include some news about Poppy in the hopes that it might trigger some paternal instinct. He also said it's important that when Poppy grows up she knows I did everything I could to bring her father into her life, and that I didn't let my personal feelings get in the way of that. I kind of think he may be right. What do you think?

From: **Rebecca Harris 20.09.11 8:48**
To: Oliver Barker
Subject: thank you

Ols, thanks so much for picking me up last night and our chat really helped. I'll definitely think about what you said.

Poppy loved seeing you as usual and she asked me to ask you if you would take her trick-or-treating for Hallowe'en again this year – any chance?

Bex

From: **Oliver Barker 20.09.11 8:54**
To: Rebecca Harris
Subject: Re: thank you

I'm glad you felt our chat helped. Whether you take my advice or not is completely up to you, and you should probably get a second opinion as I may be talking absolute bollocks. I know this is incredibly hard on you. There must be a lot of resentment there and quite justifiably so, but if you can be big about this, then it just might help Poppy's chances of having some kind of relationship with her father in the future.

Please tell Poppy I would love to take her trick-or-treating as long as I don't have to be the slime monster again. I want a cool costume like Dracula, or that guy with all the needles in his head.

Olly x

Message sent via BlackBerry ®

26

From: **Rebecca Harris 20.09.11 8:56**
To: Oliver Barker
Subject: Re: thank you

Oh but Poppy loves you as the slime monster!

From: **Oliver Barker 20.09.11 8:57**
To: Rebecca Harris
Subject: ok

Slime monster it is, then.

Message sent via BlackBerry ®

From: **Rebecca Harris 20.09.11 8:59**
To: Oliver Barker
Subject: slime monster

☺ xx

From: **Katherine Lease 20.09.11 9:18**
To: Rebecca Harris
Subject: Re: what to do?

God you get to work early!

Bex, sweetheart, Olly is obviously a much better person than I am and you should probably listen to him. Quite frankly I wouldn't give a second thought to pushing Aeron bloody Vaughan out of an airplane without a parachute, but that's just me. Go for keeping the channels of communication open, it'll be better karma.

PS. Remind my goddaughter I'm taking her shopping on Thursday.

From: **Rebecca Harris 20.09.11 9:23**
To: Katherine Lease
Subject: Poppy

Thanks, Kat, Poppy is so excited about that. I've told her teacher you're picking her up. Are you sure it's really ok for you to take a half day?

From: **Katherine Lease 20.09.11 9:24**
To: Rebecca Harris
Subject: Re: Poppy

Half day? Pick up is 3pm? The only thing that could be a problem is finding something to do in the office between lunch and then.

From: **Rebecca Harris 20.09.11 9:47**
To: Phoebe Combes
Subject: where are you?

Phoebe,

Have you moved to Scotland or something? How come you're always so late for work? Everyone else manages to get in by 9am and as head of your department you really should be trying to set an example. Also, is it always necessary to change into a different outfit when you arrive? Can't you decide at home and then stick with that?

Anyway, I've been waiting for you because our accountants were confused over some graphs that were done in 2009 depicting our retail and service figures. They were obviously done by some temp on a post-Glastonbury binge because they make no sense at all. They also can't seem to find any similar graphs for 2008 or 2007. Do you remember if any were done?

Thanks. R

From: **Phoebe Combes 20.09.11 9:52**
To: Rebecca Harris
Subject: sorry!

Rebecca, I'm dreadfully sorry about my late arrival, I am an unbearably bad timekeeper. I know how irritating it must be for you and also terribly unprofessional of me. I inherited my tardiness from my wonderfully eccentric father whom I absolutely adored. He checked in to Claridges Hotel for his fortieth birthday and died sixteen years later, having never checked out. He sadly drank his way through the family fortune, leaving behind my mother, myself, four sisters, three brothers, two Labradors, an albino gerbil and an awful lot of unpaid bills. Anyway, I am sure you are not remotely interested and there's no reason why you should be, but I mention it because, although we did have to sell off most of our family heirlooms, my mother insisted I keep hold of his much-treasured Victorian carriage clock in the hopes that it might improve my timekeeping better than it did his. Unfortunately it just stopped on me last week and I can't find anyone who knows how to fix it.

The 2006 graphs were done by me – terribly embarrassing, especially as I'm pretty sure I gave up acid in 2006 – but I have had a few flashbacks since – ghastly experiences. Anyway, I think we decided not to do graphs for the following years because they didn't really show us anything new.

From: Rebecca Harris 20.09.11 9:56
To: Phoebe Combes
Subject: graphs

No, I can see that. I personally wouldn't have used a pie chart format to do them because although all the rainbow colours look very nice, they don't, as you pointed out, tell us anything.

The Victorian clock is obviously very special, but you might want to get a modern one that has an alarm on it – just a suggestion.

Rebecca

From: Rebecca Harris 20.09.11 9:59
To: Felicity Jones
Subject: Phoebe

Fi, why does Phoebe keep so many clothes at work and why does she always come in the morning in one outfit and then change into another? She just told me a bit about her family and now I'm putting two and two together and thinking that maybe she doesn't have anywhere to live and she's too proud to say? Could she be sleeping on the floor of a friend's house or something, and have no cupboard space? You guys know each other well. Will you check that everything is alright?

How did the interview go with Sylvia?

Any sign of Suki?

From: Felicity Jones 20.09.11 10:06
To: Rebecca Harris
Subject: new manager!

Brilliant news – Sylvia has been hired as the new manager for Kensington! She's perfect, really responsible and seems to know her stuff, which makes a nice change. She's 45 years old, which I think will be a bonus as hopefully the staff will respect her. We touched briefly on the pacemaker issue, which was awkward as fuck, but she says that as long as she doesn't get over-stressed she'll be fine – gulp!

Suki is still AWOL, so I thought I'd take Sylvia over to Marylebone for a bit of management training. If she seems capable then she can always fill in until Suki gets back.

You're barking up completely the wrong tree with Phoebe. She hasn't got a bean, but the reason she keeps clothes at work isn't because of that, it's because she's shagging half of London and never gets home at night.

From: **Rebecca Harris 20.09.11 10:11**
To: Felicity Jones
Subject: Phoebe

What??

I'm completely gob-smacked. I'd never have guessed that in a million years. She just doesn't look the type. She's always so, I don't know, *proper*, I really can't believe it. Phoebe?? Really???

From: **Felicity Jones 20.09.11 10:13**
To: Rebecca Harris
Subject: Re: Phoebe

Believe it. It's always the posh ones that want watching. Something to do with repressed childhoods and being bored to death in the rose garden on a Sunday in a smock dress with nothing to do but fiddle with their fannies when the governess wasn't looking. Their libidos get so built up that by the time they burst out of the stately home they're ready to shag the first poor unsuspecting bloke that walks by.

From: **Rebecca Harris 20.09.11 10:15**
To: Felicity Jones
Subject: Re: Phoebe

I think you might have read a slightly different version of *Pride and Prejudice* to me.

Anyway, I'm really happy with the work she is doing in the new PR department. We had a great meeting this morning and all her promo ideas were well thought out and clever. She is well suited to the job. What she was doing in Accounts, I have no idea. Our accountants sent over some stuff she did which they couldn't make head or tale of. I took a look at it and it's totally out there.

From: **Felicity Jones 20.09.11 10:17**
To: Rebecca Harris
Subject: Re: Phoebe

Yeah I can imagine. Putting Phoebe in Accounts is like putting a cocker spaniel in the Big Brother house.

From: **Rebecca Harris 20.09.11 10:18**
To: Felicity Jones
Subject: Re: Phoebe

I don't get it.

From: **Felicity Jones 20.09.11 10:19**
To: Rebecca Harris
Subject: Re: Phoebe

Not sure I can really explain, but the comparison just seems right. Something to do with putting an over-enthusiastic, slightly mental people-pleaser in a room full of very dull zombies.

From: **Rebecca Harris 20.09.11 10:21**
To: Felicity Jones
Subject: stuff

Oh, right. I sort of hope our Accounts department isn't full of zombies. Anyway, that is great news about Sylvia. We have a manager, now we just need to get her a team. Hopefully the Jamiraquai fan I am picking up this afternoon will be a master manicurist.

Will you check in Suki's file to see if we have any home contact number for her? She's probably just ill, but we need to know how long we're going to have to manage without her.

From: **Charles Balford 20.09.11 10:22**
To: Rebecca Harris
Subject: dinner & . . . ???

How's the sexiest manicurist I know?

Darling, I need you to be free tomorrow night, so cancel whatever you had organized because I have to see you. I'm proposing to take you out for a delicious dinner and then have my wicked way with you. I feel sure you must have run out of excuses by now and come to your senses and realize that it is perfectly acceptable to be ravished by a gentleman who has all the right intentions . . . well, maybe not *all* the right intentions, but all the ones that matter at this stage. The point is, I'm crazy about you and if you turn me down again I might start to get a complex or something, which would inevitably lead to some form of counselling. You don't want me to have years of counselling, do you? It would be such a bore to have to make up a whole load of rubbish about how my father never kicked a ball with me and my mother didn't hug me enough. I know it's all the rage, but it does seem like a fundamental waste of time and although I do love talking about myself, I would prefer it to be over a candlelit dinner with a beautiful girl – one I'd like to know a great deal better, and I'm talking biblical sense here.

No pressure, just a yes would be fine.

Charles

From: **Rebecca Harris 20.09.11 10:26**
To: Katherine Lease
Subject: Charles

Kat,

I just got an email from Charles inviting me out for dinner, and I'm worried things are moving too quickly. This will be our fourth official date and he is definitely expecting a romp in the hay this time. I don't know what it is, but my instinct tells me to hold back. I think he might be out of my league. Would I be better off cutting my losses before he shags me and then inevitably runs off with Paris Hilton to St Barts? I'm not sure my self-esteem is up to that kind of a beating. I'm still very much on the rebound from Aeron and this would really be a big set-back.

From: **Katherine Lease 20.09.11 10:30**
To: Rebecca Harris
Subject: Charles 007 Balford

Bex,

ARE YOU INSANE? Seriously, what the hell are you talking about? On the rebound? It's been four years. Besides it's hardly as if you've been celibate since. For Christ's sake, you went out with Paulo for four months and that wasn't so long ago. Darling, even Heidi was romping in the hay by the third date.

Charles Balford is sex on a plate. You could cook bacon off his backside he's so damn hot. The guy is a demi-god who has asked YOU out on a guaranteed night of passionate sex – and you're thinking of turning him down? HAVE I TAUGHT YOU NOTHING? I can tell you now, you do not say no to a guy like that. He probably doesn't even know what the word means and you can bet your Manolo Blaniks there is a whole entourage of mini-skirted minions just waiting to step into your shoes if you turn him down.

You are thinking about it too much. You need to stop thinking. Don't worry about the consequences. Charles is far more likely to get dumped by you than the other way around. You're not madly in love with the guy, so just have some great sex and deal with whatever comes later, when and if that happens. It's time to be spontaneous, take a risk, have fun and live a little.

Rebecca, best friend of mine, do not hesitate, do not pass Go, do not even bother collecting the £200. Email Balford@gorgeous.com immediately and simply tell him that although it will mean you will have to cancel your pole dancing lesson at very short notice, you are on, and you are gagging for it. Then get your butt over here so I can kit you out with a sample Armani, chain-mail dress that just came in to the press office and will look utterly gorgeous on you, not to mention have Chuck squirming with excitement in his Saville Row suit.

From: Rebecca Harris 20.09.11 10:39
To: Katherine Lease
Subject: Re: Charles 007 Balford

I know, I know, Kat, but my life just seems very complicated at the moment. I feel like I'm juggling all these balls and if I look away for one second they'll all come crashing down and Charles will just be another ball adding to the chaos.

I have to think about Poppy, too. I can't just go out with every Tom, Dick or Charles that asks me. It sends out all the wrong message to a daughter. I don't want her getting confused, or thinking that I might abandon her for some bloke who just appeared out of nowhere.

Paulo was over a year ago and we only slept together twice in that whole time.

From: Katherine Lease 20.09.11 10:44
To: Rebecca Harris
Subject: HAVE SOME FUN!!

Rebecca, please listen because you're scaring me. You have been a man-free zone, a human wasteland, planet No-Sex for a whole year and this is not for lack of suitors. They have been queuing up, but you cast them aside like the pickle in a McDonald's burger. It's not healthy, there's even been talk you might be a lesbian.

Honey, it is time. Believe me, you cannot let this opportunity go.

Poppy is more than capable of sharing a bit of you and I'm sure she would actually be happy to see you having fun, especially if it means she can stay up late with Vinca watching America's Next Top Model while you go out gallivanting on wild dates. It's not like Charles is asking to move in, he just wants to be one of your balls, tossed up in the air a few times, take you out for dinner and maybe (hopefully, hopefully) get in a bit of nookie.

Oh I'm so jealous, suddenly my life feels boring. I desperately need some excitement. Work is beyond dull now that London Fashion Week is over. The Armani show went so brilliantly that my boss thinks I walk on water. I could probably take the whole week off, she loves me so much but that's all so boring.

I'm wondering whether I've been with Marcus too long? It's been six weeks, no wonder I'm restless. I'll call him and tell him that if he doesn't want to lose me he must plan something wild and romantic immediately.

Love you, Kat xx

From: **Rebecca Harris 20.09.11 10:48**
To: Katherine Lease
Subject: worried

Kat, You're madly in love with Marcus, don't be ridiculous. The other day you were complaining that you'd had enough of going away to amazing places and you just wanted to have a relaxed weekend at home.

I know you're right about Charles and I should probably go out with him and have fun, but I just feel nervous about it. If you really want to know, I'm worried that I'm not the same as I was. I know this may sound weird to you, but I think I may not be as good as I was because I've had a baby – you know, like a bit stretched or something? Or just have a more mummy-like approach to the whole thing – that's a real turn off. What if I have the urge to use a wetwipe half way through because it's getting a bit messy? Or I might tell Charles to calm down and stop showing off. I say those sorts of things without even knowing I do nowadays. It's like a form of MaternalTerrret's and I can't control it.

I've only slept with two guys since Aeron. One was a one-night stand who never called the next day and even though I didn't want him to, I still would have liked him to have tried, and the other was Paulo. I've lost my confidence, Kat, and I'm worried that if it goes wrong with Charles, I'll never have the courage to have sex ever again. I bet Charles has never slept with anyone who's had a baby and what happens if he notices the difference and doesn't like it? He'll go around telling people that it was like waving his dick around in the Albert Hall.

PS. Who thinks I'm a lesbian?

From: **Katherine Lease 20.09.11 10:52**
To: Rebecca Harris
Subject: just go for it!

Angel, no one actually said it out loud, but I did hear a bit of chat. Of course I would have crushed any rumour immediately if I'd thought it was damaging, but lesbianism is hugely fashionable at the moment. I've even let slip a couple of times that I'm considering becoming a part-time bi-sexual.

I can see why you're worried but you did all those pelvic whatsit lifts, didn't you? Have you ever wet your pants when you've sneezed? If not, then you're fine. If you have, then that's pretty gross, but it just means you'll need to squeeze really hard so he can feel something and you might want to look into an operation at a later date. But god, I'd forgotten you've had so little sex since then. You poor thing. Anyway, it's like riding a bicycle, you don't forget. It's also fine to try some new moves, but stick to ones you know you can pull off. Don't go for anything too complicated or someone might get hurt. If you do find yourself reminding Charles to say please when he demands you take your clothes off, he'll probably find it extremely kinky, so don't worry about it. Be confident, you're a natural sex fiend, I know it. Besides it's not every day I offer up the chance to borrow one of the coolest, sexiest dresses I have ever laid eyes on in this office. Girlfriend, this is your moment – do not waste it!!

PS Going to assume our girls' night tonight is off?

From: **Rebecca Harris 20.09.11 10:57**
To: Katherine Lease
Subject: Ok!

Alright, I am going to do this. I'm going to have wild, wonderful and carefree sex with an exceedingly good-looking man who obviously thinks I'm quite good news, and Aeron can go hang himself.

Sorry to cancel girls' night. Vinca might be willing to swap nights but there's no way she would babysit two nights in a row. Do you mind?

From:	**Katherine Lease 20.09.11 10:59**
To:	Rebecca Harris
Subject:	Re: Ok!

MIND?   Sweetheart, I insist!!

From:	**Rebecca Harris 20.09.11 11:01**
To:	Katherine Lease
Subject:	bless you

You're my best friend in the world and I'm changing my will so you get all my shoes. Oh and I've never wet my pants when I've sneezed, so I'm good to go on that front ☺

From:	**Katherine Lease 20.09.11 11:03**
To:	Rebecca Harris
Subject:	erm . . .

Can I have your Valentino jacket instead? I'm not mad about your shoes.

From:	**Rebecca Harris 20.09.11 11:05**
To:	Katherine Lease
Subject:	WHAT??

Are you serious? It's VINTAGE! Plus it's the only piece of designer clothing I have. Paulo gave me that jacket to soften the blow when he drop the bomb that he was gay. Do you remember? I was at his house and he was cooking me spaghetti carbonara and I thought I was finally over Aeron. We sat down to eat and he gave me a glass of wine, then told me he was homosexual. I thought he was saying "home is sexual" (he had quite a strong accent). Then it hit me and I realized why he had been so understanding when I hadn't been ready to go to second base. I've never been able to eat carbonara since. That jacket was his compensation gift for breaking up with me and stamping on my newly healed heart. You can't really expect me to part with it?

From: **Katherine Lease 20.09.11 11:14**
To: Rebecca Harris
Subject: no?

How bad do you want the dress?

From: **Rebecca Harris 20.09.11 11:17**
To: Katherine Lease
Subject: Re: no?

It's yours.

From: **Rebecca Harris 20.09.11 11:18**
To: Charles Balford
Subject: Re: dinner & . . . ???

Hi Charles,

I would love to have dinner tomorrow night and you never know, if you play your cards right, I just may let you hold my hand on the way home.

Your sexy manicurist

Xxx

PS. I would think counselling might do wonders for you!

From: **Charles Balford 20.09.11 11:20**
To: Rebecca Harris
Subject: Can't wait

Cheeky tart.

From: **Rebecca Harris 20.09.11 11:21**
To: Katherine Lease
Subject: 007

Kat, I said yes and Vinca said Ok and the date/shag is a go for tomorrow night!!!!!!

From: **Katherine Lease 20.09.11 11:22**
To: Rebecca Harris
Subject: Re: 007

That's my girl, now go forth and multiply! K x

From: **Rebecca Harris 20.09.11 11:24**
To: Rick Van Shear RVS@panache.com
Subject: booking

Dear Mr. Van Shear,

I spoke to your assistant Monique last week about you possibly doing the flowers for a party I am organizing for my boss, Barbara Foreman. It is an opening party for The Nail Bar Ltd's fourth nail bar in Kensington. I was told by Monique that you were busy with another function that day. At the time I didn't mention Ms Foreman's name. She is a huge fan of yours and is always promoting you to all her VIP friends both in Europe and the US. I know she would be thrilled if it were at all possible for you to re-arrange your prior engagement so you were available on the 30th September.

I look forward to hearing from you.

Best wishes,

Rebecca Harris

From: **Rebecca Harris 20.09.11 11:56**
To: Barbara Foreman
Subject: News from The Nail Bar

Barbara,

The graphs you requested unfortunately don't exist, and the ones that do are way off comprehension. If it isn't too urgent, I can get some much more comprehensive ones drawn up and have them with you by the end of the week?

I sent an email to Rick Van Shear telling him that the flowers were for your party, so I am sure he will make himself available.

We have employed a new manager – she is called Sylvia and is full of enthusiasm and experience. She was running a chain of nail bars in the north of England and then did a two-year stint with Clarins, so she knows exactly what she is doing. Felicity is taking her to Marylebone this afternoon to get a feel for how we operate.

Rebecca

From: **Rebecca Harris 20.09.11 12:02**
To: Office Staff
Subject: Joe Doyle

If Joe Doyle calls, please make sure you put him through to me immediately. I need to speak to him urgently. Thank you

Rebecca

From: **Monique De Veaux** MdV@panache.com **20.09.11 12:13**
To: Rebecca Harris
Subject: Re: booking

Mme Harris,

I regret to tell you of the impossibility for Mr. Van Shear to do your soirée. He is at present in Denmark for a royal engagement and then he returns himself to England for a celebrity birthday. Monsieur Van Shear has many VIP clients whom he tries to accommodate, but of course it is not always possible. His diary – she is full to the bursting until the end of the year and I look at next year, she is the same. We have a small window of chance in the middle of May next year. If you would like Panache for a party then, it is possible to arrange.

Please tell Madam Foreman of our unfortunate regret.

With sincerity

Monique De Veaux

Panache

From:	**Rebecca Harris 20.09.11 12:17**
To:	Clara Harris
Subject:	Urgent crisis

Clara, please just say yes to the following as am truly fxxxed if you don't: we have two weeks 'til the opening party for the fourth nail bar and we have no florist to do the flowers. My boss Barbara is flying in from New York and is already freaking out about things not being perfect. She wanted Rick Van Shear from Panache to do them because he did a party in the Hamptons that she went to and now she is obsessed with him. Rick can't do it as he's doing Cruise Beckham's birthday party, and it seems every other florist has a wedding that weekend – I told Barbara that it is under control but this is obviously far from the truth! You're brilliant with flowers, your flat always looks so nice and it's not a huge job. Please, please can you do it?

I'm off on another date with Charles tomorrow, yippeeeeee! Things have been going really well with us and I'm starting to think that I'm actually ready for a proper relationship. I know you only met him briefly but didn't you think he was great? Kat thinks he's gorgeous and I was hoping to invite him to Mum's party – what d'you think?

By the way, do you know what kind of hat Jay Kay from the band Jamiraquai wears?

Bex

From: **Clara Harris** <u>claraharris@yahoo.com</u> **20.09.11 12:21**
To: Rebecca Harris
Subject: Re: Urgent crisis

Bex, have you forgotten that I have my Nutrition exams mid October? The ones I have spent the last two years working towards? I will be revising like crazy over the next two weeks. I have said no to all social invitations, cancelled my cable subscription and even put my gym membership on hold. I don't intend to come up for air over the next 14 days. Flower arranging for your party is completely out of the question. If you had given me more notice I might have been able to do something, but this is just impossible timing. You should also know that being able to put flowers in a vase at home and make them look nice does not come close to qualifying as a professional florist.

Lucky you going on a date. I know this sounds awful, but I can't remember which one Charles is? I know you introduced me at the pub but I was pretty upset with Jason not turning up and a bit self-consumed. I was so determined to drown my sorrows in a pint of gin and tonic that I wasn't concentrating on much else. Although I met a lot of your friends that night, I hardly talked to anyone apart from Olly. He was being so lovely, chatting away and trying to distract me from looking at my watch every three minutes. I got so horribly drunk that night and he was such a gentleman, calling me a cab and practically carrying me into it and all the time assuring me that I was behaving perfectly respectfully – humiliating but lovely. Anyway, I'm sure Charles is terrific. As long as he wasn't the guy with the floppy hair doing the Ricky Martin impression by the jukebox, then you're probably onto a winner. It's great that you're dating again, and about time too!

Jason has gone to Miami again on business. He's not back 'til Friday so I'm feeling pretty lonely, but at least it's giving me time to focus on my studies.

Oh, and don't forget, if your boss does kill you for this flower situation, you promised me your Valentino jacket.

PS Who on earth is Jay Kay?

Charles *was* the floppy haired, Ricky Martin guy! Were you kidding? Didn't you like him? He was only mucking around because everyone tells him he's a dead ringer for Ricky, so when *Livin La Vida Loca* came on he did a quick impression. I'm sure if you'd spoken to him you would think he's great. Everyone loves him, he's very popular, good looking, successful, and most importantly he thinks I'm sexy, so he must be a good bloke, right? ☺ I'm going to bring him to Mum's so you can get to know him better.

Clarabelle, don't stress about your exams. You've studied harder than any of your classmates. You may even be in danger of over-studying. I can't imagine there is anyone who has learnt to spell echinacea backwards, or tried to find a tertiary use for melatonin. It's not like they're going to try and make you do the Pepsi challenge with sixteen different brands of vitamin C, and even if they did you could probably nail it. You're a saint and you like doing saintly things. Please tell me that you were just making me sweat for a minute but you're really going to help me out?

I'm sorry Jason is away so much, but I actually think you seem happier when he's not around. It's not like the guy makes you laugh much . . . . what jacket?

From: Clara Harris 20.09.11 12:26
To: Rebecca Harris
Subject: back to urgent crisis

I swear if I fail these exams it is on you and I expect you to be at Covent Garden crack of dawn on the morning of the party to help me carry everything. Bex, I'm serious, you owe me big time for this and don't give me shit about "what jacket?"

Also, can you please try to remember that Jason is my fiancé, not just a boyfriend. I love him dearly and he is only not around much because he has a very demanding job and is forced to travel a great deal. Your long-suffering sister, Clara

From: Rebecca Harris 20.09.11 12:27
To: Clara Harris
Subject: fantastic!!!

Clarabelle, you're the best sister in the world! I can't thank you enough. I love you, you're the greatest – the jacket is yours, but don't tell Kat as I sort of promised it to her as well.

From: **Rebecca Harris 20.09.11 12:36**
To: Barbara Foreman
Subject: News from The Nail Bar

Barbara,

I have just heard back from Rick Van Shear and unfortunately it was impossible for him to change his previous booking. However, I have some great news – my sister has agreed to do the flowers. She's a brilliant florist and is in constant demand, so she has done us a HUGE favour. Do you have a colour scheme in mind or should I let her run with it?

Rebecca

From: **Rebecca Harris 20.09.11 12:39**
To: Oliver Barker
Subject: hi again

Olly,

Your ears should be burning, Clara and I were just discussing you. She thinks you're hot; so if you could dump the latest Brazilian model and tear her away from her dreadful boyfriend who never treats her well, I would be eternally grateful.

On another subject, I need to know what kind of hat Jay Kay from Jamiraquai wears – no one seems to have the faintest idea? I know your office is next to HMV – is there any chance you could have a quick look at a CD cover on your lunch break and let me know?

Thanks, Bex

From: **Oliver Barker 20.09.11 12:42**
To: Rebecca Harris
Subject: Re: hi again

Jay Kay wears a different hat every day of the week as far as I can gather, don't need to go to HMV, just Google him (band name has an 'o' not an 'a' in it, as in Jamir o quai) – is this some kind of blind date?

I thought your sister was very nice, but Carmen, who is Spanish by the way, with a very Latino temper, would have my balls for breakfast if I even looked at another girl. Anyway, isn't Clara's so-called "boyfriend" actually her fiancé? If he's really bad news, I do

know a guy who knows a guy who could have this Jason guy knee-capped for a couple of grand, if you like?
Ols

From: **Rebecca Harris 20.09.11 12:44**
To: Oliver Barker
Subject: Re: hi again

Didn't know the world of architecture was so rough and tough – very sexy! Will keep you posted should we need your guy.

Don't forget the new nail bar opening party is on the 30th. I need all the support I can get, so please promise me you'll be there, and feel free to bring the Brazilian.

The JamirOquai fan is actually a Czechoslovakian manicurist who is coming for an interview. However, funny you should mention dates, I do have one lined up with a dead hot banker I've sort of being seeing recently.

Love, Bex

From: **Oliver Barker 20.09.11 12:45**
To: Rebecca Harris
Subject: ??

Bex, I really hope you're not referring to that wanker Charles Balford? He's a renowned womanizer, pathetically arrogant and will use you and then dump you. Don't be an idiot. If you think Aeron is bad news, let me tell you this guy is in a different league.

PS Date is in diary and I will bring Carmen.

From: **Rebecca Harris 20.09.11 12:46**
To: Oliver Barker
Subject: oh really?

I think you're jealous.

From: **Oliver Barker 20.09.11 12:47**
To: Rebecca Harris
Subject: wanker

Probably, but it doesn't mean I'm not right.

Does he know about Poppy?

From: **Rebecca Harris 20.09.11 12:49**
To: Oliver Barker
Subject: Charles

Yes, as a matter of fact he does, and he doesn't have any problem with her either.

From: **Oliver Barker 20.09.11 12:51**
To: Rebecca Harris
Subject: Balford

Good, well as long as he realizes how important Poppy is to you. Charles isn't exactly renowned for putting other people first.

From: **Rebecca Harris 20.09.11 12:53**
To: Oliver Barker
Subject: Charles

I think you're being a bit unfair. I have never held back on telling anyone about Poppy. I'm not ashamed of her, so why would I? You're also making assumptions about Charles that have no grounds at all and it's slightly pissing me off.

From: **Oliver Barker 20.11.11 12:56**
To: Rebecca Harris
Subject: sorry

You're right, I'm sorry, that was totally unfair of me and it's actually none of my business who you go out with. I may not be crazy about the guy but I hope you have a fun time, I really do, you more than deserve it. X

From: **Rebecca Harris 20.09.11 12:58**
To: Oliver Barker
Subject: Re: sorry

It's just a date, we're not getting married, but don't worry – I will be on my guard for wankerishness.

From: **Barbara Foreman 20.09.11 14:01**
To: Rebecca Harris
Subject: News from The Nail Bar

Rebecca,

Cole & Peterson are preparing a mid-year report for Nail Corp that should hopefully be more than sufficient, but if you feel that your graphs will add to the picture then go ahead and get them sent over. I am doing a presentation to the Nail Corp Board of Directors next week and I'd like some good visual representation, so I will rely on you to provide this element.

Nail Corp have huge plans for manufacturing an extensive new nail care range in China, and I would like to reassure my people that The Nail Bar UK will be a strong contender to carry this range. I will be going to Guangdong on Thursday for two days, followed by a day in Hong Kong. Should everything go well, we plan to open more nail bars worldwide, and continue to grow the UK chain. The pressure is on you, Rebecca, to justify our expansion plans, so I hope you are feeling the full weight of that? These reports will confirm whether or not we were right to put you in charge of our UK project. What do you mean, your sister is doing the flowers for the party? I thought she was a psychiatrist.

Barbara

From:	**Rebecca Harris 20.09.11 14:03**
To:	Barbara Foreman
Subject:	Re: News from The Nail Bar

Well, actually she's training to be a nutritionist, but the reason why she's still training is because she's in such demand for her flower arranging that she never has time to study.

Expansion plans sound exciting and I feel absolutely confident that you will be delighted with the mid-year reports.

Rebecca

From:	**Rebecca Harris 20.09.11 14:05**
To:	Phoebe Combes
Subject:	new graphs needed!!!

Phoebe, I need your help right away!!!!!! Barbara needs me to produce some new graphs that really blow the roof off. The past three years' figures are on your computer in Excel format, which is how I need them. Can you send them over? I'm going to work on them and then work with you to produce a really good creative. I know you are focusing on promos, but this is a kind of promotion. Barbara is doing a presentation to the Nail Corp Board of all the Nail Bars, showing which ones have performed the best over the last three years She is including us in the presentation, so we want to make sure we come out well.

| From: | **Phoebe Combes 20.09.11 14:10** |
| To: | Rebecca Harris |

Subject: new graphs needed!!!

Right, yes, definitely, this sounds serious. I can pass over to Carol what I'm working on now and be with you in a sec.

From:	**Roberto Sodom** robsod@nicetime.couk **20.09.11 14:16**
To:	Rebecca Harris
SPAM:	***Staying power***

Penis Pilates £7.99 (does not include exercise mat or miniature weights) A step-by-step guide to improving your sexual performance.

******GET HARD AND STAY HARD*******

http://www.pumpyourpecker.com/

From:	**Rebecca Harris 20.09.11 14:18**
To:	Tania Cutter
Subject:	SPAM

Tania, I've started to receive SPAM mail again. I thought Graham had sorted the problem out? I've only received one so far but it looks just like last time, so the onslaught will be on its way. I just can't afford to have the whole system crash again, so please be quick.

Rebecca

From:	**Tania Cutter 20.09.11 14:21**
To:	Rebecca Harris
Subject:	Re: SPAM

Rebecca,

I distinctly remember Graham warning you that if you went onto pornographic websites you would receive these kind of lurid emails. Quite frankly I don't know where you find the time? I find it all quite distasteful, especially as the association drags us all down. This is the third time we have had to call Graham. I should think we're a laughing stock at *Computer Companions.*

Tania Cutter PA

The Nail Bar Ltd

From:	**Rebecca Harris 20.09.11 14:23**
To:	Tania Cutter
Subject:	Re: SPAM

Tania, I can assure you I have not been surfing porn on the net.

Graham actually said that it could be anyone in the office as all our computers are linked. Anyway, I'm pretty sure the guys at *Computer Companions* have dealt with a lot worse than this and I really don't give a damn what they think. We need to pre-empt a technological meltdown, so if you could possibly stomach it I would like you to call Graham NOW.

Thank you

Rebecca

From: **Jonathan Banks 20.09.11 14:30**
To: Rebecca Harris
Subject: Charles Balford

Hi Bex,

I meant to tell you, I gave a guy in our office, name of Charles Balford, your email address a couple of weeks ago. I don't actually know him very well but he's in his late 30s, pretty sure he's not married, can't vouch for any illegitimate children, dresses like a ponce but doesn't beep the gay'dar (apparently), reasonably good at his job, and according to the girls in the office "he's very good-looking", so I thought I'd risk it. Sorry I didn't tell you earlier. I was in the Middle East last week and meant to tell you before I left. If he turns out to be a tosser then I owe you lunch.

Johnny

From: **Rebecca Harris 20.09.11 14:33**
To: Jonathon Banks
Subject: Re: Charles Balford

Hi Johnny,

How are you? I haven't seen you in ages. No problem about Charles, I've been seeing him quite a bit recently and I think he's great, so I probably owe *you* lunch.

By the way, I am organizing a birthday party for my mum at her house on Friday. It's just going to be a very relaxed dinner. I would love it if you came?

Bex

From: **Jonathon Banks 20.09.11 14:34**
To: Rebecca Harris
Subject: Party on Friday sounds great, would love to come. See you then.

From: **Rebecca Harris 20.09.11 14:38**
To: Oliver Barker
Subject: Mum's birthday

Ols, just a reminder about my Mum's birthday party this Friday. I'm afraid it's no longer a BBQ on my roof as this rain is forecast to stay all week, so it's now a dinner party at her house. Can you still come? You're welcome to bring Sofia too.

From: **Oliver Barker 20.09.11 14:50**
To: Rebecca Harris
Subject: Re: Mum's birthday

Bex, *Carmen* and I would love to come but I'm afraid we could only be there for drinks beforehand as I have a flight to catch to Hong Kong that night. Is that ok?

From: **Rebecca Harris 20.09.11 14:51**
To: Oliver Barker
Subject: Re: Mum's birthday

Oh Olly, I can't believe you're off again. You've only just got back from Hong Kong. I'm starting to think you have a secret family out there, a Susie Wong wife and a couple of cute little Eurasian kids. Am I close?

I was sort of hoping you were going to be around this weekend so you could come and look at the progress (or lack of) at Kensington. I'm having such a nightmare with my builders and I wanted to get your opinion on whether you think things are being done well. I'm so worried we're not going to be finished on time and I'm having serious communication problems with my contractor.

Is there any chance you could come by before you go?

From: **Oliver Barker 20.09.11 14:53**
To: Rebecca Harris
Subject: Kensington

Unfortunately, it's all work, work, work and it's making me a very dull and permanently jet-lagged boy. Actually its quite exciting stuff. We are doing a huge commercial project in Kowloon. Our firm has won the rights to design a massive new mall with over a thousand shops in it, so it's a big deal. It does mean that I'm going to be out there a lot this year and might even have to relocate, so Susie Wong is not an entirely implausible scenario ☺. You should come out some time while I'm there and bring Poppy. It would be cool to show her the country you lived in when you were her age.

Sorry I can't see the nail bar this weekend, but if you like I could come by after work tonight and give my opinion, for what it's worth. I am meant to be meeting one of our project managers then, but I could see if he was on for swinging by your nail bar first. He would have a much better idea whether your guys are doing a good job or not, but we would have to be quite quick.

PS If that doesn't suit, I will probably be at The Hound Dog later, so you could talk me through the situation there.

From:	**Rebecca Harris 20.09.11 14:55**
To:	Oliver Barker
Subject:	Re: Kensington

Olly, it would be amazing if you could come with your project manager. I was intending to be there between 6 & 7pm but I'll go whatever time suits you.

I would love to take Poppy to Hong Kong one day but at the moment I'm so busy I hardly have time to take her to the park.

Can't come to The Dog as have switched Vinca's babysitting night to tomorrow, but I think you might bump into Kat and Marcus there.

Thanks so much.

Bex

From:	**Rebecca Harris 20.09.11 15:03**
To:	Joe Doyle
Subject:	Kensington Building Works

Joe, I don't know if you've been to Kensington today but the new manicure chairs have arrived. Please could you make sure that the plastic doesn't get taken off, I don't want them to get dirty.

Rebecca

From:	**Rebecca Harris 20.09.11 15:20**
To:	Phoebe Combes
Subject:	figures please!!

Phoebe, I still haven't received the figures. I thought you were going to send them right away? Perhaps I didn't stress the urgency of this, but I need them RIGHT NOW.

Bex

From: Phoebe Combes 20.09.11 15:20
To: Rebecca Harris
Subject: Re: figures please!!
Attach: August sales figures

Oh, right, I forget sometimes what a stickler Barbara is. Poor you, having to deal with her directly, I know I'd be terrified. I remember at my primary school we had a terribly frightening needlework teacher called Mrs. Kimmons. She would point her knitting needle at any girl who was talking in class and say, "Don't make me poke you with this, young lady, because I can assure you it will hurt". One day I asked my friend Katie Wiggly if she could pass the tissue box because I had a cold. Mrs. Kimmons heard and immediately turned her cold grey eyes on me and pointed her long sharp needle and before she even spoke the dreaded words, I'd wet my pants. I'll never forget it.

Anyway, I'm sure Barbara isn't as horrible as Mrs. Kimmons, but I'm still very glad you deal with her rather than me.

Sending figures right now.

From: Rebecca Harris 20.09.11 15:30
To: Phoebe Combes
Subject: Re: figures please!!

Um, thanks Phoebe, I'll let you know.

From: Joe Doyle 20.09.11 15:31
To: Rebecca Harris
Subject: Re: Kensington Building Works

Automated response: Joe Doyle is out of the office until next week.

From: Felicity Jones 20.09.11 15:33
To: Rebecca Harris
Subject: sales training with Sylvia

Bex, I'm heading over to do some sales training at Marylebone in about half an hour, gonna take Sylvia with me to give her a feel for things. I'll also grill the shit out of the elusive Coco for more info on the whereabouts of Suki.

From: Rebecca Harris 20.09.11 15:35
To: Felicity Jones
Subject: Re: sales training with Sylvia

Aren't you meant to be interviewing Katya this afternoon? I'm meeting her in an hour, aren't I?

From: **Felicity Jones 20.09.11 15:36**
To: Rebecca Harris
Subject: Re: sales training with Sylvia

Bollocks!! I forgot about Katya. Any chance you could do the interview?

From: **Rebecca Harris 20.09.11 15:38**
To: Felicity Jones
Subject: Katya

Christ, Fi, I'm up to my eyeballs already. I'll take her to Kensington with me but I'll just have to do the interview in the car as I need to go over a lot of things with Joe this afternoon.

From: **Felicity Jones 20.09.11 15:40**
To: Rebecca Harris
Subject: Re: Katya

Great, thanks. She doesn't speak English, so there's not really much you can discuss.

From: **Rebecca Harris 20.09.11 15:45**
To: Tania Cutter
Subject: DHL
Attach: Figs for 2007, 2008

Tania, what is the deadline for DHL to pick up some documents so that they go today? R

From: **Tania Cutter 20.09.11 15:48**
To: Rebecca Harris
Subject: Re: DHL

You've missed it.
Tania Cutter PA
The Nail Bar Ltd.

From: **Rebecca Harris 20.09.11 15:50**
To: Tania Cutter
Subject: Re: DHL

I thought it was 5pm?

From: **Tania Cutter 20.09.11 15:54**
To: Rebecca Harris

Subject: Re: DHL

It is, but I am in the middle of something which I will need to finish before I can get around to calling them.

Tania Cutter PA

The Nail Bar Ltd.

From: **Rebecca Harris 20.09.11 15:56**
To: Tania Cutter
Subject: Re: DHL

Tania, I'm going to put this as nicely as I can: please could you arrange for DHL to come to the office just before 5pm today. If you delay to the point where it is too late, I will kill you.

From: **Tania Cutter 20.09.11 15:58**
To: Rebecca Harris
Subject: Re: DHL

I find that quite threatening and extremely unpleasant.

Tania Cutter PA

The Nail Bar Ltd.

From: **Rebecca Harris 20.09.11 15:59**
To: Tania Cutter
Subject: Re: DHL

I'm glad nothing was lost in translation.

From: **Felicity Jones 20.09.11 16:00**
To: Tania Cutter
Subject: sales figures

Tania, I'm off to do sales training at Marylebone. Could I have the figures for nail polish sales from all the nail bars this year to date? Felicity

From: **Tania Cutter 20.09.11 16:03**
To: Felicity Jones
Subject: Re: sales figures

Felicity, I should have the figures for you by the end of the day, or perhaps tomorrow morning, and a 'please' and 'thank you' once in a while would be appreciated.

Tania Cutter PA

The Nail Bar Ltd

From: **Felicity Jones 20.09.11 16:04**
To: Tania Cutter
Subject: Re: sales figures

You have them right there on your computer so just send them over. Please and bloody thank you.

From: **Tania Cutter 20.09.11 16:07**
To: Felicity Jones
Subject: Re: sales figures

Simply not possible, and must all your emails contain a completely unnecessary expletive? I have many other assignments today which have been requested of me prior to your demands. I will therefore work through each one in the order in which I received them. In future, should you wish for something to be completed by mid afternoon, I suggest you put it on my desk the night before, or, at best, first thing in the morning.
Tania Cutter PA
The Nail Bar Ltd.

From: **Felicity Jones 20.09.11 16:09**
To: Tania Cutter
Subject: Re: sales figures

Tania, I don't know what you're going on about, but I need the figures NOW. I am trying to manage 38 under-25-years-old, high-maintenance, low IQ, non-English-speaking female manicurists. It's called multi-tasking. You should FUCKING try it sometime.

From: **Tania Cutter 20.09.11 16:11**
To: Felicity Jones
Subject: Re: sales figures

I don't think that warrants a response.

From: **Rebecca Harris 20.09.11 16:17**
To: Joe Doyle
Subject: Kensington Building Works

Joe, you need to cancel the automated response on your computer. Every time I send you an email I get a reply saying you are out of town for the week, which can't be true? I'll be at Kensington just before 5pm so PLEASE DON'T LEAVE before I get there.
Rebecca

From: **Rebecca Harris 20.09.11 16:17**
To: Tania Cutter
Subject: Re: URGENT!!!!!!!!!

Tania,

I've just spoken to Andrea who told me that you didn't call her about sending a member of staff to Marylebone! What part of my "URGENT" email did you not understand? Marylebone is without a manager, they're fully booked, in desperate need of more staff and all you seem to be doing is filing your nails?
Rebecca

From: **Tania Cutter 20.09.11 16:19**
To: Rebecca Harris
Subject: Re: URGENT!!!!!!!!!

Rebecca,

In response to Phoebe Combes's internal memo, I am testing the new glass nail file so that I can give her feedback for her press release (even though PR is meant to be her new job, not mine) so your tone is very uncalled for.

Yes I did see your email was titled URGENT but so was her's, as are most of the ones that come to me, except, I might point out, your one regarding DHL which, if it had been, you would have got a different response from myself and presumably not had to go to the lengths of threatening my life.

I had to inform Felicity earlier and I will now do the same to you; I am operating on a system of dealing with each requirement in the order that it comes in. I prefer to complete one job before moving on to the next so as to ensure that each job is done properly. This is a method I have always used and it allows me to keep abreast of my workload, and to leave on time each day, or earlier, as is the case today, due to the 45 minutes owing to me from going to Marylebone in my lunch break yesterday.
Tania Cutter PA
The Nail Bar Ltd

From: **Joe Doyle 20.09.11 16:23**
To: Rebecca Harris
Subject: Re: Kensington

Automated response: Joe Doyle is out of the office until next week.

From: **Rebecca Harris 20.09.11 16:23**
To: Tania Cutter
Subject: Re: URGENT!!!!!!!!!

Tania, I am your boss. <u>Anything</u> that comes from me you can assume is urgent.

The next two weeks are going to be completely manic. I have Barbara breathing down my neck and I am trying to deal with an absent manager at Marylebone, a building contractor who seems to have gone missing in action, and an opening party for 200 people as well as all the usual problems with running this company.

I'm now extremely late to pick up an interviewee and you are meant to be my assistant: so please can you assist.

Rebecca

From: **Rebecca Harris 20.09.11 16:25**
To: Felicity Jones
Subject: Re: Katya

Fi, shouldn't you have left? You aren't going to have much time to do management training. I'm running late to pick up Katya. Do you have a mobile number for her? And in your search for staff, if you find someone who could pass as an office assistant, grab her. Tania is driving me to drink.

From: **Felicity Jones 20.0911 16:27**
To: Rebecca Harris
Subject   Fw: email from taniacutter@thenailbar.co.uk

Tell me about it. The reason I haven't left is because I'm waiting for Tania to give me some figures that I want to take with me. I'm forwarding the email she just sent me. The woman is so full of shit and so anally-retentive, I don't know how the whole thing doesn't blow?

I'll send Katya a text.

From: **Rebecca Harris 20.09.11 16:28**
To: Felicity Jones
Subject: Re: your email

Couldn't see her email but I agree with you, she is unbelievably irritating.

From: **Felicity Jones 20.0911 16:30**
To: Rebecca Harris

Subject   Fw: email from taniacutter@thenailbar.co.uk

Re-sending her email.

Irritating? She should be hospitalized.

From: Tania Cutter 20.09.11 16:42
To: Rebecca Harris
Cc: Felicity Jones
Subject: I resign

Rebecca and Felicity,

I would like to inform you both that your last email correspondence was also copied to me. As you can imagine, I am extremely upset by your childish and hateful comments and I intend to make a full report to the Nail Corp management about this.

Rebecca, as my boss, I find your comments the most hurtful, even though Felicity's are, unsurprisingly, more vulgar. It is of course impossible for me to work in this office under these conditions and I will notify Ms Foreman immediately, who I am sure will be most sympathetic. I will spend the rest of the afternoon gathering my things and then I will be off. I do not intend to return until I have received an official apology from both of you and some substantial compensation.

Tania Cutter PA
The Nail Bar Ltd

From: Felicity Jones 20.09.11 16:44
To: Rebecca Harris
Subject   Tania

Fuck me, that was unexpected!!

From: Rebecca Harris 20.09.11 16:45
To: Felicity Jones
Subject: Re: Tania

Oh my god!!!!!!

From: Felicity Jones 20.09.11 16:46
To: Rebecca Harris
Subject: Re: Tania

Bex, this situation is looking a little tricky. I am almost positive that you would be better at dealing with this than me.

From: **Rebecca Harris 20.09.11 16:47**
To: Felicity Jones
Subject: Re: Tania

This is a bit more than tricky!

What I don't understand is how on earth it happened? I didn't press any wrong buttons, did you?

From: **Felicity Jones 20.09.11 16:49**
To: Rebecca Harris
Subject: Re: Tania

Think it might have been me. When I tried to forward Tania's email to you, I think I might have just forwarded our emails to her. Piss.

From: **Rebecca Harris 20.09.11 16:51**
To: Felicity Jones
Subject: Re: Tania

Right, well, I'm going to try and sort it out and see if I can persuade her to stay.

From: **Felicity Jones 20.09.11 16:53**
To: Rebecca Harris
Subject: Re: Tania

Persuade her to stay? Are you mad? Isn't it a case of good riddance to the witch from hell?

From: **Rebecca Harris 20.09.11 16:57**
To: Felicity Jones
Subject: Re: Tania

I think you'll find it's not that easy. Tania isn't stupid. She's going to get straight onto Barbara, who thinks she's the best thing since peanut butter met jelly, and then we're probably going to hear from her lawyers about abuse in the workplace, or cruelty to office assistants. We're going to be up to our eyeballs in this if we're not VERY careful. Besides, as dreadful as she may be, we are seriously under-staffed in all departments, so it's not ideal to be losing another member of staff just at this moment.

I'm going to send an email to her and I'll copy you in. Please just read, don't comment, I'm so nervous of any wrong emails going to Tania again.

From: **Felicity Jones 20.09.11 17:01**
To: Rebecca Harris

Subject: Re: Tania

You're absolutely right. Sorry. Let me know what I can do to help. Will just observe from a distance.

From: Rebecca Harris 20.09.11 17:09
To: Tania Cutter
Cc: Felicity Jones
Subject: apologies

Dear Tania,

You have every right to feel offended by the email correspondence between Felicity and myself. It was incredibly childish of us and very unprofessional and we are both truly sorry. The pressure is very much on at the moment with the new nail bar opening approaching and I think tempers are probably flying higher than usual. In this case it has resulted in things being said that under different circumstances would not have been. You are a fantastic Personal Assistant and we really couldn't run this company without you. Why don't the three of us go out for a drink after work and have a good time and forget all about it?
Rebecca

From: Felicity Jones 20.09.11 17:13
To: Rebecca Harris
Subject: Re: drink after work???

Oh god, couldn't we just make it a coffee in the meeting room? Brian and I have got friends coming for dinner and I haven't done the supermarket shop yet!

From: Rebecca Harris 20.09.11 17:15
To: Felicity Jones
Subject: Re: drink after work???

Fi, I thought you weren't going to comment? I don't mean to state the obvious here, but when we have a problem with a member of staff, ideally you're meant to step in and smooth things over, especially when you are in part responsible for the problem. I know Tania is a nightmare at the best of times, but you have to admit she is quite efficient and she gets the job done, albeit in the most teeth-grindingly frustrating way, but most importantly we don't have time to recruit a new assistant at this stage.

Anyway she hasn't responded yet and she's still packing up her things, so you may be in luck.

From: **Tania Cutter 20.09.11 17:21**
To: Rebecca Harris
Cc: Felicity Jones
Subject: Re: apologies

Rebecca,

I do not believe that the way I have been insulted can be resolved over a trip to the pub, and I find it insulting that you think it could. I will leave it in the hands of Nail Corp to decide how to handle the situation and what kind of sanctions to impose.

If you need to correspond with me while I am on leave you can use my other email address littleturtle@hotmail.com

Tania Cutter PA

The Nail Bar Ltd

From: **Felicity Jones 20.09.11 17:23**
To: Rebecca Harris
Subject: Re: drink after work???

She's bluffing, there's no way she would walk out on the back of this.

From: **Rebecca Harris 20.09.11 17:30**
To: Felicity Jones
Subject: quick!!

Can you get onto the temping agency ASAP? She is walking out the door now!

From: **Felicity Jones 20.09.11 17:31**
To: Rebecca Harris
Subject: Re: quick!!

Oh crap. By the way, what's with "Little Turtle"?
Is it a sort of Red Indian thing like "Sitting Bull" or "Swimming Fish"?

From: **Rebecca Harris 20.09.11 17:32**
To: Felicity Jones
Subject: Re: quick!!

I guess so. I would have gone for something more glamorous like "Soaring Eagle" or "Flying Dragon".

From: **Felicity Jones 20.09.11 17:34**
To: Rebecca Harris
Subject: Re: quick!!

I agree, or in Tania's case something more appropriate like "Mad Cow" – but I guess that was already taken. Calling temp agency now.

From: **Rebecca Harris 20.09.11 17:36**
To: Felicity Jones
Subject: Re: quick!!

Good, and remind them that we now qualify for their discount. Can't believe we are in the middle of a massive recruitment drive and so far we have managed to lose one member of staff, have another missing in action and . . . . . . OH MY GOD, I FORGOT ABOUT KATYA!!!!!!!!!!!

Wednesday 21st September 2011

From: **Rebecca Harris 21.09.11 9:04**
To: Joe Doyle
Subject: Where are you?

Joe,

I was at Kensington yesterday afternoon and again there was only one guy working, not the same guy I met in the morning, who obviously found the whole thing just too much. This guy, who called himself Karl, said he thought you were in MAJORICA!! Please tell me Karl has just had one too many collisions with his hammer and doesn't know what he's talking about?

Rebecca

From: **Joe Doyle 21.09.11 9:06**
To: Rebecca Harris
Subject: Re: Where are you?

Automated response: Joe Doyle is out of the office until next week

From: **Rebecca Harris 21.09.11 9:14**
To: Felicity Jones
Subject: Re: Darren?

Fi, Who is the slightly weird-looking bloke wearing makeup at Reception? This isn't Darren from the agency, is it?

Bex

From: **Felicity Jones 21.09.11 9:16**
To: Rebecca Harris
Subject: Re: Darren?

It is. It's a fuck up. On Darren's CV he stated that he was gay, so I automatically assumed he would be good looking and didn't bother checking with the agency. I will tell them we need a replacement ASAP.

Fi

From: **Rebecca Harris 21.09.11 9:18**
To: Felicity Jones
Subject: Re: Darren?

It's not the look that's the problem. It's the fact that he's walking around with a feather duster in his hand singing Bette Midler songs!

From: **Felicity Jones 21.09.11 9:20**
To: Rebecca Harris

Subject   Re: Darren?

I agree. It's totally out of hand. We already have so many high-maintenance staff, the last thing we need is a queen on Reception. I'll go talk to him.

From: **Ellemis Blevin** ellemis@jwp.co.uk **21.09.11 9:21**
To: Rebecca Harris

SPAM   ***Flavour of the Month***

****WONDERCUM, 11.99 USD for 12 tablets!! ****

- **Make oral sex more fun – add a flavour to your cum!**
- **Do not exceed recommended dosage or semen may become discoloured**
- **Tablets must be taken aurally**
  http//www.yumcum.com

From: **Rebecca Harris 21.09.11 9:22**
To: Felicity Jones
Subject: Re: Spam

Did you just get that SPAM about strawberry-flavoured semen?

From: **Felicity Jones 21.0911 9:23**
To: Rebecca Harris
Subject   Re: Spam

Nope, but sounds like it might make a nice change.

From: **Rebecca Harris 21.09.11 9:24**
To: Felicity Jones
Subject: Re: Spam

Why am I the only one in this office who gets all the SPAM mail? Tania was meant to get Graham in but that obviously got put to the bottom of her extensive 'to do' list and there doesn't seem to be any listing for *Computer Companions*.

From: **Felicity Jones 21.09.11 9:26**
To: Rebecca Harris
Subject: Re: Spam

Darren's CV says that he is computer literate. Maybe he can help you.

From: **Rebecca Harris 21.09.11 9:33**
To: Darren Bennett
Subject: Spam

Hi Darren,

Hope you are settling in ok? I'll come by and say hi in a moment, but in the meantime I'm getting a lot of SPAM emails and I don't know how to block them. Do you have any idea how to do that? If not, could you get me the number of our software support company? It should be somewhere in Tania's files.

From: **Darren Bennett 21.09.11 9:35**
To: Rebecca Harris
Subject: Re: Spam

Hiya, I'm fab, thanks. Loving the whole fabulousness of The Nail Bar Headquarters, soooo professional and yet soooo fabulous.

I can take a break from colour-coding paper clips and have a little scavenge in the roller decks for you, but if the number is on Tania's computer I'm going to have trouble. That little vixen has a password in place that must be onomatopoeic because there are no normal words left. Believe me, I have tried!

I'm afraid I wouldn't have a clue how to block something even if it was about to hit me in the face, and the only spam I'm familiar with is the kind you would find in a pack lunch (reference to school pack lunch, not the other kind . . . giggle giggle).

From: **Rebecca Harris 21.09.11 9:39**
To: Darren Bennett
Subject: Re: Spam

Ok, thanks Darren.

From: **Darren Bennett 21.09.11 9:40**
To: Rebecca Harris
Subject: Re: Spam

Pleasure treasure ☺

From: **Rebecca Harris 21.09.11 9:43**
To: Felicity Jones
Subject: Darren

Fi, Darren just sent me an-email saying "pleasure treasure" – he's 19 years old! I'm really not sure this is going to work out.

From: **Felicity Jones 21.09.11 9:45**
To: Rebecca Harris
Subject: Re: Darren

That's totally inappropriate, I'll sort it out.

From: **Rebecca Harris 21.09.11 10:20**
To: Katherine Lease
Subject: OMG

Kat, I can't go out with Charles, I'm too fat. If I don't lose at least 4lb by this evening I'm going to have to cancel.

I started my crash diet last night. I know everyone says they don't work, but I had no choice. There is no time for a sensible game plan. Everything was going really well until about 10pm last night. I had 7 cups of green tea, 2 apples, three of Poppy's cheesy dip snacks (not too bad, only 87 calories and 2 grams of fat each) and a mini pack of organic raisins. Then I got into bed – this is where it gets really ugly, so brace yourself – of course I couldn't sleep because of all the green tea, so I got up again and it was like a dark force was pulling me towards the fridge and my light saber was out of batteries. I swear it was out of my control. Even Luke Skywalker would have had trouble resisting and he's a Jedi Knight – I've had absolutely no training at all!

Before I knew what was happening I was piling scoops of vanilla & macadamia nut ice cream into an enormous bowl and – wait for it, wait for it, because this is where it gets incredible – covering the ice cream with more chocolate sauce than you can shake a stick at, and then just to really rocket-launch the glycaemic index into space, I covered the whole bang lot in multi-coloured Sprinkles and scoffed it all without even sitting down. I then waddled back to bed, careful not to burn off any calories at all on the way back, and went sound asleep.

I was woken this morning by Poppy, who wanted to know why I had Sprinkles on my pillow and face. The house rule is we are only allowed Sprinkles at the weekend. I tried to explain it to her but she was having none of it and insisted that she was allowed to have Sprinkles on her toast and in her Rice Crispies, otherwise it wouldn't be fair. What could I do?

I'm coming towards Kensington at lunchtime to see how the building site is progressing. Are you on for lunch? Obviously I won't be eating, but I'd like to be near a pizza in the hopes of achieving satisfaction by osmosis. What is it about diets that make me want to eat ten times more than I normally do? It's like my brain goes into panic mode as soon as I even contemplate it and immediately thinks, "STORE, STORE, FOR FUCK'S SAKE STORE, SHE'S PLANNING A CUTBACK!!"

Who wants to be a size 8 anyway? Men all think Eva Longoria is sexy and she must be at least a size 10, right?

From: **Katherine Lease 21.09.11 10:25**
To: Rebecca Harris
Subject: Re: OMG

Just got in to work. Thank the Pope my boss is in Milan and hasn't called in yet. My status as teacher's pet was short-lived. I didn't get back to the office after our lunch until 5 o'clock yesterday. I was intending to go straight back but I noticed one of those walk-in dentist places offering a free teeth-whitening session. Suzanne was marching around the office in a bate looking for me when I got back. She flipped when I practically blinded her with my smile, which I thought was an overreaction, especially as she should really be pleased. I mean this is Armani, for god's sake! I'm expected to look good and that takes time and money. She of all people knows that. Quite frankly, she should be grateful that I didn't expense the treatment on the company account.

Darling, you're not too fat and you were obviously hungry, even if that was a little excessive. You have an extremely stressful job, a child to raise, you've just received correspondence from your bastard ex-lover/father of your child and you are shortly moving in with your mother (social suicide), so you're obviously panic eating. I'm sure it's very normal.

Kat xx

From: **Rebecca Harris 21.09.11 10:26**
To: Katherine Lease
Subject: Re: OMG

God, when you put it like that I feel even worse!

I know you think I'm mad moving in with my mum, but I just can't afford not to. The offer on my place was too good to turn down, and anyway my flat is just too small for Poppy and me. When Poppy wants to start having friends for sleepovers there'll be no room –

there's hardly enough room for me to have a friend for a sleepover! Mum suggests that when I move in I should cut Vinca's time down to just two days a week plus babysitting. She reckons she's happy to take responsibility for Poppy the rest of the time! That's a huge cost-saving for me and I can start looking for a place near a park and a decent school. Poppy and my mum think it's a brilliant plan.

Looking forward to seeing the teeth.

From: **Katherine Lease 21.09.11 10:30**
To: Rebecca Harris
Subject: Re: OMG

Well, I think you're amazing. My mother and I have not been able to live under the same roof since I was 15, but then we're talking about a woman who insists on washing and re-using cling film, has a dishwasher but refuses to use it, eats a banana with a knife and fork and won't allow a TV in her house because "the wireless is perfectly adequate".

I'm feeling extremely weird, by the way – is it possible to get high on effervescence?

From: **Rebecca Harris 21.09.11 10:31**
To: Katherine Lease
Subject: Re: OMG

What do you mean? Did the dentist give you something weird?

From: **Katherine Lease 21.09.11 10:34**
To: Rebecca Harris
Subject: hangover cure

It wasn't the dentist, it was self-administered. I was so hung-over this morning I took three Alka Seltzers and two Redoxin to try and sort me out, and I think I might have ODd? This morning on the tube coming to work I'm sure I was hallucinating. I kept feeling a dog licking my feet, but whenever I looked there was nothing there. Also, whenever I leaned over to have a look I got a massive head rush, burped and started giggling. You know I find burping really disgusting and not remotely funny, so isn't that weird? It was absolutely mortifying, especially as it happened to be the first time in my commuting history that I was sitting next to someone who could actually be described as good-looking. At first I thought it might even be Ewan McGregor. Obviously it wasn't, but could well have been his brother.

From: **Rebecca Harris 21.09.11 10:36**
To: Katherine Lease
Subject: hot tube travel

In my expert medical opinion, I probably would have settled for just three Alka Seltzer, but I think you'll survive. How come you always manage to come across these sexy men? I never randomly sit next to anyone hot on the tube.

Nurse Harris

From: **Katherine Lease 21.09.11 10:39**
To: Rebecca Harris
Subject: Re: hot tube travel

Honey, I have been travelling to work on the godforsaken Circle line for the past four years and never, not once, has there ever been anyone who would score above four in an out of ten classification for good looks. What are you talking about? I always run into cute guys? It is virtually unheard of for a hot guy to travel underground. This is why the planting of brother McGregor on a seat beside me while I was having cold sweats and trying not to vomit everywhere was borderline conspiracy theory. I have made up my mind, I'm switching to the bus. I don't care if it increases my commute time by an hour. I have had it with the London Underground. Four years of loyalty and bad skin and this is the thanks I get. That's it, no more, I'm coming up for air.

Patient Kat

From: **Rebecca Harris 21.09.11 10:40**
To: Katherine Lease
Subject: Re: hot tube travel

You go, girl! Throw caution to the wind. You need to see more of the world and the world needs to see more of you.

I am prescribing The Bus, to be taken five times a day.

Nurse Harris

From: **Katherine Lease 21.09.11 10:43**
To: Rebecca Harris
Subject: Re: hot tube travel

By the way, talking about hot guys, I bumped into Olly last night. He is looking seriously cute at the moment. There was no sign of a girlfriend and it's been four years since the Caris heartbreak, so he must be ready to get down and dirty? My advice – have a quick fling with Ricky Martin, but then move swiftly on to the architect.

I can definitely meet for lunch – Pizza Express on Kensington High Street 12.45pm. Serious carb craving, might even be one of those family size, deep pan, quarto formaggio days. Very happy not to share.

Oh, and darling, the answer to your question of "who wants to be a size 8 anyway?" – is NOBODY. Women in my business would kill themselves if they were anything more than a 4. Believe me, if Eva Longoria was ever accused of being a size 10 she would tear her own heart out and feed it to the wolves of Wisteria Lane.

From: **Rebecca Harris 21.09.11 10:46**
To: Katherine Lease
Subject: Olly

What? I thought any size less than an 8 was a reference to age?

Olly does have a girlfriend, although I can't remember her name. She's a South American model of some sort, which suits Ols down to the ground because she's only here for a short while and there's no commitment required from either of them. Olly's love for Caris hasn't changed, I'm pretty sure. In fact he's been over to Ireland a couple of times recently to visit her. She's in the process of finalizing her divorce. Once that goes through he'll kick the Argentinean into touch and be on a boat to Ireland before you can say "Ah, there goes a good-looking architect if ever I saw one".

PS By the way, do you know how to block SPAM emails?

From: **Katherine Lease 21.09.11 10:49**
To: Rebecca Harris
Subject: Re: Olly

Darling, I work in fashion. If I even pretended to have any kind of computer skills, I'd be fired. It's a miracle you receive my emails.

Can't bear it about Olly – double rehab, divorcee who led him on in the first place – doesn't deserve such a catch.

What a WASTE!!!!!

Kat

From: Rebecca Harris 21.09.11 10:56
To: Katherine Lease
Subject: Re: Caris

All I hope is that she was worth waiting for. Olly's capacity to love is so inspiring, it would be properly tragic if Caris doesn't love him back with an equal intensity. What I wouldn't give to have a guy love me like that! It's only in hindsight that I realize Aeron and I never came close. At least it's reassuring to know that that kind of love does actually exist. With Aeron I was so excited to be pregnant I never questioned how he really felt about me. I just assumed that he loved me madly but was not the type to show it.

Caris, on the other hand, assumed she wasn't liked unless she was told otherwise on a constant basis. She wanted to know who adored her and how far they would be prepared to go to show it. People tended to flock to her naturally because she was so full of energy and fun. Although she sometimes veered on the psychotic side in my opinion, I have to admit the sun definitely shone brighter when you were near Caris. The flip side was she could be quite cruel when she wanted to be. Her mood swings were fairly wild and unpredictable. Luckily, I was never of much consequence to her because she saw me as Aeron's girlfriend and therefore not capable of giving her enough attention and as such not worth bothering with. She was perfectly nice to me but I was never really in the "gang". It suited me fine as I was always way too knackered at the weekends to gallivant around the place being wild and wonderful. Olly, on the other hand, was brilliant at keeping Caris on an even keel. She adored him the most because she knew he knew her faults and loved her anyway. Caris surrounded herself with sycophants because she couldn't bear to be criticized, but she let Olly tell her off all the time. She trusted him completely because she knew he loved her the most.

From: **Katherine Lease 21.09.11 11:05**
To: Rebecca Harris
Subject: Re: Caris

So why did she go off and marry Craig?

From: **Rebecca Harris 21.09.11 11:10**
To: Katherine Lease

You mean Keith. I have no idea. We were down at the O'Briens' for the weekend when the news came through by text message to Caris's mum that she'd gone and got hitched. Olly had just arrived and I was excited to see him to show him my bump. He knew I was pregnant because I'd phoned him a few weeks before, but it had been a long-distance call and a bad line so we hadn't been able to hear each other properly. I knew he would share my enthusiasm about the baby and I was hoping he might be able to talk to Aeron – help him get used to the idea of becoming a dad. Unfortunately, when Olly arrived he was in a terrible mood. I think he knew, or at least had a pretty good idea, what Caris had done. When the text came through and the shit hit the fan, Olly and I went to the garden to give the O'Briens some space. We stayed out there for hours, talking about Caris and the baby and everything. Olly got quietly plastered and I ate about 15 packets of Twiglets. He eventually opened up and told me how he had fallen in love with someone he could now never have and he'd been such an idiot for waiting too long to tell her and now he'd missed his moment and lost her. He couldn't bring himself to even say her name. We had all known for ages how he felt about her and we all just assumed they would end up together. I think he was biding his time because he thought Caris wasn't ready for a serious relationship and he didn't want to just be one of her flings.

Caris was big on one-night stands and was always saying how boring and suburban it would be to get married. God, it was so sad, Kat, I can't tell you, he just looked absolutely crushed.

The following morning, before I woke up, he had gone. The next I heard he had left for the States.

It's only since he got back at the beginning of this year that we've become good friends again. In fact much better than we ever were before, but we almost never talk about Caris. I think he doesn't want to say anything about her until he knows for sure that she feels the same way. Anyway, if you wanna hear more, you'll have to wait 'til lunch, gotta go. x

From: Katherine Lease 21.09.11 11:13
To: Rebecca Harris

Subject: Re: Caris

Do I wanna hear more? Sweetie, I'm bored out of my mind at work. I can't wait to hear more. Practically leaving for lunch now . . .

From: Rebecca Harris 21.09.11 11:16
To: Phoebe Combes
Subject: graphs

Hi Phoebe,

Were you able to produce a good visual from the figures I sent over this morning?

From: Phoebe Combes 21.09.11 11:18
To: Rebecca Harris
Subject: Re: graphs

Hmm, I wouldn't say good, no.

From: Rebecca Harris 21.09.11 11:18
To: Phoebe Combes
Subject: Re: graphs

Oh, what seems to be the problem?

From: Phoebe Combes 21.09.11 11:20
To: Rebecca Harris
Subject: Re: graphs

Well, I watched National Geographic last night and these graphs look a bit like the seismograph readings the worried scientists were poring over. Of course, I am not in any way equating the company with a natural disaster, or indeed suggesting the nail bars are volcanoes waiting to erupt, or earthquakes about to reduce the whole place to a pile of rubble, but the figures are a bit erratic. Anyway, I'm sure we can make them look great with a bit of adjustment.

From: Rebecca Harris 21.09.11 11:22
To: Phoebe Combes
Subject: Re: graphs

That doesn't sound ideal. How about if we increase the amortization and depreciation to 10 years. Would that help?

From: Phoebe Combes 21.09.11 11:23
To: Rebecca Harris
Subject: Re: graphs

It's already at 10 years.

From: **Rebecca Harris 21.09.11 11:24**
To: Phoebe Combes
Subject: Re: graphs

Oh. Any other suggestions?

From: **Phoebe Combes 21.09.11 11:25**
To: Rebecca Harris
Subject: Re: graphs

20 years?

From: **Rebecca Harris 21.09.11 11.26**
To: Phoebe Combes
Subject: Re: graphs

I think that might be pushing it. I'll come over in a minute and take a look.

From: **Rebecca Harris 21.09.11 11:30**
To: Oliver Barker
Subject: Kat

Morning, Ols,
I hear you bumped into Kat last night. Did you have a fun evening? I wish I could have come along.
Bex xx

From: **Oliver Barker 21.09.11 11:36**
To: Rebecca Harris
Subject: Re: Kat

Morning,
I did bump into Kat last night, or rather she bumped into me, several times! Your friend was a disaster, very funny, but a disaster all the same. At one point in the evening she tried to climb over our table to get to hers and in doing so managed to knock over every single glass on the way. She then attempted to clean the whole lot up using her skirt, which Doug thought was great, especially as most of the drink had gone on him. It was a fun night but we missed you and it was absolute hell getting home. There were no taxis so I ended up walking all the way back. The wind was unbelievably strong. If you'd been there you would definitely have been blown away. Luckily, being built like a brick shithouse I was fine.

How was your evening?

Ols x

From: **Rebecca Harris 21.09.11 11:39**
To: Oliver Barker
Subject: quiet night

Poppy and I did Shrinkles.

By the way, can you thank Doug for me – he was so great looking over everything at the nail bar yesterday. I knew my builders had screwed up that ventilation system. I will also point out the other million errors to them when I get there. Do you think we will realistically be open for business on 1st October?

Bex xx

PS Presumably the 'brick shithouse' would have held on to me so I didn't fly away?

From: **Oliver Barker 21.09.11 11:41**
To: Rebecca Harris
Subject: opening date

1st OCTOBER . . . ARE YOU OUT OF YOUR MIND??????

From: **Rebecca Harris 21.09.11 11:44**
To: Oliver Barker
Subject: Re: opening date

Oh my god, are you serious?! I mean, I know it looks bad, but the builders have promised me it will be done on time. You *are* serious! What am I going to do? It's essential that Kensington opens on schedule. We're paying an astronomical rent for the place and every day that we're non-operational we're losing buckets of cash. Barbara keeps reminding me that I'm still on trial. When I persuaded her to promote me she said she'd give me a year to prove myself. If I don't produce the goods I won't even get my job back as financial manager. Charlotte (previous director) screwed up so badly that Barbara has gone all Mayor Guliani and no one is getting any second chances.

I can't lose my job. I recently took out a bank loan the size of a small country's GDP, which was blatantly irresponsible of both me and HSBC. You're right, it's never going to be finished on time.

Oh Olly, I'm seriously doomed.

Bex, sweetheart, I was joking. Of course I know you're opening on 1st October and I have absolutely no doubt that you will achieve this. If anyone can do it, *you* can. I'm so sorry, it was thoughtless of me to joke when I know how important this is to you.

Try to keep it all in perspective and you'll be just fine. You have a tendency to panic and freak out, you little passion fruit, but when you stay calm you are truly brilliant at what you do. I seem to remember that you have already proved yourself to Barbara with the triumphant opening of the Marylebone nail bar in the first month of your promotion? I'm pretty confident that Barbara isn't going to boot you out that easily, zero tolerance or not. You are not doomed, quite the opposite in fact. You're sharp, thoughtful, intelligent, extremely easy on the eye (I know that's not really relevant, but its true) and more than qualified to get the job done, so don't underestimate yourself.

I'm your friend and I am here to do whatever I can to help, but I don't think you will need it. You're doing a fantastic job for the company and they are bloody lucky to have you. I would bet my house that The Kensington Nail Bar does brilliantly and the shareholders all receive obnoxiously large dividends within a year.

Your friend Olly x

PS Yes I would have held on to you.

PPS What's a Shrinkle when it's at home?

Thanks, Ols.

You know your support means the world to me, it really does.

Shrinkles are little pictures on plastic sheets that you colour in and cut out. Then you put them in the oven and they shrink.

Cool! Those are definitely going on my Christmas list.

From: **Tania Cutter 21.09.11 12:03**
To: Rebecca Harris
Cc: Felicity Jones
Subject: your flowers

Dear Rebecca,

I would like to acknowledge the flowers sent by you and Felicity. I am sure you understand that your gesture, although a step in the right direction, does not make up for the grievance that I have suffered. I accept your apology, but I am still considering whether a return to The Nail Bar would be a step down for someone with my level of expertise. Sometimes we make a conscious decision that it is time for a change, and sometimes that decision is thrust upon us. In either case it is important to take heed and reflect on the different paths that one can take in one's life. These critical moments cannot be rushed, Rebecca. I know you are probably frantic without me and I am sure the office is in chaos, but I will not make a decision of this magnitude lightheartedly or under duress.

I ask for your patience and understanding at this time.

Yours sincerely

Tania Cutter PA

The Nail Bar Ltd

From: **Clara Harris 21.09.11 12:07**
To: Rebecca Harris
Subject: Ken. nail bar

Bex, I have just been past your new shop and the huge awning that was on the outside has torn off and is half hanging on the pavement. The police are there and have cordoned off the area. This was all going on at about 9.45 this morning. I tried to call you but your number is permanently engaged! It must have been torn off in the storm last night – so stupid of the builders to leave it open. Sorry to deliver bad news. Clara

From: **Rebecca Harris 21.09.11 12:09**
To: Clara Harris
Subject: Re: Ken. nail bar

Jesus Christ, it's not possible!! I must be jinxed. I receive more bad news a day than *The Daily Mail* dishes out in a year. That awning cost four thousand pounds! I've spent months getting the design right and the logo printed on it. What's worse is, it wasn't the builders who left it open, it was me. I was showing it off to Olly and his project manager last night. I was so pleased because it was the only thing that looked any good in this whole catastrophe of a nail bar. Oh Clara, what am I going to do? Were the builders helping the police?

From: **Clara Harris 21.09.11 12:12**
To: Rebecca Harris
Subject: Re: Ken. nail bar

I hate to tell you this, but there weren't any builders on site. Look, try not to panic, they are probably there now and it might well be salvageable.
Can't believe it cost four thousand pounds?

From: **Rebecca Harris 21.09.11 12:14**
To: Darren Bennett
Subject: GET OFF THE PHONE!

Darren, could you get off the phone, NOBODY CAN GET THROUGH!

From: **Darren Bennett 21.09.11 12:18**
To: Rebecca Harris
Subject: Re: GET OFF THE PHONE

Oops, soz.

From: **Rebecca Harris 21.09.11 12:20**
To: Joe Doyle
Subject: !!!!!!

Joe, I'm now completely freaking out. I've not heard from you since last Friday and I'm about to go beyond ballistic. What the hell is going on? This is absolutely unacceptable. I have informed my boss in America who is on the brink of bringing a lawsuit against you. Of course I would rather deal with this in a civilized manner, but if I don't hear from you today you'll leave me no choice. Last night I went along to the nail bar to discover that the dust level had reached Pompeic proportions, with no dust sheets protecting anything. The beautiful new manicure chairs had been unwrapped (although I had specifically asked for them not to be) and were lying underneath it all. If this wasn't bad enough, after the storm last night the brand new awning has blown off and is lying on the sodding pavement.

I know this is not your fault but I was informed of this by my sister who was passing by, and she said there were no workman on the premises to sort the situation out – it was 9.45am! I'm on my way there now. I expect you to be there when I arrive.

Rebecca Harris

From: **Joe Doyle 21.09.11 12:22**
To: Rebecca Harris
Subject: Re: !!!!!!

Automated Response: Joe Doyle is out of the office until next week

From: **Rebecca Harris 21.09.11 14:42**
To: Katherine Lease
Subject: carb overload

Kat, that lunch was a huge mistake. Feeling really sick, initial carb high has passed and now full of regret and remorse.

I can't believe I ate my whole pizza, half the salad bar and most of the dough balls. Does the dress, by any chance come in a bigger size? There is no way I am going to fit into it at this rate.

Fat bum Bex

From: **Katherine Lease 21.09.11 14:46**
To: Rebecca Harris
Subject: Re: carb overload

Bex, I have to say, you didn't exactly hold back, did you? I mean don't get me wrong, I ate double what you did, but I'm not trying to get into a dress made for Disco Barbie. I'm afraid it's a sample, so there's only one.

From: **Rebecca Harris 21.09.11 14:46**
To: Katherine Lease
Subject: Re: carb overload

Oh god I did, didn't I? I told you diets make me eat like crazy. I also blame my builder who is making me insane. I can't think straight and that makes me eat like a nutter. I find that if I make myself so full that I can hardly breath it makes me calm and helps me focus.

From: **Katherine Lease 21.09.11 14:48**
To: Rebecca Harris
Subject: Re: carb overload

That's quite weird. Not feeling remotely full, even picked up one of those caramel fudge sundaes from Maccy D's on the way back to the office. I don't care, Marcus loves me and he thinks fat bums are sexy. It's all about defining your space and dancing within it. Anyway, you still have around 5 hours to starve before your date.

From: Rebecca Harris 21.09.11 14:52
To: Joe Doyle
Subject: Re: Ken. crisis

Joe,

As I expected, you didn't show at Kensington to help with the crisis situation. I was mildly placated by the fact that Karl was there with TWO others – wonders will never cease! I've seen from your payment schedule that the third instalment of cash is due to you at the end of this week.

I'm afraid that I will be withholding all payments forthwith if I have not heard from you before then.

Sincerely

Rebecca Harris

From: Rebecca Harris 21.09.11 14:58
To: Barbara Foreman
Subject: News from The Nail Bar
Attach: Product order form

Dear Barbara,

Here is the latest product order form. We are running a big promotion on *Purple Rain* which I feel sure will be a huge hit. All the magazines are showing that this winter purple is the new black and the look is very gothic. All our staff have been instructed to have purple nails this week and the clients are following suit, so we're confident that sales will go through the roof.

Phoebe has come up trumps and has got *The Mail on Sunday* interested in doing a feature on the new pedicure chairs at Marylebone. A journalist is going to the Marylebone Nail Bar on the 20th with a photographer to take pictures and do an interview. I don't know how quickly they turn these stories around but hopefully it will come out the Sunday before the opening.

I have been to Kensington and apart from the bad weather throwing up a few problems, everything is on track and looking good.

Rebecca

From: **Andrea Moleno** andrea.mayfair@thenailbar.co.uk **21.09.11 15:08**
To: Rebecca Harris
Subject: problem at Mayfair

Hi Rebecca,

Sorry to bother you, but I'm having a bit of trouble with a member of staff here at Mayfair, Janine Azame. She's been bossing the other girls about and is being aggressive with clients. Some of the staff have been reduced to tears and clients have started requesting not to have her. This has been going on for a while and I've given her several warnings, but I think something in writing from you might be needed? I should also let you know that she took a two-hour lunch break today and when I told her that this wasn't acceptable she said I was picking on her because she's black, but she doesn't look black to me.

Please advise.

From: **Rebecca Harris 21.09.11 15:12**
To: Andrea Moleno
Subject: Re: problem at Mayfair

Andrea,

I have forwarded your email to Felicity. She'll come back to you on this.

From: **Felicity Jones 21.09.11 15:22**
To: Andrea Moleno
Cc: Rebecca Harris
Subject: Re: problem at Mayfair
Attach: WRITTEN WARNING

Hi Andrea,

I'm afraid that Janine has always been a pain in the arse. She was the reason Bianca, the last manager of Mayfair, left. She gave Bianca a black eye for telling her off after she arrived 2 hours late for work. She also had her boyfriend call Bianca at home with death threats, which was totally uncool. I'm sure this won't happen to you, so don't worry, but you might want to consider changing your home number.

As far as being black, it's all a bit complicated; anyone can see Janine is as white as Ready Brek. But apparently (this is according to Janine), she is somehow related by blood to Eddie Murphy and she's incredibly proud of this, so we go along with it to keep her happy.

The important thing is that we deal with this the right way so that if things get any more psychotic, we can legally fire her. If she has received previous verbal warnings from you, then the next step has to be a written warning (please see attached). What we want to avoid is a freak out with clients around, so if you print off the letter I have written, tell her to go to the staff kitchen and read it privately. Then go and have a quiet word with her afterwards. Rebecca seems pretty sure that she'll feel full of remorse after this and immediately start being more of a team player again. I wouldn't count on it, but it's worth a try.

In the meantime you're doing a great job, so hang in there.

LETTER OF WARNING

Dear Janine,

It has come to my attention that your recent behaviour at The Mayfair Nail Bar has been less than ideal. You have been disruptive to other members of staff, and worse still you have been rude to clients.

I am sure you are aware that the idea behind The Nail Bar is to create a tranquil and relaxing environment where clients come to unwind and be pampered. Our customers do not wish to be ordered around or treated in a rough manner. I also do not wish to lose other members of staff who are finding it increasingly difficult to work around you.

Unfortunately, this is not the first time your behaviour has been brought to the attention of Head Office.

Please take this letter as an official warning that will go on your record for the remainder of your time at The Nail Bar Ltd.

Should any further incidents be reported, I am afraid more drastic measures will have to be taken.

Yours sincerely

Felicity Jones

Head of Personnel

The Nail Bar Ltd

From:	**Rebecca Harris 21.09.11 15:29**
To:	Felicity Jones
Subject:	WRITTEN WARNING

Good letter, Fi!!!

From: **Felicity Jones 21.09.11 15:31**
To: Rebecca Harris
Subject: Re: WRITTEN WARNING

I know! I cribbed it from a letter that was given to me at my old job –
the bastards at *Big Boys* magazine really knew how to get heavy.

From: **Rebecca Harris 21.09.11 15:32**
To: Felicity Jones
Subject: Re: WRITTEN WARNING

Oh, right, well I hope it wasn't for doing anything too bad?

From: **Felicity Jones 21.09.11 15:35**
To: Rebecca Harris
Subject: Re: WRITTEN WARNING

No, they just weren't the understanding type. Brian and I were
going through a bad patch. I was stalling on setting a date for the
wedding and he thought I might be having second thoughts, which
I wasn't. I just couldn't decide what time of year I wanted to get
married. Anyway, there was quite a bit of f'ing and blinding down
the phone which wasn't appreciated, and eventually my boss
banned me from making personal calls during work hours – a total
overreaction on his part. Anyway, I told Brian this but he thought it
was just me making excuses not to talk to him. One day he left a
message for me to call him back and when I didn't he came
storming into the office and we ended up having a screaming row in
front of everyone. Brian asked for the engagement ring back and I
said that in that case I wanted back the shirt he was wearing as it
was a birthday present from me. He ripped it off, tearing all the
buttons, which I thought was so cool, and threw it at me. I pulled off
my ring and flung it at him. Unfortunately at that moment my boss
came out of his office and it hit him in the eye. The swearing, the cut
eye and the semi-naked man in the office was all a bit much for my
boss Gerald, and the letter arrived on my desk the next day. As I
said, not very understanding people.

From: **Rebecca Harris 21.09.11 15:37**
To: Felicity Jones
Subject: Big boys?

Yes, that doesn't sound very reasonable. Clearly you guys were just working your way through some engagement stress. Anyway, I'm very glad that you and Brian sorted things out. What is *Big Boys* magazine by the way? It sounds a bit dodgy?

From: **Felicity Jones 21.09.11 15:38**
To: Rebecca Harris
Subject: Re: Big boys?

No it's not. It's just straightforward porn.

From: **Rebecca Harris 21.09.11 15:40**
To: Felicity Jones
Subject: Re: Big boys?

Oh, right, that sounds ok then.

From: **Barbara Foreman 21.09.11 15:41**
To: Rebecca Harris
Subject: explain, please

Rebecca,
I have just received an email from your secretary with a copy of a correspondence between yourself and one Felicity Jones from Human Resources along with a request for compensation on her subsequent "forced resignation".
Please explain immediately.
Barbara

From: **Rebecca Harris 21.09.11 15:42**
To: Felicity Jones
Subject: Help!!

OMG – the eagle has landed. Tania cc'd our mis-sent email correspondence to Barbara and she wants an explanation.

From: **Felicity Jones 21.09.11 15:43**
To: Rebecca Harris
Subject: Re: Help!!

Oh shit. Think best tactic is overboard apologetic. Harder to drop the axe when someone is a grovelling wreck.
Good luck.

From: **Rebecca Harris 21.09.11 15:44**
To: Felicity Jones

Subject: Re: Help!!

Do you really think I could get fired for this?

From: **Felicity Jones 21.09.11 15:45**
To: Rebecca Harris
Subject: Re: Help!!

It's possible, what with the "Babs-the-bitch" email on Monday and now this. You may be pushing it, especially as Americans aren't exactly renowned for their sense of humour.

From: **Rebecca Harris 21.09.11 15:48**
To: Felicity Jones
Subject: Help!! Panic!!

I really can't imagine Barbara would get rid of me that easily? I mean, she knows how committed I am. As far as she's aware, everything is on schedule for Kensington and our takings for this year are up 20% on last year. I know she's a bit trigger happy, but surely this isn't a firing offence? She can't fire me, I have a child to support, for goodness sake! I'm selling my flat and moving in with my mum as it is. Not to mention I have a bank loan that is completely inappropriate for someone on my income.
This is ridiculous. Surely this is ridiculous? I'm not going to panic, I have enough things to panic about. This is definitely not something to panic about . . . right?

From: **Felicity Jones 21.09.11 15:51**
To: Rebecca Harris
Subject: Re: Help!! Panic!!

Definitely not. You're moving in with your mum? – Fuck me, THAT is something to panic about.

From: **Rebecca Harris 21.09.11 15:52**
To: Felicity Jones
Subject: Re: Help!! Panic!!

Thanks, Felicity, that's really helpful.

From: **Rebecca Harris 21.09.11 16.00**
To: Barbara Foreman
Subject: apologies

Dear Barbara,
I have looked back on the emails that you referred to and I

would like to say how mortified I feel at the juvenility of the correspondence.

Of course both Felicity and I were horrified when we discovered that our emails had gone to Tania by mistake.

We both immediately apologized and tried to make amends, but obviously it was not enough. I was hoping that the matter would just blow over and she would be back at work today, but this has not been the case. As a result I have sent her some flowers and a note in the hopes that this might make up for the unkindness we showed her.

In the meantime we have a very presentable and highly efficient replacement by the name of Darren who is handling all of Tania's workload.

Sincerely

Rebecca

From:	**Barbara Foreman 21.09.11 16:10**
To:	Rebecca Harris
Subject:	Re: apologies

For crying out loud, Rebecca, I'm not looking for you to grovel. I just want to know why the hell your staff is involving me in their pathetic lives. Get them under control or get rid of them.

From:	**Andrea Moleno 21.09.11 16:35**
To:	Felicity Jones
Cc:	Rebecca Harris
Subject:	another problem at Mayfair

Dear Felicity,

I'm so sorry that I'm always bothering you, but things have not gone so well here. I did as you said and gave the letter to Janine. She took it downstairs to the treatment room to read it. Soon afterwards she returned, grabbed a large bottle of nail polish remover, smashed it on the floor, looked at me and screamed "RACIST BITCH!" She then stood on Mrs. Richardson's beautifully polished toes and stormed out the door.

Felicity, I don't understand. I may have grown up in England and I do have an Italian grandmother but I am a black South African. If she's claiming to be black, then how can I be racist?

Of course, this is something you probably don't want to be disturbed by and I'm sure everything will be fine, but do you think I should expect her back in a little while or should I cancel the rest of her clients for the day?

One other bit of bad news (sorry). A very loyal, slightly elderly client, Lady Eleanor Deane, was sitting nearby when the nail polish remover exploded, and her red suede Prada shoes received a direct hit. She is expecting the Nail Bar to pay for a new pair.

Apart from this episode, everything else is going fine and lots of pots of *Purple Rain* have been sold. The promotion poster that Phoebe put up yesterday afternoon has made a huge impact..

Yours sincerely

Andrea

From: **Rebecca Harris 21.09.11 16:40**
To: Felicity Jones
Subject: Re: another problem at Mayfair

Fi, Just looked at Andrea's email – doesn't sound great, does it?

Andrea seems to be remaining weirdly calm over the whole thing, but can you find someone to go to Mayfair for the rest of the day to help out?

From: **Felicity Jones 21.09.11 16:46**
To: Rebecca Harris
Subject: Re: another problem at Mayfair

No prob. It's always the same old thing with Janine. I did warn Andrea that Janine can be tricky, but I held off telling her she hadn't seen the half of it. If she knew the full scale of what that woman is capable of, she'd almost certainly do a runner.

Mayfair must be critically understaffed having already lost Charlene to Marylebone to cover for Suki, who we still have not heard from, by the way. Let me check if someone from Westbourne can replace Charlene at Marylebone so she can go back to Mayfair to help with Andrea.

Have no idea how much Prada shoes cost but reckon they'll make quite a big dent in the old profit margin.

How did it go with Barbara, by the way?

Fi

From: Rebecca Harris **21.09.11 16:50**
To: Felicity Jones
Subject: Re: staffing probs

We're in the clear with Barbara. As long as our turnover of staff is not affecting our turnover of cash she doesn't care. However, we're now down one PA and one manicurist, and we have a manager who has disappeared off the face of the earth. Not an ideal scenario considering we're meant to be expanding our workforce, not reducing it. At this rate any new staff we get for Kensington will have to be used to fill the increasing number of vacancies arising in our existing nail bars.

I thought I couldn't feel any worse when I came in this morning. How wrong I was.

Rebecca

From: Felicity Jones **21.09.11 16:54**
To: Rebecca Harris
Subject: staffing check in all nail bars

I'm just inhaling a really fucking disgusting Cornish pasty from Charlie's Bakery, brilliant for hangovers as it's guaranteed to make you chuck up everything from the night before.

Let me just finish this and then I'll head off to check on all nail bars. I'll assess just how chronic the staff situation is in each and give you a full report tomorrow. I'm going to take Sylvia with me so she can see how the other nail bars run and meet the other managers. We'll finish up at Marylebone and stay there, so I won't be back in the office until tomorrow.

In the meantime, I just saw Phoebe's mock-up for the *Orange Crush* promo and it's fantastic.

From: Rebecca Harris **21.09.11 16:57**
To: Felicity Jones
Subject: Katya

Great! Will you ask her to leave it on my desk so I can take a look at it when I get back from Kensington?

Oh my god, I almost forgot, what did you think of Katya? I'm sorry but I almost died when she appeared at South Ken tube. I can't believe she described herself as the one wearing the Jay Kay hat. That's like a Harlem Globetrotter describing himself as the one in the red T-shirt. I mean your eye doesn't naturally go towards a dark green trilby when the person wearing it happens to have fourteen studs in each ear and a pierced tongue with a chain hanging off it connecting to a ring in her eyebrow. Definitely not one to get stuck behind at airport security!

I left her info on your desk along with a photo of her screaming her head off on a rollercoaster, her idea of a good choice to go with her CV! Anyway, she did an excellent manicure so I employed her.

From: **Felicity Jones 21.09.11 16:59**
To: Rebecca Harris
Subject: Re: Katya

I wouldn't have bothered with the manicure, the photo totally sealed the deal for me. I'll let Vanessa know that she'll be training there until the opening.

From: **Rebecca Harris 21.09.11 17:01**
To: Felicity Jones
Subject: what's with Darren?

Talking of slightly alternative appearances, is Darren wearing a gardening apron? And what's with the hoovering?

From: **Felicity Jones 21.09.11 17:05**
To: Rebecca Harris
Subject: Re: what's with Darren?

Yes, he is. According to Phoebe (whom he's totally bonded with), he's a "herbivore", so when he saw the state of the plants in the office he had a hissy fit, muttered something about us all being savages and murderers and rushed off to the garden centre. He came back half an hour ago with more kit than you can shake a stick at and he hasn't sat down since. I think that might actually be a lawnmower. I better go talk to him.

From: **Rebecca Harris 21.09.11 17:07**
To: Felicity Jones
Subject: re: what's with Darren?

I think that might be a good idea.

From: Rebecca Harris   **21.09.11 17:14**
To: Office staff
Subject: computer literacy

Is there any one AT ALL in this office who:

a) Knows our technical support number?
b) Considers themselves technically minded?
c) Has taken a computer studies course?
d) Has a friend who knows something about computers?
e) Knows somebody down the road who knows something about computers.

If so, please contact me IMMEDIATELY.

Rebecca

Thursday 22nd September 2011

From: **Joe Doyle 22.09.11 8:45**
To: Rebecca Harris
Subject: Re: !!!!!!

Hello Rebecca,

Just came back from taking the missus to Majorca. Celebrated our 20th wedding anniversary, very nice too. I can highly recommend it, lovely beaches, beautiful food, Pina Coladas with little umbrellas, the works. My Caroline came back looking ten years younger. That's the secret, Rebecca, make sure you marry a good looking bloke who doesn't skimp on luxury holidays. Don't let some toffee-nosed geezer fob you off on a crappy fishing weekend in Scotland. Make sure it's a holiday abroad – foreign languages, foreign food and plenty of sun. That's where the romance is, take it from me, 20 years and Cazza and I have never been happier.

Now I see you've been busy filling up my mail box while I've been away and getting a bit over-excited. Well, no need to worry, I'll be heading over to Kensington this morning to check on progress. If you'd like to meet me there, I'll be happy to put your mind at rest about anything that's bothering you. You can bring a cheque with you for the third instalment.

Joe

From: **Rebecca Harris 22.09.11 9:07**
To: Joe Doyle
Subject: c u at Ken.

Joe,

I'm very relieved you're back especially as I didn't know you were going away in the first place. I'll see you at Kensington in about half an hour

Rebecca

From: **Tania Cutter 22.09.11 9:10**
To: Rebecca Harris
Subject: your PA

Rebecca,

You may have noticed that I'm back. I have had time to get over my initial outrage at yours and Felicity's behaviour and have put it down to a certain level of immaturity in both of you. I am willing to let bygones be bygones and give you a second chance to prove that we can all co-exist in a civilized manner.

I will need until 10.30 to get myself settled and then I will be ready to resume my normal duties.

Tania Cutter PA

The Nail Bar Ltd

From: **Rebecca Harris 22.09.11 9:16**
To: Tania Cutter
Subject: welcome back

Dear Tania,

I'm delighted that you're back after a well-deserved break. No doubt the office will run much more smoothly with you in it.

Rebecca

From: **Rebecca Harris 22.09.11 9:19**
To: Felicity Jones
Subject: Tania

Fi, heads up, "Little Turtle" is back. Where are you, by the way?

From: **Felicity Jones 22.09.11 9:24**
To: Rebecca Harris
Subject: URGENT ATTN. FLOOD AT MARYLEBONE

BEX, THERE'S BEEN A DISASTER AT MARYLEBONE OF MONUMENTAL PROPORTIONS. THE WHOLE PLACE HAS FLOODED AND EVERYTHING IS FUCKED.

The storm on Tuesday night followed by that torrential downpour last night must have blocked the drains and all the rain is just bloody pouring through the shop. I came to open up with Sylvia this morning, whom I've had to throw in at the deep end (literally) because of Suki's continued absence. We arrived to find the place under about half a foot of water. I can't tell you how bad it is. It's like one of those CNN reports from Bangladesh after a typhoon – total fucking devastation.

The other girls have all arrived now and are helping to channel the flow out through the front door, but it's like farting against thunder – completely ineffectual. The chances of being operational today are minimal. I'm sending as many clients as possible to Mayfair and Westbourne, so could you warn Andrea and Vanessa.

I've got two girls coming in to the office this morning for interviews.

Could you take them on for me? One is for a senior and the other for a junior manicurist position. I can't remember either of their names or which one is for which, but if you go to my desk the two CVs are sitting on it.

I knew Little Turtle must be back because the agency called me to say that someone had dismissed Darren rudely and they were pretty upset about it. Apparently she walked straight up to him and said, "Little man, I suggest you pack your bags, your entrée into the big league is over." Quite harsh I thought, even for Tania.

Fi

From: **Rebecca Harris 22.09.11 9:28**
To: Felicity Jones
Subject: Re: URGENT ATTN. FLOOD AT MARYLEBONE

This is just too much.

Thank god you're there. I will get onto the other managers straight-away and do the interviews. Be sure to keep me posted on the salvage operation. We need to get Marylebone up and running as soon as possible.

From: **Rebecca Harris 22.09.11 9:32**
To: Tania Cutter
Subject: Re: URGENT ATTN. FLOOD AT MARYLEBONE

Tania,

Could you phone Andrea and Vanessa immediately and tell them to expect an influx of probably quite unhappy clients from Marylebone? There's been a flood and Marylebone will be non-operational for the rest of the day. The majority will go to Mayfair, I imagine, so if that is the case then could you ask Vanessa for any girls she can spare to go over there. Also, if someone arrives for an interview, will you send them into the meeting room.

Thank you so much.

Rebecca

From: **Rebecca Harris 22.09.11 9:40**
To: Joe Doyle
Subject: problem

Something urgent has come up, will be with you around 12.30.

Rebecca

From: Clara Harris 22.09.11 9:46
To: Rebecca Harris
Subject: Mum's birthday!!!

Bex,

Where were you? You forgot Mum's birthday, how could you? I can't believe you can be so self-absorbed, especially as it was your idea to do her a birthday breakfast in the first place? Mum and I were at your flat by 8am this morning, as we'd discussed we would be, but you'd already left for work? Vinca and Poppy were there and they said you hadn't even mentioned it. Honestly, Bex, it's not every day our mother turns 60 and you know how she gets around this time, she misses Dad terribly. I'm just amazed you could forget. It's really unfair of you to let her down like this. You're much too wrapped up in that nail bar of yours and it makes you forget what's important in life.

As it was, I whipped up pancakes (you don't even own a whisk, so it wasn't easy) and we all walked Poppy to school, which Mum enjoyed, but I think you should at least go and see her after work. Her friend Marjorie is taking her out to dinner, but it would be nice if you had a drink with her beforehand. Clara

From: Rebecca Harris 22.09.11 9:49
To: Clara Harris
Subject: Re: Mum's birthday!!!

Oh Clara, I feel so terrible. I can't bear that I forgot her breakfast. I was thinking about it all day yesterday so I can't believe I didn't remember this morning. What kind of awful daughter am I? Was Mum really upset? Shit! Everything is going wrong today. I'll call her now and go round after work to see her.

From: Clara Harris 22.09.11 9:52
To: Rebecca Harris
Subject: Re: Mum's birthday!!!

I'm presuming you haven't forgotten about the party we are giving for her tomorrow night? I think we should make it a buffet as numbers keep changing. I'm going to go and get everything ready in the afternoon, but I have to pick Jason up from the airport (he lands at 7pm) so we will be a little late. Could you make sure you get there early so Mum isn't hosting by herself?

From: Rebecca Harris 22.09.11 9:55
To: Clara Harris
Subject: Re: Mum's birthday!!!

Of course I haven't forgotten about her party. That is the actual day of her birthday after all. I think that was a bit unfair of you and I do know what's important in life. Mum is hugely important to me, of course she is, but so is Poppy and at the moment I am trying to make ends meet so I can support my child, and it's scaring the hell out of me. I know I obsess with the nail bar and it takes up more of my time than I would like it to, but as so much is going on at the moment with the new shop opening, I can hardly keep track of what day it is. So if I screw up occasionally, I'm sorry.

I can definitely get there early tomorrow evening. The painting of Poppy isn't going to be ready until next week so I'm going out at lunch to find Mum something that she can open tomorrow. Do you want to go halves?

From: Clara Harris 22.09.11 9:58
To: Rebecca Harris
Subject: Re: Mum's birthday!!!

Bex, I know you're having a stressful time, but I feel very protective of Mum. This is her first party since the Fu Rama hotel incident with Joy and Dad. She vowed never to have a party again after that and it's taken ten years to convince her otherwise. You know this, Bex, and you know how important it is for things to go without a hitch. We're the ones who persuaded her, so we're responsible for her having a good time. I just want everything to go right so that she doesn't regret going along with us on this.

Anyway, it's great that you can see her tonight.

I already gave her a pair of earrings and a cashmere jumper from Brora this morning.

How was your evening with Charles? I think your decision to hold off sleeping with him is absolutely right. There is no point rushing these things and you're obviously not ready yet. I never hear of anyone regretting holding back, whereas you hear the opposite time and again. Well done you, not giving in to pressure.

From: Rebecca Harris 22.09.11 10:04
To: Clara Harris

My date couldn't have been better. We had a great time and you're so right about not giving in to pressure. I know it was the right thing to do. I like him more and more each time we see each other – isn't that great? I really think this is going to go well and I went ahead and asked him to Mum's party. Whad'ya think?

From: Clara Harris 22.09.11 10:10
To: Rebecca Harris
Subject: fantastic!

I think it's GREAT. You obviously feel strongly about the guy to invite him to Mum's, so that's fantastic. I can't wait to meet him.

From: Katherine Lease 22.09.11 10:20
To: Rebecca Harris
Subject: your bloody date!!

Darling you're keeping me in suspenders. I'm gagging to hear about the date. Was Charles hung like an elephant? Did he wine and dine you and then take you down a dark alley and do extremely ungentlemanly things to you? Any dressing up or toys involved? Contact me immediately and I don't want you to spare any of the gory details.
Bored to death at work.

From: Rebecca Harris 22.09.11 10:28
To: Katherine Lease
Subject: THE date

Hi Kat,
The date was brilliant and Charles is totally gorgeous. I was in a hugely excited mood about it when I got up this morning. I didn't even give my builder a hard time when he casually told me he'd been in Majorca all week.
However, things have taken a bit of a downturn and I'm struggling to hold on to the euphoria. The Marylebone nail bar flooded in the night and a day's sales have just been wiped off the board. I also forgot my Mum's birthday breakfast which I was meant to be hosting.
Anyway, that's all so boring. Here are the details!
He picked me up at 9pm in a silver Porche – woooo hooo! He looked

sooo sexy, it didn't even matter that he was an hour late. He booked the Ivy for dinner but friends of his called on the way to say they were having a party in Notting Hill so we went there instead. When he thought I looked a bit disappointed about not going to the restaurant, he said he would take me next time – there's going to be a next time! He obviously sees this as a long-term thing – YIPPEE.

Anyway, we got to this really cool party with size zero models everywhere drinking Mohitos. Thank god I managed to squeeze into your dress. It was definitely a good thing that we missed dinner, even though I was starving.

We didn't get home until 4 in the morning, completely plastered. I told Charles that I wasn't ready to sleep with him yet as it was still too soon for me. I know we talked about it, but Kat, when it came to the moment, I just realized it was still too soon. I could tell he was disappointed, but hopefully he will respect me more for it.

Definitely think this has got long-term potential.

From: **Katherine Lease 22.09.11 10:36**
To: Rebecca Harris
Subject: WHAT???!!

Are you NUTS? Respect you? Forget respect, we're talking about opportunities here and you may well have just blown yours. You're thirty years old, you can't afford to let a single potential shag slip you by. There is no knowing when the next opportunity might arise, it could be weeks, months, or god forbid, YEARS. Not to mention that you can be damn sure that Charles would have gone straight back to that party and picked up the first willing anorexic and taken her home.

The NUMBER ONE GOLDEN RULE is keep 'em in your bed, because if they're not in yours they're in someone else's. Sweetheart, I promise you, you have to listen to me sometimes because in matters of the bedroom, I really do know my shit. You've been seeing Charles for three weeks now. Do you honestly think a man like Charles goes that long without sex? NOT A CHANCE. You're only hope is that he's channeling a ferocious porn habit rather than getting his rocks off with someone else. Honey, you just may be able to salvage the situation, but if not Marcus has got this cousin who's coming over from Zambia. He thinks you two would get on brilliantly, so when he gets here we'll all go out on a double date and you can get laid then.

Love you. K

From: **Rebecca Harris 22.09.11 10:39**
To: Katherine Lease
Subject: Re: WHAT???!!

Kat,

I promise you, I really think Charles would have been impressed by my abstinence. I don't want him to think of me as a quick fling. Also it's not like I'm being a deliberate prick tease. I want to be sure that he's the right guy for me. I'm not in desperate need to have sex. What I want is to have a relationship, something with a bit of meaning and longevity. I'm not talking marriage or anything heavy but I'd like to be with a guy who wants to hang out with me and cares about me rather than someone who just wants to get my knickers off.

I'm sure he wouldn't have gone all the way back to the party? Anyway, I'm not going to fret about it yet. If he hasn't called by midday then I'll start worrying.

From: **Katherine Lease 22.09.11 10:40**
To: Rebecca Harris
Subject: If you say so . . .

I totally understand. I obviously can't relate in any way but I do understand.

From: **Andrea Moleno 22.09.11 10:42**
To: Rebecca Harris
Subject: Marylebone clients

Dear Rebecca,

I am sorry to disturb you but we seem to be receiving a great many clients who have come from Marylebone saying their appointments were cancelled there and moved to this nail bar? Unfortunately no one told me about this so I cannot accommodate all of them. However, Janine came back in this morning and is acting as if nothing happened, so I have given some of these clients to her. I hope this is ok?

Andrea

From: **Rebecca Harris 22.09.11 10:44**
To: Tania Cutter
Subject: Marylebone extra clients

Tania,

WHAT THE HELL HAPPENED? Andrea said no one called to tell her about the extra clients?

Rebecca

From: **Tania Cutter 22.09.11 10:47**
To: Rebecca Harris
Subject: Re: Marylebone extra clients

Rebecca,

If you look back to the email I sent you first thing you will see that I very clearly said that I needed until 10.30 to unpack my stationery and arrange my desk. At 10:34 your interviewee arrived and I have settled her in the meeting room as requested. I am now back at my desk ready to call Andrea, followed by Vanessa. I cannot see how any confusion could have arisen? Quite frankly I have to say I am quite disappointed that we are slipping right back into the haphazardness that seems to be representative of the way this office is run. I can't imagine what this place was like during my absence?

Tania Cutter PA

The Nail Bar Ltd

From: **Rebecca Harris 22.09.11 10:50**
To: Tania Cutter
Subject: Re: Marylebone clients

Tania, if you could be so kind as to make those phone calls it would be much appreciated.

Also, while I am doing these interviews, could you please get Graham to put a block on these SPAM emails that I'm still receiving, and if you could do it NOW, that would be even better.

Rebecca

DIRECTOR

The Nail Bar Ltd

From: **Vanessa Deane** vanessa.westbourne@thenailbar.co.uk **11:21**
To: Rebecca Harris
Subject: problem of pong

Rebecca,

I can't get hold of Felicity so thought I should come to you – Karen Johnson (senior manicurist) has a serious body odour problem. We have all managed to get by with keeping windows open and the ventilation system on 24/7, but with all this rain we haven't been able to ventilate efficiently and the smell has reached critical level. Please advise on what The Nail Bar's normal procedure is in dealing with this kind of situation.

Also, the new girl Katya wants to know if she can offer body piercing to clients who are interested?

From: **Phoebe Combes 22.09.11 11:40**
To: Rebecca Harris
Subject: the man on my bus

Hi Rebecca,

The press release I drafted for the new Eyebrow Shaping promotion is on your desk. I left the disc on the bus this morning and went into a total panic as I hadn't made a backup copy. I ran after the bus but it was too late, it was gone and the disc with it. I got into work and had started on a new draft when the most amazing thing happened – a courier turned up with my disc in his hand! There was a note with it from this wonderful man I had sat next to on the bus. It said, *'Beautiful mystery girl, when you chose the seat next to me on the bus this morning I thought that the gods must be smiling. Your soulful eyes and*

sun-kissed skin captivated my heart and lifted my spirit so that I could surely touch the sky. When you got up to go you took my breath away with you, but you left behind this disc, which I hope finds its way back to you.'
Greg
07765431866

Isn't that such a lovely thing to say? What a nice man.

Anyway he obviously looked at the disc, saw The Nail Bar and looked us up – what luck!

You will see on the promotion that I've said a lot about Monica (the new girl at Mayfair) doing the best eyebrows in Central London and about how she is in huge demand etc etc. Let me know if you are happy with it and I will get it sent out today. Phoebe

From: **Tania Cutter 22.09.11 11:56**
To: Rebecca Harris
Subject: PERSONAL phone calls

Rebecca,

You had three personal calls while you were in the meeting room, two from that strange friend of yours, Katherine Lease, and one from your mother who told me that today is her birthday; obviously she wanted me to remind you of this.

On the work front, Vanessa called from Westbourne looking for you and either Felicity or Phoebe left a press release on your desk which I have read, corrected the rather disappointing grammar, and approved for her to send out.

I have also spoken to Andrea, who says the situation at Mayfair is manageable now that Tracey has come to her from Westbourne.

Tania Cutter PA
The Nail Bar Ltd

From: **Katherine Lease 22.09.11 12:04**
To: Rebecca Harris
Subject: Paree for mee!

Where are you? Can't get you on the mobile and that weird secretary of yours just said you were "unavailable at present" – what century is she living in?

Anyway, guess what? Marcus just called me to say he had a surprise for me. I thought he was going to tell me he'd bought me a car, as

I've been hinting at it, but it wasn't that; he's taking me away to PARIS for a dirty weekend at an amazing hotel which I can't remember the name of. I think I might be in love. I mean not only is he big, black, gorgeous and loaded, which is usually enough for me, but he's romantic too!

Going to Top Shop at lunch for a splurge. Come and join me. Kat xx

PS Any word from Charles?

From: **Rebecca Harris 22.09.11 12:07**
To: Tania Cutter
Subject: Re: PERSONAL phone calls

Tania,

For future reference, I would have quite liked to have seen the press release before you attacked it. I'm leaving in a few minutes to meet the builders at Kensington so I won't be back until this afternoon. Could you draft up an acceptance letter for Maria Sanchez. We would like to offer her a job as a junior manicurist. I've left her CV on my desk and have written the salary offer on the top. When you've finished, could you leave a copy of this on Felicity's desk. The other girl, Sinead, as you know was looking for a waitress job, so was no good.

If Barbara calls before I get back, please tell her to try me on the new number at Kensington. She's leaving for a trip to China today so will probably want to speak to me before she goes. Please make sure she gets the message.

Rebecca

From: **Rebecca Harris 22.09.11 12:09**
To: Phoebe Combes
Subject: Re: the man on my bus

Phoebe, the press release looks great, thank you.

You should probably call that guy, he sounds very charming and is obviously smitten.

From: **Phoebe Combes 22.09.11 12:10**
To: Rebecca Harris
Subject: Re: the man on my bus

I did, we're meeting for lunch in half an hour!

Thank you for taking an interest. What a lovely boss you are.

From: **Rebecca Harris 22.09.11 12:11**
To: Katherine Lease
Subject: Paris

No Charles hasn't called. But I'm going to be cool about this and extend the deadline until after lunch.

How great about the dirty weekend, you lucky sod. Maybe if things go well with Charles we will be off for wild weekends in Europe too! Does that mean you're not going to come to my mum's party tomorrow night? I totally understand if you can't.

I would love to do a Top-Shop-spend-a-thon but I have to meet the building contractor at Kensington, and then I've got to find Mum a birthday present, so unfortunately there's no way I can.

Bex

From: **Katherine Lease 22.09.11 12:16**
To: Rebecca Harris
Subject: Top Shop

Sweetheart, Top Shop is brilliant for mums – get her a present there. Anyway we have to celebrate your wonderful, despite unconsummated, date and my guaranteed sex-fest weekend.

Go and see the builder and meet me at 1pm at Luigi's off Oxford Street for lunch. We can whip through Top Shop and be back in the office by 2.30.

Not going to Paris until Saturday morning so can still come to your mum's.

From: **Rebecca Harris 22.09.11 12:17**
To: Katherine Lease
Subject: Re: Top Shop

Ok, I'm in, see you there.

From: **Felicity Jones 22.09.11 13:45**
To: Rebecca Harris
Subject: URGENT x10

Bex, nightmare – the bloody journalist from *The Mail on Sunday* turned up at Marylebone to take photos of the pedicure chairs and do an interview with you. I'm afraid to say that the place looked like shit – wet, muddy towels everywhere, kit all piled up on the Reception desk. Some of the girls were sitting on the manicure tables eating sandwiches, taking a break from flood control, and I was out getting a coffee. This left Sylvia to deal with the situation. As you can imagine, it didn't go brilliantly. When the journalist lost her temper, Sylvia went into a total panic. She tried to explain that she was new, which pissed the journalist off even more. The woman, whose name was Helen something, then got more heated, causing Sylvia to burst into tears. Not a good scene, all in all. I got back in the middle of all this and tried to placate everyone, but I'm afraid the photographer took loads of pictures and the journalist left saying she was going to write all about us. I tell you, if this goes airborne, we're seriously up the Kaiser.

We've now got the situation under control and the place will be operational in an hour or so. I'm heading back to the office shortly. Sylvia has swallowed a packet of beta blockers and says she is calm enough to resume managing the place for the rest of the day.

From: **Barbara Foreman 22.09.11 14:02**
To: Rebecca Harris
Subject: important stats

Rebecca,

While I am away I would like you to gather some statistics from various Nail Bar competitors and other major nail product retailers around London. When we first opened in the UK there were so few worthy competitors we hardly needed to take notice of them. However, more and more nail bars seem to be opening up and a few of them are manufacturing their own products on a fairly major scale. I would like Nail Corp to be fully briefed on these companies so they appreciate that the UK Nail Bars need to carry the full range of all new products that we are bringing out of China, in order to remain at the forefront of our competitors. This information needs to be with me in time for the presentation next week, along with the graphs.

I am on my way to the airport. Please get in touch immediately.
Barbara
Message sent via BlackBerry ®

From: **Tania Cutter 22.09.11 14:25**
To: Rebecca Harris
Subject: important stats for Barbara

Rebecca,

I see you are still not back from lunch.

Barbara called and wanted to know where you were. Luckily, I have covered for you by offering her my services collecting the information she needs, so there is no need for you to contact her. However, I will be very busy over the next few days gathering the statistics she has requested and will obviously need to be out of the office a great deal for this assignment. You might want to hire a temp to cover my workload for the next two days?

Graham has been in and managed to clean up the extraordinary amount of SPAM emails on your computer. He informed me that should you continue to surf pornographic websites then you will once again receive filth emails. In fact, he said you would put our entire computer system at risk. I assured him you would not want to do this.

Tania Cutter PA

The Nail Bar Ltd

From: **Barbara Foreman 22.09.11 14:42**
To: Rebecca Harris
Subject: Re: important stats

Rebecca,

In your continued absence I have resorted to communicating with your secretary, who I thought had resigned? Anyway, she seems to have re-instated herself and is once again running the office. I was informed that she has no idea of your whereabouts, which I find extraordinary. I have therefore passed over the job I wanted you to do to her as she seems more than capable. However, may I suggest you read the report she puts together as it would be beneficial to you to be marginally aware of what your competitors are up to.

Barbara

Message sent via BlackBerry ®

From: **Rebecca Harris 22.09.11 15:02**
To: Felicity Jones
Subject: Re: URGENT x10

Fi, I THINK I'M GOING TO BE SICK. This is a total catastrophe. If this article comes out I am DEAD.

That journalist was meant to be coming in tomorrow. I don't know how this happened? It is absolutely crucial that those pictures don't get published or we're seriously screwed. I'm hoping to god Phoebe is friends with someone at *The Mail on Sunday*, preferably the Editor.

From: **Felicity Jones 22.09.11 15:03**
To: Rebecca Harris
Subject: Re: URGENT x10

I know, it's a shocker isn't it?

So glad you're back, by the way. Tania has been poncing about like she owns the place. She seems to think she's in charge when you're not in the office. Phoebe says that she left a press release on your desk and Tania returned it to her covered in red pen marks and "sp" circles – what's that about? When I got back from Marylebone, I found her going through my pile of CVs. She said that she wanted to make sure there were no applicants who thought they were interviewing for waitress jobs and wasting everybody's time.

How did the interviews go, by the way?

From: **Rebecca Harris 22.09.11 15:05**
To: Felicity Jones
Subject: Re: URGENT x10

One of your interviews, a girl called Maria, seemed really good, so I asked Tania to draft an acceptance letter and put it on your desk. The other one, Sinead, didn't get past Reception. Tania gave her hell and accused her of being a spy for another nail bar. In fact she was a waitress looking for a job in a bar. She just hadn't read our ad properly. I found the poor thing with mascara running all over her face, trying to convince Tania that the Union Jack nails she was sporting were done by a friend of hers and not herself.

There's also a small issue at Westbourne. One of the staff has a B.O problem which has gone beyond the level of tolerance, and Vanessa wants to know what is the correct protocol to follow in this kind of situation. I know we've got bigger problems to deal with, but I think I'll hand this one over to you.

Andrea informed me that Janine came back in to work this morning as if yesterday's freak-out never happened. Would you just check all is going smoothly with that?

Also I think we should put Suki's salary on hold for next month. I'm getting a nasty feeling she ain't coming back.

From: **Rebecca Harris 22.09.11 15:08**
To: Barbara Foreman
Subject: Re: important stats

Dear Barbara,

I hope this gets to you before you take off. If not, then welcome to China. I hope the weather is good there?

I'm sorry I was out of the office when you called – I was having a long meeting with Joe at Kensington. We had a great deal to cover as I wanted to make sure that all the electric sockets get put in the right places and detailed carpentry work is according to spec.

I am sure Tania will do an excellent job gathering the required statistics.

Rebecca

From: **Rebecca Harris 22.09.11 15:11**
To: Tania Cutter
Subject: workload

I don't think I could have made it clearer that you were to tell Barbara I was at Kensington if she called.

Thank you for offering to do Barbara's report, but I'm afraid I cannot spare you from the office for days on end. Firstly, we have already spent a fortune on temps this month, and secondly, due to your recent unexpected holiday, there is a huge backlog of office work to catch up on. Please could you gather as many of the required statistics as possible by phone, and any "field" work that needs to be done can be shared among the managers whose competitors are in close proximity.

In response to Graham's grave warning, I will try and keep my passion for porn under control.

Rebecca.

From: **Tania Cutter 22.09.11 15:14**
To: Rebecca Harris
Subject: Re: workload

Rebecca,

If you feel it is appropriate for the managers to be doing this sort of work then I am not the one to question your judgment. However, I would like to point out that one of the problems with this company is that people are too often asked to do jobs that would not normally

107

fit their job description. This can lead to an unhappy workforce. But of course that is just my opinion.

Tania Cutter PA
The Nail Bar Ltd

From: **Rebecca Harris 22.09.11 15:16**
To: Tania Cutter
Subject: Re: workload

Acknowledged.

From: **Felicity Jones 22.09.11 15:21**
To: Rebecca Harris
Subject: pong problem

Bex, with regards to the Westbourne body odour problem, I've always taken quite a straightforward approach to this kind of thing and just given the girl a deodorant and told her to use it.

I will check on Andrea re Janine.

PS did you get the phone number of the friend?

From: **Rebecca Harris 22.09.11 15:23**
To: Felicity Jones
Subject: who?

From: **Felicity Jones 22.09.11 15:24**
To: Rebecca Harris
Subject: Union Jack girl

From: **Rebecca Harris 22.09.11 15:25**
To: Felicity Jones
Subject: Re: Union Jack girl

No, damn, I didn't think about that.

From: **Felicity Jones 22.09.11 15:26**
To: Rebecca Harris
Subject: Re: Union Jack girl

No worries, I'm just befriending Sinead on Facebook now. The search for the friend is already underway.

From: **Rebecca Harris 22.09.11 15:27**
To: Felicity Jones
Subject: Re: Friend??

Slick, but wouldn't a phone call be easier?

From: **Felicity Jones 22.09.11 15:28**
To: Rebecca Harris
Subject: are you joking?

Tania has just torn Sinead a new arsehole – she's not exactly going to offer up her friend, is she?

From: **Rebecca Harris 22.09.11 15:29**
To: Felicity Jones
Subject: Re: are you joking?

Christ! No, I guess not.

From: **Rebecca Harris 22.09.11 15:31**
To: Phoebe Combes
Subject: Mail/Sunday PR disaster

Phoebe, there has been a serious PR disaster at Marylebone. The journalist from *The Mail on Sunday* that you organized for the interview somehow got the wrong day and turned up at Marylebone today in the midst of everyone trying to clear up the flood damage. As you can imagine, this didn't look too good, and to compound the situation Sylvia was the only one on hand to deal with the crisis.

I have her down in my diary as Helen Carmichael, coming in at 1pm on the 20th September. Is that what you have too? Apparently her photographer took loads of photos and she left saying she intended to write about us anyway. I don't need to tell you the damage this kind of bad press would do to us. It is essential that this article does not get published. Do you by any chance know this Helen woman, or anyone at *The Mail* you could talk to and get this thing dropped? Rebecca

From: **Phoebe Combes 22.09.11 15:34**
To: Rebecca Harris
Subject: Re: Mail/Sunday PR disaster

Wow! That's a terrible shame, especially as Helen Carmichael really is awful. One of my friends at *The Mail* says she's known as Rocky V – nothing to do with the Sylvester Stallone movies but rather a nickname derived from the name Rockweiler which she was known by when she worked at the *News of The World*. She's a shredder. We couldn't really be at the mercy of a more cutthroat journalist if we tried. She was recently taken on by *Mail on Sunday* as a freelance journalist to try and spice it up a bit. Rebecca, I hate to tell you this, but Helen is lethal. If you even try and get her to drop this piece on us she'll smell panic, and before you know it there'll be blood everywhere. Our only hope is that a B-list celebrity gets caught in some sort of lesbian-love-triangle and it hits the front pages on the same day so no one gets round to reading about us.

I'm afraid I don't keep a diary, but I think that date rings a bell.

From: **Rebecca Harris 22.09.11 15:36**
To: Phoebe Combes
Subject: Re: Mail/Sunday PR disaster

Jesus Christ, Phoebe! I was worried before, now I'm completely petrified. The woman sounds like a monster. Why on earth did we agree to the interview in the first place? You never warned me that I was being served up as potential Pedigree Chum. This couldn't be worse. If Barbara finds out about this she will self-combust. We have to try something. Please could you draft a letter of overwhelming apology to Ms Carmichael, explaining that we were the victims of a natural disaster and there was nothing we could have done to prevent the flooding. Send this along with a huge bunch of flowers, a massive goodie bag and gift vouchers for every service we offer.

Tell me if you get any favourable reaction from this at all.

Rebecca

From: **Phoebe Combes 22.09.11 15:39**
To: Rebecca Harris
Subject: Re: Mail/Sunday PR disaster

That's a good idea, and don't worry, I'm sure she's not as bad as people say. When *The Mail* contacted me, I wasn't informed that it was going to be Carmichael doing the interview. They just told me that they were interested in doing a piece on us. It was only once it was all confirmed that they dropped the bombshell. I didn't tell you about her because I thought it would make you nervous and I was sure that she would like you anyway, so it wouldn't matter. I'm so sorry, I shouldn't have taken such a huge risk.

I think the flowers are a great idea. Everyone loves flowers and she can't not be delighted by a fully-loaded gift voucher. I'll also write her a letter.

Greg was absolutely lovely, by the way.

110

From: **Rebecca Harris 22.09.11 15:40**
To: Phoebe Combes
Subject: Greg

Oh yes, great, I'm glad to hear that.

From: **Felicity Jones 22.09.11 15:42**
To: Vanessa Deane
Subject: body piercing

Vanessa,

Rebecca passed on your email to me. I'll sort out the Karen Johnson problem. I'm afraid Katya cannot do any body piercing at the moment because we don't have a licence for it. If she shoots for a lobe and gets a neck artery it wouldn't be cool. If she's really mad for it then find out what sort of profit margins could be achieved and I'll check out the licensing.

From: **Rebecca Harris 22.09.11 15:52**
To: Joe Doyle
Subject: Kensington Building Works

Joe, I came to Kensington at 12.30 and there was no one there! I waited for half an hour and not a single one of your guys appeared. Since your return from sunny Majorca, the work ethic of your men has gone from disappointing to completely crap. How is this possible?

Rebecca

From: **Joe Doyle 22.09.11 15:58**
To: Rebecca Harris
Subject: Re: Kensington Building Works

Rebecca luv, calm down. I took a couple of the lads out for a pie at lunch to get morale up a bit. They've been working in this rain all week and needed a bit of a boost. Always look after your staff, Rebecca. I've had my business for sixteen years and never lost a good man yet. Keep the working hours short, Christmas presents for the wives and kids and the occasional free lunch. That's what breeds loyalty, take it from me.

I've had a chance to look at progress and we're going to have to push completion date back to 3rd October due to the rain.

I couldn't find the cheque so you must have forgotten to leave it. Just be a good girl and put it in the post, will you?

Cheers.

Joe

From: **Rebecca Harris 22.09.11 16:03**
To: Joe Doyle
Subject: Re: Kensington Building Works

Joe, the last thing your "lads" need is a morale boost. They've been laughing their heads off in your absence, taking extended lunch and tea breaks and most of the time not even bothering to turn up to work at all. This is the reason progress has been minimal, not the rain. There is no way we can push completion date to the 3rd as that's the day of the opening party. How could we possibly get the place cleaned, let alone set up for the party?

I didn't leave the cheque because I don't intend to pay you until I see some serious progress.

Rebecca

From: **Rebecca Harris 22.09.11 16:07**
To: Joe Doyle
To: Phoebe Combes
Subject: the rockweiler

Phoebe, Can you find out if the rock . . . Helen Carmichael has a husband and kids, and if so send them some gifts too?

Thanks.

From: **Phoebe Combes 22.09.11 16:09**
To: Rebecca Harris
Subject: Re: the rockweiler

That's a jolly good idea.

From: **Clara Harris 22.09.11 16:17**
To: Rebecca Harris
Subject: oh god

Bex, I don't know what to do! I called Jason's hotel room in Miami and the phone was answered by a woman with a sleepy voice. I could hear Jason in the background urgently saying "don't answer it, put the phone down!" and then the phone went dead. Oh Bex, what do you think that means? I mean, I know what it means but do you think it definitely means that? Should I phone back and confront him, or should I wait until he gets back tonight and then say something, or should I pretend nothing happened?

Do you think maybe it was just his assistant doing morning dictation in his room? Do you think I should tell him he can't come to Mum's birthday anymore? I'm not going to pick him up from the airport, that's for sure. Or maybe I should and bring him to Mum's as well and then tackle the whole thing at the weekend so we don't ruin Mum's birthday?

I'm in a real state, please help.

From:	**Rebecca Harris 22.09.11 16:20**
To:	Joe Doyle
To:	Clara Harris
Subject:	Re: oh god

You poor thing. That little shit. I'm so angry, but not surprised. Clara, Jason is a rat. I'm sorry, but he is. I have to say I think this is a blessing. Now you can see what a true pig he is and get rid of him. Don't even think about picking him up at the airport, and definitely don't bring him to Mum's. Go home and put all his stuff in a bin bag and dump it outside the door, then get the locks changed to your apartment and he'll get the message loud and clear.

I know you're really upset and I'm sure you were hoping that I'd tell you that you should forgive him and all that, but I'm not going to. It's been too long and you've put up with too much crap.

Clara, if you were 22 years old you would have dumped him ages ago, you know you would. The only reason you've tolerated his behaviour is because you're worried you won't find someone else, and the old biological clock is ticking. But believe me, you don't want to have kids with someone as selfish as Jason. Life would be miserable.

There really are plenty more fish in the sea. God knows where they are, but Kat seems to find a new bloke every week, and we've got a girl in the office who met a guy on the bus this morning and shagged him by lunch, so they must be out there somewhere.

I'm stopping in to see Mum after work. Come over to me after that, around 8'ish. We can have supper and talk about what to do with that bastard. Be strong, Clarabelle. See you this evening.

From:	**Clara Harris 22.09.11 16:24**
To:	Rebecca Harris

You are absolutely right. He doesn't deserve me, and what's more I'm pretty sure this has been going on for a while. Last time he came back from Miami he was looking really tanned and fit and had a new pink shirt on (he's never worn pink before) and he didn't look at all like he'd been at an insurance conference. I'm going to go home now and chuck all his stuff in the bin.

I'll see you for supper later, thanks so much.

From: Bettina Harris 22.09.11 16:54
To: Rebecca Harris
Subject: he . lloo

Sweetheart . . . how are you?? this is yourrrr mum here. writing on a blackcurrant ----cannn you believe it it? my   nice friend rodney from bridge clubbb g   for my birthday so now you can,,, tell everyyy yone how with-it your ol d mum is.ssss

now Beccy,,, your sister called clled called mand she is very upset about Jason who apparently   ,,,,, has been doing a little @@#playing away....;; i.. told her that it's very normal forr   men to get a litttttle skittish before they get married and for her not ^^not to read toooooooooooooooooo much into it.

best thing forrr her to do is pretend — — —   nothing 9999 happened and it will all //blow overthethethe chances are he'll forget all about that tramp he left behind in miami when he sees her smiling face at the airport(((

i think Clara might call you for advise tooooo so make sure you say the same thing.

so loooooooooking for ward to the party tomorr night. apart from rodney and marjorie,;;;;; i have invited   two others from my bridge clubb@@ sally perkins and herrr husband and the marshes from nexxx door....cccccccccclara tells me about six ofyour friends are coming too so we will be 144444 in all which is suppper. That handsome friend ddof yours Jonathan banks said he was coming and I hope the lovely oliver is too?

lotsoflovvvvemummy

ps...sorry don't knoww how to delete eth mistakes

Message sent via BlackBerry ®

114

From: Tania Cutter 22.09.11 17:00
To: Rebecca Harris
Subject: your PERSONAL phone calls

Rebecca,

You had two personal calls: one from your sister and the other from your mother (second time today) who wanted to know if you got her email? Over the next few days I will be making and expecting a great number of calls in order to gather statistics for Ms Foreman. Could you therefore try and keep your personal calls to a minimum as it makes it very hard for me to do my job?

I am leaving now as I only took a half-hour lunch today to make sure that I would be here if Barbara called. Would you like me to put the answer machine on?

Tania Cutter PA

The Nail Bar Ltd

From: Clara Harris 22.09.11 17:01
To: Rebecca Harris
Subject: Jason

Hi Bex, I've just been speaking to Mum and I think she's right, I can't dump Jason just like that. I don't even know for sure if he's done anything wrong. Mum says the concierge may well have put me through to the wrong room and that's perfectly possible, right?

I've decided to give him the benefit of the doubt and if it happens again then I swear I will dump him immediately.

Can I still come over?

Clarabelle

From: Rebecca Harris 22.09.11 17:05
To: Joe Doyle
To: Bettina Harris
Subject: Re: he . . lloo

Mum, you can't possibly be serious? This isn't the 1920s. Women have a few more rights now and one of them is to demand a faithful partner. After what Dad did to you I'd have thought you would feel adamant that this kind of behaviour is unacceptable. Jason walks all over Clara and it makes me sick. She's got to face up to him and let him know that she's not going to stand for this.

By the way, I know we spoke earlier, but I just wanted to say sorry again about forgetting breakfast this morning. I really feel so awful about that and I promise to make it up to you. We're really going to celebrate this year, Mum. It's time to put the past behind you and have some fun, so make sure you invite whichever friends you like. Clara is going to do the food and I'll bring the wine and champagne. It's going to be a great evening.

Lots of love,

Beccy

From: **Rebecca Harris 22.09.11 17:08**
To: Joe Doyle
To: Clara Harris
Subject: Jason

Clara, Please don't listen to Mum. She's basically telling you to turn a blind eye, sit tight and hope he comes running back to you.

Do not do or say anything to Jason until we have had a chance to talk tonight.

From: **Bettina Harris 22.09.11 17:16**
To: Rebecca Harris
Subject: Re: he . . lloo

Dddda rling,,,,i was///   born in 1942 but but i have to say the advice   that   yourrrrrr   grann   dmother   used toooooooooooooooooooooo give me was   to acceptt thaaat men men are veryy different   ;;;;   from women anddd not to judege then too harshly obviously worked well with gGrandpa and iiis certainly the reason you 555r father and i had 35 wonderful years together despite his infidelities....see you you yo yyyyyu

Seeyou iiin a while

much lovemummy

Message sent via BlackBerry ®

From: **Joe Doyle 22.09.11 17:19**
To: Rebecca Harris
Subject: give the bugger what he needs

Rebecca luv, your last five emails have all come in to my mailbox, which I'm sure must be a mistake?

I would like to say though, your grandmother was spot on. Men are very different from women. We need to be rewarded even when we haven't behaved well. We respond much better that way. You may think this J needs a good slap, but if your sister gives it to him, he's

116

gonna go straight back to the hot Hispanic chick who's just waiting on the other side of the Atlantic to give him a good old aromatherapy foot massage.

What she needs to do is give that poor over-worked bastard a well-deserved blow job and a hot meal.

From: **Rebecca Harris 22.09.11 17:24**
To: Joe Doyle
To: Tania Cutter
Subject: Graham's number!!!!!

I NEED GRAHAM'S NUMBER NOW!!!!!!!!

Joe Doyle has somehow become my default address – every time I try to send an email to someone, it automatically gets sent to Joe. Graham obviously messed up my computer when he came to "fix it".

From: **Joe Doyle 22.09.11 17:26**
To: Rebecca Harris
Subject: Re: Graham's number!!!!!

Rebecca, I wouldn't mind Graham's number either, I could do with a good tech guy. One of our computers has been playing up. My brother took it apart to get a better look and for the life of him can't figure out how to put it back together.

Once you've finished giving the poor sod an earful, maybe he could stop by Doyle Bros?

From: **Felicity Jones 22.09.11 17:28**
To: Rebecca Harris
Subject: Hygiene regs for all nail bars
Attach: HYGIENE REGULATIONS

Bex,

It turns out that Karen Johnson is the sensitive type. Vanessa reckons if we just put a deodorant on her manicure table she might walk, so I've drafted up quite a professional-looking Hygiene Regulations notice (as a disguise to get the message across – see point 8) to go in all the staff kitchens.

Here is a copy. I think it's bloody brilliant. Just let me know if you are happy with it and I will fax it over to all the nail bars.

We saw that Tania left, so Phoebe and I have cracked open a bottle of wine she had left over from her birthday – want to join us?

HYGIENE REGULATIONS

All staff are required to comply with the following rules during working hours at The Nail Bar:

1. Regulation Nail Bar uniform must be worn at all times and be in good condition i.e. clean and well ironed.
2. Sensible home shoes may be worn, but heels must be less than 5 inches and glitter and sparkle kept to a minimum. No dominatrix-style boots are permitted.
3. Jewellery must not be excessive and large bangles that jangle while doing manicures must not be worn.
4. A maximum of three earrings can be worn in each ear, and nose piercings to hold a simple ring or stud. Any other body piercings must be removed or covered; this includes belly buttons.
5. Nails should be well manicured and painted at all times.
6. Hair must be clean and tidy and worn away from the face. No Mohicans and no shaved heads.
7. Makeup is expected but should not be of a "Gothic" nature.
8. If you have a tendency to sweat profusely,

PLEASE CARRY DEODORANT AT ALL TIMES AND APPLY REGULARLY.

Felicity Jones
Human Resources
The Nail Bar Ltd

From: **Rebecca Harris 22.09.11 17:32**
To: Joe Doyle
To: Felicity Jones
Subject: Re: Hygiene regs for all nail bars

Not sure how well disguised that is but the message should be quite clear.

By the way, did we get a refund from the agency for Darren, and any luck on Facebook?

From: **Felicity Jones 22.09.11 7:34**
To: Rebecca Harris
Subject: Sinead

No, they said we have to give 24 hours' notice for a cancellation or we have to pay full whack.

Huge progress on Facebook. I'm pretty sure I've found her. She lives in Watford, goes by the name of Brochetta Tingle and works at a place called Club Beaver – I kid you not. Don't think she's going to be quite right but we'll keep her on the reserve list if things get any more desperate. In the meantime I have 42 new friends in Watford and a free entry to Club Beaver this Friday – you in?

From: **Rebecca Harris 22.09.11 17:38**
To: Joe Doyle
To: Felicity Jones
Subject: Club Beaver

Can I think about that?

Friday 23rd September 2011

Jane Johnson 23.09.11 8:15
To: Rebecca Harris
Subject: Poppy
Attach: The Importance of Suitable Adult Attire

Dear Ms Harris,

I would like to draw your attention to an unwritten rule that we have here at Stepping Stones Pre-Primary, regarding "suitable dress" required by adults at collection time. Yesterday afternoon we were delighted that Poppy was being picked up by her godmother, as indeed was Poppy herself. However, our delight turned to disappointment and concern when said godmother arrived in what can only be described as "wanton" attire. I will not go into too much detail as there is no need to expose you to the same level of offence that we here at SSPP experienced, but suffice it to say she wouldn't have looked out of place in the red light district of Soho late on a Friday night.

Collection and drop-off can often be quite an emotional time for youngsters, and the last thing we need is for anything unpredictable or untoward happening that might "upset the apple cart" as it were, and Ms Lease was definitely in danger of bruising some fruit.

I do believe it would be a bit of a nonsense to have to issue a clothing rule to parents and guardians; after all, we have not needed to do so for the children. I also feel very confident that I will not need to remind you about this again. I will, henceforth, consider the matter closed.

On a separate note – Miss Baines informed me that Poppy came to school with only one ballet shoe and therefore was unable to take part in the class. Poppy was most disappointed by this – unsurprisingly. I do think it's a shame to have our little ones suffer on account of their parent's negligence.

We look forward immensely to seeing you at the Coffee & Biscuits Morning on Thursday week.

Warmest regards
Jane Johnson
Head Teacher

From: **Clara Harris 23.09.11 9:30**
To: Rebecca Harris
Subject: Jason

Hi Bex,

Any word from Charles? Thanks so much for listening to me going on and on about Jason. I have done all my crying now and I feel much stronger. You were absolutely right about everything you said.

There was a message from him on the ansafone when I got home last night giving me his flight details and telling me not to be late picking him up – no "how are you?" or "I miss you" or even "looking forward to seeing you". He is a total arsehole and whether

121

he is having an affair or not I know that he will never really make me happy, he's WAY too selfish.

I'm going to spend the morning in the library and then go and do the shopping for Mum's party. My plan is to keep my mobile switched off the whole time so he can't get hold of me.

See you tonight.

From:	**Rebecca Harris 23.09.11 9:34**
To:	Clara Harris
Subject:	Re: Jason

Clarabelle,

You're doing the right thing, I promise.

No news from Charles, and if that isn't bad enough I received a really narky email from Poppy's headmistress. I can't stand that woman or her silly, stuck-up school with its completely outdated rules – ugh. The sooner I get Poppy out of there the better.

From:	**Clara Harris 23.09.11 9:36**
To:	Rebecca Harris
Subject:	Re: Jason

I'm feeling so strong about breaking off my engagement with Jason. Quite frankly I don't care if I never see him again.

Why don't you move her to that other school you said was really good?

From:	**Rebecca Harris 23.09.11 9:37**
To:	Clara Harris
Subject:	Poppy

She's on the waiting list . . . along with about 30,000 other kids.

From:	**Andrea Moleno 23.09.11 9:48**
To:	Felicity Jones
Cc:	Rebecca Harris
Subject:	HYGIENE REGULATIONS

Dear Felicity,

Thank you for the "Hygiene Regulations" notice which I received last night and put up here in the Mayfair staff kitchen this morning. Unfortunately Janine had just arrived and when she read it she went completely berserk. She thinks that it was written specifically for her because she wears lots of jewellery, very high heels, and she has a pierced belly button (which she showed me) and she usually wears quite heavy makeup. She ripped the notice up and tore it to pieces and then screamed, "I'm not the one who needs deodorant, I'm not the one who stinks, it's this fxxking company that stinks". Then she walked out.

The rest of the staff didn't seem too bothered about the notice so should I put up another copy or would it be best to leave it?

Janine only had a few bookings so it hasn't been too much of a problem to re-arrange her clients.

From: **Felicity Jones 23.09.11 9:52**
To: Rebecca Harris
Subject: Re: HYGIENE REGULATIONS

That psycho bitch is way the fuck out of control. She has to go . . . surely?

From: **Rebecca Harris 23.09.11 9:54**
To: Felicity Jones
Subject: Re: HYGIENE REGULATIONS

Fi, let's not overreact. I know she is a loose cannon and I think this time she has definitely over-stepped the mark. We need to have a proper talk with her, but we're so short of staff already I don't want to lose any more if we can help it. Why don't you schedule a meeting with Andrea, Janine and yourself and try and see if you can get her under control?

From: **Felicity Jones 23.09.11 9:57**
To: Rebecca Harris
Subject: Re: HYGIENE REGULATIONS

Under control? Janine is a certified maniac – believe me, there is no "controlling". Rebecca, you have to get serious. She went beyond the mark and into the danger zone when she whacked Bianca over the head with a nail dryer. If you don't fire her we risk losing a great many more staff – and I am not talking about resignations either.

From: **Rebecca Harris 23.09.11 10:00**
To: Felicity Jones
Subject: Re: HYGIENE REGULATIONS

Maybe you're right. If you really think there is no other option, then I'll get Tania to draft up a letter of termination.

From: **Felicity Jones 23.09.11 10:02**
To: Rebecca Harris
Subject: Re: HYGIENE REGULATIONS

There is no other option!!

From: **Rebecca Harris 23.09.11 10:06**
To: Tania Cutter
Subject: T of E letter

Tania,

Please could you draft a "T of E" letter to Janine Azame citing the following reasons:

- Inappropriate and often aggressive behaviour towards clients
- Unkind treatment towards other members of staff
- Persistent late arrival to work and extended lunch breaks
- Threatening and volatile behaviour towards management
- Swearing at staff and management

She has received countless verbal warnings and also a written warning prior to this. Her details, including home address etc, are on file.

Thank you.

From: **Felicity Jones 23.09.11 10:15**
To: Rebecca Harris
Subject: Suki

Bex, you made the right decision.

I'm at Marylebone, by the way, and guess what? Suki is back – but wait for it –

I gave Sylvia the keys to the nail bar yesterday so she would be able to open up this morning, which she did. She was busy doing the till reports, and had locked the front door for security reasons, when Suki turned up. Suki banged on the door and demanded to be let in, but as Sylvia didn't recognize her she wouldn't comply. Suki then started shouting all sorts of stuff in Mandarin which made Sylvia all the more convinced that she shouldn't let her in. After 15 minutes of this, one of the other staff arrived and explained to Sylvia that the crazy Chinese girl outside is actually the manager of the shop. Sylvia immediately unlocked the door, but by then Suki was already demented and demanded that Sylvia get out. Two clients had turned up by this point and Sylvia didn't want to make a scene so she took her handbag and left. She called me from a coffee shop nearby, all hyperventilating and upset, to tell me this.

I went and met Sylvia and we came back to the nail bar together to confront Suki. Sylvia is waiting in the staff room while I talk to Suki. I'll fill you in later – same shit, different day, right!

PS Wouldn't like to be at Mayfair when Janine gets the T of E!

From: **Rebecca Harris 23.09.11 10:19**
To: Felicity Jones
Subject: T of E

Actually, Fi, I think it would be appropriate if you *were* at Mayfair when Janine gets her T of E, don't you?

Did Suki give any explanation why she is 5 days late?

From: **Felicity Jones 23.09.11 10:21**
To: Rebecca Harris
Subject: Suki

Haven't heard the excuse yet. Will head over to Mayfair shortly.

From: **Katherine Lease 23.09.11 10:22**
To: Rebecca Harris
Subject: Poppy

Sweetie, any news from Charles??

Loved my afternoon with Poppy yesterday!! Everything went brilliantly. I arrived on time, dressed perfectly (totally nailed the trendy but tasteful "mummy" look), chatted to some of the other mums who were all boring sloanes, but I still made an effort. Poppy and I took a cab up to Oxford street and shopped the hell out of Accessorize. That place has the coolest stuff (I'm currently supporting a fake Tinkerbelle tattoo on my arse.) Then we went and mucked about with the toys at Hamleys. Did she show you her Build a Bear? Went to the Hard Rock café for hamburgers, chips, chocolate fudge sundaes and vanilla milkshakes, disgusting but oh sooooo good. Poppy was the best companion, we laughed loads, I love that daughter of yours, I really do.

From: **Rebecca Harris 23.09.11 10:25**
To: Katherine Lease
Subject: Re: Poppy

Kat, you're the best. Poppy was bouncing off the walls when I got home. She was full of excitement and sugar. I eventually got her into bed at 8pm with her Build a Bear (who she has called Kat, by the way).

Just a small point – Poppy's headmistress wasn't as gung-ho on your outfit as you were, I'm afraid. The woman is a real stiff, so don't worry too much, but you might have to tone it down a bit for Sport's Day.

No, Charles has not called.

From:	Katherine Lease 23.09.11 10:26
To:	Rebecca Harris
Subject:	Re: Poppy

WHAT? I looked awesome. The woman must be a dinosaur. I was wearing a beautiful Armani sea-green wrap skirt, teamed with a skinny T and Balenciaga biker jacket, white fishnets (ok, a bit risqué but not hard core) and Stella McCartney ankle boots. What the hell's wrong with that? Anyway, Poppy loved it, and that's all I care about.

Darling, hang in there. Charles will call, I know he will.

From:	Tania Cutter 23.09.11 10:23
To:	Rebecca Harris
Subject:	your PERSONAL calls

Rebecca,

You have had three personal phone calls and each one of them came with a message:

1. Vinca (your child's nanny, I believe) wants to know if she should take Poppy straight to your mum's house after school or bring her home first and then you will take her with you?

2. Your mother wants to know if Vinca is bringing Poppy to her house straight from school or if she is coming later with you?

3. Vinca (again) wants to know if Poppy is staying with your mother for one night or two as she is trying to pack her a bag.

May I suggest that you give Vinca and your mother their respective telephone numbers so that I may get on and write this letter of termination for Janine Azame.

Tania Cutter PA

126

From: **Phoebe Combes 23.09.11 10:25**
To: Rebecca Harris
Subject: Kensington etc

Hi Rebecca,

I just got back from Kensington. I'm afraid I couldn't put up the opening notice on the inside of the window because the shop was locked. You said the builders would be there to let me in but they weren't. I waited for an hour but no-one showed, so I came back to the office.

I've called around the other nail bars to see how the various promotions are going and at Westbourne they said there has been a small increase in demand for pedicures from people wanting to take advantage of the free pot of *Orange Crush*, but this hasn't been the case in Mayfair or Marylebone. However, all three nail bars say that the sales of *Purple Rain* have been huge. It's still too early to say how the Eyebrow Shaping promo is going.

My friend Saskia, who writes the horoscopes for *You* magazine at *The Daily Mail*, said that Helen Carmichael's desk is piled high with all the nail bar freebies we sent her, and this morning she was telling everyone that it showed how terrified we obviously were about the article she is going to write – so that tactic seems to have backfired, which is a shame. I can't think what else we can do, can you?

From: **Rebecca Harris 23.09.11 10:30**
To: Phoebe Combes
Subject: Re: Kensington etc

Phoebe, sorry about the builders, something must have gone wrong, they definitely should have been there.

This is not good at all about Helen Carmichael. Could you check with your horoscope friend what is in store for Sagittarians for the next couple of weeks as I think I need to be mentally prepared if things are really going to go pear shaped!!

Thanks.

From: **Phoebe Combes 23.09.11 10:34**
To: Rebecca Harris
Subject: Re: Kensington etc

That's a very good idea. I've mentioned to her before what a nice person you are, and as she usually just makes up most of her predictions, I'm sure she'll do you a really positive one.

127

From: **Suki Leung** suki.marylebone@thenailbar.com **23.09.11 10:39**
To: Rebecca Harris
Subject: Suki back, what you want?

Rebecca,

I come back from Shanghai but still sick with hepatitis. I come back to show loyalty to nail bar, even though mother and doctor say long journey very bad for sickness. Rebecca, I very unhappy about replacement with old lady who take my job. I tell her "Suki back, she go home now" but she look angry. Rebecca, you tell me, you want me or you want old lady manage this nail bar?

Also nail bar smell like wet dog, not good for client. Staff tell Suki two nail dryers broken in flood and light not working in kitchen.

Rebecca, you see, nail bar not working when Suki go away, maybe Suki need pay rise to feel happy again and make hepatitis go away.

Suki Leung

From: **Rebecca Harris 23.09.11 10:46**
To: Suki Leung
Subject: welcome back

Dear Suki,

I am very sorry for the confusion this morning. I did not know when you would be back and so I put the new manager for Kensington into Marylebone as a temporary measure. Of course I am delighted that you are back, although I am very sorry to hear you have not been well. I know that now you are here everything will once again run smoothly at Marylebone.

I'm afraid the flood at your nail bar has caused some significant damage, but we are trying our best to sort it out as quickly as possible. I will try and get to Marylebone today to take a look, or if not, I will come by at the weekend.

I will talk to Felicity about a pay rise for you, which I'm sure you deserve, and I hope you feel better soon.

Best wishes,

Rebecca

From: **Felicity Jones 23.09.11 10.51**
To: Rebecca Harris
Subject: Suki

I'm now at Mayfair and luckily there's no sign of the mentally deranged Janine anywhere. Andrea is her usual calm self and things are running as smoothly as ever.

I had a long chat to Suki and it's all cool, but she refuses to do management training with Sylvia due to what she calls a "loss of face" or something, and she also claims she's still too weak from hepatitis to teach anybody anything – like hell! The long and the short of it is, that Sylvia (whose pacemaker is really getting a good arse kicking) is now going to work with Andrea at Mayfair until Kensington opens.

Heading back to the office.

From: **Rebecca Harris 23.09.11 10:57**
To: Felicity Jones
Subject: Re: Suki

Thanks, Fi.

I had an interesting email from Suki in the meantime who reckons that arriving back 5 days late from holiday and freaking out on other members of staff somehow entitles her to a pay rise, can you believe it? . . . Of course, I said yes.

From: **Felicity Jones 23.09.11 10:59**
To: Rebecca Harris
Subject: Of course

From: **Rebecca Harris 23.09.11 11:02**
To: Katherine Lease
Subject: Re: Charles

Kat, he still hasn't called. You were right I should have slept with him. I'm such an idiot – there I was thinking that he would really respect me for holding back, but no one holds back anymore, do they? What should I do? Do you think I should send him a text or something to say "thanks for the date" to see if he replies?

From: **Katherine Lease 23.09.11 11:04**
To: Rebecca Harris
Subject: Re: Charles

Definitely worth a try, although if he doesn't reply you then look like a right prat. Make sure you word it so that it doesn't warrant a response, then it doesn't matter too much if he doesn't come back to you.

From: **Rebecca Harris 23.09.11 11:06**
To: Katherine Lease
Subject: Re: Charles

Ok, but the whole point of contacting him in the first place is to get a response, isn't it?

From: **Katherine Lease 23.09.11 11:08**
To: Rebecca Harris
Subject: Re: Charles

Yes, of course it is, and personally I would send an email telling him that I was sitting at my desk with no knickers on, feeling so turned on there was a strong possibility I might slip off my seat, and wondering if he wanted to meet at the Knightsbridge Hotel in his lunch break, room 12 . . . that is how you guarantee a response from a horny stockbroker. However, I know you and you would probably prefer a more subtle approach, which is fine, but of course it runs the risk of rejection.

Good luck and let me know how it goes.

From: **Rebecca Harris 23.09.11 11:10**
To: Katherine Lease
Subject: Re: Charles

You know, you're quite disgusting sometimes . . . does that really work?

From: **Katherine Lease 23.09.11 11:11**
To: Rebecca Harris
Subject: yes

Of course it does. By the way, I bought your Mum a Neil Diamond CD for her birthday. Is that spot on or what?

From: **Rebecca Harris 23.09.11 11:12**
To: Katherine Lease
Subject: Mum's prezzie

Thanks, Kat. Mum loves Neil (as she calls him) and his *Greatest Hits* CD was in her car when it got stolen last year and I know she hasn't got around to replacing it.

I think I'm just going to wait a bit longer to see if Charles calls.

From: **Clara Harris 23.09.11 11:16**
To: Rebecca Harris
Subject: Jason

Bex, I was just wondering, do you think I should maybe pick up Jason from the airport after all? The thing is, it is a bit mean just to leave him standing there waiting and not knowing that no one is there to meet him. Of course I shall make it clear that I am furious and that he is not welcome at the flat, but at least I could then take him to his mum's place or something.

Do you think pink champagne would be nice to drink tonight, or is it only the girls who like it? What about a cocktail – Moscow Mule or something, not sure what is the "in" drink at the moment?

From: **Rebecca Harris 23.09.11 11:20**
To: Clara Harris
Subject: Re: Jason

Clarabelle, the whole idea is that Jason is *meant* to be left waiting. He knows it was you on the phone in the hotel room, so he knows you know about the other girl. If you show up at the airport it sends him a clear message that he can screw around as much as he wants and you will still come running. You must stand firm, he has to be taught a lesson.

By the way, do you think it's weird that Charles hasn't called me yet? I haven't heard from him since our date and he's meant to be coming tonight.

I would go for Moscow Mules and I'll pick up some wine on the way home as well. Tom said he's bringing some wine as his present to Mum, so I think we're covered.

From: **Clara Harris 23.09.11 11:25**
To: Rebecca Harris
Subject: Re: Jason

You're right, I know you're right; I won't go to the airport.

I wouldn't worry about Charles, he's probably just busy. I seem to remember that brokers are really busy in the mornings, then they go out for long lunches and in the afternoon they just hang out, so you will probably get a call around 3 o'clock. In the meantime, it might be nice to just send a quick email saying thank you for the date last night and confirming tonight.

From: **Rebecca Harris 23.09.11 11:27**
To: Clara Harris
Subject: Charles

It wasn't last night, it was the night before.

From: **Clara Harris 23.09.11 11:29**
To: Rebecca Harris
Subject: Re: Charles

Oh Bex, I am sorry, that's quite a long time for him not to have contacted you. Are you sure the date went well? Did you argue? You can be quite argumentative sometimes.

From: **Rebecca Harris 23.98.11 11:31**
To: Clara Harris
Subject: Re: Charles

No we didn't argue.

From: **Clara Harris 23.09.11 11:34**
To: Rebecca Harris
Subject: Re: Charles

Were you being very opinionated? You can be very opinionated.

From: **Rebecca Harris 23.09.11 11:35**
To: Clara Harris
Subject: Re: Charles

Er no, I don't think I was being particularly opinionated.

From: **Clara Harris 23.09.11 11:36**
To: Rebecca Harris
Subject: Re: Charles

How about showing off? You do have a tendency to get over-excited when you drink.

From: **Rebecca Harris 23.09.11 11:37**
To: Clara Harris
Subject: Re: Charles

No, I don't recall any dancing on the tables or drunken exhibitionism. Does this list go on for much longer?

From: **Clara Harris 23.09.11 11:39**
To: Rebecca Harris
Subject: Re: Charles

I was just trying to rule out any possibilities because I can't understand why he hasn't called. You're such a great person and Charles should be falling over himself trying to make you feel a million bucks. You know what? I bet he's lost your email. I think you should email him because it would be polite to thank him for taking you out, and then I'm sure he'll get back to you right away. Be sure to put your mobile number on as well, because he may well have lost that too.

From: Rebecca Harris 23.09.11 11:42
To: Clara Harris
Subject: Re: Charles

Thanks, Clara, I think I'll do that.

From: Rebecca Harris 23.09.11 11:45
To: Charles Balford
Subject: just checking

Hi Charles,
Thanks so much for Wednesday night, I had a really good time and I thought your friends Phil and Cindy's party was great.
I just wanted to check if you were still on for tonight – my mum's birthday? I will understand completely if it's not your scene or if you have other plans.
Love, Bex

From: Rebecca Harris 23.09.11 11:47
To: Katherine Lease
Subject: Charles

Kat, I just emailed Charles to thank him for the date and ask him if he wants to come to Mum's birthday dinner tonight.
I'm now feeling a bit sick about it – d'you think it was a huge mistake? Will it look like I'm desperate? Will he think the idea of going to a 60th birthday really lame? He takes me to a hip party in Notting Hill and I offer that? I should be asking him to something cool, like a Bryan Adams' concert or something, not my mum's birthday, for crying out loud. I'm such an idiot, no wonder I'm single, I'm so horribly boring!

From: Katherine Lease 23.09.11 11:50
To: Rebecca Harris
Subject: Re: Charles

Bex, darling, you're not horribly boring but you do scare me when you use words like "cool" and "Bryan Adams" in the same sentence.

I have to admit that your approach was a little suicidal, but as you said before, I don't know Charles's type, so you may be fine. Anyway, it's done so there's no point worrying about it.

Marcus just sent a package to me in the office with some Agent Provocateur underwear in it. Off to the bathroom to try it on.

Kit Kat xx

From: **Rebecca Harris 23.09.11 12:00**
To: Joe Doyle
Subject: Ken. Building Works

Joe,

Please enlighten me as to why on earth there is no-one at Kensington this morning? How can we possibly have the building works completed on time if your men do not even show up to work? You obviously have no control over your team and you can be sure I will tell everyone I know never to use Doyle Brothers Construction. I am so angry, and I can promise you I will have a team of lawyers onto you before you can blink, if you don't have a very good reason for this.

You're right about men and women being different; women have some integrity and a much better work ethic.

Rebecca

From: **Bettina Harris 23.09.11 12:02**
To: Rebecca Harris
Subject: t..;rrrrrr;;;;;e
Message sent via BlackBerry ®

From: **Barbara Foreman 23.09.11 12:04**
To: Rebecca Harris
Subject: my requirements

Rebecca,

I have arrived in Guangzhou after a 19 hour flight and there was no one to meet me at the airport. I eventually managed to find a taxi whose driver spoke no known language, and consequently it has taken two hours to get to my less than adequate hotel. The reason I am telling you this is I seem to remember that you grew up in China, so presumably you know the country quite well. Not to mention there is a twelve-hour time difference between here and New York and so Nancy is not in the office yet. It therefore falls on you, Rebecca, to assist me for the next two hours in this godforsaken place – obviously I am not expecting too much.

Firstly, I need you to find me another hotel. I am currently in the Ambassador. It is filthy and the lighting is terrible. I must be somewhere central, but not noisy, in a top floor suite with a view, internet access, a fully-stocked mini bar, bed sheets must have a minimum thread count of 400, and most importantly, hotel staff who speak English. I would like to move tonight.

Secondly, I need a full-time driver who has a clean licence and knows the city well. He must, of course, understand English and be a non-smoker,

Thirdly, Nancy was meant to fax through my itinerary and the product pictures to the hotel, but the fax machine is out of order here. When Nancy wakes up please give her the fax number of the new hotel so she can send the stuff through. I do not want it in email form as I cannot print anything off, and I need to be able to see the product pictures clearly.

Barbara

Message sent via BlackBerry ®

From: **Oliver Barker 23.09.11 12:07**
To: Rebecca Harris
Subject: present for your mum

Hi Bex,

I thought I might get your mum a tablecloth from Designer's Guild for her birthday. I remember that at Clara and Jason's engagement dinner Jason spilt red wine on the table and your mum was a bit upset because the tablecloth was ruined. I'm near the King's Road this afternoon and I know my mum always goes on about Designer's Guild being so great – what do you think, is it too boring?

From: **Rebecca Harris 23.09.11 12:08**
To: Oliver Barker
Subject: Re: present for mum

She'll love that, wish I had thought of it. I have bought her the most stupid present – a gypsy skirt and some beads (the sort of thing a 13-year-old would love) from Top Shop, which she will never wear.

By the way, my boss is in Guangzhou and she is staying at a hotel called the Ambassador, which she says is terrible. She wants me to find her a nice hotel and a driver who speaks English. She thinks, for some reason, that because I used to live in Hong Kong that I should know how to help her?! I left Asia when I was 8 years old and we went to China once during that time and even then it was only for the day. I remember eating some very slippery noodles, crying in the wet market because all the animals looked so sad, then throwing up on the overnight ferry on the way home. Do you have any idea about hotels in that area? I know you usually go to Hong Kong, but you probably have a way better idea than I do? It is already 8 o'clock there and she wants to move hotels tonight!!!!

From: **Oliver Barker 23.09.11 12:11**
To: Rebecca Harris
Subject: do my best

I have been to Guangdong but I don't know it very well. I'll try and get hold of my Chinese colleague Joseph in Hong Kong, he travels to China pretty frequently.
I don't know what a gypsy skirt looks like but I'm sure your mum will love it.

From: **Joe Doyle 23.09.11 12:16**
To: Rebecca Harris
Subject: Re: Ken. Building Works

Rebecca luv, I'm afraid I had to pull my boys off your job as we had another one starting in Hull today. I had to assume that as you were not intending to pay us the money we are owed that you were officially terminating your contract. We have a very strict policy here at Doyle Brothers Construction about late payment. If payment is more than four days outstanding and a client has been given plenty of notice, then work stops immediately on that project. I am sorry, Rebecca, but my brother Kenneth, who does the accounts, is a real stickler for detail. Of course I told him you were a lovely girl an' all but he said "rules are rules, Joe", so my hands were tied.
Best wishes. Joe

From: **Rebecca Harris 23.09.11 12:18**
To: Joe Doyle
Subject: Re: Ken. building works

Joe, there has been a huge misunderstanding. Of course I don't wish to terminate our contract with you. I have been having quite a stressful day and so I was just a little unhappy when I heard there was no one at Kensington this morning. Now I know why that is, I am perfectly happy to drive over to your office immediately with the cheque for the outstanding payment. I can be there in twenty minutes.

Rebecca

From: Joe Doyle **23.09.11 12:21**
To: Rebecca Harris
Subject: Re: Ken. Building Works

Keep your hair on, luv. As long as Kenneth gets the cheque today, I'm sure I can get my men back on the job by tomorrow morning.

From: Rebecca Harris **23.09.11 12:22**
To: Joe Doyle
Subject: Re: Ken. Building Works

Sorry to be difficult, but is there any chance of someone getting in there today? I am just a bit concerned about works being completed on time?

From: Joe Doyle **23.09.11 12:25**
To: Rebecca Harris
Subject: Re: Ken. Building Works

I doubt it. I am running a sensible business here, Rebecca. I can't just miracle a team of highly skilled professional builders out of the sky. These things take time to organize. I also don't want to upset my men by moving them all around the place. Take it from me, the way to run a successful business is people management. Your workforce need to know who is in charge and what is expected of them. If you keep changing your mind and telling them one thing one moment and then another thing another, you can be sure as roses are roses that there's gonna be a breakdown of communication, and that can only lead to one thing – a loss of respect, and without respect, Rebecca, you've got nothing. I don't want you to have nothing and I understand that you are feeling a bit jumpy at this stage, so I will see what I can do for you.

I am going out for my lunch now and when I get back I will try and sort out your predicament.

From: **Bettina Harris 23.09.11 12:26**
To: Rebecca Harris
Subject: ~~

…;hhee;;..if you can sally that that would belovely..\ \ \ \
Message sent via BlackBerry.

From: **Oliver Barker 23.09.11 12:28**
To: Rebecca Harris
Subject: new hotel

The best hotel to stay in Guangdong is The White Swan – Joseph
says that it's very central and the concierge speaks English. I went
one step further and asked him to book a suite there under your
name (couldn't remember your boss's) and to organize a driver to
pick her up from the Ambassador and take her to The White Swan.
I just need your boss's name and what time she would like to be
picked up. All the details for The White Swan are on their website
www.thewhiteswanhotel.com.ch.
Hope this helps

From: **Rebecca Harris 23.09.11 12:30**
To: Oliver Barker
Subject: Re: new hotel

That is all perfect, my boss is going to think I am a genius. Her name
is Ms Barbara Foreman and I think she is ready to leave right now,
so if a driver can pick her up immediately that would be great.
Thanks so so much.

From: **Oliver Barker 23.09.11 12:31**
To: Rebecca Harris
Subject: Re: new hotel

No problem. See you tonight.

From: **Rebecca Harris 23.09.11 12:34**
To: Barbara Foreman
Subject: Re: your requirements

Barbara,
A car and driver are on the way to your hotel now to pick you up
and take you to The White Swan. I have booked you a suite with a
great view. The hotel has come highly recommended from a reliable
source. I have had a look at the website and the rooms are spacious
and clean and the concierge speaks English.

I have also sent a message to Nancy with the personal fax number for your new room.

Please let me know if there is anything else I can do for you.

Rebecca

From: **Rebecca Harris 23.09.11 12:36**
To: Bettina Harris
Subject: Re: ~~

Mum, your email to Sally came to me.

From: **Barbara Foreman 23.09.11 12:37**
To: Rebecca Harris
Subject: my hotel

Excellent. Well done, Rebecca.

By the way, how did the interview with that journalist go?

Barbara

Message sent via BlackBerry®

From: **Rebecca Harris 23.09.11 12:38**
To: Barbara Foreman
Subject: the interview

The interview went well, but I don't think the article will be out before the opening as apparently these journalists work months in advance of publication.

Rebecca

From: **Bettina Harris 23.09.11 12:40**
To: Rebecca Harris
Subject: Re: ~~

Oops, sorrrr::/y darling.

From: **Barbara Foreman 23.09.11 12:41**
To: Rebecca Harris
Subject: magazine article

Good, well, send me a copy of the magazine when it does come out.

Message sent via BlackBerry ®

From: **Rebecca Harris 23.09.11 12:42**
To: Phoebe Combes
Subject: the article

Phoebe, any news from your friend at *You* magazine?

From: **Phoebe Combes 23.09.11 12:43**
To: Rebecca Harris
Subject: Re: the article

Not since this morning, I'm afraid. I'll give her another call and see if there's been any update. Perhaps Helen Carmichael is right now painting her nails with a coat of *Purple Rain* and realizing how utterly fabulous it is and that she can't possibly bring herself to destroy the company that created such a masterpiece – fingers crossed.

From: **Rebecca Harris 23.09.11 12:45**
To: Phoebe Combes
Subject: PR

Here's hoping.

Could you also give me an update on replies for the party and any news on whether Tara and Laura can attend? We also need to put a notice on our website telling people when Kensington is going to be open for business (5th October), and put the Mayfair number for advanced bookings on it so Sylvia can deal with that as she is at the Mayfair Nail Bar now. If you have anything else PR-wise that might be exciting, put that on the website too.

Thanks, Fi

From: **Phoebe Combes 23.09.11 12:47**
To: Rebecca Harris
Subject: Re: PR

We only had one "yes" today which came by email, but I couldn't work out who it was from as the person who sent it didn't seem to know how to work his or her BlackBerry very well. Anyway I will work it out by default from the invite list closer to the time.

No news from the "It" girls' agents.

Oh, I almost forgot – Vanessa called a little while ago to say that Kylie Minogue dropped in to the Westbourne Nail Bar and bought a bottle of Purple Rain, so I am trying to get hold of her agent to see if we can get a signed photo from her saying "Kylie loves The Nail Bar" – wouldn't that be fantastic?

Phoebe

From: **Rebecca Harris 23.09.11 12:49**
To: Phoebe Combes

Subject: Re: PR

That's brilliant. I love Kylie. Send her an invite to the opening party. She won't come, but at least we can tell everyone that she wanted to but her schedule was just too busy.

I think the "yes" from the BlackBerry might have been my mum; she just got it today and is rather over-excited about it.

From: **Phoebe Combes 23.09.11 12:50**
To: Rebecca Harris
Subject: your mum

Is your mum called "bbbbbbetty,1arris"?

From: **Rebecca Harris 23.09.11 12:51**
To: Phoebe Combes
Subject: Mum

Yes, but she prefers to go by Betty Harris.

From: **Rebecca Harris 23.09.11 12:52**
To: Tania Cutter
Subject: awning

Tania,

Could you contact the company who made the awning at Kensington and ask them to come to The Kensington Nail Bar and pick it up to be repaired. It got damaged in the storm the other night and has a big tear in it. Hopefully they will not charge too much for this and if there is any chance that it can be mended in time for the opening, that would be amazing.

I'm going to Marylebone to have a look at the damage done by the flood.

Rebecca

From: **Tania Cutter 23.09.11 12:54**
To: Rebecca Harris
Subject: your PERSONAL calls

Fine. You had another personal call from your mother who wanted to know if the email she sent through replying to the Kensington opening party via her BlackBerry had been received – I checked with Phoebe and let her know that it had, and she seemed very excited.

I will be leaving for my lunch break in ten minutes.

Tania Cutter PA
The Nail Bar Ltd

From: **Rebecca Harris 23.09.11 14:52**
To: Felicity Jones
Subject: Suki, pay rise?

Hi Fi, I have just come back from Marylebone and the damage caused by the flood is far more extensive than I had feared. I know you and the girls did the best you could, but the treatment rooms downstairs are a disaster. The flooring has all come up and the bottoms of the walls have muddy water stains on them. I checked in the storeroom and three boxes of emery boards are ruined, plus a whole load of gift vouchers. I have also turned off the heating system downstairs as there is a funny smell coming from them, which seems a bit dodgy.

On the up side, Suki has somehow got the place heaving with customers again and everybody seems to be having a good time. She certainly doesn't look like someone recovering from hepatitis, and as soon as she saw me she came straight over and reminded me that I had promised her a pay rise. She has somehow turned the whole situation around and is attacking us for being disloyal to her for putting Sylvia in her place while she was gone – incredible! Can you look into what we can afford?

From: **Felicity Jones 23.09.11 14:55**
To: Rebecca Harris
Subject: Re: Suki, pay rise?

I already have and I think we can take her up by 20%. This will mean she is substantially better paid than both Andrea and Vanessa so it is crucial that the others don't find this out. We also need to be careful, as Christmas bonuses aren't so far away and we need to have something left over for that.

From: **Rebecca Harris 23.09.11 14:58**
To: Felicity Jones
Subject: pay rise

Blimey, Fi, that seems a lot. Are you sure that this isn't going to completely wipe out our profit margin?

From: **Felicity Jones 23.09.11 14:59**
To: Rebecca Harris

Subject: Re: pay rise

I've no idea, I'm just going on the basis that as we keep losing staff we must have some spare cash around to pay the existing ones.

From: **Rebecca Harris 23.09.11 15:01**
To: Felicity Jones
Subject: Re: pay rise

Well, that makes sense, but it's not very scientific. Let me have a quick look at our P&L and if it's doable then you can let her know.

From: **Rebecca Harris 23.09.11 15:04**
To: Clara Harris
Subject: Charles

Clara, I haven't heard back from Charles and I emailed him hours ago. It's now after 3pm and he's had plenty of time to get some work done and have a humungous lunch. I mean, even if you threw in a cheese plate and a glass of port, surely he'd be finished by now? Unless – I've just thought about this possibility – he likes cigars??? Stockbrokers quite often smoke cigars on Fridays, don't they? Ok, I'm going to wait for him to have a cigar and then expect an email by 4pm.

From: **Clara Harris 23.09.11 15:07**
To: Rebecca Harris
Subject: Re: Charles

Hi Bex, I'm over at Mum's. We have made very little progress with tonight's dinner because Mum keeps making me send emails to her new BlackBerry.
Mum and I both think you should just call Charles. In fact Mum is offering to call for you right now! Don't wait for an email, just do it. When he hears your voice he'll be delighted, you'll see.
By the way, don't kill me, but I left a very brief message on Jason's mobile saying I wasn't going to pick him up at the airport. I wasn't going to, but Mum says that if a girl behaves courteously, even when the man doesn't deserve it, then she has the upper hand, and I think I agree with that.
Mum and I made amazing canapés for tonight but we ate them all for lunch, so can you pick up some crisps or something on your way here?

From: **Rebecca Harris 23.09.11 15:10**
To: Clara Harris
Subject: Re: Charles

Sure. I'm going to wait for him to finish his cigar and then I'll call.

From: **Rebecca Harris 23.09.11 15:18**
To: Tania Cutter
Subject: insurance cover

Tania,

Can you get onto our insurance company to see what kind of cover we have for flood damage at Marylebone?
Rebecca

From: **Rebecca Harris 23.09.11 15:20**
To: Joe Doyle
Subject: Ken. Building Works

Joe, I just wanted to check whether you had managed to get anyone over to Kensington yet?
Rebecca

From: **Joe Doyle 23.09.11 15:24**
To: Rebecca Harris
Subject: Re: Ken. Building Works

Alright luv, give a man a chance to have his lunch, will you?
As it happens, Karl has a bad back so he didn't go to Hull. He's done you a big favour by going to your nail bar instead. He's there now.
Joe

From: **Rebecca Harris 23.09.11 15:26**
To: Joe Doyle
Subject: Re: Ken. Building Works

Thanks, that's really appreciated. I need to go over a few things with you, such as the ventilation system which I think hasn't been installed quite correctly, and various other things too.
Is it possible for you to meet me there in an hour? I will have the cheque with me.
Rebecca

From: **Joe Doyle 23.09.11 15:30**
To: Rebecca Harris
Subject: Re: Ken. Building Works

144

Anything for my favourite client. I will see you there.

From: **Charles Balford 23.09.11 15:34**
To: Rebecca Harris
Subject: hi

Hi, Gorgeous,

You looked so good the other night, everybody loved you. I'm glad you had fun.

As it happens, I can come to your mum's tonight, but I have to leave early as I have another party to go to – mind you, as your mum's is a 60th birthday party it will probably be well over by then!

What's your dad like, by the way? I seem to remember you saying he was in the armed forces? He's not an ex Navy Seal or a heavy-duty retired Brigadier General who's going to give me the third degree, is he? . . . tell me I'm wasting time in the city and I should be out there serving my country, getting my head blown off or sweating to death in a tent in Helmand province?

Charles

From: **Rebecca Harris 23.09.11 15:36**
To: Charles Balford
Subject: Re: hi

Well, he was a Colonel in the Army so he probably would if he was coming. My parents are divorced. My father now lives in Singapore with his second wife Joy. But don't think you get off lightly – my mum will definitely grill you!!!

From: **Charles Balford 23.09.11 15:37**
To: Rebecca Harris
Subject: Re: hi

Joy sounds like fun . . . sorry, couldn't resist that ☺

From: **Rebecca Harris 23.09.11 15:38**
To: Charles Balford
Subject: Joy

Yeah, unfortunately neither could my father.

From: **Charles Balford 23.09.11 15:40**
To: Rebecca Harris
Subject: hi again

I look forward to meeting your mum and will try my best to

convince her that I am just what her beautiful, funny, sexy-as-all-hell daughter needs. Charles

From: **Rebecca Harris 23.09.11 15:42**
To: Charles Balford
Subject: Re: hi again

That should be fun to watch!

From: **Rebecca Harris 23.09.11 15:45**
To: Katherine Lease
Subject: Charles

He replied AND he's coming tonight AND he called me beautiful! YIPPEEEEEE.

From: **Rebecca Harris 23.09.11 15:48**
To: Clara Harris
Subject: Charles

He's coming; oh my god I am so excited.
Please cook something amazing, Clarabelle?
What are you wearing, by the way?
I can't believe you and Mum ate all the canapés. We can't just serve crisps – I'll go to the deli on Kensington Church Street and get some good stuff.
Love you. Bex

From: **Katherine Lease 23.09.11 15:57**
To: Rebecca Harris
Subject: OMG!!!!!

Bex,

You are not going to BELIEVE what has just happened to me! For the last 30 minutes, while everyone else was carrying on with their normal lives, I have been stuck in the bathroom. I went to try on my new sexy underwear from Marcus and ended up having a total nightmare experience I was in the bathroom with my back to the door, I had my hands behind my back doing up my bra, when somehow the hook on the bra got stuck in the door lock so I was attached to the inside of the door by my back. I hadn't put the knickers on yet so I was butt naked from the waist down. As you can imagine, I became fairly frantic at this stage and I started kicking around, trying to get myself free, when all of a sudden the door

146

swung open with me attached to it! I found myself facing the entire office, impaled on the door with only my bra on. It wouldn't have been so bad as we are an entirely female office and the bra is seriously cool, but the coffee machine had broken this morning and we had a guy from maintenance down on his knees fixing it – I don't need to tell you the proximity of the coffee machine to the bathroom but let's suffice it to say that if the bloke hadn't put his hand out, I would have badly scalded quite an important part of my anatomy. As it was, I had a random bloke's hand on my completely bare fanny; beyond humiliating.

Anyway, very pleased for you that Charles is coming.

See you tonight.

From: **Rebecca Harris 23.09.11 16:06**
To: Katherine Lease
Subject: Re: OMG!!!!!

Wow, Kat, I can't imagine anything worse, except maybe if the bra hadn't been so cool. Hope the guy from maintenance had clean hands?

See you tonight.

From: **Charles Balford 23.09.11 16:12**
To: Rebecca Harris
Subject: sex kitten

Did I mention that you looked seriously hot the other night?

From: **Rebecca Harris 23.09.11 16:14**
To: Charles Balford
Subject: Re: sex kitten

You might have done. I wasn't paying too much attention.

From: **Charles Balford 23.09.11 16:16**
To: Rebecca Harris
Subject: Re: sex kitten

Oh baby, I love it when you play hard to get.

Pay attention, you bad girl: you are sexy as hell and I may well jump on you tonight, so I hope your mum can handle that!

From: **Rebecca Harris 23.09.11 16:17**
To: Charles Balford
Subject: Re: sex kitten

Ok, now you have my attention.

I look forward to that but Mum may well have a heart attack, so try to be reasonably discreet ☺.

From: **Suki Leung 23.09.11 16:45**
To: All Staff
Subject: pay rise

I remind you, Rebecca, you promise pay rise to me. Felicity tell me you decide for extra 20% each month. I think I happy with that.
Suki

From: **Rebecca Harris 23.09.11 16:48**
To: Felicity Jones
Subject: URGENT

FI, is it my imagination or did Suki just send that email to ALL STAFF?

From: **Felicity Jones 23.09.11 16:51**
To: Rebecca Harris
Subject: Re: URGENT

It looks that way.

From: **Rebecca Harris 23.09.11 16:56**
To: Felicity Jones
Subject: F******URGENT!!

SHHHHHHHIIIIIIIITTTTTTT. Can you try and do something? The other managers are going to freak when they see how much more Suki is being paid. I can't think right now, but maybe we can deny we know anything about this if the other staff start calling? I have to go to a meeting at Kensington and I'm late already, so can I leave this with you?

From: **Felicity Jones 23.09.11 16:59**
To: Rebecca Harris
Subject: Re: F******URGENT!!

Putting shit–hits-the-fan tactics into play as we speak, and following normal emergency procedures of denial. Drafting an assortment of response emails so I will be armed and ready when the first vulture attacks.

You go, and don't worry about it.

Have a nice weekend.

From: **Tania Cutter 23.09.11 17:04**
To: Rebecca Harris
Subject: pay rise?

Rebecca, I have recently received an email which has drawn my attention to another member of staff's remuneration package. Needless to say, I am rather surprised to see how this compares to my own. I have analyzed the work load, level of responsibility and duration of employment of said member of staff, and there is a huge discrepancy. Consequently I would like to have a discussion with you about this in the meeting room, immediately if possible.

Tania Cutter PA

The Nail Bar Ltd

From: **Rebecca Harris 23.09.11 17:07**
To: Felicity Jones
Subject: Re: pay rise?

That was quick.

From: **Felicity Jones 23.09.11 17:09**
To: Rebecca Harris
Subject: Re: pay rise?

Surprise, surprise, first vulture on the scene is our friend Little Turtle.

From: **Rebecca Harris 23.09.11 17:11**
To: Felicity Jones
Subject: Re: pay rise?

Fi, thank you for dealing with this, you're a saint.

See you Monday.

Bex

Monday 26th September 2011

From: **Barbara Foreman 26.09.11 8:59**
To: Rebecca Harris
Subject: travel arrangements

Rebecca,

I have decided not to fly back to New York tonight as I need an extra day to go to Hong Kong to look into some potential business and meet with another equipment manufacturer. Please could you book me on a flight (I do not wish to travel on China Airlines) departing late this evening for Hong Kong, arrange for a car to pick me up at Chep Lak Kok and take me to the Mandarin Oriental Hyde Park. Book me a suite with a harbour view and please arrange a massage for 7.30am tomorrow morning in my suite, followed by a manicure/pedicure and a wash and blow dry.

I need a table for two by the window at The Grill for 12.45pm tomorrow. Have a car on standby to take me around in the afternoon. I will then need to be on a Cathay Pacific, first class flight back to New York tomorrow night.

When you have done this, please email Nancy so she knows where I am, and tell her to contact Chantal at the Armani Press Office and arrange for them to have the shop in Hong Kong send over a navy trouser suit, blouse and shoes to my suite for me to wear to a drinks party I am attending tomorrow night before my flight. There is a good jewellery shop in the Mandarin, so tell her to inform the concierge that I need to borrow something from there as well.

Barbara

From: **Tania Cutter 26.09.11 9:06**
To: Rebecca Harris
Subject: remuneration package

Rebecca,

I took the opportunity this weekend to have a meeting with my stepfather, who is a financial adviser by profession, and he has confirmed that I am indeed underpaid. I have to say, it is disappointing that I have had to point this out to you when really you should have been aware of this yourself and taken immediate measures to put my salary up to the appropriate level. As it is, you will now have to do this anyway (should you wish to keep me), but because it wasn't initiated by you, I'm afraid there will naturally be some resentment on my behalf.

I am aware that you are pre-occupied with the opening of The Kensington Nail Bar, especially as things seem very chaotic, and therefore I am willing to let this lack of professionalism go. However, I must make it clear that a future oversight of this kind could well render you minus a pivotal member of staff. In fact, only the other day a friend of mine let me know that a friend of his was on the look-out for a highly efficient PA.

I had a less than satisfactory meeting with Felicity on Friday afternoon regarding this subject (the aforementioned remuneration package) and it was quite obvious that she does not recognize the value of my work input or longevity of employment. She was quite rude and said she didn't have time to have a discussion with me at that time, but shortly afterwards I saw her talking on the phone, and it was clearly a personal call so she can't have been that busy. I think therefore, it would be better if I had this meeting with you.

The insurance company said we are not covered for the flood damage at Marylebone and we have to be responsible for making sure the drains outside the backdoor are not blocked. Apparently there was a rubbish bin sitting over one and the other was filled with cigarette ends, obviously left there by staff smoking outside the back door – unacceptable, I'm sure you will agree.

There is also an invoice here for a pair of Prada Shoes for £850?

Tania Cutter PA

The Nail Bar Ltd

From: Rebecca Harris 26.09.11 9:13
To: Tania Cutter
Subject: Re: remuneration package

Tania, It's completely ridiculous that the insurance company is saying they won't pay. Of course we are covered for flood damage. That is absolutely standard in their 'Premium' package. When you go back to them, put in a claim for the Prada shoes as well as they were a client's that got damaged by nail polish remover.

I'm afraid that your remuneration is definitely something you have to discuss with Felicity. I really can't get involved, but I'll let her know that I think you're doing a good job.

Rebecca

From: **Phoebe Combes 26.09.11 9:17**
To: Rebecca Harris
Subject: on time!!!!

Hi Rebecca,

It worked!!!! You were absolutely right – I bought myself an alarm clock at the weekend and here I am, on time!!!! It's one of those fantastically modern ones on wheels and when it goes off the wheels get going and it goes flying off the side table and motors all around the room so you are forced to get out of bed and run after it. When I saw it in the shop I thought it was hysterical, but it was a lot less funny at 7.45 this morning! Can you imagine the scene – I had my ear plugs in, but it was still so loud I thought I was having a brain seizure. I leapt out of bed without thinking to lift up my eye mask and tripped over my toy rabbit collection (I get a fluffy rabbit every year from my grandmother who thinks I still collect them, and I don't have the heart to tell her that I stopped liking cuddly toys when I was 7 years old.) I managed not to fall flat but didn't recover quickly enough to avoid smacking my face into my wardrobe – quite painful. I never actually found the alarm clock (I think it went somewhere under the bed) so I had to leave my flat with it still going off – my flatmate is going to kill me.

It wasn't the best start to the morning, but I really am absolutely delighted that I made it to work on time, even if I do possibly have a broken nose.

Some more really good news is that Saskia emailed me your horoscope at the weekend. Here it is:

SAGITARIUS 23rd – 29th September

'You are stronger than you think so don't be afraid to battle those ogres. You are primed to continue your journey to wherever it is that you are meant to go. Do not feel threatened by having to make unconventional choices; there could be a financial gain. Love will come from an unusual source – embrace it. Closing time waits for no shopper.'

So that all sounds really positive, doesn't it? Saskia is honestly the best astrologer I know. She's actually the only astrologer I know, although I did have a boyfriend once who was into planets and everything to do with the cosmos. He even got a star named after me to celebrate our first week of dating, which I thought was wildly romantic. I couldn't wait for the second week, I thought I might get a planet, but we didn't make it to the second week, unfortunately. Anyway, Saskia is usually right on the mark. A couple of years ago she told me that I would find the man I'm going to marry when I least expected it. I thought that might have been that nice guy I met on the bus the other day because that's quite an unexpected place to meet your husband. He was terribly sweet (his name escapes me) but sadly he turned out to be engaged. So as it is, I am still waiting to find my dream man. But I do think Saskia is right. I really have a feeling it will be when I least expect it.

The Express on Sunday supplement featured a bottle of *Purple Rain* in their Essential Beauty section and also mentioned the opening of the new nail bar at Kensington. Unfortunately they insinuated that we were already open for business, so we will probably get a whole load of people turning up looking for manicures, which is a bit of a pain.

I am going to get a managers' report on the Eyebrow promo today. I will keep you posted.

From:	**Rebecca Harris 26.09.11 9:24**
To:	Phoebe Combes
Subject:	ok

That's great news about *The Express* and I'm not too worried about clients turning up at Kensington. With this rain they're much more likely to call first and make an appointment rather than just show up. The phone at Kensington is directed to Mayfair where Sylvia is, so she can deal with any enquiries.

I seem to remember the man's name was Greg.

From:	**Phoebe Combes 26.09.11 9:25**
To:	Rebecca Harris
Subject:	Greg

Greg, that's right! Such a nice man.

From:	**Rebecca Harris 26.09.11 9:37**
To:	Katherine Lease
Subject:	did it!!

Kat! Wait for it . . . I slept with Charles on Friday night after my mum's birthday dinner and it was WILD. I'm so excited I might throw up.

You know he left Mum's early to go to a party? Well, I was a bit upset that he didn't ask if I wanted to go too, but I guess he assumed that I would want to stay with Mum. Anyway, he turned up on my doorstep in the early hours of the morning and I let him in – thank god Poppy was having a sleepover at Mum's! He was pretty drunk, but being really cute and kept telling me how sexy I was. We finished off a bottle of wine and the next thing I knew he was taking off my clothes with his teeth . . . actually that's an exaggeration, but it felt like that.

We stayed in bed all Saturday morning, then had a pub lunch followed by a romantic walk in the rain in Battersea Park – perfect.

Kat, I'm so excited, our relationship has really moved forward. He told me all about himself, his plans for the future – he's so ambitious and really wants to succeed in the city. He has all these great ideas about holiday homes he wants to buy and exotic places he's going to go to. He's been working for Carringtons Bank for eight years and he thinks he's going to be made head of his desk next year, which will be a huge promotion. He's completely passionate about golf, which I can't relate to at all, but he's really close to his family, so that's very sweet. His mum sounds like an amazing woman, fantastic cook, always looks immaculate and totally dotes on her husband and Charles and his older brother.

How was your weekend in Paris? I am dying to hear all about it. Marcus was so lovely to give Mum those earrings. She's mad about them and said that he was "charming" and a "delight" to sit next to at dinner.

Finding it so hard to concentrate at work and have completely lost my appetite; only had a skinny cap for brekky.

PS I had my horoscope done professionally and it said that "love would come from an unusual source". I have never dated a city guy before, so that must mean Charles.

From: **Katherine Lease 26.09.11 9:42**
To: Rebecca Harris
Subject: Re: did it!!

You filthy slut. Well done and about bloody time, but I want to hear about the SEX, not his plans for the future? Details, darling, details. I'm waiting (im)patiently . . .

155

From: **Rebecca Harris 26.09.11 9:43**
To: Katherine Lease
Subject: Re: did it!!

Ok. Well, we did it in the kitchen, which was fun and definitely a first for me. I would have preferred to do it on the sofa in the sitting room where I had candles burning and Bon Jovi playing – slightly more romantic and my bum wouldn't have been nearly so cold, but I guess these things never turn out how you fantasize they will. It was very different from Aeron, much more spontaneous and exciting and just altogether more passionate. I don't actually think Aeron really liked having sex much, whereas Charles is obviously mad for it.

From: **Katherine Lease 26.09.11 9:46**
To: Rebecca Harris
Subject: Re: did it!!

That doesn't surprise me at all, he's got sex written all over him. Love a kitchen shag, there's something about being surrounded by whisks and wooden spoons that really gets me going. Keeping out of earshot from Jon Bon Jovi was probably a good move – might have been slightly off-putting for Charles to have another bloke singing about wanting to lay you down on a bed of roses while he was desperately trying to lay you on the kitchen counter.
Anyway, back to the party (which was great, by the way) although Charles and Olly seemed a bit unfriendly towards each other. I thought they were meant to be mates?
That Carmen girl was amazing-looking, and annoyingly she seemed quite nice too – but I'm very suspicious of those types, there's always a hidden fault somewhere and it's usually a real shocker. Bet she bludgeoned her granny to death at a family picnic, or was born with an extra toe. Mark my words, there'll be something, there always is.
Paris was excellent, I've just been showing my boss all the photos I took from the weekend and she thinks Marcus should do some modelling in the Armani show we're putting together for the Spring collection. The hotel was beautiful, and although it rained a bit it didn't matter at all. We ate delicious food, shopped like nutters, went for windy walks down the Champs Elysées and watched movies in bed – fantastique. There was a small, panicky moment

when I thought Marcus might propose at the top of the Eiffel Tower, and another when he threatened a tour of the Louvre, but aside from that it all went brilliantly and I loved every minute.

Marcus is madly in love with me and I have even agreed to go to the opera with him tomorrow night, so I'm obviously madly in love with him too!

PS Don't read too much into your horoscope. In today's *Guardian* my sign said "Do not worry that the past two weeks have felt somewhat lacklustre because exciting times are in store". I'm sorry, but there's certainly been no lack of lust in my life. In fact, if things get any more exciting I will have to consider vaginal rejuvenation! K

From: **Rebecca Harris 26.09.11 9:48**
To: Katherine Lease
Subject: yuk!

Yuk! What the hell is that?

Paris sounds wonderful. I can't believe you avoided the Louvre, I would kill to go back there. My granny took me when I was fourteen and I've been dying to go back ever since. Kat, if Marcus does ever propose you better say yes. He's gorgeous and by far the best guy you've ever gone out with – I'll be furious with you if you let him get away.

Did you really think Carmen was so great? I mean, I know she's got a good figure and everything, but she's quite tough and I didn't find her very friendly.

Olly doesn't think much of Charles, but he really doesn't know him very well. I certainly wouldn't call them "mates" at the moment, but I'm sure when they get to know each other better, they will be.

From: **Katherine Lease 26.09.11 9:50**
To: Rebecca Harris
Subject: Re: yuk!

I don't know, Carmen definitely oozed Latino sex appeal and confidence and Olly seems pretty happy with his lot, but by then I had drunk about ten Moscow Mules, so even your mum's friend Rodney with the terrible comb-over, seemed pretty cool.

Vaginal rejuvenation is what everyone in Hollywood is doing at the moment. It was mentioned on Californication last night, so it's kinda on my brain at the moment.

Sorry to disappoint about the Louvre, but museums make me itchy.

From: **Rebecca Harris   26.09.11   9:54**
To: Katherine Lease
Subject: Re: yuk
Attach: letter to Aeron

How can you talk about vaginal whatever and then say museums make you itchy?

Oh, I almost forgot, I wrote my reply letter to Aeron on Sunday and I think it's quite good. It's the fifth attempt so it oughta be.

I have attached it, so let me know what you think.

> Dear Aeron,
>
> It was good to hear from you after such a long period of silence and I'm delighted that you are in good health. I think marriage will suit you well and I have always thought you'd make a good father, even though you were adamant that you wouldn't. It sounds like Miranda and you have a good set-up, and although I never saw you as a Sussex person it obviously works for you.
>
> For my part, the business is going well, and as you quite rightly said, I am probably working a bit too hard, but I am managing to have lots of fun too.
>
> Just over six months ago I was given a promotion and I am now running the UK side of The Nail Bar Ltd. The added responsibility has been great but also pretty stressful, especially as we are about to open our fourth nail bar and my boss is coming over from America for the launch.
>
> With my promotion came a pretty huge pay rise, so I've decided to invest in the property market. I've currently got my eye on this amazing place in Barnes. It has four bedrooms, a beautiful garden with its own weeping willow tree and a Wendy house. I'll probably put an offer in for it, unless something even bigger comes up. I love the idea of Poppy having somewhere to run around and ride her bicycle.
>
> I was disappointed, bewildered and hurt, but unfortunately not surprised, that you did not ask after Poppy in your letter. Although you have never shown even the remotest interest in your child I guess I am still shocked by it, and so ashamed of you for that. Are you not at all curious to know about your own flesh and blood? Well, I will tell you anyway.
>
> Poppy turned 4 on July 5th and we celebrated her party with an "Under the Sea" theme so that we could decorate the table with the shells she collected from Cornwall last summer. She is the best in her class at reading and she loves ballet and swims like a fish. She hates My Little Pony and Barbie but loves make-up and jewellery, and when she grows up she wants to be a mermaid.
>
> I talk to her about her father from time to time, usually when she asks, which is not very often. However, there may well come a day when she

wants to know more about you and may even want to meet you. I hope if and when that day comes around you will not let her down as you have done so far in her life.

Regards. Rebecca

What do you think? Too brutal?

From: **Katherine Lease 26.09.11 9:58**
To: Rebecca Harris
Subject: letter to Aeron

Brutal???????

I think you're amazing. If it was me I would send a post-it note with:

I DON'T GIVE A TOSS ABOUT YOU, YOU USELESS BASTARD

and DHL it to him.

But well done you for being brilliantly grown up.

From: **Rebecca Harris 26.09.11 9:59**
To: Katherine Lease
Subject: Re: letter to Aeron

Why DHL?

From: **Katherine Lease 26.09.11 10:00**
To: Rebecca Harris
Subject: Re: letter to Aeron

Because, darling, Fed-Ex is sooo yesterday.

By the way, what do you mean about investing in the property market? I thought you were moving in with your mum because you want to save money?

From: **Rebecca Harris 26.09.11 10:02**
To: Katherine Lease
Subject: Re: letter to Aeron

Yes, but there's no way I'm going to tell Aeron that.

From: **Katherine Lease 26.09.11 10:03**
To: Rebecca Harris
Subject: Re: letter to Aeron

Oh I see. The Wendy house was a nice touch! I think you're nuts not making him pay child support, but I understand it's important to you to be independent and I love you for it, girlfriend. Now get an email off to Charles and forget about Aeron. xxx

From: **Charles Balford 26.09.11 10:06**

To: Rebecca Harris
Subject: call me!!

Rebecca Harris, you sexy little minx, where are you and what are you wearing? I can't stop thinking about you and that gorgeous bottom of yours. Why haven't you called, you wicked witch? You're killing me!

From: Rebecca Harris 26.09.11 10:08
To: Katherine Lease
Subject: Charles

He beat me to it, yay!

From: Katherine Lease 26.09.11 10:09
To: Rebecca Harris
Subject: YAY!

From: Rebecca Harris 26.09.11 10:10
To: Charles Balford
Subject: Re: call me!!

Hi Charles,
You can't be getting much work done if you're thinking about my bottom!
In answer to your question, I am in the office and I am wearing my old school uniform, which of course is much too small for me ☺☺
Rebecca The Witch Xxx

From: Charles Balford 26.09.11 10:14
To: Rebecca Harris
Subject: gymslip & navy knickers?

I knew it, you naughty strumpet. School uniform, hey! So I'm thinking straining buttons over voluptuous breasts, a hint of that great arse as you lean forward for your pencil sharpener, striped tie and slutty hold-up stockings – am I right, please tell me I'm right?
If I am, then I'm coming over there right now!

From: Rebecca Harris 26.09.11 10:15
To: Charles Balford
Subject: Re: gymslip & navy knickers?

You're dead right.

From: Charles Balford 26.09.11 10:17
To: Rebecca Harris

160

Subject: must see you!

You are so the witch for me.

Have dinner with me tonight.

From: Rebecca Harris 26.09.11 10:19
To: Charles Balford
Subject: Re: must see you!

I would love to but I can't. Vinca (Poppy's nanny) can only babysit on Tuesday and Friday nights.

I have nothing on tomorrow night.

From: Charles Balford 26.09.11 10:22
To: Rebecca Harris
Subject: Tuesday it is

Wow, I didn't think you could top the school uniform, but "nothing" definitely takes the edge. Tomorrow night it is.

How about a movie?

From: Rebecca Harris 26.09.11 10:23
To: Charles Balford
Subject: Re: Tuesday it is

A movie sounds great.

From: Rebecca Harris 26.09.11 11:42
To: Oliver Barker
Subject: Hong Kong

Hi Olly,

I hope you got your flight on Friday night; you were cutting it quite fine? Thanks so much for stopping by at Mum's. She always loves seeing you and she said the tablecloth was her favourite present. I hope Carmen had a good time. She seems really nice, she must hate that you travel so much?

What did you do at the weekend? Did you get a chance to go surfing on Big Wave Bay beach, like I suggested? Are you at the Mandarin Oriental? My boss is on her way there this evening.

PS There is this great place in Hong Kong called Stanley Market where you can get amazing silk pyjamas. If you go there, can you get me some?

From: Oliver Barker 26.09.11 11:48
To: Rebecca Harris

Subject: Re: Hong Kong

Hi Bex, I'm actually staying over on Kowloon side so probably won't be bumping into your boss.

Drinks last Friday was great. I wish we could have stayed for dinner, despite that arsehole Balford being there.

I thought your Mum looked happy and well and I'm glad she liked the present. Unfortunately Carmen and I got into a bit of a fight on the way to the airport and by the time we got to Heathrow we had decided to call it off. She's a great girl, but we just didn't see eye to eye on so many things.

I worked most of Saturday and on Sunday I went for a walk out at this place called Shek O, which I think is near your Big Wave Bay beach – absolutely beautiful, and a side to Hong Kong I never knew existed.

I've been picturing you here as a little girl, running around with the wind in your hair. I bet you were cute as hell – naughty, but very cute!

I would love to buy you some silk pyjamas.

From: Rebecca Harris 26.09.11 11:50
To: Oliver Barker
Subject: Re: Charles

Olly,

I wish you would stop slagging off Charles. I know you don't like him, for some unknown reason, but I do and I don't like him being called an "arsehole", especially from someone who hardly knows him. I don't know what your problem is with him but whatever it is I don't want to hear about it. You're meant to be my friend and that means you shouldn't be rude about people who are important to me, no matter how you feel about them.

PS I was quite cute but I'm annoyed with you at the moment so I'm not going to go into it.

From: Oliver Barker 26.09.11 11:52
To: Rebecca Harris
Subject: Re: Charles

Bex, I do have my reasons for not liking Charles, but I will keep them to myself. Sorry to have offended you. Believe it or not, it's because I don't want you to be dicked around by yet another waste of space bloke who won't give a damn about hurting you.

From: **Rebecca Harris 26.09.11 11:54**
To: Oliver Barker
Subject: Re: Charles

I think you should give me a bit more credit than that. Not every guy I've gone out with has been a waste of space. In fact I think you're the one being a bit of an "arsehole" here, Olly.

From: **Oliver Barker 26.09.11 11:56**
To: Rebecca Harris
Subject: Re: Charles

Bex. I've obviously upset you, which was far from my intention, I assure you. For what it's worth, I'm sorry.

From: **Tania Cutter 26.09.11 11:57**
To: Rebecca Harris
Subject: petty cash

Rebecca,

I think you should be aware that Felicity Jones is taking money from petty cash and not filling in the ledger correctly. This makes it extremely difficult for me to tally up the figures at the end of the month. I also find that I am constantly going to the bank to top up the float because she "borrows" such excessive amounts each week. Not only is this a considerable waste of my time, but I also believe that she is deliberately fudging the ledger to deceive me as to what the money is being used for. I noticed the other day that she took out £2.10 from petty cash before lunch and after lunch she came back with a brand new *Hello* magazine which, when I checked on my way home, costs exactly £2.10. I have also never seen Felicity on the tube (her apartment is very near mine in Earls Court) going to or from work, and I am pretty sure she is using company money to commute to the office by taxi.

It is clear that the sensible thing to do in this situation is to simply ban Felicity from accessing petty cash altogether. I would of course notify her myself of our decision, but as you insist she is the one I must talk to about bringing my salary up to the correct level, were I also the one to be imposing sanctions on her, it could be somewhat awkward. I will therefore leave this area to you.

In response to your last email: we do not have the Premium package with the insurance company, only the Standard package, and this does not cover flooding or damage to clients' property.

Tania Cutter PA

The Nail Bar Ltd

From:	**Rebecca Harris 26.09.11 11:59**
To:	Tania Cutter
Subject:	Insurance

Tania, what are you talking about? I know we have the Premium package because I set it up myself – it was the first week we were in business, before you joined the company.

From:	**Tania Cutter 26.09.11 12:01**
To:	Rebecca Harris
Subject:	Re: Insurance

Rebecca,

I am aware of that, but you are forgetting that last year, on 16th April, you called a staff meeting. In that meeting (at which I took the minutes) you addressed the issue of "cost cutting" (point four), in which you very clearly asked all staff to look at ways of reducing overheads in both the office and the nail bars. Unlike the rest of your staff, I actually did something about this and one of the first things I noticed was the amount of insurance we were paying. I immediately reduced all shops to the Standard package and saved us a total of £16.66 per month. I also introduced other economizing measures such as switching from chocolate Hobnobs to Rich Tea biscuits for the kitchen, making sure the heating is only on for two hours a day in winter and teaching staff to always use both sides of the fax paper.

I wrote you a memo, shortly after this, which clearly stated all the improvements I had made. I have to say I am a little disappointed and actually quite concerned that you don't remember.

Tania Cutter PA

The Nail Bar Ltd

From:	**Rebecca Harris 26.09.11 12:02**
To:	Felicity Jones

Fi, LOCK THE WINDOWS, I'M THINKING ABOUT JUMPING!

Tania is driving me completely insane. I feel like that girl in The Exorcist movie – you know, the one whose head starts spinning around and she's screaming and vomiting all at the same time? Help me!

From: **Felicity Jones 26.09.11 12:04**
To: Rebecca Harris
Subject: Re: suicidal!

Oh god, I've got a meeting with her in 5 minutes to discuss her salary, which I'm completely dreading. Can I tell her to sod off?

From: **Rebecca Harris 26.09.11 12:05**
To: Felicity Jones
Subject: Tania

Annoyingly I don't think you can, we just can't afford to lose anybody at the moment, but make the increase minimal.

Did you know that a pair of Prada shoes cost £865? What the hell are they made of?

From: **Felicity Jones 26.09.11 12:06**
To: Rebecca Harris
Subject: Re: Tania

Iguana tongue, I think?

Seriously, Rebecca, why do you put up with Tania's shit? She's a nightmare and we all know it. Wouldn't we be better off with nobody than with her?

From: **Rebecca Harris 26.09.11 12:10**
To: Felicity Jones
Subject: Re: Tania

I've never told you this because I'm pretty sure Tania wouldn't want everyone to know, but when Charlotte was fired as Director of the company, she didn't just take the contents of her desk with her, she took Tania's husband too.

From: **Felicity Jones 26.09.11 12:12**
To: Rebecca Harris
Subject: Re: Tania

Fuck me, I never knew Tania was married! How did that happen (reference to both Tania finding a husband and Charlotte getting her mitts on him)?

From: **Rebecca Harris 26.09.11 12:15**
To: Felicity Jones
Subject: Re: Tania

She never talks about him, so not many people know. Derek met Charlotte at the Mayfair opening party and they got on like a house on fire. A few months later they saw each other again at the office Christmas party. Shortly after that they began an affair. The first Tania knew of it was right after Charlotte was fired. She got a call from Derek saying he was leaving her and going to live in Spain with Charlotte who was planning to set up her own rival nail bar chain in Soto Grande. They opened one nail bar but it soon went belly up. Charlotte got bored with both Spain and Derek and came back to London. Derek moved to Ibiza and apparently works as a bouncer in one of those clubs. He occasionally sends drunken SMSs to Tania asking her to come and join him, but she doesn't respond.

From: **Felicity Jones 26.09.11 12:17**
To: Rebecca Harris
Subject: Re: Tania

Bloody hell, poor Tania. It's incredible she found *one* husband, the chances of a second would be nothing short of a miracle. What's her love-life situation now?

From: **Rebecca Harris 26.09.11 12:20**
To: Felicity Jones
Subject: Re: Tania

I don't know, she doesn't confide in me anymore. When I moved up to take Charlotte's position, Tania turned, and no longer saw me as a natural confidante. She had actually been one of the people to put me forward for the management position.

Fi, the only reason I'm telling you this is so you understand why I keep her on, but I've stopped cutting her as much slack as I used to and I do come down heavy when she gets carried away. Please keep what I told you confidential.

From: **Felicity Jones 26.09.11 12:22**
To: Rebecca Harris
Subject: Yeah, course I will.

From: **Rebecca Harris 26.09.11 12:27**
To: Tania Cutter
Subject: Re: Insurance

Tania,

I don't remember the memo and if I had read it at the time I'm sure I wouldn't have agreed to cut our insurance policy. However, the damage is obviously already done.

As far as your accusations towards Felicity go, your ledger is an absolute nightmare to fill out and as Felicity needs petty cash frequently, for very legitimate reasons, it is incredibly annoying for her to have to fill it in every time. The *Hello* magazine she bought the other day was because The Nail Bar was mentioned in their beauty page and she needed a copy to give to Phoebe, and the reason she doesn't take the tube to work is because her husband drives her.

Rebecca

From: **Tania Cutter 26.09.11 12:30**
To: Rebecca Harris
Subject: Re: Insurance
Attach: Memo. 18th April 2011

Please see copy of attached memo.

I must say I find your tone unnecessarily hostile.

Tania Cutter PA

The Nail Bar Ltd

From: **Barbara Foreman 26.09.11 12:33**
To: Rebecca Harris
Subject: travel arrangements

Rebecca,

It is over two hours since I emailed you and I have not heard back. Please confirm immediately that you have my flights and hotel reservations booked.

Barbara

Message sent via BlackBerry ®

From: **Rebecca Harris 26.09.11 12:35**
To: Barbara Foreman
Subject: Re: travel arrangements

Barbara,

I'm so sorry not to come back sooner; it's been a very busy morning. I have booked a suite at the Mandarin Oriental with a harbour view,

and I'm just waiting for the travel agent to come back to me with your flights, which of course I will let you know immediately.
Rebecca

From: **Joe Doyle 26.09.11 12:39**
To: Rebecca Harris
Subject: Ken. Building Works

Rebecca luv, there are over 20 people queuing outside the front door of The Kensington Nail Bar waiting for appointments? It might be a good idea for you to put some information on that nice website of yours letting your customers know that you're not open yet. It would be a shame to lose business before you've even opened, and I can tell you, this lot are starting to look pretty unhappy.

Don't forget, Rebecca, it only takes a couple of people to say negative things about your company and then those people tell their friends and they tell their friends and well, you can see where I'm going, can't you?

You'll be pleased to know that my lads have been working round the clock and the floor tiles are now down in all the treatment rooms downstairs.

Joe

From: **Rebecca Harris 26.09.11 12:41**
To: Phoebe Combes
Subject: URGENT!! Kensington

DROP WHATEVER YOU ARE DOING AND GO IMMEDIATELY TO KENSINGTON. There are clients swarming the pavement outside thinking they are going to get a manicure today! Felicity and Tania are in a meeting and I have to book flights, hotels and god knows what for Barbara in the next 5 seconds, so there is no one else. I know you are trying to do a million things already, but can you also squeeze in a bit of crisis management?

Grab money from petty cash for a cab and don't waste any time filling in the ledger.

Thanks a million
Rebecca

From: **Phoebe Combes 26.09.11 12:44**
To: Rebecca Harris
Subject: Re: URGENT!! Kensington

Don't worry at all, Rebecca, I am on my way. I am surprisingly good at this sort of thing. I was once at a Macy Gray concert with my sister. We were queuing to get in and it was raining. There was a group of teenagers without umbrellas giving the bouncer a really hard time because they were getting wet. I remembered that McDonalds was doing a promotion, giving away free 'Mac bags' (Macintosh in a bag) to anyone who could say "Big Mac, Fillet o Fish, Quarter pounder, French fries, ice coke, milk shake and apple pie" in less than 5 seconds. There were all these hand actions that went with it, but I had been practising all week and was really good at it. I went into Maccy Ds and did the challenge seven times, then came out and gave the Macintoshes to the teenagers. They loved them and stopped making a racket. The bouncer swapped our tickets for front row ones and even gave me his phone number. We went out a couple of times but it didn't work out.

I'll keep you up to date on how it goes, but crowd control is definitely my forte, so I'm confident all will be fine.

Phoebe

From: **Rebecca Harris 26.09.11 12:46**
To: Phoebe Combes
Subject: Re: URGENT!! Kensington

Thanks Phoebe, I'm obviously sending the right "man" for the job.

From: **Rebecca Harris 26.09.11 12:49**
To: Barbara Foreman
Subject: Re: travel arrangements

Barbara,

I have got you on a Dragon Air flight leaving Guangdong at 21:07 local time which gets you in to Hong Kong at 22:00, so it's nice and quick. They don't have First Class so I have booked you a window seat in Business.

The Mandarin Oriental is sending a car to pick you up at the airport and the driver will hold up one of those signs with your name on it. The spa wanted to know what kind of massage you wanted, so I went for Lymphatic Drainage, which sounded amazing and especially good if you've been flying. They also had a really good one with hot stones, but it was an hour and a half so I didn't choose that, but they said you could have it the next day if you wanted.

My friend is in Hong Kong at the moment and the weather is really great, but the pollution is apparently quite bad.

The concierge has a car lined up for you to use tomorrow and you are booked in to The Grill for lunch.

We have been having some fantastic press coverage here from *The Sunday Express* and *Hello* magazine and last Friday Kylie Minogue came in to the Westbourne Nail Bar and bought a bottle of *Purple Rain*!

By the way, my friend works for the Armani Press Office in London so when you come over for the opening, if you want to borrow something, let me know and I can arrange it.

I have sent an email to Nancy with all the info you requested and you are booked on CX251 departing at 23:55 on the 26th (you check in tomorrow night but you actually leave 15 minutes into the following day) for New York.

You should probably leave pretty soon for the airport as your flight leaves in 2 hours.

Rebecca

From:	**Rebecca Harris 26.09.11 12:55**
To:	Joe Doyle
Subject:	Re: Ken. Building Works

Joe, thank you for your advice, we do actually have information about the opening on our website, but *The Sunday Express* did a feature on us saying we were open for business, which is why all these people have turned up at Kensington. I have one of my staff on her way there now to sort it out.

I am pleased progress is being made, although I had a slight panic attack when you said you had put the tiles down in the treatment rooms because I know you know we are carpeting those and tiling everywhere else, but I realized it must just be a typing error, right?

Rebecca

From:	**Barbara Foreman 26.09.11 12:56**
To:	Rebecca Harris
Subject:	Re: travel arrangements

Rebecca,

I appreciate you are not used to doing secretarial work for me, but for future reference, when you only give me two hours to change, pack, check out and get to the airport, please try to keep your emails short and to the point.

Barbara

Message sent via BlackBerry ®

From: **Joe Doyle 26.09.11 12:58**
To: Rebecca Harris
Subject: Re: Ken. Building Works

I don't know anything about any carpet, luv. On the brief right here in my hands, which has your signature at the bottom, it clearly says Flooring (basement and ground) dark grey, rectangular slate tiles. Now if you want to make some last minute, costly changes, then be my guest, but I have to warn you, you are cutting it quite fine if you want things to be ready for that big bash of yours.

Joe

From: **Rebecca Harris 26.09.11 13:00**
To: Joe Doyle
Subject: Re: Ken. building works

Joe, last month you and I had a meeting at Kensington at which I pointed out to you that there had been a mistake, one admittedly I had overlooked in the original brief, regarding the flooring in the treatment room. I told you that I wanted carpet instead of tiles because it would give the rooms a warmer feel. You then told me, and I remember it clearly, that this would not be a problem and you would try and find a carpet that was the same colour as the grey slate. You can't now tell me you don't remember this conversation?

Rebecca

From: **Joe Doyle 26.09.11 13:03**
To: Rebecca Harris
Subject: Re: Ken. Building Works

Rebecca,

All I know is that I have a brief here telling me to put tiles down in all the rooms. I'm following that brief and if you want to make changes, well, that's all well and good, and we would be happy to accommodate you, but if you're going to start calling me a liar, well then, we're going to start having problems.

You're a nice lady, Rebecca, and that is why I've bent over backwards for you in the past, but even I have my limits, so please don't make me regret taking on this job.

Now, there are two things we can do here. Either we can pull up these tiles and make a whole load of mess, re-cement the floor and then put down carpet, which will take about a week, and I will have to come up with a new costing for you, or we can just leave it as it is? I'm going back to the office now so you better have a think and contact me there later.

Joe

From:	**Jonathan Banks 26.09.11 13:05**
To:	Rebecca Harris
Subject:	last Friday

Hi Bex, thank you so much for a great dinner last Friday, I really enjoyed myself. You, your sister and your mum all did a great job, and the food was excellent. It was strange to see Charles there as I have never seen him socially before, but I'm glad things are obviously going well for you two.

It was so good to see your sister again, who I hadn't seen for nearly three years! She looked fantastic despite what must have been a fairly awful last 24 hours – she told me about her fiancé. Actually, I was wondering whether she might like to go out for a drink or something to cheer her up. What do you think?

Johnny

From:	**Rebecca Harris 26.09.11 13:07**
To:	Jonathan Banks
Subject:	Re: last Friday

Hi Johnny,

So glad you had a good time and Clara was the one who did all the cooking, not me. I think she would love to go out for a drink with you. Her email address is: claraharris@yahoo.com

Things are going really well between Charles and me. Does he sit near you in the office? If so, tell him I said Hi.

From:	**Jonathan Banks 26.09.11 13:09**
To:	Rebecca Harris
Subject:	Charles

Yes he does and I will. Thanks for the address.

From:	**Rebecca Harris 26.09.11 13:12**

To: Joe Doyle
Subject: Re: Ken. Building Works

Joe, I'm not calling you a liar. I'm just very concerned as there has been some kind of breakdown in communication between us and now I have tiles where I would have ideally liked carpet. I'm going to be at Kensington in a while so I'll see what it looks like and I'll email you when I get back.

Rebecca

From: **Rebecca Harris 26.09.11 13:15**
To: Tania Cutter
Subject: where to find me

I'm going to Westbourne and then Kensington. The answering machine is on, please switch it off when you come out of your meeting with Felicity.

Rebecca

From: **Rebecca Harris 26.09.11 14:24**
To: Phoebe Combes
Subject: all sorted?

Hi Phoebe, how did it go?

I was hoping to get to Kensington but got delayed at Westbourne.

From: **Phoebe Combes 26.09.11 14:30**
To: Rebecca Harris
Subject: Re: all sorted?

Things went pretty smoothly turning people away, although I did have a little bit of trouble with one lady which took me by surprise. She was about 65 years old and absolutely determined to get in. She started being really quite unpleasant, even though I patiently explained to her that it wasn't possible for her to have a pedicure. I even took her inside so she could see downstairs where most of the ceiling was lying in a pile of rubble on the floor, but she said she didn't care because, according to her, her feet were in a worse state than our nail bar. She then took off her shoe to show me (they really were disgusting, she either had early stage gangrene or advanced athlete's foot – yuk), but again I said no, and this time she threw her shoe at me and it hit me on my sore nose!

I am sorry, Rebecca, but this was a bit much, especially as her pop sock came with it and stuck to my lip. I'm afraid to say I

173

slapped her. I know it wasn't a very nice thing to do and of course I believe in respecting my elders and I do not condone violence, but sometimes a bit of force is necessary. It wasn't too hard, just a short sharp slap on the cheek. Anyway, it seemed to do the trick. She left quietly, and after that everyone else behaved very well.

I am printing off a notice explaining the mistake made by *The Express* so that Fi can put it in the window of Kensington on her way to Harrods.

I will get on now with finding out how the Eyebrow promo is going.

From:	**Rebecca Harris 26.09.11 14:34**
To:	Phoebe Combes
Subject:	Re: ??

Gosh, Phoebe, that all seems quite extreme, but I guess if you think everything is ok, then . . . well . . . great.

Thank you for sorting it all out.

I am a bit concerned about you saying the ceiling was on the floor downstairs – that doesn't sound right? What were the builders doing about it?

From:	**Phoebe Combes 26.09.11 14:38**
To:	Rebecca Harris
Subject:	builders

Well, I got there just before 1pm and they weren't there (luckily I took the office key), and they only turned up when I was leaving, so I didn't get a chance to ask.

From:	**Tania Cutter 26.09.11 14:45**
To:	Rebecca Harris
Subject:	messages

Rebecca,

I am relieved you are back. You didn't delete the old messages from the answering machine before you put it on and consequently the memory was full after only three calls. The phone was therefore ringing off the hook the entire way through my meeting with Felicity, which as you can imagine was extremely tiresome.

We eventually had to cut the meeting short after only forty minutes so I could get back to my desk.

One of the messages on the machine was from the awning company who said they could give us a plain red canvas and install it this week at a cost of £1,998.

Suki called to say that clients are complaining about being too cold in the treatment rooms at Marylebone and they are losing business because of it.

I think you should know that Phoebe has only just got back from lunch.

Tania Cutter PA

The Nail Bar Ltd

From: Rebecca Harris 26.09.11 14:52
To: Joe Doyle
Subject: Ken. Building Works

Joe, I didn't make it to Kensington, but one of my team did and said that none of your men were on site between 1 and 2pm. I thought we discussed this? Do you not think it makes sense to have them take their breaks in shifts? I have also been informed that for some reason the ceiling has been torn down downstairs?

From: Joe Doyle 26.09.11 15:04
To: Rebecca Harris
Subject: Re: Ken. Building Works - ceiling

Rebecca,

I am running a business in which I employ grown men, men who are perfectly capable of making grown-up decisions – now if they decide that it works better for them to take their lunch at the same time as each other, well then that's their decision. I can't tell my men when to eat no more than I can tell them what to eat. This is the real world, Rebecca, where men go about their business as they see fit and I think it's best if we leave them to it, don't you?

Now, the ceiling is down because you weren't satisfied with the ventilation system, which is a shame as it was a very reliable, economic one that I have used many times in the past. Luckily, I was able to get hold of some new, state-of-the-art ventilators, last minute, from a friend of mine in the business, but they're not cheap, I can tell you. They also require a great deal more space to be installed, which is why we have had to tear the ceiling down.

From: Rebecca Harris 26.09.11 15:08

To: Felicity Jones
Subject: Tania

Fi, How was the meeting with Tania?

I just saw a girl leave the office – was she an interviewee, and if so was she any good?

Do you by any chance know of a good cheap builder who we can get to Marylebone ASAP to repair the flood damage? I don't want to ask Joe's team, partly because he is a nightmare to deal with, but also because he will undoubtedly use it as an excuse for being late with Kensington and we can't afford any more delays.

From: Felicity Jones 26.09.11 15:14
To: Rebecca Harris
Subject: re: Tania/Annette

Bex, the girl you just saw leaving is my friend Annette, not an interviewee. She had a fight with her partner last night and they started throwing each other's stuff out of the window. She was in the middle of pushing his favourite armchair out when he grabbed hold of it and ended up going out of the bloody window with it. Luckily it was only two floors up so he suffered a few cracked ribs and a broken arm but nothing more, and quite frankly he deserves it, the bastard has been a real shit to her.

Anyway, she's now in a state because he wants to press charges, so she came to see me for some advice.

Unfortunately, I have no more interviews lined up all week and we still need an extra member of staff to replace Janine at Mayfair. Looks like I'm going to have to get down and do the dirty and poach some staff from somewhere else. Harrods have a big beauty salon and they always recruit good people, and that Al Fayed's meant to be a bit of a pig, so I wouldn't feel too guilty about it – what do you think?

I increased Tania's salary by what we discussed. She said she had expected double the offer – the woman is delusional. I agreed to a Christmas bonus if all goes well.

I can't tell you how painful it was sitting there listening to her rabbit on and on about why the office couldn't function without her and her huge plans for making the company run more smoothly. She had a whole prepared speech that she was reading from. She was in such free flow that she didn't even notice when I slipped out to go to the toilet halfway through. I was just about to get up again and go get my Ipod when she suddenly came to an abrupt stop and mumbled something about it being impossible to concentrate with all the phones ringing, and then she marched out. Anyway, she seems content with the new salary and I tried to be as nice as possible after what you told me, but god, she doesn't make it easy.

Our staff costs are definitely starting to escalate as we have to pay all the new girls straightaway to make sure we don't lose them before the opening.

Weirdly enough, Annette's partner is actually a builder, but I guess he won't be much help at the moment.

From: **Rebecca Harris 26.09.11 15:17**
To: Felicity Jones
Subject: Harrods

Wow, poor Annette, I thought *I* had problems.

Definitely go to Harrods. Al Fayed doesn't own it any more but don't let that stop you. Grab the whole team if you can, and when you're there can you get me some of those gourmet jelly beans – I'm not really eating at the moment but those are fat free, so they don't count.

From: **Felicity Jones 26.09.11 15:18**
To: Rebecca Harris
Subject: Re: Harrods

Sure, any particular flavour?

From: **Rebecca Harris 26.09.11 15:17**
To: Felicity Jones
Subject: Re: Harrods

A mixed bag would be great, but no butter popcorn or licorice if possible. Thanks.

From: **Charles Balford 26.09.11 15:42**
To: Rebecca Harris
Subject: a piccy perhaps?

I'm wondering if you have a camera on your computer so you can take a picture of yourself in your school uniform. I can't stop thinking about it and I need visual gratification.

From: **Rebecca Harris 26.09.11 15:44**
To: Charles Balford
Subject: re: a piccy perhaps?

Charles, you need to get over it, I'm wearing jeans and a jumper –
and not a very nice one at that – sorry to disappoint.

From: **Charles Balford 26.09.11 15:45**
To: Rebecca Harris
Subject: jumper

Ok. I am a tiny bit disappointed, but are we talking quite a tight
jumper?

From: **Rebecca Harris 26.09.11 15:46**
To: Charles Balford
Subject: Re: jumper

Extremely

From: **Charles Balford 26.09.11 15:47**
To: Rebecca Harris
Subject: Re: tight jumper

Bra?

From: **Rebecca Harris 26.09.11 15:48**
To: Charles Balford
Subject: Re: tight jumper

No bra.

From: **Charles Balford 26.09.11 15:47**
To: Rebecca Harris
Subject: Re: tight jumper

Rebecca Harris, I think I might be in love with you.

From: **Rebecca Harris 26.09.11 15:50**
To: Charles Balford
Subject: Re: tight jumper

Charles Balford, I think you are perhaps too easily pleased.

From: **Charles Balford 26.09.11 15:51**
To: Rebecca Harris
Subject: Re: tight jumper

Quite possibly, but you please me all the same. Until tomorrow....

From: **Rebecca Harris 26.09.11 15:51**
To: Charles Balford

Subject: ☺ ☺

From: Rebecca Harris 26.09.11 16:28
To: Clara Harris
Subject: sex at last!!!

Hi Clarabelle, guess what? I have some seriously exciting news . . .
Johnny Banks asked me for your email – he wants to ask you out!
The other deliriously exciting news is Charles and I hooked up on
Friday night after Mum's B/day dinner and he spent the night! Do
you remember he had to go off to a party early? Well, later that
night he showed up at my door and it all went from there. I have to
tell you – the sex was amazing! It's funny, it's like riding a bike, isn't
it? You just get straight back in there. Actually, I think I might have
improved with abstinence. I definitely tried harder than I used to – I
mean not too hard, but I was very open-minded and experimental.
We're not talking "9½ Weeks" or anything, but we did do it in the
kitchen, which was a slightly more advanced level of kinkiness than
I would have been comfortable with in the past.
I'm so happy, Clara, I can't tell you. I had such a fear about sleeping
with someone after it being so long, but it was great and Charles
made me feel totally relaxed. I'm crazy about him.
He keeps sending me funny emails and we're going out again
tomorrow night.
I'm dying to hear what you thought about him. Was he nice to sit
next to at dinner? I can't believe I've gone almost a year without sex.
Now I don't think I can last a whole day – gagging for it!
Loads of love, Bex

From: Clara Harris 26.09.11 16:41
To: Rebecca Harris
Subject: Oooops

Bex, don't die, but Mum just read the email you sent me. I'm so
sorry, but I'm staying over at her house and she wanted to practise
sending emails from her BlackBerry, and when she went to check
that it had gone through, she read your email. I was in the hall at the
time but I heard her gasp, so I rushed in and saw her (hand on heart,
eyes wide open) staring at the screen like Tesco's had announced it
was no longer doing home deliveries or something. I'm afraid she is
not taking it brilliantly. I think it was the bit about gagging for it that

really threw her. I didn't really know what to say but I made her a cup of tea and she has gone to lie down upstairs, so hopefully it will all just blow over.

From: Rebecca Harris 26.09.11 16:44
To: Clara Harris
Subject: Re: Oooops

OH MY GOD CLARA YOU HAVE GOT TO BE FUCKING KIDDING ME? I feel sick. This is our mother, Clara!!!! Information like this should never be read by mothers about their daughters, it's all wrong, just WRONG.
I'M SO EMBARRASSED.
How can I face her?
Why are you sleeping at Mum's?

From: Clara Harris 26.09.11 16:49
To: Rebecca Harris
Subject: Jason

Don't be too embarrassed. Mum isn't as innocent as she pretends to be. I once overheard her telling Marjorie about a swingers party she and dad went to in the sixties. Even though they apparently left early, she claimed she witnessed some "fairly racy behaviour".
I'm over at Mum's just for the night because Jason has turned off the gas and electric supply to the flat. He left a message on my mobile letting me know that if he wasn't allowed in the flat then he didn't see why he should pay the bills. It has all gone really nasty. I called him on Sunday to try and see if we could work things out, and he told me he feels relieved that the wedding is off and that it had all been a huge mistake for him. He said that he had been seeing Samantha (the girl from Miami) on the quiet for the past six months and that they were madly in love. When I asked him why he hadn't told me sooner, he said that he needed somewhere to stay in London until he and Samantha could find somewhere together (she is moving here apparently), and he knew I would throw him out of our apartment if he told me.
Bex, I can't tell you how awful he was, there was absolutely no emotion there at all. It would have been ok if he had been a bit remorseful about it, or even angry that I had found out, but he wasn't. It was as though he felt nothing at all. I feel so stupid. How

180

could I have thought that he loved me and wanted to spend the rest of his life with me? I obviously don't know men at all.

Anyway, Mum has been amazing and I am already feeling so much better, and that's great that Johnny wants to go out with me. I'd forgotten what a nice guy he is, and much better looking than I remember.

Charles seems very nice and I'm glad the sex was good, although to have waited a little longer might have been advisable, especially as he does come across as a bit of a player. I don't mean that too negatively. It's just that he is very good-looking and assertive and confident, which is great, but I think he is quite aware of his attributes. Just be careful, Bex. Men like Charles often love the chase but tire very easily once they have their prey.

From: **Rebecca Harris 26.09.11 16:53**
To: Clara Harris
Subject: Charles

Clara, that's all very David Attenborough of you and I know where you're coming from, but for once in my life I actually feel that he might like me as much as I do him. To put it in a National Geographical context – I am more likely to eat him than he is to eat me. He has sent me three emails already today.

From: **Clara Harris 26.09.11 16:57**
To: Rebecca Harris
Subject: Re: Charles

Well, that is absolutely as it should be and I am so pleased to hear it. I just wanted to tell you one thing. I know it probably doesn't mean anything, but were you aware that Charles told Carmen to come along to the party he was going to after she dropped Olly at the airport? I was standing nearby and I overheard – he was probably just being friendly, but Olly heard and definitely looked pissed off.

I went to the library this morning and saw lots of people outside your Kensington shop. What was that all about?

From: **Rebecca Harris 26.09.11 16:59**
To: Clara Harris
Subject: Re: Charles

Don't worry, I'm not at all bothered about Charles asking Carmen to the party. He and Olly have this sort of rivalry thing going on and he would just have said it to piss Olly off. I know it's not very nice but it would have been Charles's idea of a joke. Anyway, I have already had an earful from Olly about what he thinks of Charles, and quite frankly I am sick of everybody being so negative about him. He is sexy and he makes me laugh, so what more could a girl want?

But I'm so sorry about Jason, you poor thing. I hope him and that Samantha slut rot together! God, to think he could have been part of the family – Clara, you made a lucky escape.

We had a bit of a situation at Kensington with clients thinking we were open already, but it's been sorted out.

By the way, do you know of a good builder who would be willing to take on a small job at short notice?

From: **Clara Harris 26.09.11 17:01**
To: Rebecca Harris
Subject: builder

No, but will ask around

From: **Jane Johnson 26.09.11 17:03**
To: Rebecca Harris
Subject: Poppy
Attach: Parenting Advice

Dear Ms Harris,

I find myself writing to you again in what seems a relatively short time since our last correspondence.

It has come to my attention that Poppy has been unusually overtired today, falling asleep in both Music Appreciation and Story Time, and openly yawning in Morning Prayers, which I found particularly disconcerting as I was taking it.

An exasperated Mrs Bates (Stepping Stone's music teacher) questioned the child as to why she was so fatigued and was informed that Poppy had been to a grown ups' birthday party on Friday night and stayed up until 11pm, of all things! Now far be it, Ms Harris, for me to interfere in what goes on in people's homes, or to cast judgment on how others choose to rear their offspring, or offer forth my opinion on parenting. However, should you care for some advice on the matter from someone with a BA in Elementary Education & Childcare, then I would say, quite firmly, that children under the age of six should not be out of bed after 8pm even on weekends, and I have always found it unadvisable to allow the young to partake in adult festivities.

Individually, an incident of this nature would not give me too great a concern, but when put together with all the other situations concerning Poppy, I find myself questioning your commitment to this establishment. This is not to say that we wish Poppy to move on at this stage, but just that I think it would be wise to keep the channels of communication between ourselves open, so that things are not allowed to get too much out of hand.

Warm regards
Jane Johnson
Head Teacher

From: **Katherine Lease 26.09.11 17:11**
To: Rebecca Harris
Subject: flicks?

Marcus and I are going to see the new Jane Eyre movie at the Leicester Square Odeon. I know this is not Vinca's night on, but we're planning to get the 6.40 show which ends at 8.15, so I thought she might be willing to hang on 'til you get home, or we could bring Poppy to the movie? Let me know soon as I'm trying to impress Marcus by booking the tickets online. He has bet me £10 I can't do it, cheeky little shit. Kat xx

From: **Rebecca Harris 26.09.11 17:12**
To: Katherine Lease
Subject: Re: flicks?

Hi Kat, I still have so much work to do and I don't think Vinca will stay past 7.30. She's pretty cool most of the time but I don't want to push it. Also, Poppy's headmistress has been giving me an earful about not getting her to bed earlier and saying Poppy falls asleep at school. I really can't stand the woman, she acts like this happens all the time and that I'm some kind of negligent mother. I'm not a bad mother, am I? Poppy goes to bed at 7pm every night except Fridays and Saturdays when she is allowed to stay up until 8 – I think that's normal, don't you? Last Friday was an exception because of Mum's birthday. The reason why Poppy was tired on Monday was because she had tummy ache on Sunday night and didn't sleep well. I got an email from the wretched woman this morning and it made me so mad – she has a way of saying shitty things without actually saying them. She even threatened to expel Poppy in the email and then signed off with "warm regards" – how toxic is that? I'm getting really desperate to get her out of there.

From: **Katherine Lease 26.09.11 17:13**
To: Rebecca Harris
Subject: Poppy's headmistress

I know! I met Jill Johnson or whatever she's called, for all of three seconds, and I walked away with a sensation not dissimilar to having wet sand in my knickers. Very unpleasant.

From: **Phoebe Combes 26.09.11 17:22**
To: Rebecca Harris
Subject: Eyebrow promo

Rebecca,

All the shops are reporting back that the Eyebrow promotion is going brilliantly. Monica did one of the Sultan of Brunei's niece's eyebrows this morning and was given a £100 tip. Her mother called this afternoon to say how happy she was with her daughter's new look and has block-booked Monica to do 7 other members of the family tomorrow morning.

From: **Rebecca Harris 26.09.11 17:24**
To: Phoebe Combes
Subject: Re: Eyebrow promo

That's fantastic news. Well done, Phoebe!

From: **Rebecca Harris 26.09.11 17:33**
To: All Staff
Subject: builder needed. DESPERATE

If anyone knows of a builder who might be available this week to do some work at Marylebone, please could they let me know.

From: **Tania Cutter 26.09.11 17:36**
To: Rebecca Harris
Subject: Re: builder needed. DESPERATE

Rebecca

My brother is a building contractor and has recently set up his own company. I'm sure it would not be too much trouble for me to ask him if he might be able to take on the Marylebone job. I cannot of course guarantee that he will be available.
Tania Cutter PA
The Nail Bar Ltd

From: **Felicity Jones 26.09.11 17:38**
To: Rebecca Harris
Subject: bloody French dragon

I just got totally bloody busted at Harrods – nightmare. I booked in for a manicure and a bikini wax to see if I could find a good manicurist and beauty therapist. Things went really well with the manicurist, who said that she wanted to leave Harrods because they pool all the tips and the manager is a real dragon. So I got her number and then went for my wax. In the middle of my treatment (knickers off, one leg in the air), in walks the sodding dragon, who is French and up her own arse. She starts shouting at me and calling me a "sneaky cochon" and demands that I get dressed and bloody well leave there and then. I was so embarrassed as I still had wax all over me and was forced to put my knickers and jeans on anyway. The bitch then marched me out like I was a fucking shoplifter or something, and told me I was never welcome there again. I can't tell you how painful the walk to the bus stop was. I may well have done myself some permanent damage. I'm now sitting here dying for a pee and too scared to pull my trousers down in case my whole sodding inner thigh comes off.

From: **Rebecca Harris 26.09.11 17:43**
To: Felicity Jones
Subject: Re: bloody French dragon

Ooh Fi, that sounds nasty. Maybe call Collette at Mayfair. I would say she's our best beauty therapist and I'm sure she'll know what to do. I remember she was brilliant when Janine screwed up that guy's Back, Sack & Crack wax last year; could have been a major lawsuit but she calmed him down and he didn't end up with any major damage.
You didn't by any chance remember the jelly beans, did you?

From: **Felicity Jones 26.09.11 17:44**
To: Rebecca Harris
Subject: No

From: **Felicity Jones 26.09.11 18:11**
To: Rebecca Harris
Cc: Phoebe Combes
Subject: bikini wax

Please don't either of you two tell anyone what just happened in there. Brian is going to completely freak out. He's a pretty understanding husband but he had a very strict Catholic upbringing and already finds me quite extreme. Last Valentine's I surprised him with a Brazilian bikini wax and he nearly had a heart attack, so this could potentially kill him.

From: **Rebecca Harris 26.09.11 18:14**
To: Felicity Jones
Cc: Phoebe Combes
Subject: Re: bikini wax

I promise, Fi, I won't tell a soul.
I have to say, I don't think Collette's advice about using the nail polish remover was particularly helpful.
Phoebe, on the other hand – you were brilliant. That duct tape was inspired, obviously not as accurate as wax, but certainly did the job!
By the way, Tania suggested that her brother might be able to do the repair work at Marylebone. Apparently he's a builder – have either of you met him? I'm a bit nervous about taking him on if he is anything at all like his sister!

From: **Felicity Jones 26.09.11 18:17**
To: Rebecca Harris
Subject: Re: bikini wax

In so much pain. Must go home. Never met brother.

From: **Phoebe Combes 26.09.11 18:24**
To: Rebecca Harris
Cc: Felicity Jones
Subject: Re: bikini wax

Thanks, Rebecca. I actually find masking tape better as it's a bit more gentle. I used to use it when I was a student and on a budget. Actually I still do use it when I'm caught short for some reason or other and haven't had time to go to a salon. But duct tape was all I could find. Sorry it hurt so much, Fi, and don't worry, of course I won't tell anyone.
Never met the brother either.

From: **Rebecca Harris 26.09.11 18:29**
To: Tania Cutter
Subject: Re: builder needed. DESPERATE

186

Tania,

Thank you for suggesting your brother. That would be great. Would you find out if he could meet me at Marylebone tomorrow morning?

Rebecca

From: **Tania Cutter 26.09.11 18:30**
To: Rebecca Harris
Subject: Re: builder needed. DESPERATE

Rebecca,

I don't know what you three have been doing in the loo all this time, but I am now extremely late leaving. I need to talk to you about overtime pay as this is getting ridiculous.

I will call my brother and text you later if the appointment is possible for him.

Tania Cutter PA

The Nail Bar Ltd

From: **Rebecca Harris 26.09.11 18:53**
To: Oliver Barker
Subject: so sorry

Hi, Ols,

you're probably asleep, but I just wanted to say I'm sorry I was so busy biting your head off for being rude about Charles that I didn't focus on the fact that you and Carmen broke up. I was feeling pretty defensive about what you said and it just didn't register. I know I only met her briefly but she seemed really nice. I hope you are not feeling too down about it?

From: **Oliver Barker 26.09.11 18:58**
To: Rebecca Harris
Subject: glad you emailed

Hi Bex, I'm awake. I've been feeling totally knackered all day and now it's the middle of the night and I'm wide awake, very annoying. At least I'm getting some work done, and looking out at the Hong Kong skyline at night is pretty incredible.

I'm sorry again for what I said about Charles. You're absolutely right to be pissed off with me and I'm glad you told me so. In fact, it's one of the many things I like about my straight-talking little friend.

Thanks for saying that about Carmen. I am a bit sad about it, more for the fact that it marks another failed relationship than Carmen being the love of my life. I'm getting a bit bored with the fact that I keep getting it wrong with women – or keep getting the wrong woman, not sure which, or possibly it's both? Those people who meet and marry the loves of their lives in their twenties – is that just luck or are they just less picky? I am turning 35 (I know, you would never have guessed, right!) this year and I had far more clue what kind of girl I liked when I was in prep school. When I was 9 years old there was this girl called Jenny Taylor in my class at school and I was crazy about her. One day I plucked up the courage to go up to her and tell her she had nice hair and she smiled at me and said "thanks". I can honestly tell you it was the happiest moment of my life. I was absolutely certain that I would marry her after that and I probably should have done, but she was the first of many to slip in and out of my life. Tragic, isn't it?

Anyway, I'm boring on and you're probably frantically trying to finish up and get home to Poppy. What are you still doing at work anyway? Bex, you work too hard. Go home and call a taxi to take you. I don't like the idea of you taking the bus when it's dark.

From: **Rebecca Harris 26.09.11 19:04**
To: Oliver Barker
Subject: Re: glad you emailed

Olly, I'm so glad you're awake. I'm having a nightmare and I need someone to vent my frustration on. My boss is using me as her secretary, travel agent and slave; my secretary is trying to take over the company; my builder counsels me on the ways of the world at the same time as trying to con me any which way he can; my Mum is having heart palpitations because she thinks her youngest daughter is a sex deviant; I have one nail bar that is meant to be opening in a week but looks like a bomb went off in it, and another with major flood damage and no insurance cover because my moron of a secretary downgraded our package in a misguided attempt at economizing, and half the staff are demanding pay rises which I can't afford to give them – help me!!

I'm sorry about Jenny Taylor, what a bummer. Do you think she was The One? I always thought I would marry Johnny Banks until at the age of six he suggested that if I showed him mine, he would show me his. Naturally I didn't hesitate, but then he reneged on the deal and ran off and told everyone that I flashed him – actually, funnily enough, he just asked me for Clara's email address. I must warn her!!

I think the best way to deal with the ones that got away is to assume they're now fat, incredibly boring, and wearing polo neck jumpers with ducks embroidered on them, then put it all down to valuable experience and assume the next one will be a winner.

From: **Oliver Barker 26.09.11 19:07**
To: Rebecca Harris
Subject: Re: glad you emailed

Brilliant advice, except Jenny is now an extremely successful news reporter for CNN living in New York and looks like a million bucks. But still, I will try to apply the embroidered duck theory to the others.

I have to say, I'm impressed and not just a little envious that Johnny pulled off such a genius stunt at so young an age. I had no idea he was such a devious little bastard and your Mum obviously has good reason to be worried about you!

From: **Rebecca Harris 26.09.11 19:09**
To: Oliver Barker
Subject: Re: glad you emailed

I thought you were meant to be on my side? Anyway, I miss you, when are you coming home?

From: **Oliver Barker 26.09.11 19:07**
To: Rebecca Harris
Subject: c u soon

I get in on Wednesday morning.
I miss you too.
Goodnight.
Olly

Tuesday 27th September 2011

From: **Rebecca Harris 27.09.11 10:04**
To: Tania Cutter
Subject: Jeremy

Tania,

I met Jeremy this morning at Marylebone and he's great, just what we're looking for. It's a shame he isn't doing Kensington for us but I told him when we open the fifth nail bar we would definitely let him pitch for the business. He's gone back to the office now to work out a quote, and if we are all agreed then he will start work this afternoon which is fantastic, thank you.

Rebecca

From: **Tania Cutter 27.09.11 10:07**
To: Rebecca Harris
Subject: Re: Jeremy

Rebecca,

Yes, it is a pity you didn't ask my advice on construction firms in the beginning. I could have saved you a great deal of trouble. Doyle Brothers were so transparently not up to the job. Anyway, what's done is done and I am glad you are happy with my brother who, you will not be surprised to hear, is extremely reliable and efficient.

It has been a busy morning – here are my notes:

1. Barbara has called twice.

2. Felicity arrived at work at 9:55. She gave a doctor's appointment as her excuse so I have had to cover her workload as well as my own.

3. Phoebe has some exciting news that she is bubbling to tell you but is unwilling to share with me, which all seems a bit childish.

4. Andrea called and wants you to contact her.

5. A man called Charles Balford rang. A PERSONAL call, I believe.

6. We received a letter from a law firm called "Stratford, Errington and Bond" who have filed a lawsuit against The Nail Bar on behalf of Janine Azame.

As you can see, I have been run off my feet, so I am sure you will be grateful that I have decided to opt for overtime pay rather than taking time off. While on that subject, should I just submit a slip (calculations done on hourly rate based on percentage of my new salary) to Accounts and get them to write me a cheque?

Tania Cutter PA
The Nail Bar Ltd

From: **Rebecca Harris 27.09.11 10:14**
To: Tania Cutter
Subject: letter from law firm

Tania,

Can you bring me the lawyer's letter immediately and I assume you told Barbara that I was at Marylebone?

Rebecca

From: **Tania Cutter 27.09.11 10:16**
To: Rebecca Harris
Subject: Barbara

No, I told her you were in the loo, as I thought that is what you preferred I tell her.

Tania Cutter PA
The Nail Bar Ltd

From: **Rebecca Harris 27.09.11 10:17**
To: Tania Cutter
Subject: Re: Barbara

TANIA, what do you mean you told her that? Why the hell would you do that when you knew perfectly well where I was?

From: **Tania Cutter 27.09.11 10:19**
To: Rebecca Harris
Subject: Re: Barbara

Yes, I did know where you were. However, the last time Barbara called and you weren't around you specifically told me that I should have told her you were in the "toilet". I mentioned at the time that I thought this was rude, but you didn't see it that way.

Tania Cutter PA
The Nail Bar Ltd

From: **Rebecca Harris 27.09.11 10:21**
To: Tania Cutter
Subject: Re: Barbara

THAT IS BECAUSE I *WAS* IN THE TOILET, FOR CHRIST'S SAKE!!!!!!!!!!!!

Dear Rebecca,

Sorry to bother you but I thought you should know that Janine came back again this morning and insisted that she have her work station back. I didn't want her causing a scene so I gave it to her. I tried to steer clients away but there was one waiting. She saw Janine was free and insisted on having her.

Throughout the client's pedicure, Janine was slagging off the company, saying she was underpaid and treated really badly, and all the while talking in a really loud voice. I tried to call you an hour ago but I was told you were in the toilet.

Janine is now with another client doing the same thing, and I am a bit worried because the Sultan of Brunei's daughters are due any minute to see Monica for their eyebrow shaping. As they are all coming together, some of them will have to wait for quite a while and they will be in close proximity to Janine.

Sylvia also says that Janine shoved her when she was making a coffee in the kitchen and called her something rude. I'm not sure what, but it was obviously bad and she is looking quite shaky. I don't know if you know this, but apparently Sylvia has some kind of heart condition? I did a CPR course three years ago and I think I remember most of it, so hopefully that will be adequate should we encounter a problem. I just thought you should know.

Should I just let Janine carry on, or try and convince her to leave?

Andrea

Fi, have you just read that email from Andrea? You're not going to believe this, but this morning we got a letter from Janine's lawyer saying that she intends to press charges against us, citing both "unfair dismissal" and "racial discrimination" and now she's back at work – is that legal?

By the way, how did Brian react and what did the doc say?

From: Felicity Jones 27.09.11 10:37
To: Rebecca Harris
Subject: a f****** mess all round

Hi Bex, the doctor said I would be fine but "uncomfortable" for a few days, which is the under bloody statement of the year, and I'm "off games" for a week. Luckily Brian hasn't seen it yet as last night he went to pick up Annette's partner Dave who was being discharged from hospital, and he didn't get back 'til late.

Yes, I read Andrea's email and my initial thought was how fucking cool that she can do CPR if Sylvia has a heart attack – that's just the sort of skillset we need in a company like this.

I'm not exactly sure what is and isn't legal when it comes to working for a company while suing them, but let me have a look at the letter and I'll see if I can make sense of it. In the meantime you might want to get some legal advice yourself.

Phoebe said she hadn't seen you all morning. Have you been in the toilet all this time?

From: Rebecca Harris 27.09.11 10:39
To: Felicity Jones
Subject: Tania's bruv

No, of course not! I was over at Marylebone with Tania's brother who couldn't be more different from her, completely normal, very professional and seriously easy on the eye, which obviously came as a huge surprise. I think he is going to do a great job with the re-furb.

From: Rebecca Harris 27.09.11 10:42
To: Andrea Moleno
Subject: Re: Janine

Andrea, Janine has actually filed a lawsuit against us, so I'm going to talk to a lawyer about whether it is legal or not for her to be working with us. In the meantime, if you can try to keep the situation under control as best as possible, that would be great. If you think Sylvia can't handle the stress and feels threatened by Janine, then see if she would prefer to go over to Westbourne. Let me know how it goes?

From: Andrea Moleno 27.09.11 10:46
To: Rebecca Harris
Subject: Re: Janine

Rebecca, don't worry, the Sultan's women have just shown up accompanied by two of the most enormous bodyguards I have ever seen in my life. Sylvia has gone to sit near them, so I think she will be fine. I think Janine might also quieten down a bit now.

Andrea

From: **Rebecca Harris 27.09.11 10:50**
To: Charles Balford
Subject: film

Hi Charles,

I heard you called. I still don't have your mobile number, will you text it to me? I called your office number (I know it from Johnny Banks) but was told you were busy.

My friend Kat, who you met at my mum's birthday, saw the new Jane Eyre movie last night and said it was pretty good. Shall I book that?

Can't wait to see you.

From: **Charles Balford 27.09.11 10:53**
To: Rebecca Harris
Subject: how bout some action, hint hint!

Hi Darling,

I have to tell you, I would rather slam my cock repeatedly in a drawer than sit through a period drama, even if it does have Mia Wasiwhatsit in it. How about an action film, or at least nothing with over-earnest English actresses in, especially not Emma Thompson.

Anyway, let's move on to more exciting stuff. Have you got nothing on today, like you promised? The thought of it has been distracting me all morning.

I've been reminiscing about our night together, and apart from a niggling feeling that Bon Jovi might have been playing in the background, it was a very, very repeatable experience.

You are a much naughtier girl than I realized and I can't wait to see you either. All of you, that is.

Charles

From: **Rebecca Harris 27.09.11 10:55**
To: Charles Balford
Subject: Re: how bout some action, hint hint!

Charles, I know you're trying to get me to write a dirty email to you, but I'm not going to because knowing my luck I will send it to my mother by mistake, and anyway I am trying to book cinema tickets and I have loads of work to do. I'm not going to allow myself to be distracted.

How about the new Bruce Willis film? Can't believe you don't like Emma Thompson? She's a fantastic actress and I'm pretty sure she's won a Golden Globe. She also graduated from Cambridge and is an active environmentalist.

From: **Charles Balford 27.09.11 10:58**
To: Rebecca Harris
Subject: Willis

Well, now I <u>really</u> don't like her.

Bruce Willis can single-handedly beat the shit out of a heavily-armed, hardcore terrorists' cell, drive a car at 100mph through Central Park without hitting a tree, abseil down the side of an 80-storey building using a telephone cord AND manage to look cool in a vest, which is not easy! The man is a legend and he doesn't need any awards or degrees to prove it.

From: **Rebecca Harris 27.09.11 11:00**
To: Charles Balford
Subject: Re: Willis

Plus he nailed Demi Moore in her prime when the likes of Rob Lowe and Judd Nelson were swarming around her like bees to honey, which proves he's a total super stud.

From: **Charles Balford 27.09.11 11:01**
To: Rebecca Harris
Subject: Re: Willis

Beautifully put, and you're absolutely right. Loving the fact that you are so in touch with your masculine side.

From: **Rebecca Harris 27.09.11 11:03**
To: Charles Balford
Subject: Re: Willis

Yes it's something I really pride myself on.

I'll see you and Bruce around 7.45pm.

From: **Charles Balford 27.09.11 11:04**
To: Rebecca Harris
Subject: I'm looking forward to it.

From: **Barbara Foreman 27.09.11 11:10**
To: Rebecca Harris
Subject: update required

Rebecca,

I assume that you are back from the Ladies' room by now?

I want an update on the progress being made at the Kensington Nail Bar. An acquaintance of mine from Chicago was in London yesterday and went to have a look through the salon window. She said, and I quote, "Barbara, if that place is up and running in a week, I'll eat my hat". Needless to say, this has not filled me with a great deal of confidence, especially as I have spent the last five days making sure that the new product range will be shipped to London in time for the opening.

I would appreciate a response sooner rather than later.

Barbara

From: **Rebecca Harris 27.09.11 11:14**
To: Tania Cutter
Subject: my whereabouts

Tania, let me be very clear here to avoid any possible confusion in the future – if Barbara, or indeed anyone calls me, please always tell them the truth about where I am unless I have specifically asked you to lie for me. If I actually happen to be in the toilet, then perhaps you could say something like I am on the other line and will call them back shortly. Is this understood?

Rebecca

From: **Tania Cutter 27.09.11 11:19**
To: Rebecca Harris
Subject: never-ending phone calls

Rebecca,

I am not a child and I resent being treated as one.

I don't think you realize quite how difficult my job is. For a start, I have never worked in an office where there are quite so many in-coming PERSONAL calls, and these of course have to be treated differently from work-related calls. On top of this, I get different requests from everyone in the office about how they want me to answer these calls. For example: Phoebe has told me that she cannot take calls from Stewart (who rings at least four times a day), Matthew, Grant, Heath, Richard or Louis, but anyone called Simeon, Mark (except her bank manager Mark Derrek), John, Pasqual, Ian or Harry is fine.

Felicity always wants me to put Brian through but not any member of his family unless they are calling to tell her that something has happened to Brian.

When your sister calls she only wants to speak to you if you don't "look busy" and your mother calls but doesn't want to speak to you at all – she just wants to check if you have received her latest email. To be frank, I am sick of lying for everyone, and from now on I will answer each call as I see best. I do not tell you how to do your job so please do not tell me how to do mine.

I am going out now to get my morning coffee, which I normally get at 11am but have been too busy on the phone to do so until now.

Tania Cutter PA

The Nail Bar Ltd

From: **Rebecca Harris 27.09.11 11:20**
To: Tania Cutter
Subject: re: never-ending phone calls

Tania, I'm afraid that is the nature of the job.

Can you get me a non-fat blueberry muffin while you're at it?

From: **Phoebe Combes 27.09.11 11:21**
To: Rebecca Harris
Subject: lots of news!!

Hi Rebecca,

I've been waiting for you to come in as I have some great news and some not-so-great news, but luckily the great news I think outweighs the not-so-great news . . . The great news is that Kylie's agent called and asked for 20 bottles of *Purple Rain* nail polish to be sent around to her office this morning. This means that we can officially release a statement saying "Kylie Minogue cannot live without *Purple Rain*", and her agent is sending round four signed photographs for each of the nail bars. How cool is that?

The not-so-great news is that someone from *The Mail on Sunday* phoned Suki and asked for some basic facts about The Nail Bar for the piece they're writing – this must have been one of Helen Carmichael's researchers, so she is obviously going ahead with her article.

I need to take an Eyebrow promo poster up to Marylebone today as theirs got ruined in the flood. Let me know if there is anything else that needs to go?

From: **Rebecca Harris 27.09.11 11:24**
To: Phoebe Combes
Subject: Re: lots of news!!

Phoebe, the "great" news really is great, but the "not-so-great news" is shockingly awful. When will we know which Sunday the article is coming out? I am praying like hell that it is not this coming one as not only is it the one before the opening, it also happens to be the day Barbara flies in to London. Can you try and find out?

Before you go to Marylebone, I need to give you a cheque for the new builder who is going to repair the flood damage there. I don't know the amount yet, so can you wait a bit until I find out?

What is the reply count for the party, and are there any high profile "yes's"?

From: **Phoebe Combes 27.09.11 11:27**
To: Rebecca Harris
Subject: party replies

No problem, just let me know when you have it ready.

So far we have 84 "yes's", 22 "no's" and no high profiles, but they never reply until the last minute and sometimes they just show without replying at all. Anyway, I have given the press a list of some major celebs who I've said are coming, so they are working themselves into a frenzy of excitement, which hopefully means some good coverage.

From: **Rebecca Harris 27.09.11 11:28**
To: Phoebe Combes
Subject: Re: party replies

Is that such a good idea? Won't they be annoyed when they find out the celebrities weren't even invited?

From: **Phoebe Combes 27.09.11 11:31**
To: Rebecca Harris
Subject: Re: party replies

Not at all, this sort of thing happens all the time. Anyway, they *have* been invited – I invited them, but it's just not very likely that they'll come. I've invited these same celebrities to other events I've organized in the past and they didn't come, but I figure if I ask them enough, eventually they will feel bad about having turned me down so many times that they'll just have to say yes out of guilt. My strongest contender is Brian Adams. He was very sweet when I sent him an invitation to my 21st birthday. He wrote a hand-written reply saying he was on tour in America and unfortunately couldn't make it. I've invited him to all my birthdays since and each time he responds charmingly, and one time even sent me a signed copy of his Anthology album. I have high hopes for Stephen Fry as well. I've asked him to all sorts of different events and the last one, my mum's annual, Open Gardens day party, he was genuinely sorry that he wasn't able to make it but he had a terrible cold and was worried he might pass it on to the other guests. Others like Bono and Sting are not likely as they always have their publicists respond. I did get a couple of actors from East Enders to come to a party I organized for friends of mine who had come down from Devon for the "Countryside Alliance" march, which I thought was quite an achievement. I actually fancied one of them but the timing wasn't right because I was with the love of my life at the time and completely smitten. I tried getting them again for my "Save our Scottish Salmon Farmers" rally, but they were a no-show.

Anyway, I've asked the whole cast of East Enders this time, and of course Kylie as well. The thing is, it's always worth a try because you never know, and the worst that could happen is they say no, and even then you might get a CD out of it.

From: **Rebecca Harris 27.09.11 11:33**
To: Phoebe Combes
Subject: what love of your life?

I thought you hadn't met the love of your life yet?

No, not this year, but I've still got three months to go, so fingers crossed!

From: Rebecca Harris 27.09.11 11:43
To: Barbara Foreman
Subject: News from The Nail Bar

Barbara,

I hope you have been having a productive day in Hong Kong and that the lymphatic drainage massage got you off to a good start. Apparently it's very good for varicose veins.

You will be pleased to hear that everything is going extremely well over here and I am more than confident that Kensington will be finished on schedule, so I hope your friend has a strong digestive system!

The reason Kensington looked so bad when she went past was because we had to replace the new ventilation system. We had been wrongly advised that the new system was a superior model, and it was only once it had been installed that it became apparent that this was not the case and that it was completely inadequate for the job. There was no way it had the capacity to dispel all the toxic smells from the nail polishes and removers that accumulate during a busy day. I took an executive decision and ordered Joe to upgrade the entire system. I checked that this would in no way delay our schedule, and as this error was entirely Joe's fault (I had clearly specified from the outset what we needed), he assured me that he would still finish on time.

I'm very excited about the new products. We're really in need of a fresh look for our retail. On the subject of retail, I have already had to place another order with Nancy for *Purple Rain* because it has been selling so fast, and Kylie has been back to bulk buy!!

Most of the party invitees have come back with a positive response and we are expecting a lot of press to show, due to our high-profile guests. I have organised outdoor heaters to go on the street to allow for the overflow, as numbers seem to be getting bigger and bigger. Unfortunately the new awning, which looked amazing, got torn off in a huge storm we had last week, but luckily there will be another one up for the night, just not with our logo on it. The storm also caused some flood damage at Marylebone, but I have a builder in there today doing repairs.

The Sultan of Brunei's eldest daughter went to the Mayfair Nail Bar yesterday to take advantage of our Eyebrow promotion and was so happy with her new look that today all the daughters and half his harem are in there getting themselves done.

We have had a small issue with one of our staff whom we had to get rid of last week due to a series of incidents. Unfortunately this girl believes that she was wrongfully dismissed and is trying to bring a lawsuit against us, but as she has absolutely no grounds for her claim of racial discrimination, I am not at all worried about it.

I am in constant touch with all the people involved with the party, from food to flowers to wine and waiters, and all is on track. Pink Mango want to confirm our canapé list which I sent to you last week. When you get back to New York could you email it back to me with your choices (think Peking duck rolls sound yum) – thanks.
Rebecca

PS The varicose vein comment wasn't meant to insinuate that you had varicose veins, I'm sure you don't, not that there's anything particularly wrong with them, but that's just what the therapist told me when I booked.

From: **Barbara Foreman 27.09.11 12:00**
To: Rebecca Harris
Subject: absolutely NO lawsuit

Rebecca,

Lawsuits involving racial discrimination are the worst. I am seriously concerned and so should you be. It does not matter if you think this girl has no grounds for her accusations, you still need a damn good lawyer to crush her case before it even gets off the ground. Contact Nancy immediately and tell her to put you in touch with someone in Dan Bernstein's office. Dan is a shark of a corporate lawyer who could sort out this mess in a flash, but you would have to sell your house to pay for him (which if it comes to it, I am sure you will be willing to do). In the meantime you will have to settle for one of his juniors taking on the case. Rebecca, I do not like this, it is bad for business and bad for the company's reputation – get it fixed!

The new range is due to arrive in the UK on Thursday morning, so should clear Customs and be with you early on Friday. The majority of the Nail Care products and all of the electrical equipment are being dealt with by the Hong Kong manufacturer, and I plan to set up a small logistics office here for processing paperwork and dealing with orders. The products that concern you therefore will be coming out of Hong Kong, so we will be changing your whole ordering system. But I will give you details on all that when I get back to New York.

Barbara

From: **Rebecca Harris 27.09.11 12:03**
To: Barbara Foreman
Subject: Re: absolutely NO lawsuit

Fantastic! We will be on standby to receive the new products on Friday.

My friend's boyfriend is a lawyer and he also happens to be black, so I might try him first as I am sure he would be happy to give me some free advice.

Rebecca

From: **Barbara Foreman 27.09.11 12:06**
To: Rebecca Harris
Subject: Re: absolutely NO lawsuit

Good, get on to him immediately.

From: **Jeremy Cutter** jcutter@cuttingedge.bis.uk **27.09.11 12:10**
To: Rebecca Harris
Subject: quote
Attach: Marylebone Nail Bar

Hi Rebecca,

Good to meet you this morning. I have attached the quote for you to take a look over. If you're happy with it then we can get started pretty much immediately. If it's alright with you, I might head over there now with a couple of my guys to show them what needs doing? Please could you also let the manager know that there will be a fair amount of noise from downstairs? Those treatment rooms you have down there will be out of action for the next three days. Do you have a spare key to the shop, because we will try to do most of the more noisy work out of shop hours?

Regards, Jeremy

From: **Rebecca Harris 27.09.11 12:18**
To: Jeremy Cutter
Subject: Re: quote

Dear Jeremy,

The quote looks fine, thank you for being so quick. I will let Suki, the manager at Marylebone, know you are coming and I am sending a girl from the office with the key and your cheque for the deposit.

Rebecca

From: **Rebecca Harris 27.09.11 12:21**
To: Phoebe Combes
Subject: new builder @ Marylebone

Phoebe, Jeremy (the new builder) is going to be at Marylebone in about two hours. Can you meet him there with a spare key to the salon (Tania has it) and give him the cheque?

From: **Phoebe Combes 27.09.11 12:23**
To: Rebecca Harris
Subject: Re: new builder @ Marylebone

No prob.

From: **Rebecca Harris 27.09.11 12:27**
To: Suki Leung
Subject: Re: new builder @ Marylebone

Suki, there is a builder called Jeremy coming to your nail bar this afternoon to repair the flood damage. He says he will need three days, so I am afraid the treatment rooms downstairs cannot be used until Friday, or maybe Thursday afternoon – check with him. I am giving him a spare key so that he can let himself in out of hours. You will need to show him how the alarm works.

From: **Suki Leung 27.09.11 12:35**
To: Rebecca Harris
Subject: Re: new builder @ Marylebone

Rebecca, you tell me this but I not happy. You put strange man in my nail bar when I not here. I not take responsibility if he steal money from till. Why you not use my uncle, he very good builder, much better than English man? You tell English man go home, I call my Uncle Li.

From: **Rebecca Harris 27.09.11 12:39**
To: Suki Leung
Subject: Re: new builder @ Marylebone

Suki, I understand your concern, but the builder is Tania's brother so he is very trustworthy and I am not worried about him stealing. Thank you, and next time maybe I will use your uncle.

From: **Suki Leung 27.09.11 12:41**
To: Rebecca Harris
Subject: Re: new builder @ Marylebone

Rebecca,

Why you use Tania's family, not my family? This is my nail bar, you not use my family now I lose face. This man give you good discount? My uncle very cheap and work hard like me. You cancel English man and I call Uncle Li.

From: **Rebecca Harris 27.09.11 12:44**
To: Suki Leung
Subject: Re: new builder @ Marylebone

Suki, I cannot cancel Jeremy, I've already offered him the job, so please don't call Uncle Li. I sent out an email to everyone yesterday asking if they knew a builder and you did not say anything, so I'm afraid it is too late. It is only a small job and we employ many members of your family who are all great, but we just can't do it this time. I'm sorry.

From: **Suki Leung 27.09.11 12:46**
To: Rebecca Harris
Subject: big pay rise

Suki not happy, if pay rise not big maybe Suki look for other job and take family with her.

From: **Rebecca Harris 27.09.11 12:48**
To: Phoebe Combes
Subject: Suki

Phoebe, when you go to Marylebone, will you just hang around for a little bit as I want to make sure that Suki doesn't give Jeremy a hard time? She is pissed off that I didn't employ her uncle to do the job and I'm worried she might be difficult. She's being very over-dramatic, and as usual is threatening to leave.

From: **Phoebe Combes 27.09.11 12:50**
To: Rebecca Harris
Subject: Re: Suki

Sure. I rather like hanging around at the Marylebone nail bar, it's always buzzing and Suki makes me laugh with her crazy shouting and the way she bosses the clients around, telling them what treatments they should have regardless of what they want. I once saw her whack a woman on the leg with a foot file because she was taking too long to decide on what colour polish to have. Suki took the two colours away that the client was deliberating over and gave her another one that was completely different, saying "you choose very bad for you, make feet more ugly, you use this one, maybe you get lucky later with rich guy, then he give you diamond necklace and you thank Suki, she know much better than you". Amazingly the woman accepted this and even thanked Suki for caring so much. Anyway, I will try to make sure that Jeremy stays out of her firing range.

From: **Bettina Harris 27.09.11 12:54**
To: Rebecca Harris
Subject: li /ttl/e chat

Dddarling   I   thought weeeeeeeeeeeeeeeeeee could have lunch today. I'd like......\\ a little chat with yyou??? How about t h a t nice French restaurant by me at 1:::30??
Love mummmmy

Message sent via BlackBerry ®

From: **Rebecca Harris 27.09.11 12:57**
To: Katherine Lease
Subject: cover for me

Kat, remember that girl Janine I told you about? Well, she's been causing trouble again and I was wondering if I could get some legal advice from Marcus?

Forgot to tell you, my mum intercepted an email I sent to Clara with details of my night with Charles in it – nightmare! I am absolutely mortified. She just asked me if I wanted to have lunch but there's no way I can face her. I'm going to have to tell her I'm having lunch with you. I feel awful lying but I'm far too much of a coward to do anything else.

From: **Tania Cutter 27.09.11 12:57**
To: Rebecca Harris
Subject: your PERSONAL calls

Your mother called to see if you received her email.
I am going for lunch. The machine is on.
Tania Cutter PA
The Nail Bar Ltd

From: **Katherine Lease 27.09.11 13:03**
To: Rebecca Harris
Subject: lunch & don't spare the details

Bex, I can't believe that Clara got the sex details and I didn't?
Marcus isn't a lawyer, he's a sports manager. You're thinking of Meka, my last boyfriend before Noah who was the one before Antoine.
You *are* having lunch with me so you're not lying – I've already booked it – Casa Mexicana in 20 mins. See you there.

From: **Rebecca Harris 27.09.11 13:05**
To: Katherine Lease
Subject: Re: lunch & don't spare the details

OK, great, but it will have to be quite a quick one as I need to buy ballet shoes for Poppy.
Is there any chance I could talk to Meka?

From: **Katherine Lease 27.09.11 13:08**
To: Rebecca Harris
Subject: Re: lunch & don't spare the details

I'd rather you didn't. I told him I was moving to Vietnam when he threatened to leave his wife for me, so I don't want him to know I still live in London. Anyway, he's a divorce lawyer so he wouldn't be able to help you.

From: **Rebecca Harris 27.09.11 13:10**
To: Barbara Foreman
Subject: Lawyer re lawsuit

Barbara,

It turns out that my friend's boyfriend isn't a lawyer, he's a sports manager, so I will contact Nancy immediately.

Rebecca

From: **Barbara Foreman 27.09.11 13:12**
To: Rebecca Harris
Subject: Re: Lawyer re lawsuit

Why does that not surprise me?

From: **Rebecca Harris 27.09.11 13:13**
To: Bettina Harris
Subject: Re: lunch

Mum,

So sorry but I don't really have time for lunch today as I have to buy ballet shoes for Poppy and things are so busy at work. I thought I would just grab a sandwich with Kat then head back to the office – do you mind? Next week, once the opening is out the way and things have calmed down a bit, I would love to meet for lunch.

From: **Bettina Harris 27.09.11 13:20**
To: Rebecca Harris
Subject: Re: lunch

        ...darling ooof course   we ccan, don''''t worry at   all... poor you working so h a rd. Why ddon''t I byu the b allet shoes andd you h   ave a nice luncccccch wit kat?

Love yoou

    mummmmmmy

Trying to write faster buut making a a a few m ore mistakesss
Message sent via BlackBerry ®

From: **Rebecca Harris 27.09.11 13:14**
To: Bettina Harris
Subject: Re: ballet shoes

Oh Mum, thanks so much but don't worry, I can do it.

From: **Andrea Moleno 27.09.11 14:35**
To: Rebecca Harris
Cc: Felicity Jones
Subject: a few problems, sorry

Dear Rebecca,

We have had a small crisis here I'm afraid. The Sultan of Brunei's

208

second favourite daughter is missing an eyebrow. She was the last one to go in for shaping, and I think Monica was quite tired because she accidentally spilt a large blob of wax on her left eyebrow and when she tried to remove it the entire thing came off. The Number Two wife (whose daughter it is) has gone ape shit and wants to see you.

The other slight problem is that Monica was hugely upset by all this and felt she had lost her confidence, so Sylvia suggested that she "get straight back on the horse" and do an eyebrow wax on her. Unfortunately, Monica's hands were shaking and Sylvia now looks like a Geisha. Sylvia made a heroic effort to keep her hysteria under control but eventually it got the better of her, so I have sent her home. Of course, Janine has got involved and is now telling all the Arabs about how racist this company is and how this was probably done deliberately to them and they shouldn't stand for it. They are demanding to see the boss of the company, so I was wondering if you could come here? There are 11 of them, plus two bodyguards, which leaves very little room for the other customers, and they are refusing to leave until you get here, so if you could come as soon as possible, that would be great.

Sorry to bother you with all this.

Andrea

From: **Felicity Jones 27.09.11 14:40**
To: Rebecca Harris
Subject: Arabian Frights

Bex, I'm glad you're back. If you've read Andrea's email, don't panic, things are a little better since then. I've spoken to Andrea several times over the last 45 minutes and she has been brilliant. She managed to persuade Nayla (Number One Sultan wife) to move the extended family to the Bistro up the road. She bought them all an enormous lunch and told them to wait for you there. Apparently they're all happily eating and plotting to tear you and the company apart. Good luck.

From: **Rebecca Harris 27.09.11 14:48**
To: Felicity Jones
Subject: Re: Arabian Frights

God, Fi, I've had two margaritas and a glass of wine. I'm not sure how to cope with this at all. What about Sylvia, is she ok?

From: Felicity Jones 27.09.11 14:51
To: Rebecca Harris
Subject: Re: Arabian Frights

You lucky cow. Brian and I are trying not to drink on Mondays and Tuesdays and it's making me insane. I can't even hear the word "margarita" without getting twitchy. Anyway, it's a good thing – you definitely wouldn't want to approach this situation sober.

My advice is, have a quick flick through the fashion mags on Phoebe's desk to see if by any chance the "no eyebrow" look is in. Failing that, grab a whole load of the goodie bags from the cupboard and just pile them with freebies.

I called Sylvia at home. She's had a hell of a first few days with us, but she says if her eyebrows have grown back a bit, she will come to the opening party. She'll start at Kensington after that but she doesn't want any more "training" until then, which I think is fair enough. As for Janine, you better find out whether we can legally throw her out. She is seriously bad for business!

From: Rebecca Harris 27.09.11 14:55
To: Felicity Jones
Subject: Re: Arabian Frights

I know. I'm going to contact Barbara's lawyer. See you later. Wish me luck. Bex

From: Felicity Jones 27.09.11 15:00
To: Rebecca Harris
Subject: Best of British . . !!

From: Clara Harris 27.09.11 15:12
To: Rebecca Harris
Subject: Johnny

Hi Bex, just got a really sweet email from Johnny Banks asking me out to dinner. I'm actually quite nervous as I haven't been on a first date in two and a half years, yikes! What shall I wear? I'm also quite pleased because Jason wants to come to the flat after work to get the rest of his stuff, and this gives me an excuse to be out. X x

From: Oliver Barker 27.09.11 15:25
To: Rebecca Harris

Hi Bex, just checking in. Hope today is going more smoothly than yesterday? It's 11.30pm and I'm at the airport trying not to fall asleep, waiting for my flight which I've just been told has been delayed by 45 minutes, apparently caused by chronic weather conditions in London. Doesn't sound good.

You'll be pleased to hear that I got your silk pj's, wasn't sure what colour you wanted so I went for white? I also picked up some cool stuff for my flat, a Chinese jacket for my Mum and a jade necklace for my sister, so definitely a worthwhile trip to Stanley Market.

I get in seriously early. How about meeting me for breakfast at The Brasserie?

Lots of love, Olly

Message sent via BlackBerry ®

From: Joe Doyle   27.09.11 15:42
To: Rebecca Harris
Subject: you got the wrong wall

Rebecca,

It turns out that the wall you wanted the glass display shelves put up on wouldn't support the weight. We only discovered this once we put them up and half the wall fell off and most of the shelves got broke. A lot of surrounding plaster came off too. Do you want us to order some more shelves and put them up on a different wall, or should we get a free standing unit instead?

Joe

From: Suki Leung   27.09.11 16:01
To: Rebecca Harris
Subject: DOUBLE URGENT

Rebecca, you phone me immediately. I very upset, more upset than in whole life. English man builder he go to storeroom with Phoebe and not come back for long time. I go see what the matter, door lock, so I go get key. Inside I see English slut and English builder making sex all over storeroom products.

This my nail bar Rebecca, not happy happy house. People no respect for nail bar mean no respect for Suki. You use Uncle Li and no problem, now very big problem. I very unhappy.

Suki

From: **Tania Cutter 27.09.11 16:10**
To: Rebecca Harris
Subject: ABUSIVE PHONE CALLS

Rebecca,

I don't know where you are but Suki has called five times and the last three calls she would only speak in Mandarin, but I could tell she was swearing. I don't like to be on the receiving end of abusive phone calls, especially in a foreign language, and especially when one is in one's own country. It's very disconcerting. If I was in a bar in Beijing I might expect it, but I am not, and I find it extremely unnerving. I would appreciate it if you could have a word with her about this.

Tania Cutter PA
The Nail Bar Ltd

From: **Rebecca Harris 27.09.11 16:16**
To: Felicity Jones
Subject: Brace yourself

Fi, SUKI HAS JUST CAUGHT PHOEBE AND JEREMY, TANIA'S BROTHER, SHAGGING IN THE STOREROOM AT MARYLEBONE!!!!!!!!!!!!!! Suki has naturally gone ballistic and is only conversing in Mandarin. She's taking it as a personal affront and blames me for using Jeremy instead of her Uncle Li. The whole situation is so completely out of order I don't even know where to begin. Obviously Phoebe needs to be talked to, but I don't know what to do about Jeremy? I don't want to fire him because we desperately need the work done, but if I don't, Suki will go insane. Have you ever had a situation like this in other companies you worked for, and if so, how did Personnel deal with it?

I actually don't know whether to be completely horrified or seriously impressed with Phoebe's ability to get laid. How does she do it?

From: **Felicity Jones 27.09.11 17:07**
To: Rebecca Harris
Subject: Re: Brace yourself

I've never worked in Personnel before now. At *Bad Boys* mag I did the music and movie reviews. Prior to that I was a technical assistant for a theatre group in the West End, and before that I was self-employed as a pavement artist in Covent Garden. Did I not tell you that?

Shagging in the storeroom is quite hardcore, I agree, but I have to tell you, I'm not surprised. Phoebe is legendary. She only has to look at a guy and he starts frothing at the mouth. Suki should be bloody grateful you didn't employ her Uncle Li!

Why don't you get Tania to talk to Jeremy – that will give her something to sweat about, and you can deal with Suki. Phoebe is pretty much a lost cause – sex is like breathing for her, she can't function without it. I think that is why she is good at Public Relations, she "relates" to the public better than anyone I know.

How did it go at Mayfair?

From: **Rebecca Harris 27.09.11 17:11**
To: Felicity Jones
Subject: Sultanas

I think in your interview you might have omitted the bit about being a pavement artist?

The whole Sultan situation was exhausting. By the time I got to the Bistro they had had enough of lunch and were ready for tea and thought the Dorchester Hotel sounded nice! So we climbed into three limousines and headed off. Once we were there I gave them each a goodie bag and apologized profusely, and then the most amazing thing happened; an elderly Japanese couple walked past our table and the woman pointed to the Sultan's eyebrowless daughter and said something to her husband. The husband then came over and asked, in very broken English, where she had her eyebrows removed because his wife wanted to have the same thing done. I gave them my card and they smiled, bowed and walked on. This of course was brilliant, and I immediately explained to the Brunei contingent how, in England, everything Asian was huge at the moment and the "no-eyebrow" look was right at the forefront of fashion. Anyway they seemed to swallow this, along with three thousand cucumber sandwiches and a truckload of scones with cream and jam, all courtesy of The Nail Bar, so I think we are off the hook.

From: **Felicity Jones 27.09.11 17:13**
To: Rebecca Harris

Bloody hell, can't believe you got to have tea at the Dorchester! I'm starving, could fucking murder a scone. I actually went to get one from Coffee Republic about an hour ago. The place was packed and there was nowhere to sit but I didn't feel like coming straight back to the office so I perched on a radiator, momentarily forgetting that I was missing at least three layers of skin from my nether regions. As soon as my raw bum made contact with the hot metal I screamed my head off and threw my scone and cup of tea across the room. Everyone in the coffee shop jumped, and almost all of them spilt their drinks. The manager rushed over, felt the radiator, realized it wasn't too hot and that he couldn't be sued, and promptly marched me off the premises, telling me I would not be welcome in his establishment again – bastard! Now my only option is Starbucks and their scones are crap.

From: **Rebecca Harris 27.09.11 17:16**
To: Felicity Jones
Subject: scones

Ooh Fi, that all sounds nasty.

From: **Rebecca Harris 27.09.11 17:18**
To: Tania Cutter
Subject: Jeremy

Tania,

I am afraid I have some rather disturbing news: The reason why Suki has been calling so frantically is because this afternoon she caught Phoebe and your brother having sex in the storeroom at Marylebone. Of course, different families operate under different moral codes, but even so I think this is outrageous, and obviously Suki does too. It goes without saying that this kind of behaviour is completely unacceptable, and frankly I am not sure how to deal with it. I'll be talking to Phoebe, but I think it would be best if you talk to Jeremy. This is all pretty embarrassing, Tania, especially as you were adamant that your brother was professional and reliable.
Rebecca

From: **Tania Cutter 27.09.11 17:27**
To: Rebecca Harris
Subject: Re: Jeremy

214

Rebecca,

I don't know what to say except that I am beyond humiliated. I will of course speak to Jeremy immediately about his completely unacceptable behaviour. If you feel it necessary, I will tender my resignation at once, although I do feel that this office needs me enormously and Barbara is still relying on me for that report, and of course I have been extremely loyal to this company.

I expect you intend to fire Phoebe as her conduct is the most shameful of all, considering she is an established employee, whereas Jeremy is not and can be excused to a certain level for not knowing company policy.

I would like to add that although Jeremy and I are related, we do not share the same ethics when it comes to relations with the opposite sex. I cannot begin to fathom how two people can copulate without even knowing each other. I have a strict code of conduct about when a relationship advances to the level of heavy petting, which I can assure you does not happen until several months into a courtship. I have never had a one-night stand and I am completely appalled by Jeremy's and Phoebe's conduct.

Tania Cutter PA

The Nail Bar Ltd.

PS As it is almost time for me to leave, I think I will speak to Jeremy from home and let you know about it tomorrow.

From:	**Rebecca Harris 27.09.11 17:30**
To:	Joe Doyle
Subject:	Re: you got the wrong wall

Joe,

I don't understand why you put up the shelves without first assessing that the walls could take the weight? Surely there must be a way of checking the strength of the structure before you just go ahead and bang a nail into it? It comes across as very amateur, and I'm pretty upset that the shelves are all now smashed. I suppose you expect me to pay for them?

Rebecca

From:	**Joe Doyle 27.09.11 17:36**
To:	Rebecca Harris
Subject:	Re: you got the wrong wall

Rebecca luv,

You're wasting time moaning about the broken shelves when what you should be doing is putting your energy into making a decision about what you would like to do about them.

I'll repeat the question: do you want the same glass shelves put up on a different wall or would you prefer a free-standing unit?

Joe

From: **Rebecca Harris 27.09.11 17:38**
To: Joe Doyle
Subject: shelves or unit

Joe,

I do believe I have a right to feel a little bit irritated by this and to vent my frustration, but in the interest of keeping to schedule, I will try and make a decision as soon as possible, but I'm currently dealing with a staff situation so I haven't had time to think.

Rebecca

From: **Rebecca Harris 27.09.11 17:40**
To: Phoebe Combes
Subject: conduct unbecoming

Phoebe, I saw you sneak in. Don't you think you have a bit of explaining to do?

From: **Phoebe Combes 27.09.11 17:41**
To: Rebecca Harris
Subject: Re: conduct unbecoming

Yes, I absolutely do, Rebecca, and I was just about to email you. I am so so sorry about the incident in the storeroom, it was completely out of character. I really don't know how it happened. I am so embarrassed, you must think . . . well, I don't know what you must think, but please know that I certainly wasn't thinking at the time.

From: **Rebecca Harris 27.09.11 17:44**
To: Phoebe Combes
Subject: Re: conduct unbecoming

Phoebe, I'll tell you what I think; I am gob smacked that you had the audacity to have sex in a completely packed nail bar, in the middle of the afternoon with a virtual stranger. I can only imagine that, like you said, you weren't thinking. I know it's not the worse thing in the world, but to be honest, if this or anything like this happens again, I will have to let you go. You should also know that Suki is seriously upset so you need to make a major apology to her.

From: **Phoebe Combes 27.09.11 17:47**
To: Rebecca Harris
Subject: Re: conduct unbecoming

Do not worry I will apologise to Suki and it won't ever happen again, I guarantee it. Thank you for being cool about it.

What a surprise that Tania's brother turned out to be such a complete stud muffin. I mean, he really is a walking sex machine, all testosterone and biceps and a butt you could crack a nut in. I took one look at him and I just knew I had to have him. I am amazed you resisted? The sex was out of control – some men just really know how to use it, don't they? Thank goodness the treatment rooms downstairs weren't being used because there was no way I could stop myself screaming out in ecstasy. I can't tell you what a completely unreal experience it was.

I don't know if you are in a relationship, Rebecca, but if not you really should go for Jeremy, he is utterly gorgeous. Personally, I'm not looking for anything long-term at the moment so I wouldn't mind at all if you wanted to have a crack at him.

Anyway, I've got to run as I have a date tonight. A lovely Puerto Rican guy called Alberto is taking me salsa dancing. I've always wanted to learn to salsa, it just seems so wonderfully romantic.

See you tomorrow, and again I really am sorry.

From: **Rebecca Harris 27.09.11 17:49**
To: Phoebe Combes
Subject: Re: conduct unbecoming

Thank you for that very detailed explanation. I really don't know how I resisted such a "stud muffin"? I obviously wasn't focusing properly. I am actually in a relationship, but thank you for, um, offering to share Jeremy.

We can probably now consider the matter closed.

From: **Felicity Jones 27.09.11 17:50**
To: Rebecca Harris
Subject: Brian is downstairs, see you tomorrow.

From: **Charles Balford 27.09.11 17:53**
To: Rebecca Harris
Subject: sorry, Gorgeous

Bex darling, stuck in meetings 'til late, have to cancel tonight, will try and swing by yours later.
Charles

From: **Rebecca Harris 27.09.11 17:56**
To: Katherine Lease
Subject: shit no date

Kat, Charles has just blown me out for our date tonight. I was really looking forward to seeing him and I even bit the bullet and told Vinca that I probably wouldn't come home tonight, so now she not only thinks I'm a slut but that I'm a loser slut on top of that. I'm feeling really flat, not helped by the onset of a hangover from lunch and everything going wrong in the office. I also feel horrible because Olly sent me an email earlier today telling me he'd bought me some silk pyjamas. He went miles out of his way to get them and I didn't even have the decency to email back a thank you because I was so busy getting drunk with you and celebrating an obviously misjudged level of confidence that Charles was crazy about me. It's now too late as he's on a plane heading back to London. He must think I'm an ungrateful cow.

I also lied to my Mum about lunch today, saying I was working, so not only am I a horrible, hungover, hateful person but I'm also a rubbish daughter.

I'm being punished for being so awful.

From: **Katherine Lease 27.09.11 17:58**
To: Rebecca Harris
Subject: Re: shit no date

Oh darling, poor you, I would suggest we go to the pub and get smashed, but it's opera night with Marcus and I'm so nervous I'll do something uncool like drop my popcorn everywhere and all the opera buffs will recognize me for the philistine I am.

You're not being punished or jinxed or anything and you're not awful. Charles is a shit for cancelling so late. Don't worry about your mum, what she doesn't know won't hurt her, and if she did know I'm sure she would understand and you can always have lunch with her tomorrow. As for Olly, he is more than cool and I'm sure he bought you pyjamas (sounds quite intimate, do we need to talk about this?) because he wanted to and not because he wanted thanks for doing so. Anyway, you can always send him a text now and he'll get it when he lands.

And for good measure, you're the best mum I know, so chin up, sugar pie, it ain't so bad. Kat xx

From: **Rebecca Harris 27.09.11 18:02**
To: Katherine Lease
Subject: cheers

Thanks Kat, you're a great friend. I will see what Clara is up to.

Don't get excited about the pyjamas, it wasn't a spontaneous romantic gesture on Olly's part. I asked him to get them for me, which makes my not thanking him even worse, but I will send him a text now.

By the way, I'm pretty sure you are not allowed to eat popcorn at the opera, so hopefully you will remain incognito.

From: **Rebecca Harris 27.09.11 18:06**
To: Clara Harris
Subject: hi, sis

Clarabelle, I'm sitting in the office on my own after another crappy day and I just got an email from Charles saying he can't make tonight (we were meant to be going to the movies). He's stuck in meetings but said he might be able to see me later. I know he can't help it if he has to work late, it's just I'm feeling a bit vulnerable about the whole thing. I haven't seen or spoken to him since we slept together and it just feels weird. I'm sure, as soon as I do, it will all be great again, but in the meantime I'm just feeling a bit low about it. Can we meet for a drink or is Johnny picking you up early?

From: **Clara Harris 27.09.11 18:11**
To: Rebecca Harris
Subject: hi to you, sis

Oh Bex, I'm sorry about Charles, but don't hang around at home waiting for him because he might be very late or not show at all, and anyway, it would be good for him to know you have a busy social life. It's very normal to feel a bit insecure at the beginning of a relationship. I have never felt secure in any relationship, beginning, middle or end, but as soon as you see Charles I'm sure he will tell you he adores you and you will be back on cloud nine.

I'm afraid I can't have a drink as Johnny is picking me up any minute. So excited. I'm wearing jeans and I splashed out on a new top from Joseph which I think is quite funky. Does that sound good?

Clarabelle xx

PS Ask Mum to the movies, I'm sure she'd love to go.

From:	**Rebecca Harris 27.09.11 18:15**
To:	Clara Harris
Subject:	hi again

Outfit sounds perfect.

I'll give Mum a call. I blew her out for lunch, which I'm not feeling brilliant about, so it would be good to take her to the movies.

Have fun. xx

From:	**Rebecca Harris 27.09.11 18:19**
To:	Bettina Harris
Subject:	movie tonight?

Hi Mum, just finishing up here at work and was wondering if you would like to go and see a movie with me tonight? I have tickets to a Bruce Willis movie and I thought it would be fun for the two of us to hang out. We could go to that Lebanese restaurant you like afterwards?

From:	**Bettina Harris 27.09.11 18:27**
To:	Rebecca Harris
Subject:	Re: movie tonight?

Bbeccy   at bridge cccccccccccccccccccclub. Not allowed to...@@ use blaackcurrrent sooory cannnnnot come to //////;;mov11ie –wwho is bruce illis?. Take tthat nice boy Olivver instead.

Ove   #~ ~   Mmummy

Message sent via BlackBerry ®

From:	**Rebecca Harris 27.09.11 18:29**
To:	Bettina Harris
Subject:	Olly

Olly is on a plane at the moment. Think I'll just have a quiet night. Have fun at bridge. Bex

Wednesday 28th September 2011

From: Clara Harris 28.09.11 9:20
To: Rebecca Harris
Subject: where are you?

Bex, I just tried to call the office and was told you hadn't come in yet. I'm guessing Charles showed? Dying to tell you about my date with Johnny, all quite dramatic . . .

From: Rebecca Harris 28.09.11 9:24
To: Clara Harris
Subject: Re: where are you?

Hi Clarabelle, I'm a bit late as I've just been out to breakfast with Olly. He called at crack of dawn to say he'd just got in from Hong Kong and was starving, so I went to meet him at the Brasserie in South Ken.

Charles never showed or called and Mum had bridge club. I sat on my own at home just staring at the phone. I know that was a stupid thing to do, but I haven't seen Charles since Saturday and it's really starting to get to me. Anyway, breakfast with Olly was great and he had bought me a beautiful pair of silk pyjamas, so I'm feeling happy again.

Now tell me immediately about the drama.

From: Clara Harris 28.09.11 9:29
To: Rebecca Harris
Subject: J v J

Ok. The evening was great and Johnny was so totally different from Jason. It really made me realize how much crap I had put up with for the last two years. We went to a great Italian restaurant. During dinner we talked and talked and remembered funny things about when we were all little together – I never knew you flashed him when you were only nine, you tart!

Now for the drama . . . when we got back to the flat, Johnny walked me to the door, but unfortunately Jason was just walking out at the same time. He looked at Johnny and me and then went into a whole tirade about how he had always known that I wasn't so perfect with my high and mighty attitude and "bullshit hypocritical morals". He called me a whore!!! He said I was worse than him because at least he hadn't pretended to be faithful. Johnny told him to back off, which made Jason go beserk. He tried to thump Johnny, missed, and

222

then ran at him like a wild dog. Johnny just stepped out of the way and let Jason run into the wall behind, which was quite awful as Jason was running really fast. Actually I felt a bit sorry for him because one of his front teeth got knocked out and you know how vain he is. We ended up driving Jason's car for him with him sitting in the back clutching his tooth in a tissue all the way back to Samantha's place.

How's that for an eventful evening?

From: **Rebecca Harris 28.09.11 9:33**
To: Clara Harris
Subject: Re: J v J

That has totally made my day! Wish I could have seen Jason getting what he deserved. Johnny is a rock star and has seriously gone up in my estimation, even though he promised he'd never tell anyone about the flashing incident.

From: **Clara Harris 28.09.11 9:35**
To: Rebecca Harris
Subject: flasher!

Yes, Bex, we need to talk about that.

From: **Rebecca Harris 28.09.11 9:37**
To: Clara Harris
Subject: Re: flasher!

He tricked me. I was 9 years old. It's Johnny who needs the talking to, not me!

From: **Clara Harris 28.09.11 9:40**
To: Rebecca Harris
Subject: Re: flasher!

Hmmm, I'm not so sure about that?

I'm sorry about Charles. Men can be so thoughtless sometimes. Try not to read too much into it. I'm sure he is dying to see you too but is obviously snowed under with work. Anyway, its good Olly is back, he always seems to make you happy.

I'm in the library and have procrastinated enough, so I better get on and study. C-belle xx

From: **Tania Cutter 28.09.11 9:42**
To: Rebecca Harris

Subject: Report for Barbara etc

Rebecca,

I'm glad someone else has made it to work today. I was starting to think there was a public holiday I didn't know about.

Jeremy is at Marylebone working on the treatment rooms. I have emailed Suki and assured her that there will not be a repeat performance of yesterday, and Jeremy has put a note on the till for her, apologizing for the incident. After the conversation I had with my brother last night, I feel confident that he is suitably contrite and will do the work well without any further mishaps.

In the meantime I have completed the report for Barbara and left a copy on your desk. You will see that our main competitors – California Nails, Ruby Splash, and You've Nailed It, are all retailing substantially less than us. Quick Tips is doing appallingly badly and so is The Nail Emporium. However, there is a new place just opened off Marylebone High Street (only a block away from us!) called Top Tips, which is doing phenomenally well. I haven't been there, but they seem to be retailing a huge amount, and when I pretended to book an appointment, they had no availability until next Thursday.

There is a message from Adam Green at Daniel Bernstein & Associates returning your call.

Tania Cutter PA

The Nail Bar Ltd

From: **Rebecca Harris 28.09.11 9:45**
To: Tania Cutter
Subject: Re: Report for Barbara etc

Thank you, I will look over the report.

Rebecca

From: **Rebecca Harris 28.09.11 9:50**
To: Oliver Barker
Subject: pig out

Olly, thanks so much for breakfast. Let's do it again next week, but it will be my shout and you mustn't let me eat so much, I feel quite sick. I don't know what got into me, why didn't you stop me?

From: **Oliver Barker 28.09.11 9:53**
To: Rebecca Harris
Subject: Re: pig out

I did try, but you kept saying you were starving and you looked like you were having such a good time. You're surprisingly cute when you're stuffing your face. Saying that, I don't think I've ever seen a girl eat that much . . . actually I don't think I've ever seen anyone eat that much. Where the hell do you put it all?

Just running into a meeting . . .

From: **Katrina Sparrow** bumble@yahoo.com **28.09.11 10:07**
To: Rebecca Harris
Subject: Blast from the past

Hi Beccy,

It's been such a long time since I've seen you, I hope you are well? Yesterday in my lunch break I went and had a manicure in one of your amazing nail bars, and I thought of you. I have to say, it was the best manicure I've ever had, and the place looked so cool. You have obviously done a re-vamp! The look is the same, only much better. The staff were very friendly and one of them even recognized me from when I used to go to your other nail bar in Westbourne Grove. I was also given a free Top Tips nail file with my bill, which I thought was a great touch.

Big congratulations on your success.

Lots of love,

Katrina

From: **Rebecca Harris 28.09.11 10:10**
To: Katrina Sparrow
Subject: Re: Blast from the past

Hi Katrina,

I'm really well and it's so nice to hear from you, it's been ages. I'm glad you had a good time at The Nail Bar but I just wanted to double-check something; was the nail file you were given just a good one, or was it actually called a "Top Tips" nail file?

Lots of love, Beccy

From: **Katrina Sparrow 28.09.11 10:14**
To: Rebecca Harris
Subject: nail file

It was called "Top Tips", like your nail bar. Surely you know that, or have you become so important that you don't get involved in the minutiae any longer, you high-powered woman!! Actually I liked your products so much I took some of the girls from the office back after work yesterday, and we bought a whole load of stuff. I will spread the word and hopefully business will continue to boom.

Let's catch up soon.

Katrina.

From: **Rebecca Harris 28.09.11 10:21**
To: Felicity Jones
Subject: Top Tips

Fi, I am feeling quite sick, and it's not just because I've got a full English breakfast swirling round my stomach, although that isn't helping. I've just had two emails confirming that a competitive nail bar has opened up right down the road from our Marylebone Nail Bar. Not only is this place very similar in look to us (one email was from a friend who thought she was actually in OUR nail bar), but there are obviously some of our ex-staff working there too, because one of them recognized my friend from when she used to go to Westbourne! The place is called Top Tips (such a stupid name), and according to Tania's statistics report (the other email), they are already doing a huge amount of business both in services and retail. This has huge disaster potential for Marylebone as new clients might get the two places mixed up and old clients might be persuaded to try something new, especially with our treatment rooms being out of order. Can you go over there and do some covert investigation? Try and find out just how similar they are and what methods they are using to attract so many new clients?

From: **Felicity Jones 28.09.11 10:24**
To: Rebecca Harris
Subject: staffing probs

Hi Bex, I'll get over there immediately, burn the bloody place down if I have to!

I'm afraid I've got some more bad news. Sylvia phoned me this morning – she had obviously reviewed her week with us. The abuse by Suki, followed by being shouted at by *The Mail on Sunday* journalist, then physically assaulted by Janine and finally losing an eyebrow, was all just too much, and in the cold light of day she has decided the job is not for her. This puts us in quite a critical position, staff-wise, for Kensington. We have Sally and Katya – manicurists (currently training at Westbourne); Sheena – beauty therapist at Marylebone (not getting much training as no treatment rooms in operation); and Maria Sanchez, the girl you interviewed who started yesterday at Mayfair but might well end up staying there when we eventually get rid of Janine – so I am only counting her as a half at the moment. The total makes 3 ½ . Not brilliant.

By the way, were you able to find out whether what Janine is doing is illegal or not?

From: **Rebecca Harris   28.09.11   10:27**
To: Felicity Jones
Subject: Re: staffing probs

3 ½ and no manager? And only three days left?

FUCKING HEEEEEEEEEELLLLLLLL

Fi, are you taking on board just how bad this is? Phoebe is sending out flyers left right and centre telling people to book now for appointments next week, and Sylvia said that, on the back of *The Express* article, she has almost fully booked the first two days after opening. WHO IS GOING TO DO THESE APPOINTMENTS? Please assure me that you're aware of the urgency of this situation because your apparent calmness is completely freaking me out!

I haven't had a chance to speak to Adam Green (the lawyer) yet re Janine.

From: **Felicity Jones   28.09.11   10:29**
To: Rebecca Harris
Subject: The Zone

Bex, you have *got* to get into THE ZONE in situations like this, otherwise you'll lose it. I look calm to you because I'm Zoning – "functioning in a highly efficient manner while under intense duress". You must have heard about Hirsh's 'Entering The Zone' (Fredrick Hirsh, German psychologist's new book, not to be confused with The Zone Diet)? Phoebe is seriously into it and she passed it on to me, so I'll put it on your desk when I go. It's genius, I'm telling you, and really easy to do, but you don't want to try it on a full stomach, so maybe wait an hour or so. Anyway, let me reassure you that the staff situation is under control. There is no way I will let you down, not a chance – seriously. You can totally relax, it'll be fine. In fact, Chantal (the manicurist who hated working at Harrods) is coming in this afternoon for an interview, so that potentially takes us up to 4½. You see? Nothing to worry about. Going to Top Tips now. Yes, it is a stupid name.

From: **Rebecca Harris 28.09.11 10:42**
To: Tania Cutter
Subject: urgent address needed

Can you get me Adam Green's email address?
Thanks
Rebecca

From: **Rebecca Harris 28.09.11 10:51**
To: Adam Green
Subject: unfair dismissal

Dear Mr Green,

Thank you for returning my call. I was given your contact details by Barbara Foreman from Nail Corp in New York. I run a chain of nail bars here in London and one of my staff has brought an "unfair dismissal" case against the company. Ms Foreman recommended that Daniel Bernstein & Associates would be the best firm to help me tackle proceedings.

The member of staff in question, Janine Azame, was fired by us last week following several verbal warnings and a final written warning for abusive behaviour towards other staff and the occasional client. I thought we had followed the correct protocol, but we have received a letter from her lawyer saying she has a viable case against us.

Today Janine returned to work demanding that we allow her to continue with us until the case is resolved – is she allowed to do this? I should mention that Janine is black, although not visibly so, and she is also accusing the company of racial discrimination.

I would very much like your advice on what to do.

Yours sincerely,
Rebecca Harris
Director
The Nail Bar Ltd

From: **Oliver Barker 28.09.11 11:14**
To: Rebecca Harris
Subject: I'm relocating

Hi, Bex. Remember I told you at breakfast that I had a meeting this morning to discuss some quite major issues with Sebastian Wright, my business partner and co-owner of Barker Wright? Well, I've just come out of that meeting and one of the main issues discussed was that I should relocate to Hong Kong. The idea has been on the cards for quite a while as we're doing more and more jobs in the Far East, and Seb and I have both decided that it's in the best interests of the company. The last trip just confirmed it. Seb has a wife and two kids, so it's easier for me to be the one to go, plus I love it out there. I won't be going until the end of November, but I just wanted to let my best friend (you) know, so we should definitely have lots of breakfasts before then.

Ols

From: **Rebecca Harris 28.09.11 11:20**
To: Oliver Barker
Subject: Re: I'm relocating!

Oh Olly, this is terrible news. I can't bear it. I know I should be happy for you but I'm not. I don't want you to go. I'm sick of London, the business is a disaster, everyone is in Hirsch's Zone apart from me, all my friends are married or in serious relationships and even my Mum has a busier social life than I do. I need you here and so does Poppy. She adores you and looks up to you. Admittedly she's a bit confused about whether she wants you to be her father or her boyfriend, but either way you're the most significant male in her life. Why can't Sebastian go? Hong Kong is great for kids. With all the beaches and Filipino nannies, it's perfect. My parents had a field day there (my father possibly a little too much so), and I loved my childhood. I can call him and tell him all about it. Give me his number, I'm sure I could convince him. They've just built a Disneyland there, for goodness sake, what more could he ask? In fact, for him not to move is actually quite selfish on his children, not to mention that London is becoming more and more dangerous every day. I read in the paper the other day that kids as young as 10 are getting ASBOs. I don't know how old Sebastian's kids are, but he can forget holidays in Tenerife – all the kids will be electronically tagged way before they have a chance to learn to surf. Honestly, it makes sense for him to go and he'd have a much better time than you. Please tell me it's not set in stone?

Sebastian's children are three and one so he has a little time before they become knife-wielding delinquents.

I'm afraid it's pretty much set in stone, but it's very nice to know I'll be missed. As far as you having no friends and no social life, that's ridiculous. You have a million friends, plus a budding romance (I'm not saying anything), and just a couple of hours ago you were saying what a great city London is.

I hate the idea of not seeing so much of Poppy, but I'll phone regularly and I'll make sure on my trips back that I see lots of her.

How is everything in the office today and have you been back to your builder about the smashed shelves?

How are things in the office today? . . . Well, let's see. I'm in discussions with a lawyer about an impending court case. A rival nail bar has set up right next to ours and is doing a huge amount of business. The Kensington Nail Bar is not going to be finished before the opening party to which nobody is going to come anyway. We've burnt the eyebrows off one of the Sultan of Brunei's daughter's face. We have only managed to recruit three staff for the new shop, and one of the girls from the office has just been caught shagging the builder at our Marylebone Nail Bar. And now your bombshell, so I'm not exactly humming U2's "it's such a perfect day" while tapping away on my keyboard.

You're my best friend in the whole world, Olly. No one else understands me and I'll be utterly miserable if you go.

Bex, please don't say that, because I really am going. Anyway, I can't believe you think I understand you as I never have a clue what you're talking about. What on earth is Hirsch's Zone, for example? Does it exempt you from the congestion charge?

As for your day, if anyone can cope with all that, then you can. You've always operated in near catastrophic conditions and emerged not only remarkably unscathed but more often than not, triumphant . . . apart from the time you locked yourself in the Westbourne staff kitchen overnight, and even then I seem to remember things turned out alright.

I'll miss you hugely too, but as I said, I'll travel to London a lot and you could always come and visit me. Doesn't your Dad still live there? Anyway, I'm not leaving for a while, so let's forget about it until closer to the time.

From: **Rebecca Harris 28.09.11 11:43**
To: Oliver Barker
Subject: Re: you'll be fine!

Things didn't turn out alright when I got locked in the Westbourne kitchen, don't you remember? I tried to crawl out the window and got arrested for breaking and entering and spent the entire night in a police cell. I wouldn't call that alright by a long stretch!

My Dad moved to Singapore with May Lin after he retired from the army.

From: **Oliver Barker 28.09.11 11:45**
To: Rebecca Harris
Subject: Re: you'll be fine!

Your distress call came at 11pm. I was at the Central West Metropolitan police station by midnight and we were eating burgers in Ed's Diner by 12:45am. I would hardly call that all night.

From: **Rebecca Harris 28.09.11 11:47**
To: Oliver Barker
Subject: Re: you'll be fine!

Well, this is my point exactly. What will I do if it happens again and you're in Hong Kong?

From: **Oliver Barker 28.09.11 11:50**
To: Rebecca Harris
Subject: Re: you'll be fine!

Sweetheart, I would love to be the one to bail you out every time you land yourself in prison, but I'm more than sure that there are plenty of others who would happily step up to the mark. If for some reason all your millions of friends as well as numerous family members, are unaccountably detained, then I will not think twice about jumping on a plane and coming to get you. Admittedly we might not make last orders at Ed's, but we'll be first in line for breakfast at the Brasserie.

From: **Rebecca Harris 28.09.11 11:52**
To: Oliver Barker
Subject: Huh

You've still ruined my day ☹

From: **Joe Doyle 28.09.11 11:55**
To: Rebecca Harris
Subject: glass shelves

Rebecca,

I still have not heard from you.

If you had come back to me yesterday with a decision we could have got started right away, but instead you got yourself in a tizz and wasted time worrying about the problem rather than focusing on the solution. I've offered you various options on shelving but you will have to tell me what you want or I can't help. It's typical of you women, you waste so much time fussing over the problem, you can't see past it to what is so often a very obvious solution. Only the other day my missus was complaining about being exhausted because she had too much housework and I apparently "leave all my shit everywhere", so you know what I did? I went out and bought her a new, state-of–the-art Phillips washer/dryer as an early birthday present. You see, Rebecca, women look at the problem, men look at how to resolve it.

I'm at Kensington for the next half hour, so if you could come here and take a look at where you would like to put new shelves and what type of material you would like used, then we can try and get back on track with the deadline.

Joe

From: **Rebecca Harris 28.09.11 11:56**
To: Joe Doyle
Subject: glass shelves

I'll come right now.

From: **Rebecca Harris 28.09.11 12:00**
To: Oliver Barker
Subject: double Huh

. . . builder nightmare continues, have to go to Kensington. Can't tell you what Hirsch's Zone is yet as haven't read the book, but apparently my life would be much better if I was in it.

From: **Adam Green** agreen@bernstein&associates.co.uk **28.09.11 12:06**
To: Rebecca Harris
Subject: unfair dismissal

Dear Ms Harris,
Thank you for your preliminary account of the case brought against you by Janine Azame. I think it would be best for us to arrange a meeting to go over, in detail, all the facts of the case. How would 9.00am tomorrow at our offices in Holbein Place suit you?
I will need you to bring along all relevant materials relating to Ms Azame, including a copy of her employment contract, any letters of warning she received, written complaints by clients and minutes of meetings in which verbal warnings were issued to her. All these will be crucial to your case. Also all paperwork you have received from her solicitor.
Yours sincerely,
Adam Green

From: **Rebecca Harris 28.09.11 12:11**
To: Adam Green
Subject: Re: unfair dismissal

Dear Mr. Green,
I can be at your office at 9am tomorrow and I will bring all the necessary paperwork.
Kind regards,
Rebecca Harris

From: **Rebecca Harris 28.09.11 12:13**
To: Felicity Jones
Subject: Janine, disciplinary procedure

Fi, do we have any records of meetings in which verbal warnings were given to Janine, or any written complaints by clients relating to

Janine, or anything at all relating to Janine, in the files?

From: **Felicity Jones 28.09.11 12:16**
To: Rebecca Harris
Subject: Re: Janine, disciplinary procedure

Er . . . not that I know of.

Going to get a packet of crisps, d'you want one?

From: **Rebecca Harris 28.09.11 12:17**
To: Felicity Jones
Subject: Re: Janine, disciplinary procedure

Shit!

Yes, cheese & onion please.

From: **Phoebe Combes 28.09.11 12:20**
To: Rebecca Harris
Subject: Tara P-T no show

Hi Rebecca,

Just to let you know, Tara Palmer-Tomkinson's agent called to say
she wouldn't be able to make the opening party. There's a new "I'm
A Celebrity Get Me Out Of Here" series being made, this time it's
set in the South Pole. Tara is one of the celebs involved so she has
gone skiing in Klosters with Prince Charles to do some "climate
training". She isn't back until the end of next week. I am definitely
going to watch the series when it comes out. Can you imagine how
dramatic it will be if one of the celebs gets eaten by a polar bear? I
can't imagine anything worse. I spent too many childhood
Christmases freezing to death in castles in Scotland with no central
heating and having to share three inches of bath water with my
entire family to ever want to go further north than Cricklewood ever
again.

From: **Rebecca Harris 28.09.11 12:22**
To: Phoebe Combes
Subject: Re: Tara P-T no show

Phoebe, you only get polar bears in the North Pole, but I agree it
sounds like a good series.

Thanks for keeping me posted

From: **Rebecca Harris 28.09.11 12:29**
To: Katherine Lease

Subject: zoned out

Hi Kat,

Charles never showed or called last night, Olly is moving to Hong Kong permanently and apparently I'm not coping very well at work because I'm the only person who doesn't know about being in The Zone.

How are you and how was the opera?

From: Katherine Lease 28.09.11 12:37
To: Rebecca Harris
Subject: Re: zoned out

Wow, I didn't think there was anyone not in The Zone, where have you been? Anyway, don't worry, everyone is now talking about Spacializing Your Mind's Aura – a new theory by a South American sociologist who has been studying Nahuatle Indians in the Sierra Norte Mountains of Mexico and has come up with a whole new idea that is going to blow Hirsch and his Zone out of the water.

The opera was amazing, I was completely captivated. Don't get me wrong, I still prefer a good movie any day, but I was surprised at how great this was. There is something to be said for a bit of culture once in a while.

That's really bad news about Olly leaving. Marcus got on so well with him and is always suggesting meeting up with the two of you. At least you'll have an excuse to go back to Hong Kong. You're always talking about wanting to go back and visit and now you'll have a reason to, plus somewhere to stay.

Not sure what you should do about Charles. He sounds like he's being a bit of a tosser.

Going to have a foot massage in Soho over lunch, want to join?

From: Rebecca Harris 28.09.11 12:40
To: Katherine Lease
Subject: no go

Can't, meeting Joe at Kensington to discuss shelves – so glamorous!

From: Felicity Jones 28.09.11 14:04
To: Rebecca Harris
Subject: Top Tips

Bex, this might be the straw that breaks the camel's back, so prepare yourself . . . Top Tips looks almost exactly like The Nail Bar except cleaner and newer. When I got there it was packed, and I spotted three of our ex-staff working away. It gets worse – I did a bit of research and it turns out that the owner is a Mrs Diane Shaker, who used to be a very frequent client of ours at Marylebone. The manager of the place is a girl called Lin Leung – surname look familiar? It should, it's SUKI'S SISTER!!!!

As soon as I found this out I went straight to the Marylebone Nail Bar and grabbed Suki. There was no time to wait for authorization or backup, I had to go all Jack Bauer on her, but I got her to fess up. It turns out that Diane Shaker approached Suki six months ago to come and be the manager at her new nail bar. She offered Suki a ridiculously high salary that she said she couldn't refuse. However, Suki played hardball and said that once Diane was ready to open she would come and do a trial week and then make a decision. In the meantime she offered to help with design ideas and staff hiring, for a small fee.

The days that Suki was missing from us and supposedly sick with hepatitis was when she was at Top Tips doing her trial week.

When it came to the crunch, Suki decided to turn down the job because she claimed she felt guilty about leaving us, and anyway preferred The Nail Bar – yeah, right! I think Diane Shaker wasn't able to come through with the salary she promised, and Suki thought fuck that for a game of marbles I'm out of here. Apparently Diane was furious with Suki and threatened to expose her betrayal to us. Suki then came up with the idea of bringing her sister in to replace her, and Diane was happy to accept the compromise.

I've told Suki that she has really over-stepped the mark and I'd be talking to you about what we plan to do about this. I reminded her that she was in breach of her contract on several counts and we would be consulting a lawyer on the matter. She seemed suitably distressed and promised to make it up to us.

My feeling is that in light of our staff situation we don't necessarily want to get rid of Suki, but we obviously need to impress upon her that what she did was totally unfuckingacceptable.

From: **Rebecca Harris 28.09.11 14:35**
To: Felicity Jones
Subject: Re: Top Tips

This really is too much! The camel's back hasn't just been broken, the whole camel has been slaughtered. I can't believe that Diane Shaker has done this, especially after we went out of our way to do her daughter's private party at Marylebone!

Well done you for getting things done in real time.

As for Suki, she is so far out of order it's not funny. How dare she ask for a pay rise when all this time she has been in bed with the competition! The audacity of the woman, trying to make us feel bad, that we weren't more considerate of her so-called illness!

I think you're right, we shouldn't fire her but we should make her seriously sweat it out and come up with a proposal of how she intends to make it up to us. Maybe she can be pressured to find some staff for Kensington, rustle up another sister or two?

I'm going to see Adam Green, our lawyer, tomorrow morning, about Janine. I'll ask him whether we can do anything about Tops Tips copying our look.

Did you see Jeremy while you were at Marylebone and did he look like he was doing what he was meant to be doing?

From: **Felicity Jones 28.09.11 14:43**
To: Rebecca Harris
Subject: JC

Yes I did and I nearly jumped him myself. My god that guy is seriously hot!! How can he possibly be related to Little Turtle? Can't we find him something to fix or paint in the office? The carpet looks a bit shit and the cupboard door is falling off in the kitchen. We could get him in here then jack the heating up really high and hope he takes his shirt off. What do you think?

Oh, Chantal's here for the interview, better go.

From: **Rebecca Harris 28.09.11 14:48**
To: Phoebe Combes
Subject: party update

Phoebe, I'm about to contact Barbara. Can you just give me a brief update on how plans for the party are coming along?

From: **Phoebe Combes 28.09.11 14:56**
To: Rebecca Harris
Subject: Re: party update

Yes, absolutely.

Out of the 200 invitations we sent out we have now had 86 "yes's" and 23 "no's". I have prepared 140 gift bags for women and sixty for men. The men's one contains a gift voucher for a Winter Pedicure i.e. no polish plus a selection of foot products, and the women's one is as we discussed. Staff have been told to wear their uniforms, which must be in good condition, and managers can wear their own clothes. I haven't decided what I'm going to wear yet, have you? We have 40 silver helium balloons with *The Kensington Nail Bar* written in pink on them arriving on Monday morning. Also arriving sometime around lunch on Monday, will be all the wine and champagne from Goedhuis & Co, and I understand that your sister will be bringing the flowers? I plan to be at Kensington from lunchtime onwards with any staff we can spare, setting up the displays, putting up the promotional graphics and getting the place looking good. I will also make sure that any paparazzi that turn up know where they can put their cameras. I will brief them on who's coming, what the new nail bar will be providing the local community with in terms of an outstanding service, and how our presence will enhance the whole Kensington High Street area.

The only thing we haven't made a decision on is background music. How about a bit of Latino salsa? My date last night, Alberto, turned out to be a little conservative for my taste, terribly sweet but just not for me. However, the salsa teacher, Ernesto, was wonderful, and he said he would make me a CD compilation of all his favourite South American dance music, so I think that might be perfect.

From: **Rebecca Harris 28.09.11 15:03**
To: Phoebe Combes
Subject: Re: party update

Phoebe, that all sounds brilliantly organized. The only thing that is bothering me slightly is the fact that we have only 83 people coming. Should I be worried?

From: **Phoebe Combes 28.09.11 15:05**
To: Rebecca Harris
Subject: Re: party update

Oh no, that's nothing to worry about at all.

From: **Rebecca Harris 28.09.11 15:06**
To: Phoebe Combes
Subject: Re: party update

Really? Well that's great, then. Thanks

From: **Phoebe Combes 28.09.11 15:10**
To: Rebecca Harris
Subject: No problem

From: **Rebecca Harris 28.09.11 15:16**
To: Barbara Foreman
Subject: News from The Nail Bar
Attach: Blue Strawberry canapés

Dear Barbara,

I am sure it feels good to be back in the Big Apple and I trust Conrad and the children are well and happy to have you home?

We are just a few days off the opening now and everything is fitting nicely into place. The salon is looking fantastic, bookings are flooding in and we have a great team who are undergoing final training. Felicity is holding a meeting for all new staff tomorrow morning to brief them on procedures to follow on Tuesday morning, our first day of business. I will be holding a meeting for all the office staff on Monday morning and will then be ready to meet you after that, if you would like to have a tour of the new nail bar before the party?

I have been in touch with Adam Green at Daniel Bernstein & Associates and we are meeting tomorrow to discuss Janine Azame's case.

Pink Mango contacted me yesterday and said the deadline for the canapé selection was this morning, so I went ahead and made a choice. If you could take a look at what I have chosen, and if you have any strong objections, let me know. I am sure I can make a last-minute change.

Tania's report for you is complete and I have taken a look at it and feel pretty confident that we are on track, as far as our competitors go. We are definitely in the top three performing nail bars and once we open Kensington and bring in the new retail products, I feel certain that we will become the UK's number one nail bar chain. You will notice in the report that a new place called Top Tips is doing rather well, but we have already been over to take a look at them and I am pretty sure they will not be too much of a threat. They obviously did a big marketing campaign before opening, which has got them off to a good start, but on closer inspection they look pretty chaotic and I think they will very quickly begin to struggle.

The owner of Top Tips is actually an ex-client of The Nail Bar who obviously saw how well we were doing and decided she could just copy us. This is of course very annoying, but not really such bad news as I know for a fact that this woman knows nothing at all about running nail bars. She is a bored housewife from St John's Wood with a ton of money (her husband is a multi-millionaire property guy) who sees this as a fun hobby.

Is there anything you would like me to arrange for you to do on Sunday while you are here, perhaps a trip to Tate Modern or the Tower of London? Let me know and I will be happy to arrange it.

Rebecca

From: **Barbara Foreman 28.09.11 15:34**
To: Rebecca Harris
Subject: Re: News from The Nail Bar

Rebecca,

My husband and children are fine, thank you for asking.

I received Tania's extremely detailed and thoroughly well-researched report this morning. I have it in front of me now, along with her comments, which do not express the same "gung-ho" attitude as you, but a rather more sombre and, I fear, realistic analysis of the current situation of our various competitors. She quite rightly expressed extreme concern about Top Tips and I am inclined to agree with her. The fact that this Diane Shaker is married to a wealthy property developer means she will probably be getting a very good deal on her rent and will be able to find new locations to expand easily. I am also surprised that the marketing campaign she successfully undertook did not attract your attention earlier. You should have known about her months ago, and the fact that you did not means you are not keeping your eye on the bigger picture. This has always been a problem of yours, Rebecca. You have a strong tendency to micro-manage, focusing too much on the less important details rather than on what is going to make the business grow. Your canapé list is a classic example of this. Do you really think I give a damn whether we serve crab cakes or spring rolls?

That aside, I received the latest press clippings sent by Phoebe and they are indeed excellent. The interview you did with *Tatler* was particularly good, ahd there's no doubt it will be good for business too. Keep this up, Rebecca, and we just might weather this god-forsaken financial crisis after all.

Change of plans for my arrival: I want to look at Kensington on Sunday morning, not Monday. Bring the new manager, and the two of you can meet me there at 9am.

I also need you free for lunch on Sunday as I want you to meet Hilary Shellwood – Nail Corp's Vice President of International Ventures & Marketing.

On Monday I intend to drive around each of the Nail Bars, so tell the various managers to be ready for me. I do not need you to accompany me as presumably you will have your hands full with preparations.

I have decided not to go to Hong Kong until Tuesday evening as I have some business I need to attend to in London. I would like to come to your office to meet your staff – most of whom only know me by name.

You mentioned that your friend worked in the Armani Press office in London. Check if they have the new *Amalfi* trouser suit with the satin cuff in a size ten and a cream silk blouse, preferably the one that ties with the bow at the neck. Have her send it all round to the Mandarin Oriental.

No, I do not want to go to The Tower of London or Tate Modern.

Barbara

From: **Rebecca Harris 28.09.11 15:44**
To: Barbara Foreman
Subject: Re: News from The Nail Bar

Barbara,

All of that should be fine and I look forward to meeting Hilary Shellwood. Will she be coming to the opening as well?

The *Tatler* piece has been fantastic for business. Between Westbourne and Mayfair we had a 25% increase in service sales and 15% in retail in the week immediately following its publication, and

last week we were still up a good 12% on last year. We have also had several phone calls from all over the world with people wanting to buy the franchise. Do you have any interest in selling a franchise to a Mustafa Koch in Instanbul or Ismail Bin Nadim in Qatar?
I'll get that trouser suit sent over to the hotel.
Rebecca

From:	**Barbara Foreman 28.09.11 15:48**
To:	Rebecca Harris
Subject:	Re: News from The Nail Bar

Yes to Hilary coming to the party and no to franchises in Qatar and Instanbul.

From:	**Rebecca Harris 28.09.11 15:49**
To:	Phoebe Combes
Subject:	end of month figs

Phoebe, your press package was well received by Barbara. Thank you. Just to be sure, Tania is doing the end of the month figures, not you, is that correct?

From:	**Phoebe Combes 28.09.11 15:50**
To:	Rebecca Harris
Subject:	Re: end of month figs

Absolutely correct, yes.
Unless of course you would like me to do them?

From:	**Rebecca Harris 28.09.11 15:51**
To:	Phoebe Combes
Subject:	Re: end of month figs

No, that's fine. I just didn't want there to be any confusion, that's all.

From:	**Phoebe Combes 28.09.11 15:53**
To:	Rebecca Harris
Subject:	Re: end of month figs

I am not at all confused. Do you want me to check if Tania is confused? `

From:	**Rebecca Harris 28.09.11 15:54**
To:	Phoebe Combes
Subject:	Re: end of month figs

No, I'm sure she's fine. Why are you wearing glasses, by the way?

From: **Phoebe Combes 28.09.11 15:55**
To: Rebecca Harris
Subject: new image

Oh, it's just a new look I'm trying out. I felt like a change of image. I was planning on getting highlights but then I found out how expensive they were so I thought I'd try glasses instead. What do you think?

From: **Rebecca Harris 28.09.11 15:57**
To: Phoebe Combes
Subject: Re: new image

I think they look good, very intellectual. But be careful you don't damage your eyes. You shouldn't really wear prescription lenses if you don't need them.

From: **Phoebe Combes 28.09.11 15:59**
To: Rebecca Harris
Subject: new image

They're an old pair of my mum's and the lenses fell out years ago so I'm just wearing the frames, which is perfect because I have a mild case of conjunctivitis (fingers crossed I didn't give it to Jeremy) and it means I can put my eye drops in without having to take my glasses off – how convenient is that?

From: **Rebecca Harris 28.09.11 16:02**
To: Phoebe Combes
Subject: Re: new image

I'm definitely crossing my fingers, Phoebe. The last thing I need is for Jeremy to start drilling into the wrong walls because his eyes are all stuck together!

From: **Felicity Jones 28.09.11 16:05**
To: Rebecca Harris
Subject: Chantal

Bex, great news – Chantal is joining the Kensington team. She is a fantastic manicurist and a pretty good beauty therapist as well. The only annoying thing is she has to serve out two weeks' notice with Harrods, so she will not be around when we first open.

From: **Rebecca Harris 28.09.11 16:07**
To: Felicity Jones
Subject: Ken. manager needed, urgent

Fi, that really is good news, but we're still desperately short and I've just received an email from Barbara who wants to meet the new manager this Sunday!

From: **Felicity Jones 28.09.11 16:11**
To: Rebecca Harris
Subject: Re: Ken. manager needed, urgent

Oh SHIT. That might be a problem. Maybe we can just get one of the other managers to pose as the new manager and Barbara won't know the difference? Going to get a flapjack from Charlie's, do you want one?

From: **Rebecca Harris 28.09.11 16:13**
To: Felicity Jones
Subject: Re: Ken. manager needed, urgent

I thought of that, but Barbara also wants to meet all the other managers on Monday, so that wouldn't work.
Prefer a chocolate brownie.

From: **Rebecca Harris 28.09.11 16:40**
To: Katherine Lease
Subject: no CB

Kat, Charles hasn't called all day. Don't you think that's strange? I haven't seen him for four days, not since we slept together. After he cancelled on me last night I would have thought he would call, wouldn't you? I'm starting to have a bad feeling about this. Maybe I wasn't as good in bed as I thought I was? Maybe, like I feared, he doesn't like the idea of dating a mum, or maybe I'm too fat for him, or maybe he just doesn't like me full stop. Do you think he just might not like me? What should I do?

From: **Katherine Lease 28.09.11 16:47**
To: Rebecca Harris
Subject: Re: no CB

Bex, just because he hasn't called doesn't mean there is anything wrong with you. It means he's an inconsiderate arsehole. Most men are, it's not a huge deal, but you just have to be on your guard and be prepared to be disappointed. I also think he's being pretty immature and obviously doesn't understand women – again, most men don't, but at least the mature ones try. Bex, any guy would be lucky as all hell to have you so don't you dare start thinking you're not good enough for Charles. Give it another day and if you haven't heard from him we need to start working on a plan B.

In the meantime, Marcus and I are going to the Comedy Club Friday night and really want you to join us – it always makes me laugh my head off and it's just what you need. Come with us . . . and if you haven't heard from Charles by then, bring Olly. I have 4 tickets.

From:	**Rebecca Harris 28.09.11 16:51**
To:	Katherine Lease
Subject:	Re: no CB

Thanks, Kat, I would love to. I know you're probably right about Charles but we had such a good time at the weekend and I really felt that he was on my wavelength. I just don't understand it.

From:	**Katherine Lease 28.09.11 16:53**
To:	Rebecca Harris
Subject:	Re: no CB

I know darling, it really is crap. Listen, I'm off to your Westbourne Nail Bar for a manicure. I'm going to call you from there and we can have a proper chat.

From:	**Rebecca Harris 28.09.11 16:54**
To:	Katherine Lease
Subject:	Ok, thanks

From:	**Suki Leung 28.09.11 17:03**
To:	Rebecca Harris
Subject:	Suki make nice nail bar

Rebecca,

I know you not happy with me and sister Lin. You think we are devil, try to steal business idea and go work for Shaker lady, but we not like that. I work very hard, try to support big family, always send money home and not keep money for Suki. Rich lady she want to give me big money. I not say no because I think of family, not because I greedy. Suki never go expensive shopping, never eat nice restaurant, always live like shit. I know now that Shaker Lady is liar to Suki, not give money like she say, so I not go to her nail bar. She very, very angry so I give her Lin and I stay here. Lin not happy but she owe Suki big favour (I make angry boyfriend disappear so Lin not have trouble anymore) so she not refuse me.

Rebecca, I make sure Shaker nail bar not do well. Suki know ways to cause trouble. You don't think about it anymore and if somebody ask you, you say you know nothing.

English builder not so bad, work hard and not too noisy, but you tell Phoebe she not welcome here.

Suki

From: Rebecca Harris **28.09.11 17:11**
To: Felicity Jones
Subject: Suki!!!

Fi, I have just had an email from Suki that totally confirms our suspicions that she's a Triad. She basically told me that we would not have any problems from Top Tips in the future and she wouldn't be surprised if they went out of business very soon. Makes me very nervous.

From: Felicity Jones **28.09.11 16:14**
To: Rebecca Harris
Subject: Re: Suki!!!

Yeah, me too, but there's a part of me that gets a bit of a kick out of the whole death and vendetta stuff. The good news is we can now totally relax about the competition, and if Top Tips suddenly bursts into flames on Friday morning, well, we know nothing about it, right? Actually, you better delete this email and yours to me afterwards – just to be safe.

How good was your brownie, by the way? I think my flapjack might have been the most delicious thing I've eaten in my entire life.

From: Rebecca Harris **28.09.11 17:16**
To: Felicity Jones
Subject: yummy

Yeah, mine was really good too.

Thursday 29th September 2011

To: Felicity Jones
Subject: Janine

Fi, I think you're in a staff meeting but I just wanted to let you know what Adam Green said about Janine. We have two options; either we allow Janine to continue working at Mayfair while the case is being argued, or we have to pay her full salary but she doesn't work. I know she's a massive liability but I think we have to go for option one because of our staff shortage. The whole thing is so ridiculous and completely biased towards the employee, it makes me furious. The only upside is that if Janine places a foot wrong while working for us, then it could damage her case. Adam suggests that we take a hardcore approach and go in "guns blazing", demanding that the case go to court in the hopes that she backs down completely, or at worst, it all gets resolved with a small, out-of-court financial settlement. Apparently this is the best we can hope for. Anyway, I'll let Andrea know.

From: **Rebecca Harris 29.09.11 10:21**
To: Andrea Moleno
Subject: Janine

Hi Andrea,

I've just come from a meeting with our lawyer about Janine. I'm afraid we have to let her continue working with us for the time being until the case is settled, which we will of course try and do as quickly as possible. Her lawyer will have warned her that anything equating to "misconduct" could damage her case, so hopefully she won't be stupid enough to muck around. Please report to me immediately if you feel that her behaviour is upsetting clients or other staff in any way.

How is the new girl Maria doing, and has Monica got her confidence back?

Rebecca

From: **Andrea Moleno 9.09.11 10:29**
To: Rebecca Harris
Subject: golden hand

Rebecca, Janine didn't turn up today so I have asked Felicity to see if she can find someone to cover, but I think she is still in a staff meeting. There is something else that I am not sure what to do with – about 20 minutes ago a delivery truck pulled up and five guys got out carrying an enormous statue in the shape of a gold-painted hand. When I say enormous, I mean it's the size of a Smart car, and it has what I think are semi-precious gemstones on each of the finger nails. There was a card attached which reads: To all the wonderful staff at The Nail Bar. We are exceedingly grateful for the beauty enhancements you have afforded us. Our visit to the United Kingdom has been a most favourable one and we look forward to returning to your prestigious Nail Bar when we next make our presence in the great City of London. May Allah in all his wisdom grant you eternal happiness and many children. The daughters of the Sultan of Brunei.

Sorry to bother you with this, but it's taking up a huge amount of room in the entrance way. Do you have any suggestions?

Maria is doing very well and Monica is feeling much happier since the arrival of the hand.

Andrea

From: **Rebecca Harris 29.09.11 10:34**
To: Andrea Moleno
Subject: Re: golden hand

Andrea,

I think I'll have to come back to you on what to do with the hand.

From: **Rebecca Harris 29.09.11 10:37**
To: Phoebe Combes
Subject: Re: golden hand

Hi Phoebe, I've just been told by Andrea that a giant gold statue in the shape of a hand has arrived at the Mayfair Nail Bar – a gift from the Sultan of Brunei's daughters. Andrea doesn't know where to put it and I was wondering if you thought it would be a good PR move to put it outside Kensington for the opening party? I'm sure it's completely hideous, but the paparazzi might be impressed that the Sultan's family are clients of the nail bar. What do you think?

Rebecca

From: **Phoebe Combes 29.09.11 10:42**
To: Rebecca Harris

Subject: Re: golden hand

Rebecca, I think that sounds like a fantastic idea. I'll get a moving van to bring it here until Monday and then we can take it over on the morning of the party, along with all the other kit.

From: **Katherine Lease 29.09.11 11:01**
To: Rebecca Harris
Subject: bored

Hi Bex, just got in to the office. Things are pretty slow today as the boss is in Paris. Actually there's been nothing to do here since London Fashion week finished two weeks ago and I'm bored out of my mind. The girls in the office are all just sitting around reading fashion mags and hanging out. I'm eating the world's biggest chocolate croissant (Marcus says I'm too thin) and reading *The News of the World* – did you know that Honeysuckle Jones is going to give birth any day now and she's letting *OK* magazine photograph the whole thing?! Apparently Pete Jones is not entirely happy that the world is going to see his wife's noonie, but Honeysuckle is saying that it's nature and a beautiful moment to share with her fans. How totally off the mark is that?
Might go for a bit of retail therapy at lunch, wanna come along?
PS Went along to Westbourne after work yesterday. Had an excellent manicure with a girl called Katya – the girl knows how to give a good paint job! With all those cool piercings you should put her on the front desk, funk the place up a bit.

From: **Rebecca Harris 29.09.11 11:07**
To: Katherine Lease
Subject: Charles

Hi Kat. Lucky you. Opposite here, all very hectic, no way have time to shop at lunch. Would kill for a chocolate croissant as starving, but told myself if I stick to diet then maybe Charles will call.
I left a message for him yesterday but heard nothing back. It's so weird coz when we're together he's really lovely and tells me he's crazy about me and stuff. He even teases me for being hard to get and says he's much more into me than I am to him. Then when I call him he never comes back to me. I don't know how I'm meant to behave or what he really wants. It's all a bit confusing.
I didn't know Honeysuckle was pregnant? I saw a picture of her in

250

Heat mag. in August. She was topless, drinking Crystal champagne on P.Diddy's super-yacht in Saint Tropez and she didn't look at all pregnant.

Glad manicure was good. Can't put Katya on front desk as she doesn't speak English.

From: **Katherine Lease 29.09.11 11:13**
To: Rebecca Harris
Subject: Re: Charles

That's weird, I thought we had a really good conversation . . . she must be a great listener.

I remember that picture of Honeysuckle because it caused major problems at the time. One of the photographers we use also freelances for *Vogue* and he gave me the skinny on the whole thing. She had just signed a contract with Clarins to be their new SPF 50 girl and a month later they found out she was pregnant. This of course was a nightmare for Clarins because the ad campaign wasn't being shot for another three months and Honeysuckle would have been six months pregnant by then – not ideal for bikini modelling. Clarins just had to suck it up because they knew it would cause a stink if they fired her on the back of it. It was just pure luck that the P.Diddy photos hit the press shortly after because the contract firmly stipulated that Honeysuckle was not allowed to appear topless in public while she was under contract. This gave them a legitimate excuse to dump her, which they promptly did.

Bex, Charles is messing with your head and you're too good to tolerate that kind of crap. There's no way you should be starving yourself for that little shit. Anyway, sex appeal is all about confidence, not weight, so believe that you're fabulous and everyone else will too. Don't call him anymore, let him call you.

PS If you change your mind about shopping, let me know.

From: **Rebecca Harris 29.09.11 11:16**
To: Katherine Lease
Subject: Re: Charles

Wow! I am so out of touch, I had no idea about any of that Honeysuckle stuff? This is the problem with my job, I never get the chance to read magazines anymore. I'm cocooned in a world of nail polish, nightmare builders, unreliable staff and a Nazi boss, while other girls like you get to hang out with models, borrow cool clothes and chat away about celebrities. How did I get it so wrong?

I won't call Charles but I might just send him an email to check he's coming to the opening party on Monday.

From: **Rebecca Harris 29.09.11 11:25**
To: Felicity Jones
Subject: Katya/Honeysuckle

Fi, how did the meeting go?

Will you double check whether Katya can speak English?

Did you know that Honeysuckle Jones is pregnant?

From: **Felicity Jones 29.09.11 11:30**
To: Rebecca Harris
Subject: Re: Katya/Honeysuckle

Of course I did. She's about to give birth and be photographed doing it. In school I used to pretend she was my sister because we shared the same last name, but then she was caught giving a traffic warden a blow job so I quickly cut all sibling ties.

I'm going to send Karen Johnson to Mayfair to fill in for Janine today. If Janine is gone for good, then Maria will have to stay at Mayfair, bringing us back down to three staff for Kensington, which is a shame. Suki said she might have an idea, so I'll follow up on that.

PS If Katya can speak English, then I'm a leprechaun.

From: **Rebecca Harris 29.09.11 11:33**
To: Felicity Jones
Subject: "a SHAME"???

Felicity, a shame is when you break a tea cup or forget a friend's birthday. This is not a shame. This is an ALMIGHTY BLOODY CASTASTROPHE. Zone or no Zone, you do not have this in proportion. I'm going out of my mind with worry. How can we possibly open with three staff?! Where is Phoebe? We need to chuck money at the problem and get some ads in the Evening Standard NOW!

From: **Felicity Jones 29.09.11 11:37**
To: Rebecca Harris
Subject: Re: "a SHAME"???

Bex, I know it's really bad news. Derek once superglued his hand to his arse when trying to put an Ikea table together. He got an itch in his crack mid-assemble and without thinking he scratched it. The idiot ended up in Casualty; so believe me, I have this in proportion and I know what a total cock up looks like when I see one.

I spoke to our two recruitment agencies, even though we vowed we'd never use them again. They have a few possibilities but their finder's fee has gone up another 20% and we only have one month to decide if the member of staff is working out, or we don't get our money back. As you know, we have never had much success with anyone they have given us and it's always taken more than a month to realize they're no good. Anyway, as it's an emergency they are sending over two CVs for me to look at.

Phoebe has gone around to the nail bars to put up Early Closing notices for Monday and to organize moving the Hand to the office.

From: **Rebecca Harris 29.09.11 11:39**
To: Felicity Jones
Subject: recruitment

What about the new Kensington girls? Would any of them make a good manager?

From: **Felicity Jones 29.09.11 11:42**
To: Rebecca Harris
Subject: Re: recruitment

I was hoping that one of them might be good management material, but unfortunately the only one with experience in this area is Katya and I just don't think we can have someone greeting clients in a foreign language. I also think Barbara might be a bit freaked out by someone with that much facial piercing, so the search for a manager continues.

I'm about to head to Mayfair to check on Andrea.

From: **Rebecca Harris 29.09.11 11:45**
To: Felicity Jones
Subject: Re: recruitment

Have you got any more interviews today or tomorrow or anyone you are still waiting to hear back from?

Felicity Jones 29.09.11 11:48
To: Rebecca Harris
Subject: Re: recruitment

I don't have any more interviews today, but I'm still waiting to hear back from a potentially excellent girl. I didn't want to tell you about her in case you got too excited, but I'm feeling very confident that she'll accept my offer. She's called Petra and is a highly qualified beauty therapist. She said that out of all the nail bars she had seen in London, ours was definitely the place she would most like to work. She managed a chain of nail bars in Ireland, but recently moved here with her husband. She promised that I would hear back from her before the weekend, so I'll let you know as soon as I hear anything.

From: **Rebecca Harris 29.09.11 11:50**
To: Felicity Jones
Subject: Re: recruitment

Great, that sounds really hopeful, thank god!

From: **Rebecca Harris 29.09.11 11:55**
To: Joe Doyle
Subject: Ken. Building Works

Joe,
I'm going to go to Kensington at lunchtime today to check on progress and take a look at the new ventilation system. I'm assuming the ceiling is back up and painted? Will you be around?
Rebecca

From: **Rebecca Harris 29.09.11 12:14**
To: Suki Leung
Subject: your behaviour

Suki, by the time I got your email yesterday, I had already heard about how you went behind our back to go and work with Diane Shaker, and I'm not only surprised but also very angry. The fact that you encouraged ex-employees of ours to go and work with her adds insult to injury. On top of this you helped with the design of Top Tips with the result that it is an almost exact copy of us. That is about as uncool as it gets.

All of this could possibly have been forgiven if you hadn't deliberately lied to us about being sick with hepatitis while you were in fact working for them. You have blatantly deceived us and I

254

hope you realise that this is completely unacceptable.

Yesterday I had every intention of firing you, but after receiving your email, and with further consideration, I have decided to give you a second chance. However, I expect you to make this up to the company in the form of exceptionally hard work, and ultimately running a very profitable nail bar with loyal and happy staff. If you think you are capable of this then I am willing to give you this chance.

I also insist that you have no further dealings with Diane Shaker or Top Tips in any form, and your goal should be to make sure that we do not lose any customers to them. If you feel that this will not be possible in light of the fact that your sister is the manager there, then you must let me know immediately.

Rebecca

From:	**Joe Doyle 29.09.11 12:20**
To:	Rebecca Harris
Subject:	Re: Ken. Building Works

Rebecca,

I won't be in the Ken. Nail Bar today as my son is playing in a football match at his school. Karl and Phil will be there, though, so you can sort things out with them. I'll come over tomorrow to tie up any loose ends, so I'll need you to be present to sign off on everything, probably around 5pm.

Joe

From:	**Suki Leung 29.09.11 12:25**
To:	Rebecca Harris
Subject:	no worry

Rebecca,

Don't you worry, Suki make nail bar most successful nail bar in country. Plenty money for you and you forget about Top Tips shithole. Shaker lady in big trouble with Suki but you lucky, Suki like you and like company. Jeremy finish work tonight so treatment rooms ready tomorrow. You right, Jeremy very hard worker, like Suki. Phoebe poison Jeremy, make him forget mind. Now Phoebe not here Jeremy very good boy.

Suki

From: Rebecca Harris 29.09.11 12:27
To: Tania Cutter
Subject: figures for September

Tania,

I understand from Phoebe that you're doing the figures for this month. I'm sure you're on top of this, but with the party approaching and everything that has been going on, I just wanted to check. Thanks.

Rebecca

From: Tania Cutter 29.09.11 12:30
To: Rebecca Harris
Subject: Re: figures for September

Rebecca,

I have not allowed the impending party to get in the way of my responsibilities. I will be presenting a copy of the figures to Barbara at the meeting as well as a brief summary of the company's financial situation.

I will need you to supplement this month's petty cash so that I can arrange for flowers on the Reception desk and in the meeting room as well as sandwiches and good biscuits for Barbara's visit. Please could you let me know the exact time of the meeting?

I am currently drafting up the minutes of this morning's staff meeting held by Felicity.

Tania Cutter PA

The Nail Bar Ltd

From: Rebecca Harris 29.09.11 12:35
To: Tania Cutter
Subject: Re: figures for September

Tania,

You're welcome to present the figures to Barbara at the meeting, but you might leave the briefing of the overall financial situation of the company to me, don't you think? I mean, it's probably a bit more appropriate coming from the Director of the company rather than my PA – just a thought.

During your unexpected mini break at the beginning of last week, I had to get Phoebe to do some of the accountancy work that had been assigned to you, which is why I wanted to be sure that there

was no confusion as to who was expected to do it now.
Rebecca

Hi Charles, how are you? I left you a couple of messages on your mobile. Did you get them? I just wanted to check you're still able to come to the Nail Bar opening party this coming Monday? I've just come back from a site visit and things are looking a bit less ready than I was hoping – yikes! Anyway, call me, as I really want to hear from you.
Love, Bex

Bbeccy darling. I'm doing   a little s   shopping and thought....i.....might pick up something ice for Poppy your big party >> on mondy – any suggestions?
Love mummy
Message sent via BlackBerry ®

Mum, that's so kind of you, thank you. Just so you know, Poppy's favourite colour is no longer purple, it's green. I'm hoping this phase will be shorter than the purple phase as I'm not crazy about the colour on her. There was a worrying twenty minutes when she contemplated orange, so I guess we should be grateful for small mercies.

Rebecca,
I would like an update on your meeting with Adam Green and the state of play with the lawsuit.

I have attached my itinerary for the three days I am in London – you will see that I have put in suggested times for my meeting with you and the new manager on Sunday, touring the other nail bars on Monday, and coming to the office on Tuesday. If for some reason there is a problem with this, please let Nancy know, but I would prefer not to make any changes.

Barbara

From: **Rebecca Harris 29.09.11 14:33**
To: Felicity Jones
Subject: ???

Fi, if we still don't have a manager by the time Barbara wants to meet one, have you got any suggestions?

From: **Felicity Jones 29.09.11 14:37**
To: Rebecca Harris
Subject: Re: ???

Yes I do – Phoebe.

From: **Rebecca Harris 29.09.11 14:38**
To: Felicity Jones
Subject: Our Phoebe?

From: **Felicity Jones 29.09.11 14:39**
To: Rebecca Harris
Subject: Yes, our Phoebe.

From: **Rebecca Harris 29.09.11 14:40**
To: Felicity Jones
Subject: Re: Phoebe

I'm going to need some medication.

From: **Felicity Jones 29.09.11 14:41**
To: Rebecca Harris
Subject: Re: Phoebe

Bex, it's not such a bad plan. Honestly, Phoebe will be great. She's so enthusiastic the clients will love her. Anyway, we still have all of today and tomorrow to find someone, so this is not the moment to panic.

From: **Rebecca Harris 29.09.11 14:43**
To: Felicity Jones
Subject: Re: Phoebe

You're right. Why panic now when I can just as easily do it tomorrow.

From: **Rebecca Harris 29.09.11 15:35**
To: Joe Doyle
Subject: Ken. deadline

Joe,

I have just spent the last hour and a half at Kensington tearing my hair out trying to communicate with Karl and the other deadbeat you have working there. The sense of urgency they need to bring to this situation just isn't getting through to them. The place is a MESS. The ceiling downstairs has been plastered, but cannot be painted until tomorrow when it will be dry enough, and the same goes for the wall upstairs, which means the shelves can't go up until Monday, so any attempt to clean the place tomorrow is a waste of time because it will be made dusty again from the drilling.

I tried to explain to your goons, but it just wasn't computing. The place needs to be finished by tomorrow 5pm latest (as agreed in the contract) as I have an industrial cleaning company coming in straight afterwards. I need Saturday and Sunday to unpack all the electrical equipment and products, and Monday to prepare for the opening party.

I'm afraid, Joe, that your men will now have to work on Saturday because otherwise there is no way the place is going to be finished on time. I will have to try and re-schedule the cleaning company, which is a pain in the neck. I don't see how you intended to sign off on loose ends tomorrow afternoon when clearly the job won't be finished?

Rebecca.

From: **Rebecca Harris 29.09.11 15:40**
To: Tania Cutter
Subject: any calls?

Tania,

Did someone called Charles Balford call while I was out?

Rebecca

From: **Tania Cutter 29.09.11 15:42**
To: Rebecca Harris
Subject: Re: any calls?

No, but someone called Barbara did.
Tania Cutter PA
The Nail Bar Ltd

From: **Rebecca Harris 29.09.11 15:48**
To: Barbara Foreman
Subject: News from the Nail Bar

Barbara,

The meeting with Adam Green went very well and he is confident that we will be able to put this whole matter with Janine Azame behind us in no time. Our primary objective is to get her to back down, but if this doesn't work we'll try to bring about an out-of-court settlement. Adam doubts that Janine will want to go to court because even with legal aid she would have to put up a certain amount of cash to do this. Unfortunately, she is allowed to continue working at the Mayfair Nail Bar until the case is closed. However, we are keeping a close eye on her to make sure she doesn't step out of line, and the manager there feels confident that all will run smoothly.

I have spent the last couple of hours over at Kensington making sure all the finishing touches are in place and bullying the builders – you know what they're like – into getting everything shipshape so that I can spend the weekend setting up.

I have spoken to my friend Katherine at the Armani Press Office and she is getting the *Amalfi* suit sent over to the Mandarin for you.

Rebecca

From: **Rebecca Harris 29.09.11 15:53**
To: Tania Cutter
Subject: re-schedule

Tania, can you call Spick & Span, the industrial cleaning company, and ask if we can re-schedule them to come to Kensington on Saturday afternoon instead of Friday evening?

Rebecca

From: **Joe Doyle 29.09.11 16:20**
To: Rebecca Harris
Subject: Re: Ken. deadline

Rebecca luv, I'm afraid that's a "no-can-do" for Saturday. Doyle

Brothers don't operate on weekends. You can jump up and down and rant and rave but it won't make any difference, my men are on five-day contracts and that can't be changed. The best I can do is have the place finished and painted by close of day tomorrow and the shelves will have to go up on Monday morning.
Joe

From: **Tania Cutter 29.09.11 16:19**
To: Rebecca Harris
Subject: Re: re-schedule

Rebecca,
Spick & Span cannot change the appointment as they are already booked for another job on Saturday. They also said there is a 15% cancellation fee.
Tania Cutter PA
The Nail bar Ltd

From: **Rebecca Harris 29.09.11 16:24**
To: Oliver Barker
Subject: where do I stand?

Ols, I know I always complain to you, but I need help again. My builders aren't going to be finished on Friday, the date of completion in the contract. They're also refusing to work this weekend, meaning they're still going to be putting up shelves and making a mess on Monday. This is a disaster because I need the place professionally cleaned at the weekend, so the shelves must go up before then. I had organized for cleaners to come in Friday evening but have now had to cancel them and they are fully booked for Saturday. I need the weekend to set up everything, and on Monday the place will be packed with people organizing the party, so we can't have builders in there. Can I legally force Doyle Brothers (the building contractors) to work over the weekend or after hours on Friday?

From: **Oliver Barker 29.09.11 16:30**
To: Rebecca Harris
Subject: Re: where do I stand?

Bex, the only way to have any leverage over Doyle Brothers is if you haven't deviated from the original plans in any way. If you have changed your mind about how you wanted something done, then they can use that as a reason for not meeting the deadline. Nearly everybody does change something, which makes it pretty hard to put the pressure on. Generally it comes down to the goodwill of the contractors, which by the sounds of it isn't going to happen with these guys.

You mentioned that you're having some work done by a different builder at one of your other nail bars – why don't you see if you can get him in to finish off the job on Saturday? I know this means more money, but if he is a small outfit then he might be willing to do it. No big company will want to take on such a small job.

I have a friend called James who owns a professional cleaning outfit called Guardsmen Cleaners. He's usually very booked up but let me see if he could spare a couple of guys to come in at the weekend. When would be the best time?

From:	Rebecca Harris 29.09.11 16:36
To:	Oliver Barker
Subject:	Re: where do I stand?

Ols, that is a brilliant idea. I will ask Jeremy if he can work tomorrow night as he is due to finish the Marylebone job this evening. If he can, then it would be great if Guardsmen Cleaners can come in early Saturday morning.

Will come back to you as quick as poss. B xx

From:	Rebecca Harris 29.09.11 16:38
To:	Suki Leung
Subject:	URGENT

Suki, I need to get hold of Jeremy urgently. Can you go and get him and ask him to call me in the office?

From:	Suki Leung 29.09.11 16:40
To:	Rebecca Harris
Subject:	Re: URGENT

Jeremy right here, he finish job already, he help me with till so I can look after customer, making more money for company. Customer like to see handsome man in window so good for business. I tell Jeremy he come to Kensington opening party with me.

From: **Jeremy Cutter 29.09.11 16:42**
To: Rebecca Harris
Subject: Re: URGENT

Hi Rebecca, I'm just manning the till for a bit as Suki had so many customers to deal with. How can I help?

Message sent via BlackBerry ®

From: **Rebecca Harris 29.09.11 16:44**
To: Jeremy Cutter
Subject: work on Saturday?

Hi Jeremy, thank you for helping out at Reception. I was wondering if you might be able to do a small job for me at our new Kensington nail bar on Saturday morning? I need to have some glass shelves put up. The walls are being painted on Friday morning so hopefully they will be dry by Saturday morning. I know this is very late notice and it is a weekend, but I thought I would just see if you were free?

From: **Jeremy Cutter 29.09.11 16:47**
To: Rebecca Harris
Subject: Re: work on Saturday?

That shouldn't be a problem, I'm happy to work weekends. But you need to check if there are any residential properties beside or above your nail bar. If so, do you have permission to carry out construction work on Saturdays?
I will get the address off Suki and head over there now to have a look. J

Message sent via BlackBerry ®

From: **Rebecca Harris 29.09.11 16:50**
To: Jeremy Cutter
Subject: no prob there

That's great Jeremy, thanks. I know that the properties either side are occupied by a hairdresser and a clothes shop and above us are offices, so that shouldn't be a problem. I will come and meet you there, but aim to get there at 5.30 – I want to be sure that the other builders have left so they don't get uptight about me bringing you in to do the job.

From: **Rebecca Harris 29.09.11 17:04**
To: Oliver Barker
Subject: cleaners

Hi Ols, Jeremy has agreed to put up the shelves on Friday night! If Guardsmen Cleaners can come in Saturday morning, that would be amazing. I'll then have most of Saturday to get the place looking good for when Barbara comes to see it on Sunday.

I have to go back to Kensington now – can you call me and let me know what they say?

Thanks so much. B x

From:	**Oliver Barker 29.09.11 17:16**
To:	Rebecca Harris
Subject:	Re: cleaners

No problem, I'll let you know as soon as. Ols xx

Message sent via BlackBerry ®

From:	**Rebecca Harris 29.09.11 17:19**
To:	Oliver Barker
Subject:	Friday night

I also meant to ask you, would you like to come to The Comedy Club tomorrow night with my friends Kat and Marcus? The plan is to get a curry first and then head on over to Leicester Square.

From:	**Oliver Barker 29.09.11 17:22**
To:	Rebecca Harris
Subject:	Re: Friday night

That sounds great. I haven't been to The Comedy Club for years, but last time I went it was brilliant. I have to go round to a mate's house after work tomorrow to pick up my tickets for the Chelsea match this Saturday. We're going to beat the crap out of Liverpool. Let me know where and when and I will meet you at the restaurant.

Message sent via BlackBerry ®

From:	**Rebecca Harris 29.09.11 17:35**
To:	Phoebe Combes
Subject:	Suki & J

Phoebe,

Just to give you a heads up, I think Suki may have taken a shine to your Jeremy – she's bringing him to the opening. I know you were very magnanimous and offered him to me, but I wanted to be sure you weren't just saying that, you know, just being kind, sort of thing. I wouldn't want you to be surprised or upset on the opening night – or worse, try and confront Suki and end up having your front teeth kicked in!!

From: **Phoebe Combes 29.09.11 17:39**
To: Rebecca Harris
Subject: Re: Suki & J

Not at all, I think it's wonderful. Actually, I'm not entirely surprised. When Suki caught Jeremy and me in the storeroom and was going completely mental, I caught a glimpse of the way Jeremy was looking at her. I thought he would be shocked or terrified but he wasn't, it was a look of respect with just a hint of lust. I know that sounds a bit freaky, but it wasn't – Suki is very Lucy Lui when she's going ape shit and Jeremy was really digging it.

Thank you for your concern, but I couldn't be more relaxed, especially as I'm absolutely head over heels in love with Ernesto whom I've invited to the party. Hope that's alright with you?

From: **Rebecca Harris 29.09.11 17:42**
To: Phoebe Combes
Subject: Ernesto

You mean the guy from Tuesday night?

From: **Phoebe Combes 29.09.11 17:43**
To: Rebecca Harris
Subject: Re: Ernesto

Yes, my salsa teacher.

From: **Rebecca Harris 29.09.11 17:44**
To: Phoebe Combes
Subject: Re: Ernesto

But you only just met him! At the risk of sounding old fashioned, isn't it a bit early to be feeling that strongly?

From: **Phoebe Combes 29.09.11 17:45**
To: Rebecca Harris
Subject: Re: Ernesto

I know, who would have thought? I guess you just know when you know. Saskia did say I would find love in an unusual place, and a salsa class is a fairly unusual place for a girl from Northamptonshire, so she was absolutely right. He wears a gold locket with the Virgin Mary in one side and he says he's going to put a picture of me in the other, which I think is just gorgeous, don't you?

From: **Rebecca Harris 29.09.11 17:48**
To: Phoebe Combes
Subject: Re: Ernesto

Yes I do, and I'm really happy for you, Phoebe.
Can't wait to meet him at the party.

From: **Charles Balford 29.09.11 18:01**
To: Rebecca Harris
Subject: sexy arse

Darling, grab your shortest, tightest, sexiest black dress, I'm taking you to the Ivy – as promised.
Pick you up at 8.30.
Have been thinking of you constantly.
C.

Friday 30th September 2011

From: **Rebecca Harris 30.09.11 9:04**
To: Clara Harris
Subject: beyond blissful!

Hi Clarabelle, I didn't tell you what happened yesterday . . . I hadn't heard from Charles all day and was feeling really down about it, when suddenly I got an email just before I was leaving inviting me to the Ivy for dinner. I phoned Vinca and begged her to babysit and she agreed.

It was all so spontaneous and great. We had the best evening. The Ivy was amazing and soooo glamorous. Madonna was there with her daughter (forgot name?) and Kelly Osbourne looking miles slimmer than she does on TV. Charles kept going outside to make work calls so I had plenty of time to stare.

Clara, he was so charming and attentive and he made me feel like a million bucks. I've been bouncing off the walls ever since. It's really put work in perspective. How can I possibly have been getting upset about such insignificant little things like shelves falling off walls, and staff not turning up to work, when I have the hottest guy in town telling me he's crazy about me?

Life is perfect and I promise never to complain again ☺ ☺ ☺

From: **Joe Doyle 30.09.11 9:14**
To: Rebecca Harris
Subject: Ken. Building Works

Rebecca,

I've just received a call from Karl saying that some toffee-nosed git by the name of Jeremy stopped by this morning at Kensington to drop off his tools. This geezer was bloody rude to Karl and told him that because we were doing a "crap" job, he had been pulled in to sort it out. Karl is extremely upset, obviously, and has come back to the office. I will not have my men falsely accused of wrongdoing by some wanker masquerading as a tradesman. Naturally I have told Phil, Alan and Rod (who were all on their way there) to turn round and come back to the office. I don't know what you're playing at, Rebecca, but as of this minute Doyle Brothers is terminating its contract with The Nail Bar Ltd and we'll expect payment in full within the next ten days.

Rebecca, if you think you can pull the wool over my eyes and bring someone else in without me knowing, then you're a bigger fool than I thought. You have insulted me and my staff by this underhand behaviour and I am well and truly pissed off. You're obviously ignorant of the strict code of conduct amongst building contractors. We never go in on someone else's job without first informing the other firm and coming to some kind of an agreement. You don't just sneak a new firm in while another one is already hard at it and almost finished. I have gone out of my way to tolerate your whinging and moaning throughout this whole project, but this is the limit.

No doubt this new guy is doing it on the cheap. Well, Rebecca, you know the expression – pay peanuts and you get monkeys.

Good luck with getting a monkey to finish the job before your big opening on Monday.

Joe

From: **Rebecca Harris 30.09.11 9:18**
To: Joe Doyle
Subject: Re: Ken. Building Works

Joe,

You're completely overreacting, I was in no way trying to deceive or undermine you or your men. I brought in Jeremy just to see if he could possibly put up the shelves tonight because I know how busy your guys are doing the painting. I didn't intend to insult you, but I have expressed countless times how urgent it is to have those shelves up by tonight so I can get cleaners in tomorrow. My boss is coming to have a look at the place on Sunday morning and I can't have it half finished.

Jeremy is the brother of a girl in the office and he kindly offered to help out. It wasn't like I went out looking for a new firm to take over from you. I don't know why he was rude to Karl and of course I'll get to the bottom of that, but in the meantime please could you send your men back?

Rebecca

From: **Joe Doyle 30.09.11 9:22**
To: Rebecca Harris
Subject: Re: Ken. Building Works

Automated response: Joe Doyle is currently out of the office.

From: **Andrea Moleno 30.09.11 9:29**
To: Rebecca Harris
Subject: no Janine

Hi Rebecca,

I hope the preparations for the new Kensington Nail Bar are going well? We are all very excited here at Mayfair about the party, and the girls are especially pleased that we're closing early on Monday.

I'm afraid Janine hasn't showed yet again this morning. She's always late, so I normally don't book anything for her until mid morning, but I think she may not be intending to come in today at all. Maria heard her talking on the phone to her boyfriend yesterday and they sounded like they were making plans to go to a concert in Brighton today.

We're fully booked, so I was wondering if you could spare any staff from one of the other nail bars?

Andrea

From: **Rebecca Harris 30.09.11 9:33**
To: Felicity Jones
Subject: someone for Mayfair

Fi, Andrea needs another member of staff as Janine is a no-show and she's fully booked. I know we're desperately short already, but try and miracle someone from somewhere – most likely Westbourne, they always seem worryingly quiet.

Having monumental drama with Kensington builders so can't help. Has that girl Petra confirmed yet?

From: **Felicity Jones 30.09.11 9:36**
To: Rebecca Harris
Subject: Re: someone for Mayfair

Morning Bex. I'm afraid to say Petra has accepted another job and the real bastard of it is, it's with Top Tips.

From: **Rebecca Harris 30.09.11 9:37**
To: Felicity Jones
Subject: Re: someone for Mayfair

FXXXXXXXXXXXCK!!!!!!!!!!!!!!!

From: **Felicity Jones 30.09.11 9:38**
To: Rebecca Harris
Subject: Re: someone for Mayfair

270

I know. How was your dinner at the Ivy last night – see any celebs?

From: **Rebecca Harris 30.09.11 9:39**
To: Felicity Jones
Subject: Re: someone for Mayfair

Oh Fi, this is terrible news. Every time there's a glimmer of hope it gets smashed down and we're back where we started, but with less time to sort things out.
Yes, saw Madonna – she looked amazing.

From: **Felicity Jones 30.09.11 9:41**
To: Rebecca Harris
Subject: Madonna

Oh my god, you lucky cow, she's my absolute hero. Still hoping she's going to bring fingerless lace gloves back in. I bought a pair after watching Desperately Seeking Susan but never got full usage out of them as they went out so quickly.
What did she eat?

From: **Rebecca Harris 30.09.11 9:42**
To: Felicity Jones
Subject: Re: Madonna

I think it was Tuna Carpaccio, but I couldn't see properly.

From: **Felicity Jones 30.09.11 9:43**
To: Rebecca Harris
Subject: Re: Madonna

Yuk! I hate that stuff. Why would anyone go to a great restaurant with a famous chef and then order something that isn't cooked?

From: **Rebecca Harris 30.09.11 9:44**
To: Felicity Jones
Subject: Re: Madonna

No idea, not my thing either.
I promised myself I was going to keep the staff crisis in perspective today, but please, Fi, can you try and make a miracle?

From: **Felicity Jones 30.09.11 9:46**
To: Rebecca Harris
Subject: miracles are my thing!

Don't worry I'm feeling quietly confident.

From: **Rebecca Harris 30.09.11 9:50**
To: Charles Balford
Subject: last night

Hi Charles, thanks for a great night. The Ivy was amazing, as was the whole evening. I'm sorry I couldn't stay over but my babysitter was doing me a big favour and I didn't want to push it.

I can't wait for tomorrow night. I miss you already.

Lots of love, Bex xx

PS Don't forget Monday night Nail Bar opening party

From: **Rebecca Harris 30.09.11 9:56**
To: Jeremy Cutter
Subject: everything's gone wrong now

Jeremy, why on earth did you go to Kensington after 9am this morning? I gave you the key last night specifically so you could get in early, leave your stuff and not risk bumping into the other builders. My contractor has now gone ape shit. He's just emailed to say that he's pulling out of the job because I've gone behind his back and also because you insulted one of his guys. What's that all about? I know you're doing me a favour by taking on this job last minute, but quite frankly I think you owed me anyway after using my store room as a shag den, and now I have a half-painted shop and no one to finish the job.

Rebecca

From: **Rebecca Harris 30.09.11 9:58**
To: Andrea Moleno
Subject: Re: no Janine

Andrea,

Felicity is going to try and find someone to help out, so please deal directly with her today as I have a lot on. We're all excited too!

Rebecca

From: **Jeremy Cutter 30.09.11 10:03**
To: Rebecca Harris
Subject: Re: everything's gone wrong now

Rebecca, I went to Kensington at 7.45am. The reason why your contractor found out about me was because I found one of his guys asleep on the massage bed in the treatment room. I think his name is Karl? There was food all over the floor and about seven empty beer bottles lying around. There was also a small DVD player plugged in with a pretty hard-core porn movie still playing on it. Karl was completely passed out and obviously still wasted, because when I tried to wake him up he was all over the place and quite abusive. I eventually got him up and out the door and I threw all his stuff out on the pavement. He's definitely been camping out in your nail bar for some time. He then flipped me the bird and staggered off down the street. So I think if anyone should be pissed off, it's me. I will happily step down from the job, which to be honest I was only doing because my sister works for you and I didn't want my indiscretion reflecting badly on her.

Jeremy

Message sent via BlackBerry ®

From: **Rebecca Harris 30.09.11 10:07**
To: Jeremy Cutter
Subject: omg

Oh god, Jeremy, I'm so sorry. I had no idea that Karl was sleeping there. I was given a completely different story by my contractor.

Please ignore everything I said and I really don't mind that you had sex in my storeroom. It's a very underused room anyway, and you work so hard it must be difficult for you to find time to conduct a normal love life.

I know it's a lot to ask, but is there any chance you could do the painting that still needs to be done at Kensington? It's only one wall upstairs and the ceiling downstairs, but it has to be done this morning otherwise it will never be dry for putting up the shelves tonight. It may already be too late, I don't know how long paint takes to dry? There is no one else to bring in at this late stage so I'm completely stuck if you can't do it.

From: **Jeremy Cutter 30.09.11 10:10**
To: Rebecca Harris
Subject: Re: omg

No harm done. I will change my schedule and head over to Kensington shortly. Paint usually needs 24 hours to dry but I'll see what I can do. Maybe the cleaners can start downstairs in the morning while I put the shelves up upstairs?

Message sent via BlackBerry ®

From: Rebecca Harris 30.09.11 10:11
To: Jeremy Cutter
Subject: forever in your debt!

Thank you so much. I can't tell you how grateful I am, and that would probably work all right with the cleaners.

From: Rebecca Harris 30.09.11 10:16
To: Joe Doyle
Subject: Karl

Joe,

How dare you make me out to be the bad guy when I have just discovered that Karl has been squatting at Kensington for god knows how long, watching pornographic movies and guzzling beer on my brand new massage beds. No wonder shelves fall off walls and nothing gets done right by your lot, they're obviously all hung-over and cross-eyed from wanking themselves senseless all night. I can't believe that you had the cheek to make me feel guilty for hiring Jeremy. I should have got rid of you and your useless team ages ago. I'll be consulting my lawyer about whether you're entitled to your final payment or not, based on this latest turn of events.
Rebecca Harris

From: Clara Harris 30.09.11 10:22
To: Rebecca Harris
Subject: Re: CB

Hi Bex, I know you are all excited about Charles and I don't want to be a party pooper, but I have heard from quite a few people that he is a womanizer. I know it's not good to listen to idle gossip but it has come from several quite reliable sources, and it worries me. Johnny knows him reasonably well and he doesn't have much good to say about him, so I would take things a bit slow if I were you. Clarabelle

From: Rebecca Harris 30.09.11 10:24
To: Clara Harris
Subject: Re: CB

Clara, you don't know Charles from a bar of soap and just because Johnny is now saying negative things about him, even though he told me he hardly knows Charles, you're now jumping on the bandwagon saying he's trouble. Just because Jason is an untrustworthy bastard, it doesn't mean that all men are.

Anyway, have you had any thoughts about the flowers for Monday?

From: **Clara Harris 30.09.11 10:27**
To: Rebecca Harris
Subject: Re: CB

I think that's a little unfair. Of course I don't think all men are bastards. I think Johnny's great and I think your friend Olly's a really nice guy, so I certainly haven't written off all men because of Jason.

As for what Johnny thinks of Charles, I didn't want to tell you this but I think you should know – apparently Charles spends a huge amount of office time talking on the phone to various different women. This wouldn't be a big deal on its own, but when you told me that he is always too busy to call or email you it made me worried. I don't think you should dump Charles on the back of this or anything, but I just think you should have your wits about you, and make sure he doesn't take you for a ride.

As the theme for the party is silver and pink I thought big bowls of peonies would look good and maybe some silver bowls piled high with strawberries?

I have my first exam on Tuesday morning so I have to get on.

From: **Rebecca Harris 30.09.11 10:35**
To: Clara Harris
Subject: Re: CB

Clarabelle, sorry, I know you're being protective, but it's difficult when everyone is going around saying negative things about a guy I'm really into. I know Charles had a reputation in the past but he's a different bloke now. He was so sweet last night and very attentive towards me and if anything, he was being more full on than I was. I know this might come across as arrogant, but I think he could well be more into me than I am to him. Throughout the whole evening he was so over-excited and giggly and kept saying what a good mood he was in. He's not the love of my life (I think I might have to give up on that concept) but he makes me feel good and I really need that at the moment. Hope you understand?

Peonies and strawberries sound wonderful. Don't worry about your exam, I'm sure you will sail through it.

From: **Rebecca Harris 30.09.11 10:57**
To: Tania Cutter
Subject: can you help?

Tania,

I know this is very last minute but we're having a small issue with staff recruitment for Kensington. Felicity has exhausted all the avenues that she can think of and I was wondering if you had any ideas where we might be able to find one or two manicurists or beauty therapists or possibly even a manager?

Rebecca

From: **Tania Cutter 30.09.11 11:01**
To: Rebecca Harris
Subject: Re: can you help?

Rebecca,

I believe that the situation in this office is becoming faintly absurd when I am expected to do my job, Phoebe's, and now, it seems, Felicity's as well. If I had known this was going to be the case I would have asked for a more substantial pay rise.

The only thing I can suggest is that you ask Jeremy. About three weeks back in June he dated a beauty therapist who was looking to move jobs at the time. I remember her because we all thought he would marry her (he'd never gone out with anyone for more than three days before that). I think her name was Suzy, and according to Jeremy she was extremely good at her job. That's the best I can do.

Tania Cutter PA

The Nail Bar Ltd

From: **Joe Doyle 30.09.11 11:07**
To: Rebecca Harris
Subject: Re: Karl

Rebecca,

I have just read your email and frankly I'm disappointed. I would have thought a girl like you, from a nice family and all, would have looked upon a man like Karl with sympathy rather than disgust, but I obviously misjudged you. Here is a hard-working guy fallen on bad times with no family to turn to, no home and no loving wife to make him hot meals or see to his needs. He was kicked out of his council flat three weeks ago through no fault of his own, and he has nowhere else to go. If he saw an opportunity with your empty nail bar equipped with hot and cold running water, heating and a bed, well then, who can blame him?

You people are always worrying about the starving kids in Africa or the homeless in Bangladesh, well – what about a bit of charity at home? Karl didn't do anybody any harm and so what if he wants to get his rocks off now and then watching a couple of lesbians go at it. A man can't think straight if he's walking around with a loaded gun. Now Rebecca, if you don't want Doyle Brothers to finish the job that's all well and good, but don't go getting messy with lawyers and that or things could get very unpleasant. You just send over that cheque so that we're all squared off and then we can all go our separate ways, none the better, none the worse.

Joe

From:	Rebecca Harris 30.09.11 11:14
To:	Joe Doyle
Subject:	Re: Karl

Joe,

I would hardly equate Karl's situation with the chronic plight of children starving in Africa.

I want no further dealings with Doyle Brothers and I certainly won't be recommending your company to anyone else. The final, very undeserved payment will come to you next week, and if that isn't charitable I don't know what is!

Rebecca

From:	Rebecca Harris 30.09.11 11:20
To:	Jeremy Cutter
Subject:	Suzy??

Jeremy, I know this might sound strange, but we're in bit of a bad situation regarding our staff recruitment for the new nail bar. We have exhausted almost all avenues we can think of so I've been asking the staff in the office whether they know anyone in the beauty industry who might be looking for a job. Tania mentioned that an ex-girlfriend of yours called Suzy is a beauty therapist, and I was just wandering if you were still in touch with her and whether she might be looking for a job?

I know you're already doing so much for us but it would be great if you could possibly let her know that we're recruiting, and would she perhaps be interested in a managerial or senior therapist position?

From: **Jeremy Cutter 30.09.11 11:28**
To: Rebecca Harris
Subject: Re: Suzy??

Hi Rebecca, I hate to tell you this, but Suzy was a topless dancer from Spearmint Rhino, not a beauty therapist. I didn't tell my family that because they're not very open-minded. She was something else, 34 EE, with a face like an angel and an ability to wrap herself around a pole that could make a grown man weep. I thought about marrying her but she was determined to go to America and be a Country n' Western singer – I woke up one day and she had gone. There was a note on the pillow saying she'd left for Arizona, and I never heard from her again.

Sorry, Rebecca, you're obviously having quite a stressful time, what with no staff and this place looking like hell. I wish I could help.

Good luck! J

Message sent via BlackBerry ®

From: **Rebecca Harris 30.09.11 11:33**
To: Jeremy Cutter
Subject: Suzy!!

Gosh, Jeremy, Suzy sounds really something and obviously very talented. I'm sorry it didn't work out for you guys.

Thank you for your concern with my staff problem, I'm sure everything will turn out fine in the end.

From: **Katherine Lease 30.09.11 11:37**
To: Rebecca Harris
Subject: your date!!

Bex, how was the date??? I haven't heard from you all day, what's going on? Where did he take you? What did you eat? What did he eat? What were you wearing? What was he wearing? He slightly left it to the final hour, are we cool with that?

I got your message; doesn't matter at all about tonight, definitely better to use up babysitting credits on romantic dinners/shagathons.

Tell Olly that he can come with us if he wants to.

From: **Rebecca Harris 30.09.11 11:40**
To: Katherine Lease
Subject: my d a t e!!!

Hi Kat, sorry to delay on the goss. My day has been spiralling out of control.

The date was perfect, very romantic and glamorous. We went to the Ivy where . . .wait for it . . . Ciccone mother and daughter both present with Kelly Osbourne at the next door table! It wasn't a shagathon because I had only managed to negotiate with Vinca for an 11pm curfew, but we're going out again Saturday night.

Sorry about cancelling tonight but I can't ask Vinca to cover again and I really want to spend time with Poppy as I'm not going to see her much this weekend. Xx

From: **Katherine Lease 30.09.11 11:43**
To: Rebecca Harris
Subject: Re: my d a t e!!!

How cool. What was Lourdes wearing? I'm of the opinion her fashion line has potential, but needs focus. What did Madonna eat – nothing, probably?

From: **Rebecca Harris 30.09.11 11:45**
To: Katherine Lease
Subject: my d a t e!!!

Lourdes that's it! Was trying to remember her name. She looked cute in sundress and laceup boots.

Madonna ate Tuna Carpaccio (marinated raw fish).

By the way, does Marcus remember that he is bringing his outdoor heaters for the party?

From: **Katherine Lease 30.09.11 11:47**
To: Rebecca Harris
Subject: your heaters

Yes, he's getting someone to deliver them on Monday morning.

Bex, I know what Carpaccio is, for god's sake, I work in fashion, remember. Madonna only eats raw food because she's macrobiotic.

From: **Rebecca Harris 30.09.11 11:50**
To: Oliver Barker

Ols, I'm really sorry, I have to cancel tonight as I can't get Vinca to babysit. Kat and Marcus are still going and said they would love you to go with them.

I fired Doyle Brothers this morning after discovering that one of their guys was squatting at Kensington, sleeping in the treatment room and watching pornos every night. It's ok, though, because Jeremy has stepped in and gone over there to do the painting, and he'll have the shelves up by the time Guardsmen Cleaners arrive tomorrow morning, and if not he said he will work around them.

Things aren't going very well here today but I won't bore you with the details because I know you must be sick of my constant moaning. Have you got a nice weekend planned? As I remember, you have a Chelsea match on Saturday. What are you up to on Sunday?

From: Oliver Barker 30.09.11 11:54
To: Rebecca Harris
Subject: Re: so sorry can't make it

Bex, I worry about you much more when you don't moan. Are you alright? Firing your builders on the last day of the job seems a bit radical. Are you sure that was the right move? I know this is a seriously stressful time for you, but things will be a lot calmer after next week so try to keep it all in perspective.

You know I'm here to help if you need me. Guardsmen Cleaners say they can start tomorrow morning, so will someone be there to let them in?

Don't worry about tonight, I think I'll take the opportunity to do a bit of homework instead. I'm giving a lecture on Sunday to a group of Brown University students who are here on an architectural exchange programme. Not looking forward to it as I'm sure Saturday night will be large.

Are you in the new nail bar all weekend?

From: Rebecca Harris 30.09.11 11:59
To: Oliver Barker
Subject: Re: so sorry can't make it

Pretty much, I've got to be there all day on Saturday unpacking boxes and setting up as Barbara is coming to look round on Sunday morning. There was no way I could keep going with Doyle Brothers even for another minute. They were a total nightmare. I feel much more confident with Jeremy.

I'm working on the perspective thing but it's a struggle. Have a great weekend.

From:	**Oliver Barker 30.09.11 12:03**
To:	Rebecca Harris
Subject:	can I help?

Poor you, that doesn't sound like much fun. Do you want me to take Poppy to the park on Saturday morning?

From:	**Rebecca Harris 30.09.11 12:06**
To:	Oliver Barker
Subject:	Poppy

That's so kind, she would have loved that, but my mum is going to take her to Alton Towers as a special treat.

From:	**Oliver Barker 30.09.11 12:08**
To:	Rebecca Harris
Subject:	Alton Towers

Cool – love that place! ☺

From:	**Charles Balford 30.09.11 12:12**
To:	Rebecca Harris
Subject:	tomorrow

Darling, would love to have gone out tomorrow night but I'm catching the sleeper train to Scotland – off fishing this weekend with some friends near Inverness. It's been planned for months. Did I not mention it? See you Monday.

Charles

From:	**Rebecca Harris 30.09.11 12:17**
To:	Katherine Lease
Subject:	Charles

Kat, Charles just sent me an email saying he's going fishing in Scotland this weekend. He told me last night that we would go out together tomorrow evening. He can't have forgotten that so soon, surely? I know he said it because we discussed going to The River Café and I said I'd never been there and had always wanted to go. He said the Scotland trip had been planned for months, so why would he not remember he was going just two days before the event? He must be lying to me. It was probably a last-minute plan, but I don't understand why he didn't just say that? I would've been disappointed but I'd have understood.

I've now got a miserable weekend ahead with absolutely nothing to look forward to. I've starved myself all morning for nothing. I desperately need to get into Hirsh's Zone so that I can have some perspective and not get hysterical, but there's so much crap to sort out I don't have time.

From: **Katherine Lease 30.09.11 12:20**
To: Rebecca Harris
Subject: Re: that little shit

Bex, Charles can go drown himself in a loch. What a selfish bastard. Who wants to go to bloody awful Scotland anyway? You either freeze to death or get massacred by midges. Also I've heard The River Café is overrated. A friend of mine went there for her anniversary dinner and she said her Jimmy Choos kept sinking into the wet grass and there was no sign of Jamie Oliver anywhere, which was the only reason she had persuaded her husband to take her there in the first place.

Cheer up, pumpkin, Marcus and I are always around to play with. No plans yet for Sat night but will keep you posted.

From: **Rebecca Harris 30.09.11 12:22**
To: Katherine Lease
Subject: no Choos even

Thanks, Kat. I think I would feel marginally better if I at least owned a pair of Jimmy Choos.

From: **Rebecca Harris 30.09.11 12:24**
To: Tania Cutter
Subject: golden hand

Tania,

I'm going to be out for a couple of hours. Phoebe will be back in a bit with a large gold statue of a hand which she needs to store somewhere until Monday morning. Can you move the table and chairs in the meeting room against the far wall so we can put it in there? Thanks. Rebecca

From: Rebecca Harris 30.09.11 14:06
To: Phoebe Combes
Subject: the Hand

Wow! The Hand is miles bigger than I expected. I asked Tania to clear some space in the meeting room, but there's not a hope in hell it's going to fit in there. Is there any way of putting it slightly more to the back of the office so that it's not completely blocking the entranceway?

I need a final count on numbers for the party so I can tell Pink Mango.

Did Felicity ask you whether you had any leads on staff recruitment? We're really desperate.

Did all the nail bars look busy when you went around this morning?

From: Phoebe Combes 30.09.11 14:10
To: Rebecca Harris
Subject: Re: the Hand

I'm afraid the Hand can't be moved. It can't get past the gap between the filing cabinet and the kitchen, and the filing cabinet is too heavy to move. It will have to stay where it is for now and I'll get it moved first thing Monday.

Numbers for the party stand at 97 "yes's" and 31 "no's", but I'm sure it will be 200 by tomorrow.

I don't have any leads for staff but I'll ring round some friends.

Nail Bars all looked packed.

I heard about the Madonna/Osbourne sighting – how exciting. What did Madonna eat?

From: Rebecca Harris 30.09.11 14:12
To: Phoebe Combes
Subject: the Hand

Tuna Carpaccio, it's raw, marinated fish. I've never tried it and I certainly wouldn't order it, but apparently it's a macrobiotic thing and that's what Madonna's into.

From: Rebecca Harris 30.09.11 14:15
To: Amanda Brady amanda@pinkmango.com
Subject: Kensington Nail Bar party

Hi Amanda, I just want to confirm Pink Mango's arrival time for Monday. The party kicks off at 6pm and is due to end around 9pm.

Parking isn't brilliant in front of the shop, but you can probably get away with 10 - 15 minutes for loading and unloading. Our staff kitchen is about the same size as the one you saw at the Westbourne Nail Bar so I hope that will be alright? Although we have not had all the replies in, we are still expecting around 200 people as we originally agreed.

I'll be there on and off throughout the day, but there will always be someone to let you in.

Kind regards,

Rebecca Harris

From: **Phoebe Combes 30.09.11 14:17**
To: Rebecca Harris
Subject: macro diet

That's right, I watched her Blonde Ambition tour and there was a lot of talk about her macrobiotic diet, but I couldn't really get the gist of it? How can a person only live off uncooked food? What about things like crisps, or biscuits, or bread – that stuff is already cooked when you buy it?

From: **Rebecca Harris 30.09.11 14:18**
To: Phoebe Combes
Subject: Re: macro diet

I guess she doesn't eat those kind of things.

From: **Phoebe Combes 30.09.11 14:20**
To: Rebecca Harris
Subject: Re: macro diet

What about pasta, or rice, or potatoes? You can't eat those raw and you have to have some kind of carbohydrate?

From: **Rebecca Harris 30.09.11 14:23**
To: Phoebe Combes
Subject: Re: macro diet

Phoebe, I really don't know, I haven't looked into it that carefully. I really have to get on!

From: **Phoebe Combes 30.09.11 14:25**
To: Rebecca Harris
Subject: no puds?

Sorry, I know, but just one other thought – no puddings? I can't think of a single pudding that isn't cooked, can you? Imagine no puddings for the rest of your life, my idea of absolute hell!

From: **Rebecca Harris 30.09.11 14:27**
To: Phoebe Combes
Subject: Re: no puds?

I agree. Actually I would have stumbled at no crisps, but can we talk about this later?

From: **Amanda Brady 30.09.11 14:40**
To: Rebecca Harris
Subject: Re: Kensington Nail Bar party

Dear Rebecca,
We usually get there about two hours ahead of start time. We have warming ovens in the vans so we won't need to use your kitchen to do any cooking, just to store the hot and cold food. Is there somewhere our staff can change, as they will need to do this just before the guests arrive?
Amanda

From: **Rebecca Harris 30.09.11 14:42**
To: Amanda Brady
Subject: Re: Kensington Nail Bar party

Amanda,
That is no problem, they can use the treatment rooms downstairs to change. Look forward to seeing you Monday.
Rebecca

From: **Phoebe Combes 30.09.11 14:43**
To: Rebecca Harris
Subject: jelly!!

Ooh, just thought of one – jelly!! I don't think boiling water counts, so she could totally chow down on that. What a relief, I was really starting to feel awful for her.

From: **Tania Cutter 30.09.11 14:46**
To: Rebecca Harris
Subject: the hand/Barbara - requirements

Rebecca,
I am finding it very difficult to manoeuvre around my desk with this

enormous gold hand right beside me. Could you please have it moved into the meeting room, which I specifically spent half an hour clearing space for?

My brother called to say around twenty boxes have arrived at Kensington from Hong Kong, and he has moved them downstairs.

Barbara called, she wants you to go to the Mandarin Oriental Hyde Park today and have a look at the two suites they have offered her and choose the superior one. They are both the same price but have different layouts. She said for you to make the choice and confirm it with the concierge, and then email Nancy.

She wants you to remind the concierge that she will be arriving very early, and if they cannot guarantee that her suite will be ready at that time, then they must make another one ready in the interim.

I also took the liberty of making a list of things for you to check in her room.

1. Fruit bowl
2. Champagne on ice
3. Sunday newspapers: *The Sunday Times, Mail on Sunday* and *Herald Tribune.*
4. Diet Pepsi not Coke in the mini bar.
5. TV programmed to CNN.
6. Armani suit pressed and hanging in the wardrobe.

She specified points 3 and 6, the others I added myself.

Tania Cutter PA

The Nail Bar Ltd

From: **Rebecca Harris 30.09.11 14:48**
To: Tania Cutter
Subject: Re: the hand/Barbara – requirements

Tania,

Is there any chance you could go over to the Mandarin and sort all that out for me? My day is out of control busy.

Many thanks. Rebecca

From: **Tania Cutter 30.09.11 14:50**
To: Rebecca Harris
Subject: Re: the hand/Barbara - requirements

Rebecca,

Naturally I would be the first to volunteer to help, but unfortunately I am completely backed up here. Why don't you ask Felicity? She has no one to interview so is probably quite free. Your sister called while you were out.

Tania Cutter PA

The Nail Bar Ltd

From: **Rebecca Harris 30.09.11 14:51**
To: Tania Cutter
Subject: Re: the hand/Barbara – requirements

I'm sorry you're so busy you can't help with the Mandarin.

I'm afraid the Hand can't be moved. Please could you put the furniture in the meeting room back to its right place.

From: **Rebecca Harris 30.09.11 14:52**
To: Felicity Jones
Subject: recruitment

Fi, I'm having a horrible day, what are those CVs from the agency looking like?

From: **Felicity Jones 30.09.11 14:55**
To: Rebecca Harris
Subject: Re: recruitment

Um, not great. There is one for the management position, girl called Margaret who has managed a branch of Bagel Mania in Kensal Rise for the last three years but is keen to get into the beauty industry. She lists her skills as, "well organized, hard working and good with clients," her hobbies are "camping" and "chatting with friend" – can that be classified as a hobby? Then the bit that threw me slightly is at the bottom of her CV where she has added a footnote saying: "If I won the Lottery I would give all the money to help promote World Peace" – how completely ridiculous is that? I'm sorry, but not only is it a blatant lie but she's cribbed it straight off a Miss World pageant. I'm certainly not buying it and I find it annoying that she thinks we would be impressed.

My personal feeling is that Margaret should stay at Bagel Mania.

The second one, Tarla, is 19 years old and fresh from beauty school, so she knows nothing but sounds enthusiastic to learn. Her hobbies are harmless enough: she likes to walk her dog and she collects scratch n' sniff stickers. The problem is, we would have to spend the first month training her up, and if she still didn't catch on then once again we have blown the deadline for the refund.

Anyway, they are both coming in for an interview shortly so I will save final judgment until then.

From: **Rebecca Harris 30.09.11 14:57**
To: Felicity Jones
Subject: Re: recruitment

Fi, I have to say, I am not so against the "World Peace" statement, and in our current situation I don't think we can afford to be so picky. Let's see how they are in person.

From: **Clara Harris 30.09.11 14:59**
To: Rebecca Harris
Subject: oh dear

Hi Bex, I'm afraid I have some not so good news. Johnny called me earlier because he thought you should know that Charles is taking Carmen away for the weekend, fishing in Scotland. I'm sorry to have to tell you this but he is obviously playing several women at the same time and unfortunately you are one of them. I know this is a blow for you and I wish I could say something to make you feel better. I tried to call earlier because I thought it would be better to tell you on the phone, but you were out.

He's not worth your tears, so try to be strong about this.

Lots of love, Clara

From: **Rebecca Harris 30.09.11 15:00**
To: Clara Harris
Subject: Carmen?

CLARA, ARE WE TALKING ABOUT CARMEN AS IN OLLY'S EX???!!

From: **Clara Harris 30.09.11 15:03**
To: Rebecca Harris
Subject: Re: Carmen?

I'm afraid so. Apparently she took up Charles's offer to come to that party he was going to after Mum's birthday. She dropped Olly at the airport and went straight there.

Johnny has heard them talking on the phone quite a lot, but he didn't want to say anything to you because he wasn't sure. He told me about his suspicions, which is why I've been pretty skeptical about Charles.

I know this is hard for you to hear, but it's important you realize that Charles is a player and a waste of space and the sooner you move on, the better.

From: **Rebecca Harris 30.09.11 15:06**
To: Clara Harris
Subject: oh no

Oh my god, this can't be happening, how can he be with Carmen? How could he have lied to me so blatantly and made me believe that he was crazy about me? Why would anyone do something like that? Clara, I feel such a fool. I don't understand this at all. I have to go. I can't deal with this now.

From: **Felicity Jones 30.09.11 15:20**
To: Rebecca Harris
Subject: r u alright?

Bex, I just went to get Margaret from Reception – are you ok, you look really upset? Have you been crying in the toilet? If it's about the staff situation, I promise I'm going to sort it out.

From: **Rebecca Harris 30.09.11 15:22**
To: Felicity Jones
Subject: Re: r u alright?

Fi, no it's not the staff situation, it's just a personal matter, but I really don't want to talk about it.

From: **Felicity Jones 30.09.11 15:24**
To: Rebecca Harris
Subject: Re: r u alright?

Oh god, it's hemorrhoids, isn't it? I know exactly how you feel. They're so fucking painful they make you want to scream! About two years ago I had really bad flu, then I got hemorrhoids on top of it and every time I sneezed it was like farting glass. I had to eat All Bran and prunes for a month. I can't stand either of them but they sorted me out. You've got to get onto fibre and stay away from spicy food. Going to talk about World Peace with Margaret.

From: Rebecca Harris   30.09.11   15:30
To: Clara Harris
Subject: what's wrong with me?

Clara, I've done my crying and I feel a bit better. I actually feel more angry than upset now. I also feel pretty stupid. Charles and Carmen are probably laughing their socks off at what an idiot I am. I realize now why we went to the Ivy. In my brief conversation with Carmen at Mum's she told me it was her favourite restaurant. I bet Charles was meant to be taking her and last minute she cancelled so he called me. I'm obviously his reserve shag.

What is wrong with me that I always fall for these bastards? It happens every time and I'm so sick of it. Why aren't there any nice guys interested in me?

From: Clara Harris   30.09.11   15:35
To: Rebecca Harris
Subject: Re: what's wrong with me?

Bex, the nice guys are staring you in the face, but you've never been interested, you've always found the bastards more exciting. Let me tell you, Jason was a bastard and the novelty soon wears off, leaving you completely miserable.

I know I've said this before, but what about someone like Olly? He's good looking, makes you laugh and is obviously crazy about you . . .

From: Rebecca Harris   30.09.11   15:39
To: Clara Harris
Subject: Olly

I would have loved to gone out with Olly, believe me, but that was a long time ago and I've firmly killed that fantasy. Our timing has always been off and even if it hadn't been, I'm pretty sure that anyone he dates will always be a poor substitute for Caris, and I would hate to be that. After Poppy was born I really started to miss Olly and the friendship we had. I started to build up this fantasy that maybe I was in love with him. After a few months, I convinced myself that he might be in love with me too. Late one night I drunk-dialled him in America, ready to declare my love. It was a disaster. He was in the middle of trying to cook dinner for a new girlfriend, attempting to make coq au vin and didn't have a clue how to do it. He ended up putting me on speakerphone and I talked him through the whole thing. As you can imagine, it wasn't quite the moment to suggest he chuck the shallots and bacon bits in the bin, feed the chicken to the dog, down the bottle of cabernet sauvignon, tell the floozie to order a takeaway and get his bum on a plane back to Britain where the love of his life plus her one-year-old would be waiting with open arms.

Anyway, I put it down to some form of delayed post-natal depression, and after about a year I got over it.

We are now better friends than we've ever been. I really love his friendship and I wouldn't want to jeopardize it by getting romantic inclinations again. Besides, Caris is now clean and sober and I think Olly is very keen to see if there's a possibility for the two of them to have some kind of future together. The other day at breakfast he was talking about her and apparently she's really determined to get her singing career back on track. He's off to see her soon and he seems really excited about it. B

From: **Clara Harris 30.09.11 15:42**
To: Rebecca Harris
Subject: Re: Olly

Well, maybe you're right. I didn't know all that and to be honest, I don't know him very well, but he just seems like a cool guy and I like that he always cares about you so much.

From: **Rebecca Harris 30.09.11 15:45**
To: Clara Harris
Subject: Re: Olly

He does care about me, doesn't he? You know, the other day when we had breakfast together, he held my hand to cross the road to make sure I got over safely. He's always doing cool stuff like that. Do you really think he might fancy me?

From: **Clara Harris 30.09.11 15:49**
To: Rebecca Harris
Subject: Re: Olly

I don't know, but I definitely think it's possible. The most important thing is to take a break from men. Get over Charles, focus on the opening party, and then when things have settled down, have a think about what you're really looking for in a guy.

From: **Rebecca Harris 30.09.11 15:53**
To: Clara Harris
Subject: gloomy outlook

Clara, I'm a single mum and I'll be 40 in just under 10 years' time. My prospects simply aren't good. I don't have the luxury of time to get over failed relationships, I have to get straight back out there. If I allow myself time to mourn every guy that dumps me, all the decent blokes in England will be taken. I don't want to be old and alone. I want a soulmate, and most importantly I want a dad for Poppy. Anyway, god knows when I'll get the chance to meet anyone. While Charles and Carmen gallivant around the Scottish Highlands catching trout and making out behind the thistles, I'm going to be slaving away in the nail bar all weekend.

From: **Clara Harris 30.09.11 15:57**
To: Rebecca Harris
Subject: Re: gloomy outlook

You're being a little over-dramatic, don't you think? I've always been envious of how much fun you seem to have. Pull yourself together and remember all the advice you gave me when I caught Jason cheating – and he was my fiancé, for Christ's sake!
Working over the weekend is not such a hardship. I've been doing it for the past month and I'm in the library all this weekend too, so try not to feel too sorry for yourself.
Focus on the next few days, which are going to be really big for you, and then we can work on your love life later.

From: **Rebecca Harris 30.09.11 16:02**
To: Clara Harris
Subject: outlook remains gloomy

I know I should be grateful for having a job, a beautiful daughter, being healthy and all that, but I don't feel like counting my blessings at the moment. I've been two-timed or unofficially dumped by my boyfriend, I'm not quite sure which? Work is killing me and it all just feels so pointless. I've got so many responsibilities and I can't give anything or anyone enough of my time. I never see enough of Poppy, I'm so not on top of my work, I haven't been to the gym in almost a year and guys don't want to date me because I have babysitting issues and that's just way too complicated for them. I think I need to get out of London, take Poppy with me and go live on a beach in somewhere like Goa. Poppy can get her hair plaited and I can pierce my nose and learn how to henna feet, maybe even teach yoga. The only decisions to be made would be things like, shall I go swimming now or after lunch? Or should I have rice or poppadoms with that?

I really need a change, Clara, what should I do?

From: **Clara Harris 30.09.11 16:06**
To: Rebecca Harris
Subject: outlook brightening up?

I'm not sure what the best solution is, but going to live in India sounds a bit extreme. Cheer up, Bex, you're just in a slump. Next week you'll have more time and you can do some fun stuff with Pops and get some exercise, and because you have to work all weekend I'll let you off coming to Covent Garden with me on Monday morning – how's that for sisterly love?

From: **Rebecca Harris 30.09.11 16:08**
To: Clara Harris
Subject: Re: outlook brightening up?

Thanks, C-bel x

From: **Phoebe Combes 30.09.11 16:11**
To: Rebecca Harris
Subject: hemorrhoids

Hi Rebecca, I heard about the hemorrhoids – yeow! I've never had them but I called my Granny. She's brilliant with this kind of thing, and she says that you must have a hot bath and then sit on a pack of frozen peas for at least half an hour, and that should work wonders. When I was 8 years old she made me climb into a cupboard and turn around three times because she said it would get rid of the warts on my knee. Two weeks later the warts were gone, so the peas may well be the way forward.

Anyway, sorry to add to your pain, but Saskia just called and I'm afraid Helen Carmichael's article is in this Sunday's *Mail*. Saskia has seen the proof copy and it's really bad. There is a picture of Suki screaming at Sylvia who is holding a mop and crying, and another pic of the staff all sitting on their manicure tables eating sandwiches with wet towels all over the floor. There is no mention of the flood, so it just comes across that we always look like that. Helen refers to Suki as "aggressive, rude and borderline psychotic" and Sylvia as "a waste of space". The only person who comes across quite well is Felicity, who is described as "mildly competent".

Some potential good news is that Suki is apparently related to Jackie Chan in some way and she has invited him to the party! Apparently he is in town filming a movie – at least I think that's what she said?

From: Rebecca Harris 30.09.11 16:17
To: Phoebe Combes
Subject: Re: more gloom & doom

I didn't think this day could get any worse. I now know how Ebenezer Scrooge felt when the ghost of Christmas Future rocked up. I could handle having no staff, I could handle the building disasters, I could even handle Janine trying to kill people, but this article coming out this Sunday, it's all just too much. Barbara has requested a copy of the Sunday papers to be delivered to her hotel room, including *The Mail*.

I'm trying to get excited about Jackie Chan (my mum is a huge fan), but at the moment I can't see past the inevitable devastation that this article is going to reap.

Rebecca

PS I don't have hemorrhoids, but the way this day is going, I'll probably have them by the end of it.

From: Rebecca Harris 30.09.11 16:20
To: Katherine Lease
Subject: everything's crap

Kat,

Charles is cheating on me with Olly's ex – Carmen. He's not going to Scotland with mates, he's taking Carmen to the Highlands for a romantic weekend. Apparently they've been seeing each other since my Mum's birthday and I've been his bit on the side when Carmen was unavailable. I just didn't see it coming, Kat. I feel like I've been smacked in the teeth. Why would Charles lead me on like that, it seems so unnecessarily cruel? I know he wasn't the love of my life and I know we've only been seeing each other a few weeks, but it doesn't stop it hurting. My self-esteem has been kicked into next week and I feel utterly crap, and it doesn't help that I have to work all weekend.

From: **Katherine Lease 30.09.11 16:24**
To: Rebecca Harris
Subject: Re: everything's crap

Oh Bex,

You poor thing, I can't imagine anything worse than having to work all weekend, what a nightmare.

Charles is such a double-crossing little shit, how dare he do that to you! At least you had a lucky escape from the fishing weekend – what a relief! I'm sorry, but if a bloke I was dating tried to take me to Scotland for a weekend, it would be curtains. Charles is an idiot if he thinks Carmen is going to survive in her five-inch heels hiking across the moors – I give that relationship until Tuesday, max.

Don't spend a second crying over that arrogant son of a bitch, he was never right for you anyway. Get straight back out there and grab the nearest male you can find and shag his brains out. Your self-esteem will bounce straight back, believe me.

From: **Rebecca Harris 30.09.11 16:26**
To: Katherine Lease
Subject: Re: everything's crap

Who's the right guy for me, Kat?

Maybe my right guy is living with some tribe in Papua New Guinea and I'll never meet him because they have spiders the size of your hand there, so I can't possibly go. Plus, knowing my luck, I would be shot by guerillas before exiting the arrival gate and even if I did survive, John, or whatever he was called, would have to call the romance off because his commitment to his research on pygmies would surpass his love for me and even though it would break both our hearts he would assure me it was for the best.

I'm going to die a spinster.

From: **Katherine Lease 30.09.11 16:29**
To: Rebecca Harris
Subject: cheer up!!

That is ridiculous and freakily morbid. Anyway, I have a friend who went scuba diving in Papua New Guinea and she said it was great, so you can always ask the love of your life to step out of the jungle and come and meet you on the coast, where I'm sure the spiders are smaller.

I'm so happy with the green beaded top I bought at lunch, I'll probably wear it for your party. What are you going to wear?

From: **Rebecca Harris 30.09.11 16:30**
To: Katherine Lease
Subject: Re: cheer up!!

Too miserable and too busy to even think about what to wear at the moment.

From: **Katherine Lease 30.09.11 16:31**
To: Rebecca Harris
Subject: it's not that bad

Oh Angel, cheer up, I'm going to go shopping for you. I'll buy you something awesome and you'll be saying "Charles who?" before you know it.

From: **Rebecca Harris 30.09.11 16:32**
To: Katherine Lease
Subject: Re: it's not that bad

I don't know about that, but thank you.

From: **Andrea Moleno 30.09.11 16:34**
To: Rebecca Harris
Subject: Janine again

Rebecca,

I don't know how to tell you this but Janine came in after lunch (she said her baby sitter arrived late) and she saw Karen Johnson sitting at her station. Apparently they used to work together at a beauty salon in Blackheath and hated each other. Janine took one look at Karen and said "get that stinking cow out of my chair". Karen tried to stand her ground at first, but when Janine started to drag the chair towards the door with Karen on it past all the clients, Karen couldn't take the humiliation and burst into tears.

Karen has now gone home saying she will never work for this company while Janine is here, and Janine is sitting smugly back in her place. Luckily no clients felt the need to leave and I even heard one saying to her friend that the Mayfair Nail Bar was the best in town because there was always an exciting drama going on.

I'm so sorry, Rebecca, I know you were relying on me to handle Janine and I have failed, and now we have lost another member of staff. I thought maybe I could ring Karen after everyone has gone, explain that Janine is pretty much on her way out and ask if she will consider coming back when she's gone?
Andrea

From: **Rebecca Harris 30.09.11 16:40**
To: Andrea Moleno
Subject: Re: Janine again

Andrea,
This is not your fault, I know you did everything you could. I'm going to contact my lawyer now and see whether we can get rid of Janine on the back of this incident, and if you could phone Karen that would be great.
Rebecca

From: **Rebecca Harris 30.09.11 16:47**
To: Felicity Jones
Subject: Karen

Fi, we have lost another member of staff. In our attempt to sort out Karen Johnson's B.O. problem we have ended up losing her altogether. Janine turned up out of the blue back at Mayfair, took one look at Karen and called her a "stinking cow", which Karen didn't take very well and promptly left. Apparently Janine and Karen used to work together and were not the best of friends.

I'm going to call Adam Green to see what can be done. Andrea is going to call Karen after work to see if she can persuade her back.

I keep hoping this is all part of one of those hidden camera shows like You've Been Framed or something, and any minute now someone is going to jump out from behind the gold hand with a camera and tell me that this whole week has been a joke. Then my mum and sister and a whole load of school friends whom I haven't seen for years will appear and we'll all laugh and drink champagne and I'll act embarrassed but secretly pleased that I am now a C-list celebrity. If by any chance this is the case, can you tell the TV crew that now might be the moment to reveal themselves, because I'm not sure I can take any more of this.

From: **Felicity Jones 30.09.11 16:44**
To: Rebecca Harris
Subject: Margaret

Bex, keep it together, I have some good news at last – Margaret (aka Miss Bagel Mania) turns out to be employable – just. She is far off being management material but she has completed the Jessica manicure course and will be fine to start as a junior manicurist at Kensington on Monday.

The agency called to say that Tarla has decided to specialize in laser hair removal so there isn't any point her coming to us. If you're not keen on the Phoebe Plan B, then I'm afraid you might have to tell Barbara that we have no manager for Kensington yet, but we are working on it. I'm sure she'll understand.

I'll call Andrea about Karen to see if she would rather I speak with her directly.

From: **Rebecca Harris 30.09.11 16:47**
To: Felicity Jones
Subject: Re: Margaret

I'm certain Barbara will not understand, but that is good news about Margaret.

From: **Bettina Harris 30.09.11 16:51**
To: Rebecca Harris
Subject: fish t..ie

Beccy sweet   heart ii have jus t made a delicious fish t/tie from a recipe in in a bew cookbook I got for my birthday. S   hall I bring it it around tonightand the three of usssssssssssssssss can have dinner/ Mum

Message sent via BlackBerry ®

From: **Rebecca Harris 30.09.11 16:54**
To: Bettina Harris
Subject: fish pie

Thanks, Mum, that would be great and it's just what I need. I have to go and sort some stuff out for my boss at the Mandarin Oriental hotel after work, so you and Poppy start without me. Should be home about 7.15pm. See you soon. B

From: **Barbara Foreman 30.09.11 17:04**
To: Rebecca Harris

298

Subject: please confirm

Rebecca,

The new products from Hong Kong should have arrived today, please confirm.

Did you receive my request list for the Mandarin Oriental from your secretary and have you carried it out?

Leave your UK mobile number for me at Reception and I assume you still have the BlackBerry you charged on company expenses?

I am expecting to meet you and the new manager (Sylvia, is it?) at The Kensington Nail Bar on Sunday morning.

Barbara

From: **Rebecca Harris 30.09.11 17:09**
To: Felicity Jones
Subject: Barbara!

Fi, Barbara needs a name and she needs it now! Are we really going with Phoebe? Barbara is going to think it's very strange as I only recently told her we moved Phoebe from Accounts to PR.

From: **Felicity Jones 30.09.11 17:10**
To: Rebecca Harris
Subject: Re: Barbara!

Hold out a little longer, the day isn't over yet.

From: **Bettina Harris 30.09.11 17:13**
To: Rebecca Harris
Subject: Re: fish pie

Lovely, ss ee you later darling.

Message sent via BlackBerry ®

From: **Oliver Barker 30.09.11 17:14**
To: Rebecca Harris
Subject: Carmen/CB

Bex, I heard from Johnny about Charles and Carmen and I just want to say how sorry I am. I understand that Clara let you know and you were pretty upset. I'm not surprised. I wish there was something I could do to make you feel better.

If it's any consolation, I'm sure Charles really likes you, but one girl has never been enough for him. His arrogance covers up the fact that he's actually quite insecure and needs constant reassurance, which he seems to get from having multiple girlfriends.

Carmen is very like Charles in her insecurity, which I guess is part of the territory that comes with being a model. The reason we broke up is because she was so needy and insanely jealous. She was always panicking that I would leave her, and hated it if I so much as spoke to another girl. I didn't tell you this before, but after your mum's birthday drinks she laid into me about flirting with you and was convinced we were having an affair. I tried to explain that that couldn't have been further from the truth and we have never been more than friends, but she was having none of it. When we got to Heathrow I tried to suggest that we take a break from each other for a while but she got hysterical, so I changed tactic and said we would talk about it when I got back from my trip.

On arrival in Hong Kong there was a voice message on my mobile from Carmen. She was laughing and telling me to go to hell and the relationship was over. She was obviously at a party and I could hear Balford's voice in the background telling her what to say. I was relieved about Carmen, but angry as hell with Charles because I knew you liked him. I'm sorry I didn't tell you all this at the time. I realize now that I should have done.

I know hearing all this doesn't change your immediate situation, but hopefully, later down the line, you'll realize that you're much too good for a bloke like that.

I thought you might want some company this weekend and could probably use a hand with all those boxes you have to unpack, so if you like, I could come along to Kensington tomorrow and help you get your shop organized?

Lots of love, Olly

From: Rebecca Harris 30.09.11 17:19
To: Oliver Barker
Subject: no to tomorrow

Olly, thank you for saying all that about Charles and Carmen, it does help, and if you'd told me earlier I probably wouldn't have listened. I've been an idiot. So many people warned me but I didn't want to hear it.

Your offer to help tomorrow is so kind, but I know you've got the Chelsea match and there's no way you should miss that. I'll be fine.
Bex

From: **Oliver Barker 30.09.11 17:21**
To: Rebecca Harris
Subject: Re: no to tomorrow

So about 9am then? . . . and Bex, I'm intending to listen to the match on the radio while I'm there, so if you were picturing a dramatic scene of you moping around to Nina Simone looking all hard done-by, then you need to think again. Ols

From: **Rebecca Harris 30.09.11 17:27**
To: Oliver Barker
Subject: tomorrow ☺

OK, but can I at least listen to Nina at half time?

From: **Oliver Barker 30.09.11 17:25**
To: Rebecca Harris
Subject: Re: tomorrow ☺

I'll think about it. x

From: **Rebecca Harris 30.09.11 17:30**
To: Clara Harris
Subject: SO over Charles

Clarabelle, I know you're revising, but I just wanted to tell you how amazing Olly is. Johnny told him about Charles and Carmen so he emailed me to see if I was alright. He has now offered to come and help me all day Saturday setting up the nail bar, so that I'm not on my own. He has tickets to a Chelsea match and is a huge fan, but he has given them up to be with me.

Oh Clara, I'm really starting to let myself think about Olly again. I know you probably think that it's a bit soon as I've been all into Charles, but my feelings for Olly have always been there, I've just suppressed them.

I only went out with Paulo to get over Olly and the reason why I've dated so few people is because I always compared them to him and no one came close. There's no question that I'm upset about what happened with Charles, but there's a part of me that's quite relieved. All day today I've been feeling miserable, but it's not so much because of being treated badly by Charles but more because I've been such an idiot, wasting my time being with someone who was so wrong for me.

I've always known that Olly was the type of guy I should be with and I just hoped that someone like him would come into my life at some point. But I'm starting to realize that someone *like* him wouldn't be good enough, I want the *real* thing, I want *him*. I think I've always wanted him. The problem is I really don't think he sees me like that and even if he had started to fancy me I'm sure I've put him off for life by the fact that I went out with Charles, whom he loathes.

From: **Clara Harris 30.09.11 17:41**
To: Rebecca Harris
Subject: cool it, sis!

Bex, I think you need to keep calm about this. If you and Olly are meant to be together then it will happen. I don't think the fact that you went out with Charles is going to tarnish his opinion of you forever, but you may want to give it a bit of time before you begin your full-on assault. As far as Olly's feelings for you go, I can't be sure because as I said before, I don't know him very well, but things like giving up his Chelsea tickets to help you out on a Saturday means he is either a bloody good friend or he fancies the pants off you.

In the meantime, play it cool, sister.

From: **Rebecca Harris 30.09.11 17:46**
To: Clara Harris
Subject: Re: cool it, sis!

You don't understand. Olly thinks I'm a fool for falling for Charles, plus I bit his head off when he tried to warn me. I've abused his friendship and moaned to him constantly about work problems, which not only shows how incompetent I am but also must have been extremely boring for him. I must be an idiot for even thinking that he might be interested in me – when Carmen accused him of flirting with me he told her that she couldn't have got it more wrong – how clear cut is that? The fact that he has offered to help me on Saturday doesn't prove anything – Olly does that sort of thing for friends all the time.

302

Maybe I can find a way of being happy just knowing that I love him, even if he doesn't love me. Well, maybe I can't, but I'm going to be seriously grown-up about it, starting with going home, getting drunk with Mum, eating fish pie and crying about how messed up my life is.

From: **Clara Harris 30.09.11 17:48**
To: Rebecca Harris
Subject: yeah!

That's the spirit! Say hi to Mum for me.

From: **Felicity Jones 30.09.11 17:56**
To: Rebecca Harris
Subject: TIME TO CELEBRATE!

Bex, you're going to love what I am going to tell you . . . I have just got off the phone with Suki who called to tell me that her sister Lin has walked out of Top Tips (on her instruction) along with three other members of staff and they are all coming to work for us at Kensington! Lin will be the manager and the others are two beauty therapists and a manicurist. They had still to sign any contract with Diane Shaker and Top Tips, so they are under no obligation to serve out notice or anything. None of them feel any loyalty because Diane is apparently a nightmare to work for and salaries have not been as promised.

WE NOW HAVE A MANAGER AND SEVEN STAFF AND WE ARE READY TO ROLL!!!!!!!!!!!!

They're all on their way here to sign contracts and be briefed on what is to happen on Tuesday. I'll organize a further briefing sometime on Monday for the whole team – how fucking genius is that!!!!

From: **Rebecca Harris 30.09.11 18:00**
To: Felicity Jones
Subject: Re: TIME TO CELEBRATE!

IT'S ABOUT AS FUCKING GENIUS AS IT COMES. YIPPEEEEEE!!!!! – Talk about the final hour, I just can't believe it! How come Suki made such a radical move all of a sudden? I mean I know she said she owed us, but she has known about our staff shortage for a while and not said anything – what happened?

From: Felicity Jones 30.09.11 18:04
To: Rebecca Harris
Subject: Re: TIME TO CELEBRATE!

Jeremy is what happened. It turns out that you were spot on about Suki having the hots for him. He apparently called her for a chat (this happens about six times a day according to Suki, who is very proud of the fact) and told her how you sounded stressed out with building problems and a dire staff situation. Suki jumped into action immediately, obviously hoping to impress Jeremy with her resourcefulness, and dragged Lin and the other girls she got *in* to Top Tips, *out*, and informed them that they now work for The Nail Bar – simple as that.

From: Rebecca Harris 30.09.11 18:07
To: Felicity Jones
Subject: Re: TIME TO CELEBRATE!

That's incredible.

Until a few moments ago I thought I would do a Peter Cook and burst a stomach ulcer all over the office.

Thank you, thank you, thank you, you're the best. I think we should change your title to Director of Human Resources, you're too good to just be Head of Human Resources. What d'you think?

From: Felicity Jones 30.09.11 18:04
To: Rebecca Harris
Subject: Vice-President

I'm liking it, but thinking I like Vice-President of Human Resources even more!

From: Rebecca Harris 30.09.11 18:07
To: Felicity Jones
Subject: Re: Vice-President

It does have a certain ring to it, I agree, but if we go down that route then I have to be President and that would just be too weird.

From: Felicity Jones 30.09.11 18:10
To: Rebecca Harris
Subject: ok

You've got a point. I'll get some Director name cards made up.

From: Rebecca Harris 30.09.11 18:14

To: Barbara Foreman
Subject: News from the Nail Bar

Dear Barbara,

I'm just finishing up here in the office before heading over to the Mandarin Oriental Hyde Park to make sure (in person) that everything is alright for your arrival.

I do still have my BlackBerry (which I only use for office purposes) with me and I will email Nancy once everything has been confirmed.

All the arrangements and preparations for the party are in order and we have a fantastic team trained up for Kensington.

The new manager is called Lin and she and I will meet you on Sunday at Kensington. Lin is highly qualified and very excited about coming to work with us. She is the sister of Suki, our Marylebone manager, who as you know runs our most profitable nail bar, so we are expecting great things from her. In addition to Lin we have seven staff consisting of three beauty therapists and four manicurists. We also have an additional beauty therapist starting in two weeks' time, so we couldn't be in better shape.

The products from Hong Kong have arrived and I will be setting up everything tomorrow.

Building works are of course completed and an industrial cleaning company is going in tomorrow morning.

All the office staff and managers are prepared for your arrival, and the ones who haven't met you are excited to do so.

I will leave my mobile number at the hotel and looking forward to seeing you on Sunday. Hope you have a good flight.

Rebecca

Monday 3rd October 2011

Kensington Nail Bar Opening Party

From: **Clara Harris 3.10.11 9:04**
To: Rebecca Harris
Subject: party day!

Hi, Bex,

The big day has arrived!

All the flowers are in buckets of water at Kensington. I'm going to do a bit of studying in the library now and then I'll go back there at about 3pm to start arranging.

I can't believe you complain about your builders. One of them was there packing up his stuff when I arrived and he seemed so nice and SO good-looking. He even helped me carry everything in from the car. He also told me he would see me later at the party, so you can't find him that bad if you've invited him to the opening!

The place looks absolutely fantastic. You've done such a great job, although I'm not entirely sure about the gold hand?

How was lunch with Barbara? I ended up having lunch with Johnny and some friends of his at Chelsea Farmers' market.

See you later, Clarabelle

From: **Rebecca Harris 3.10.11 9:10**
To: Clara Harris
Subject: Re: party day!

Clarabelle, I've just had the best weekend of my life. I'm so over the moon, beside myself and freaked out with overwhelming joy, that I just don't know where to start.

On Saturday morning I went to the nail bar. Olly arrived shortly after me wearing a crumpled blue linen shirt and jeans with his hair all rumpled and looking out-of-this-world gorgeous. How does that happen? He's the same guy as he was yesterday, but today I find him heart-stoppingly beautiful? I know that sounds ridiculous after all this time of knowing him, but somehow something had changed. I'm not sure if it was the way he was looking at me as he walked through the door, or the vibe he was giving off, or the combination of the two, but whatever it was, it instantly changed everything.

After dropping a fourth bottle of nail polish, Olly realized I wasn't quite myself and put it down to nerves about tonight. He came over and gave me a hug, telling me that everything was going to be fine and it would all go brilliantly. He was holding me close to his chest and stroking my hair and I knew this was the moment I had waited for my whole life. Ok, that might be an exaggeration, but certainly the moment I had been waiting for all morning. I turned my face up to him, ready for the kiss, but it never came. When I opened my eyes to find out what was causing the delay, I found Olly looking at me with this concerned but slightly amused expression. Oh god, Clara, I can't tell you how much I wanted him to kiss me, but he didn't. Why?

I couldn't concentrate after that, my mind kept racing, desperately trying to work out if I had misread the signals or had just made them up completely and there weren't in fact any signals at all.

We spent the morning unpacking boxes and I kept trying to accidentally make our fingers touch – pathetic, I know, but I couldn't help it.

Around lunchtime we headed off to the pub. We both ordered a cheese ploughman's but I couldn't eat a thing, can you imagine? Olly was amazed as he knows what I can usually pack away.

In the afternoon Olly went downstairs to take the remaining treatment beds out of their boxes and listen to the Chelsea match on the radio. I waited for him to get one of the beds up and then headed down with a cup of tea. I was pretty sure that within the confines of one of those small rooms with a bed right there, something was sure to happen. Unfortunately I didn't see that there was a footbath in the way at the bottom of the stairs and I stepped straight into it. I went flying across the room, landing with my skirt around my neck, bum in the air and tea everywhere. Olly pretended not to notice, but I'm pretty sure I heard him say "nice knicks" as I headed back upstairs, humiliated to the core and ready to abandon all further fantasies.

Just as we were about to leave, Kat texted and suggested we both go and meet her and Marcus for dinner.

After dinner, Olly and I shared a cab. When we got to mine, he told the driver to wait while he walked me to the door. After the humiliation of the footbath I didn't even turn around to see him following me. I knew that he was just being polite and making sure I didn't get mugged. At that stage I probably would have welcomed the attention of a good mugging. I opened my door, turned around to tell him I was safe and he could go, but when I turned, my voice caught in my throat. Olly was right behind me, looking at me with those crinkled-eyes of his, and then he leaned in and kissed me. Yup he really did ☺☺☺. I've never been kissed like that before and no kiss has ever made me feel that way. My whole body was shaking. I didn't want it to end. I could have carried on kissing him forever. I think I actually yelped when he pulled away.

We stood on the doorstep for a while and he held my face in his hands, just looking at me with this beautiful intensity. He kept looking like he was about to say something but couldn't get the words out, or thought he shouldn't let the words. When he turned to leave he seemed slightly annoyed, and then just when he reached the taxi door he looked back and said, "Bex, you're a real heartbreaker". Then he was gone.

What do you think? I spent the whole night lying awake wondering what he meant? Does he mean heartbreaker in a positive way or a negative way? It could be either, couldn't it? Did he walk away because he thinks I'm the kind of girl who deliberately goes around breaking hearts? Or did he just intend to leave then anyway and called me a heartbreaker in the same way you might call someone a knockout?

Or am I wrong both times and it actually means something else?

I'm so excited, but I'm not sure if I should be? I don't know what to do and I have so much to do today, but I can't think straight. I also have nothing to wear tonight.

PS Builder you met was different guy from our normal builders who I kicked off the job on Friday.

PPS Lunch with Barbara was fine except she brought along a major powerhouse lesbian who I think fancied me. I tried to flirt back just to be friendly while appearing professional to Barbara, but I'm not sure how well I pulled it off.

From: **Clara Harris 3.10.11 9:19**
To: Rebecca Harris
Subject: Olly day?? ☺

Wow, Bex, that was practically a novel! If things go wrong with the nail bar you could always try your hand at a bit of chick lit.

I think it's safe to say that Olly likes you, heartbreaker or not. Just be yourself because that's obviously what attracts him to you, and try to stay calm. I know the whole thing is very exciting and I can't quite believe it myself – one minute you're devastated by Charles's two-timing you and the next you're being swept off your feet by Oliver Barker. You're a lucky girl.

I don't think Olly would have kissed you if he wasn't pretty serious about you. Remember, you and Charles haven't even officially split up and as far as he knows you're still pretty cut up about it, so it was a brave move on his part. Johnny and I haven't even got to first base yet, and I'm talking holding hands, so you have sped way past us.

Both of you have a lot to lose if this goes wrong because it would very likely ruin your friendship. I'm sure Olly is aware of that and you should be too, so be careful, but at the same time I think you should definitely get decked out tonight and knock Olly's socks off. Why don't you ask Kat for an outfit? Doesn't she work for Armani?

From: **Rebecca Harris 3.10.11 9:26**
To: Clara Harris
Subject: Re: Olly day (☺??)

You're right, you're right, YIPPEE. He wouldn't kiss me if he didn't really like me, would he? I'm not going to blow this, I promise. I'm going to make sure he knows I am totally over Charles and that all advances on his part will be most welcome, but at the same time not act like a desperate slut – this is definitely going to take some planning. Hopefully, he'll be so impressed by how well tonight goes and how calm and sophisticated I look that he'll fall madly in love with me. We'll immediately begin a very intense relationship, and because we know each other so well we can skip all that shy beginning bit, and very quickly he'll realize that he can't possibly move to Hong Kong because he can't be without me.

This is going to be perfect, I know it is. At last my life is on the right track . . . I'd better get on and start organizing.

From: **Clara Harris 3.10.11 9:34**
To: Rebecca Harris
Subject: steady does it

Easy ,tiger, you may be getting a little ahead of yourself there. As far as I remember Olly has got a pretty serious job. In fact, doesn't he own the company? Don't start going off into fantasy land too quickly. It's extremely unlikely that he's going to drop all his plans for you. I shouldn't think he took the decision to move to Hong Kong lightly, so you can't expect him to immediately do an about-turn.

Of course I can't be sure, but just take it slow, Bex, or you'll only end up hurt and disappointed.

From: **Rebecca Harris 3.10.11 9:38**
To: Clara Harris
Subject: Re: steady does it

Don't worry, everything will be absolutely fine. Anyway, I'm much too happy to think logically.

From: **Barbara Foreman 3.10.11 9:44**
To: Rebecca Harris
Subject: IMPORTANT

Good morning, Rebecca,

I hope I can assume everything is going smoothly this morning with no unexpected dramas?

Unfortunately, I can't say the same at my end as I seem to be short one Armani suit? Once this problem has been resolved I am planning on coming to your office today instead of tomorrow as I have something to discuss which concerns all of you. I will be there around 11am – I seem to remember this is when you have your morning meeting; if not, make it so it is. It is very important that you are all present.

I thought lunch yesterday went well. Even though you were appallingly under-dressed for Daphne's, you managed to make a very good impression on Hilary Shellwood. I'm sure you gathered that Hilary is responsible for the international branding of Nail Corp. She determines which new countries would be suitable for Nail Corp to have a presence in, and which ones we are already in that should be expanded. She is razor sharp, has zero tolerance for bullshit and is very hard to please, so you did well.

Barbara

From: Rebecca Harris 3.10.11 9:50
To: Barbara Foreman
Subject: Re: IMPORTANT

Barbara,

Thank you for lunch yesterday, it was very spoiling and I'm glad to hear I made a good impression on Hilary Shellwood. It may have had something to do with the numerous whisky sours she was putting away!

I'm sorry your suit hasn't arrived. I'll find out what the problem is immediately.

Everything is going well here and we'll expect you at the meeting.

Rebecca

From: Phoebe Combes 3.10.11 9:56
To: Rebecca Harris
Subject: Love that Honeysuckle!

Bex,

I'm at Kensington. Did we get away with it? We must have done. There's no way anyone in their right mind got around to reading about us, not with the sensational story of Honeysuckle Jones giving birth to a black baby all over every decent newspaper in the country. We really couldn't have planned this better! Did you see the look on Pete Jones' face when the doctor handed him the baby that was so obviously not his? What about the one of him smashing up the hospital room? Honeysuckle looked remarkably relaxed, I can only think she knew all along. I thought it was rather mean that she was so obviously loving the publicity and not caring at all that Pete was being utterly humiliated. There's still no word on the real father, although my money is on Vince Trevane, the Olympic pole vaulter. She was all over him at that New Year's Eve party held in Madam Tussaud's last year.

Now that I'm sure we are in the clear with Barbara, I can tell you I was convinced it would be heads on a plate for all of us, especially you. I hardly know Barbara, but I'm pretty sure she would have come down like a ton of bricks on this one, no question.

PHEW!

Having a bit of trouble placing the Hand. We can't get it through the door and it takes up quite a lot of the pavement. Jeremy is here, so he's helping me, but I might have to miss the morning meeting. Is that alright?

From: **Rebecca Harris 3.10.11 10:04**
To: Phoebe Combes
Subject: Re: We're off the hook!!

We are so not in the clear with Barbara. She has just sent me an email saying we're *all* requested to be at the morning meeting as she has something important to discuss with us. There's a teeny weeny chance that this has nothing to do with the flood, but I'm not very optimistic. I can't see otherwise why Barbara would change from coming to tomorrow's meeting, which was the plan, to today's.

I know the whole Honeysuckle thing really worked in our favour as far as the general public goes, but I'm not sure that someone like Barbara would have been so engrossed, especially as she's probably never heard of her.

Try not to be too late for the meeting, I don't want to give her any more reason for thinking we are all incompetent, and she'll want to hear all about the party arrangements. Maybe you can get Jeremy to deal with the Hand – I think it should be on the street, near the door, kind of like a welcoming symbol. After the meeting it might be quite good if you based yourself at Kensington to help co-ordinate all the deliveries while I stay and deal with everything on this end.

From: **Phoebe Combes 3.10.11 10:08**
To: Rebecca Harris
Subject: ouch

Oh gosh, Bex, I am sorry. I shouldn't have said that about heads rolling. Even if Barbara has seen the article, I'm sure she'll weigh that up against all the fantastic work you've been doing and know that you're brilliant at your job.

I should probably warn Fi, though, she might not fare so well.

My clothes for tonight are here at Kensington anyway, and I need to be here to arrange all the party gifts, so that suits me fine. Will tell Jeremy about THE HAND.

Be there as soon as poss.

From: **Rebecca Harris 3.10.11 10:09**
To: Phoebe Combes

Subject: Re: ouch

It's ok, Phoebe, I'm not going to panic and I'll just explain to Barbara that we did the best we could in a very bad situation.

I'll see you in an hour.

From: Rebecca Harris 3.10.11 10:11
To: Katherine Lease
Subject: Love is in the air

Kat, guess what? After you and Marcus left on Saturday night, Olly took me home and kissed me on the doorstep!!!!!!!!! Hee hee, I'm so happy, I want to jump up and down. I can't tell you how different this feels from anything else I've ever experienced. I've never felt so sure of my feelings for someone. I'm crazy about him.

I know it's soon after Charles but I don't care. What Charles and I had was a joke, completely meaningless. This, on the other hand, is the real thing, no question.

My boss is coming to the morning meeting and I'm pretty sure she's going to tear me apart, but I don't care because I'm completely, madly and passionately in love. Actually I'm shitting myself, but I'm trying not to let it blight my euphoria quite yet.

I don't have anything to wear. I've been so busy organizing I haven't had time to think. Can you help me out with something really fab? I want Olly to be blown away. B

PS Can you believe that about Honeysuckle Jones?

Oh, and what happened to Barbara's suit? It isn't at the hotel.

From: Katherine Lease 3.10.11 10:18
To: Rebecca Harris
Subject: Joyfulness!

Not sure what happened with the suit . . . I'll go and check on it in just a sec.

As for you and Olly, its just too fanfuckingtastic for words. You scored big time, girlfriend, best news EVER. We are SO celebrating tonight! Marcus and I were talking about the chemistry between you two after we left you on Saturday. We picked up the flirtation vibe big time.

I can't lend you any Armani clothes as everything has gone out for a major shoot Giorgio is doing at the Tower of London today. Shit, I

314

hope Barbara's suit didn't go with the shoot outfits – that would be a fuck up and a half!

Anyway, you have nothing to fear, Cinderella, you can still go to the ball. Your friend had a retail triumph yesterday. I bought you a super-cool, black, faux-leather corset with cream satin ribbons that will look amazing on you. You can squeeze a blouse under it for the Vivienne Westwood-milkmaid-slut look, or wear it as is for the more obvious bondage queen look. Nearly kept it for myself but it needs tits to hold it up, so it's yours, my friend. Shall I bike it round? Honeysuckle is such a whore, but you have to give the girl credit for a sensational publicity campaign.

See you later, Kit Kat

From: **Rebecca Harris 3.10.11 10:23**
To: Katherine Lease
Subject: THE SUIT

It's vital that you have the suit! Please let me know as soon as possible and then send it over to the Mandarin Oriental Hyde Park. Barbara is waiting for it. This is seriously urgent.

Thank you so much for the corset, it sounds gorgeous and it was so kind of you, but I think I need to be slightly more conservatively dressed. Do you mind if I save it for when we next go pole dancing or to a strip club?

I can probably find something at home, but the question is whether I will even have enough time to go home. I don't know why I didn't think about it before as there's no way I have time to shop today. The other girls in the office all brought their outfits in with them. What was I thinking?

From: **Katherine Lease 3.10.11 10:26**
To: Rebecca Harris
Subject: get shopping

You obviously weren't. Don't worry, you'll find the time. You have to find the time. Bex, please find the time. You need to look good tonight, you really do. It would be way uncool if you were wearing something crap.

I still think the corset would look great, but up to you.

Good luck and see you ce soir.

From: **Rebecca Harris 3.10.11 10:30**
To: Katherine Lease
Subject: Re: get shopping

Will make time, promise. Ahhhhhh the pressure.

From: **Rebecca Harris 3.10.11 10:37**
To: Tania Cutter
Subject: Important

Tania,

Just so you know, Barbara will be here soon. She's coming to the meeting.

Rebecca

From: **Tania Cutter 3.10.11 10:40**
To: Rebecca Harris
Subject: re: Important

Rebecca,

A little more notice would have been appreciated. I know I make it look easy, but preparing the meeting room is not normally something that can be done in 20 minutes. The carpets need to be vacuumed, furniture rearranged, flowers displayed, tea, coffee and biscuits prepared and stationery laid out. Of course, I will be able to get it done *and* have the figures ready, but next time, as I said, I would prefer a little more notice

Phoebe has not shown up for work today and you may not be aware that one of the supplements in *The Mail on Sunday* wrote an appalling article on The Marylebone Nail Bar over the weekend. I do not normally read *The Mail* but I happened to be at a friend's house for Sunday lunch and she had a copy. Everyone else was reading about that ghastly Honeydew Jones story, so I was forced to browse the supplements.

I would imagine that Barbara will have been informed about this article's existence and the nature of its content, and will be in a justifiably bad mood as a result? I have taken the liberty of disposing of all the office copies of the Sunday papers.

Presumably you would like me to take the minutes?

Tania Cutter PA

The Nail Bar Ltd

316

From: **Rebecca Harris 3.10.11 10:43**
To: Tania Cutter
Subject: the article

Tania,

We do not know for sure that Barbara has read the article so let's not make any assumptions yet. I saw her on Sunday and she didn't mention it, so for god's sake don't bring it up unless she does. Phoebe is co-ordinating everything at Kensington so she might be a bit late.

Yes, if you could take the minutes that would be great.

From: **Rebecca Harris 3.10.11 10:45**
To: Felicity Jones
Subject: the meeting

Fi, meeting starts in 15 minutes and Barbara is coming to it. We don't know yet whether she has seen the article but we're bracing ourselves for the worst. Please have all details of new staff on hand in case Barbara wants to know. She may also require an update on staffing in general, so be prepared to speak on that too. It's important that this meeting runs in a professional manner rather than the usual bun fight. Phoebe is running a little late so we'll leave the party briefing until last. I'll open the meeting with an overview of how the company is doing, then pass on to you. Tania will brief us on September's takings, then Phoebe on the party, and then I'll do a brief summary.

I had lunch with Barbara on Sunday and she didn't mention the article, but she said there is something she specifically wants to talk to all of us about today, so I guess that is it. If we can pull off an act of semi-professionalism convincingly, it just might take some of the edge off Barbara's inevitable freak-out.

From: **Felicity Jones 3.10.11 10:49**
To: Rebecca Harris
Subject: we're mincemeat

I'm not looking forward to this at all. If anyone is going to get crapped on it's me, no question, followed closely by you. Suki is another obvious target, but Barbara may think twice before going head to head with a ninja, at least she will if she knows what's good for her, but then again Americans aren't renowned for exercising caution. Hopefully Barbara will realize that the British public will have been completely captivated by the story on Honeysuckle Jones, and consequently our assassination will have gone virtually unread. Can you believe it about Honeysuckle's baby? That really came out of left field. I was completely gob-smacked, weren't you? I always thought Pete Jones was such a loser, but now I actually feel pretty sorry for the guy. I think the father is her ex-personal trainer. He was Nigerian and built like a tank. The two of them always looked like they were doing more than just a few laps of the running track.

Are you wearing a dress tonight or trousers and top? I decided on trousers, but Phoebe and Tania are both wearing dresses.

From: **Rebecca Harris 3.10.11 10:54**
To: Felicity Jones
Subject: hope for the best

You and I are definitely going to have to take the brunt of this, I'm afraid; our seniority dictates that.

I haven't actually got anything to wear yet tonight. I'm going to try and whiz home before the party to get changed.

Phoebe reckons the father is that pole-vaulter, Vince something or other.

From: **Felicity Jones 3.10.11 10:56**
To: Rebecca Harris
Subject: here we go!

Interesting theory, I hadn't thought of him.

I can see Tania jumping up and down. Barbara must be in the building. See you in the meeting room.

From: **Oliver Barker 3.10.11 13:15**
To: Rebecca Harris
Subject: big day

Hi, Bex,

Hope you are staying calm on this big day of yours? Remember you've done brilliantly already and Kensington looks great. Try not to get too stressed out if there are a few last-minute hiccups today – there usually are. More often than not there is very little you can do about it, so hang on in there and enjoy yourself.

Can't wait to see you

Lots of love, Olly

From: **Rebecca Harris 3.10.11 13:19**
To: Oliver Barker
Subject: so far so good

Hi, Ols,

Just came out of a company meeting with Barbara in attendance. We all sat there terrified she was going to mention the article but she didn't. I can't tell you what a massive relief it was. I'm starting to hope that she just might not have read it.

So far everything is going smoothly and I'm feeling quietly confident. The only major drama is that I forgot to bring an outfit to work to wear tonight, but I'm planning to rush home before the party and get something.

Can't wait to see you too. Love, Bex

From: **Felicity Jones 3.10.11 13:26**
To: Rebecca Harris
Subject: wow

Bex, that went brilliantly! You were so impressive and I almost got the giggles when Phoebe started talking in that posh voice – she actually sounded like she knew what she was talking about! D'you think Barbara just might not have read the article, or do you think she was so impressed she decided to let it pass?

Going to Charlie's to get a sandwich, would you like something?

From: **Rebecca Harris 3.10.11 13:29**
To: Felicity Jones
Subject: Re: wow

It did go well, didn't it? I think Barbara hasn't read the article. It's unlikely that if she had she would just let it pass. Fingers crossed, we may have got away with it.

Can I have a BLT and a packet of salt and vinegar. Thanks.

From: **Rebecca Harris 3.10.11 13:37**
To: Clara Harris
Subject: Olly

Clarabelle, I just got an email from Olly and it was really nice, but he didn't mention the kiss or anything about last night Is that a bad sign? He just wanted to wish me luck for tonight. I sent a casual email back and didn't make any reference to last night either, but I'm now feeling worried that maybe it all just meant nothing to him. Oh Clara, here I am practically planning our wedding and Olly probably doesn't even remember that he kissed me!

From: **Clara Harris 3.10.11 13:42**
To: Rebecca Harris
Subject: Re: Olly

He's making next-day-contact, which is definitely a good sign. It means he's not playing games. See how it goes tonight. I feel confident that it will all be fine, but maybe hold off deciding on kids' names just yet.

From: **Jeremy Cutter 3.10.11 13:50**
To: Rebecca Harris
Subject: wine cooling

Hi Rebecca, I'm still at Kensington as there seems to be quite a lot to organize here. Is anyone from your office coming by?
I've put that big gold hand outside the front door and it looks quite cool, sort of bling gone mad.
Your wine has arrived but it isn't cold. The fridge in the kitchen can only hold about two bottles so how are you planning to cool the rest? If you want I can go to Homebase and get a couple of big bins and then go and get a load of ice from Waitrose?
Jeremy
Message sent via BlackBerry ®

From: **Rebecca Harris 3.10.11 13:54**
To: Jeremy Cutter
Subject: Re: wine cooling

Gosh Jeremy, I didn't realize you were still there and I completely forgot about having the wine chilled. If you could go to Homebase that would be fantastic. Phoebe is on her way back now and she has petty cash with her, so she can give you some.
Jeremy, thank you also for talking to Suki about our staff problem. She really came to the rescue and I'm hugely grateful. B

From: **Jeremy Cutter 3.10.11 13:57**
To: Rebecca Harris
Subject: No problem
Message sent via BlackBerry ®

From: **Rebecca Harris 3.10.11 14:07**
To: Suki Leung
Subject: thank you!

Suki, thank you so much for setting us up with staff and a manager for Kensington, you really have been brilliant. I'm looking forward to meeting Lin and the others who'll be arriving at the office soon. I'm sorry I didn't thank you earlier, but as you can imagine it's been very busy here.

See you tonight at the party.

From: **Suki Leung 3.10.11 14:12**
To: Rebecca Harris
Subject: what you wear?

Rebecca, you know Suki always helping, always best manager at Nail Bar. I train Lin myself so she second best manager for you.

You say thank you very late. In my country we not say thank you we just remember who is good to us. I know big boss in town so you be like performing monkey and not remember anything.

Rebecca, I think good idea you wear something sexy to party tonight, not like normal shit you wear in office. You always single all your life because you don't know good dressing. Suki give you this advice free, don't need special thanks.

From: **Felicity Jones 3.10.11 14:16**
To: Rebecca Harris
Subject: let's get them up & running

Bex, I've sent the two new beauty therapists to do a few hours' training with Andrea as Janine has obviously been advised by her lawyer not to come back to work after what happened with Karen. The two manicurists have gone to Westbourne to get some training with Vanessa, and Lin is about to arrive in the office. I'll take her to the meeting room to brief her on everything, then if you want to come in and have a chat in about 45 minutes, that would be great.

Brian is coming to the office sometime soon to drop off my clothes for tonight. Will you ask him to leave them on my chair if I am still in with Lin? Thanks. Fi

From: **Barbara Foreman 3.10.11 14:36**
To: Rebecca Harris
Subject: our staff meeting

Rebecca,

I thought the meeting went well this morning and you seem to be on the right track with the business. I think the Westbourne Nail Bar could do with some attention. It is definitely your weakest link, perhaps a new manager is in order?

Phoebe seems competent and it sounds like she has done an impressive job with the PR for the new nail bar and the party, and Felicity has obviously come through with the staff.

Tania is a bit of an anomaly. I thought she was your secretary but she seems to also be the company accountant, receptionist and various other things? I imagine this is an attempt at cost cutting, but not necessarily a wise one; either employ a new secretary or a new accountant.

The meeting ran longer than I anticipated and as I was running late for a lunch appointment I wasn't able to address you all on a serious matter which was the main reason I came to the meeting. Rebecca, you may well know, or at least have a pretty good idea, of what I am talking about. As it involves all of you and possibly some of your careers, it is important that I get an opportunity to speak to you all again. However, I appreciate that tonight is meant to be fun, and therefore I suggest you find a time for us all to meet again tomorrow, and I would like the manger of the Marylebone nail bar to attend.

The Armani suit has arrived with a completely illegible, hand-written note attached, presumably an apology from your friend for its late arrival?

Barbara

From: **Rebecca Harris 3.10.11 14:44**
To: Barbara Foreman
Subject: Re: our staff meeting

Barbara,

I will of course arrange another meeting for tomorrow and let you know the time.

See you tonight.

Rebecca

From: **Rebecca Harris 3.10.11 14:48**
To: Office Staff

Cc: Suki Leung
Subject: YOU magazine

Unfortunately I have some bad news for you all. Having thought that no news was good news when it came to Barbara not mentioning the article in *The Mail on Sunday*, it turns out not to be the case. Quite the opposite in fact. The reason she did not mention it is because she considers it "a serious matter" and didn't feel she had enough time today to go into it properly. I'm not trying to scare you by telling you this because this is not something you should worry about. This is my responsibility and I am the one to shoulder the blame. I'm only telling you because I don't want you to be taken by surprise.

The meeting will be at the usual time of 11am, as this gives Suki a chance to open up her nail bar and be back before the lunchtime rush. Please let me know you can all make it.

Rebecca

From: Tania Cutter 3.10.11 14:51
To: Rebecca Harris
Subject: Re YOU magazine

Rebecca,

I do not see how this has anything to do with me. I was nothing to do with the whole fiasco and I resent being dragged into it. Please could you inform Barbara immediately that I am completely blameless and I was horrified by what took place that day at Marylebone. I have worked extremely hard for this company and I will not take the fall for other people's incompetence. I am happy to sit in on the meeting if minutes are required, but if not, I should prefer to remain at my desk.

Tania Cutter PA

The Nail Bar Ltd.

From: Rebecca Harris 3.10.11 14:54
To: Tania Cutter
Subject: Re: YOU magazine

Tania, we are all aware that you did not cause the flood and you did not get involved in any way with helping out in the situation. You are therefore entirely blameless, so relax. I'm sure that Barbara wants you to attend because you're so brilliant at doing the minutes, and that is all. Rebecca

From: **Tania Cutter 3.10.11 14:57**
To: Rebecca Harris
Subject: taking minutes

Rebecca,

You are being sarcastic and I think it is unkind and uncalled for. I am not stupid and I know that for some reason you and Felicity find my minute-taking a point of amusement. I cannot imagine what is funny about it and can only put it down to your childish sense of humour. Although you mock me I will attend the meeting, because unlike yourselves I am sure Barbara appreciates the importance of making records of events. I have checked my diary and I am free at 11am tomorrow.

Tania Cutter PA

The Nail Bar Ltd

From: **Phoebe Combes 3.10.11 15:00**
To: Rebecca Harris
Subject: waiters

Just got your message. What a monumental bummer, I thought we'd got away with it. Not much we can do about it now, so we might as well just enjoy the party.

There's been a bit of a screw up with the company All Hands on Deck – they're the ones supplying the two wine waiters. They just called to confirm for tomorrow night. I told them that they had got it wrong and the party was tonight, but they insisted we told them 4th October. I asked if they could send someone anyway but apparently all their staff are on jobs. Jeremy had just got back from Homebase and was actually the one who took the call (I was outside trying to stop a granny's border terrier from peeing on the Hand), and when I got back he told me the situation. Anyway, it turns out that Jeremy started out as a waiter at the Savoy hotel and he said he would be happy to help out. He was intending to wear a black shirt and black jeans anyway so he should look the part. I told him I would check with you first, but that I thought it sounded great.

Your sister has just arrived to sort out the flowers

From: **Rebecca Harris 3.10.11 15:06**
To: Phoebe Combes
Subject: Re: waiters

Phoebe, definitely say yes and a huge thank you to Jeremy and tell him we'll pay whatever he suggests.

From: **Felicity Jones 3.10.11 15:10**
To: Rebecca Harris
Subject: is it a hanging offence?

I just came out of the meeting room to get you and check my emails and I saw your one about Barbara. That does not sound good at all!

From: **Rebecca Harris 3.10.11 15:15**
To: Felicity Jones
Subject: Re: is it a hanging offence?

I know it's bad and I really don't know what Barbara is intending to do about it, but it's not your fault, and I'll make sure Barbara knows that. I actually toned it down a bit for the others. Her actual words were "it involves all of you and possibly some of your careers", which is quite heavy.

From: **Felicity Jones 3.10.11 15:20**
To: Rebecca Harris
Subject: It IS a hanging offence

What? She can't be serious? Brian is going to kill me if I lose this job. He had to take out a second mortgage on our house to pay for the earrings he gave me for our anniversary. Of course that was his decision and he could have said no, but I did pressure him a tiny bit. I also have a massive overdraft that he is unaware of and he still thinks that Mum is the one who splashes out on a designer handbag for me every year. What has Phoebe said about this?

From: **Rebecca Harris 3.10.11 15:27**
To: Felicity Jones
Subject: Re: it IS a hanging offence

The only thing we can console ourselves with is that she likes the new nail bar. She was very happy with how things went in the meeting this morning and she thought you did a good job with staff recruitment, so don't worry.

I think Phoebe is very much focused on tonight and is planning on worrying about it tomorrow.

Brian dropped off your clothes. I took a peek and they look great.

I'm now going in to see Lin.

From:	**Suki Leung 3.10.11 15:37**
To:	Rebecca Harris
Subject:	why she want me?

Rebecca,

Why Barbara want see me? I not do anything wrong. I not give rat's butt what journalist say, she stupid liar. She say Suki psychotic but I cannot see the future. I just normal, hard working Asian girl. English always try blame poor Asians who just want make living. I not collect social security, I not burden on society, I do honest work, but everyone try to make me their problem.

I come to meeting tomorrow and show Barbara I not borderline maniac like newspaper say.

Suki

From:	**Rebecca Harris 3.10.11 15:40**
To:	Felicity Jones
Subject:	Lin

Fi, Lin seems very nice and not at all like Suki, much more passive and controlled. Her English is worse, though, which might be a bit of a problem, but hopefully quite a lot of that is down to shyness.

I've just had an email from Suki who's ranting and raving about being asked to come to the meeting. She says she's going to show Barbara that she's not the crazy Asian that Helen Carmichael makes her out to be; should make for interesting viewing. Anyway, if it's any consolation, she definitely has more to worry about than you. After all, she's the one in the photo screaming her head off.

From:	**Rebecca Harris 3.10.11 15:46**
To:	Suki Leung
Subject:	don't worry

Suki, I know you're not anything like what Helen Carmichael says and I'm sure Barbara will see that immediately. I have just met your sister, who is great. I will be sure to let Barbara know that it was thanks to you that we got her.

Thank you for your earlier advice on what I should wear tonight. I will definitely try to look better than I do normally.

From: **Tania Cutter 3.10.11 15:50**
To: Rebecca Harris
Subject: parcel

Rebecca,

There is a large package for you here at Reception.

Tania Cutter PA

The Nail Bar Ltd

From: **Rebecca Harris 3.10.11 16:06**
To: Katherine Lease
Subject: Whoooopppeeee!!!!

Kat, you will never guess what just arrived for me by courier . . . a DONNA KAREN, RED HALTER-NECK DRESS!!!!!!!!! It's a present from Olly and it's the most beautiful thing I have ever seen in my life. The card reads: In case you don't get a chance to go home before the party. Olly x

I'm completely blown away. I've got bubbles of excitement bursting everywhere inside me. Kat, I'm so happy I want to go skydiving and bungie jumping and all sorts of things I've never wanted to do before in my life. I'm grinning so much I could get arrested. I feel like Julia Roberts in Pretty Woman without the hooker part. I keep waiting for whoever it is who sings "It must have been love" to start singing, and Olly to come cruising round the corner in a limo with a rose in his hand.

I can wait for him, Kat, I know I can. He said he wouldn't be in Hong Kong for more than two years. I can wait two years – I can wait five!

Blissful Bex

From: **Katherine Lease 3.10.11 16:11**
To: Rebecca Harris
Subject: Re: Whoooopppeeee!!!!

Darling Blissful one, that is so cheesy I need crackers. Not the waiting bit, that was very cute – unrealistic but cute. It was the Pretty Woman bit that was just too much.

You lucky sod, I know the dress you're talking about. Lindsay Lohan wore it at Donna Karen's new store opening last month. It's amazing, and you will look incredible in it. Olly is obviously pretty (woman) serious about you, girl!

Gotta run, things are a bit mad here today.

Very excited about tonight. Kat

From: **Rebecca Harris 3.10.11 16:19**
To: Phoebe Combes
Subject: Clara

Is my sister around? I want to speak to her. I've tried the phone a couple of times but it's always engaged and she's not answering her mobile. Can you tell her to call me? Thanks,

From: **Felicity Jones 3.10.11 16:23**
To: Rebecca Harris
Subject: ?????????????

DID I JUST SEE YOU WALK PAST HOLDING THE NEW DONNA KAREN HALTER-NECK DRESS IN YOUR HAND?

From: **Rebecca Harris 3.10.11 16:25**
To: Felicity Jones
Subject: Re: ?????????????

YES YOU DID ☺

From: **Felicity Jones 3.10.11 16:28**
To: Rebecca Harris
Subject: Re: ?????????????

Holy Cow, you lucky thing, how did you get your mitts on that? I'm going to look like a right tramp next to you. What time are you heading over to Kensington? I thought I might go in about half an hour? Fi

From: **Phoebe Combes 3.10.11 16:31**
To: Rebecca Harris
Subject: Pink Mango

I'm really sorry you haven't been able to get through on the phone. I'm afraid we are dealing with a pretty big disaster here. The Pink Mango catering truck took Hyde Park corner too quickly and has flipped over. The driver and two waiters on board have been taken to hospital but are apparently not too badly hurt. The canapés on the other hand didn't fare so well, in fact they're all completely ruined.

I know this is a major problem and you're probably already experiencing the beginnings of a massive coronary, but I am doing my best to resolve the situation.

I have been in constant contact with Amanda Brady's secretary, Tessa, at Pink Mango who has been trying her best to see if she can get hold of any more party food for us, but unfortunately this hasn't been possible. She hasn't been able to speak to Amanda because she is at the hospital. According to Tessa (who says it's very hush hush), Amanda has been conducting a secret affair with the waiter who was in the catering van.

However, there is light at the end of the tunnel – your sister overheard the entire conversation and has jumped into action. She has phoned your Mum and the two of them are at Marks & Spencer food hall right now buying loads of mini food. They told me to tell you not to worry, they'll sort it all out. Clara is so nice, she even said she would pick me up a prawn cocktail while she's there as I haven't had a chance to have lunch yet.

The only remaining problem is that Jeremy is now the only waiter.

From: Rebecca Harris 3.10.11 16:39
To: Phoebe Combes
Subject: Re: Pink Mango

WHAAAAAAAAT???!!!!!!!!!! You can't be serious? This simply cannot be possible. No catering truck has ever crashed en route to an event, not even in the movies. How can it have happened to us? We can't have M&S food, everybody will know and it will all be cold and Barbara will freak. Oh my god, I'm going to die.

I'm going to get hold of Amanda. I'll go to the hospital if I have to.

From: Rebecca Harris 3.10.11 16:43
To: Bettina Harris
Subject: thanks but no!

Mum,

I hear you're in M&S food hall getting food for the party with Clara. I know you're trying to help, but I don't think we can serve up cold mini sausages and quiches on tinfoil trays to 200 guests who are arriving in 1hr.15mins. I'm going to go back to the catering company and demand that they sort us out.

Thank you both for trying to help out. Beccy

From: **Rebecca Harris 3.10.11 16:47**
To: Amanda Brady
Subject: Re: Pink Mango

Amanda, I know you're at the hospital with your staff and I really hope they're ok, but could you possibly give me a call? You may not realize this but all the canapés got ruined in the crash. Of course this tragedy pales in comparison to your people being injured, but it still leaves me with a major problem.

I'll wait to hear from you. Rebecca Harris

From: **Bettina Harris 3.10.11 16:52**
To: Rebecca Harris
Subject: it's gonna be OK

Ddarling, all under control,, Clara and I have chosen a wondergful selection of delicious little eats that ii am sure..oh hold on clara wants to use the blackcurrant.

Bex (sorry, Mum was taking all day with that), listen I know this isn't ideal, but we have done quite well. We've chosen the less obviously "M&S" variety of party food so people won't know. Mum's going to take home now all the ones that need to be heated up and then bring them directly to Kensington as soon as they're ready. I'm going to stop by my friend Lucy's house who has a homewear addiction problem and borrow loads of her serving plates. I'll then join Mum at the nail bar and plate everything nicely with all the spare peonies. Promise it will work, Bex, don't panic.

Get to Kensington ASAP, need all the help I can get.

Gotta go, Clara

Message sent via BlackBerry ®

From: **Rebecca Harris 3.10.11 16:58**
To: Bettina Harris
Subject: Re: it's gonna be OK

Clara, OMG, that might actually work. Can't thank you guys enough, you're amazing. Pray Barbara doesn't catch on.

I'll head to Kensington in a few minutes. Bex

From: **Rebecca Harris 3.10.11 17:04**
To: Felicity Jones
Subject: CRISIS

Fi, what ever you're doing stop and focus, we are having a crisis.

The Pink Mango truck has crashed and all the canapés are history. My mum and sister have gone to M&S to buy mini food to serve instead, and you and I are needed to go and help put it out on plates. The two waiters that were on board the catering truck are in hospital, which leaves Jeremy as our sole waiter for the evening.

Do you have any suggestions that might help this horrendous situation?

From: **Felicity Jones 3.10.11 17:09**
To: Rebecca Harris
Subject: Re: CRISIS

Oh shit, I was about to go and pluck my eyebrows, but don't worry, it can wait. Firstly, M&S food is excellent, we had it at our engagement party and everybody ate loads, so we don't need to worry about that. Secondly, Barbara will be none the wiser as there is no M&S in America as far as I know. Thirdly, Jeremy will not be the only waiter as we have Amy and Tina from Westbourne, remember? I will also call Brian and tell him he has to help out. He used to work at Café Rouge before I met him and he's always showing me how he can do that plate-stacking thing, so now he can put it to good use. Finally, we have saved ourselves a fortune by not using professional caterers; in fact I think this may all turn out to be a blessing.

Ready to leave when you are. Fi

From: **Rebecca Harris 3.10.11 17:12**
To: Felicity Jones
Subject: Re: CRISIS

Fi, are you high or something?

Meet you at Reception in 2 minutes.

Tuesday 4th October 2011

From: **Diane Shaker 4.10.11 9:03**
To: Rebecca Harris
Subject: Staff Poaching

Ms Harris,

As you are aware, I am the owner of a new nail bar establishment off Marylebone High Street called Top Tips Ltd. I am sure you are also aware that as of yesterday I am short one manager and three members of my staff. It has come to my attention that these missing staff have found their way to your nail bars and are now currently employed by you. I do not imagine that you will be surprised to hear I find this situation unacceptable and plan to take immediate action to rectify the matter.

The most simple and obvious route would be to contact my lawyers and have them drag you through the courts for unlawful conduct. However, being a former client of your Marylebone Nail Bar has made me (for some absurdly charitable reason) decide to give you a chance to redeem yourself. If by the end of the day, my staff is returned to me, ready and willing to begin work back at Top Tips, then I will consider letting this matter drop. If not, then I guarantee things will get ugly.

Diane Shaker
Managing Director
Top Tips Ltd

From: **Rebecca Harris 4.10.11 9:07**
To: Diane Shaker
Subject: Re: Staff Poaching

Dear Ms Shaker,

I am aware of who you are and I am aware of Top Tips nail bar. I am also aware that you were the one to not only try to poach my manager in the first place but also steal all our design and concept ideas, something you might not be aware that I am aware of. The fact that you deviously stole our ideas while posing as a client, and then opened up a copycat shop just down the road from us, makes me feel no qualms at all about approaching your staff to come and work for us.

I do not feel remotely threatened by your talk of lawyers, as without signed contracts your staff are under no obligation to serve out any notice with you. I believe my case against you for copying our concept would be far stronger than your case against me.

Rebecca Harris

Managing Director

The Nail Bar Ltd

From: **Rebecca Harris 4.10.11 9:11**
To: Clara Harris
Subject: next bit of the novel!

Clarabelle, you and Mum were fantastic last night. The canapés all looked so professional, truly brilliant. Thank you for saving the day. The flowers also looked beautiful – Barbara actually said she thought Rick could learn a thing or two from you! I think the party went really well. Did you have a good time?

I still can't believe that Charles had the audacity to turn up! I know you were shocked when Olly punched him, but you didn't hear what Charles said to him. I was talking to Olly and Marcus when Charles came up to us and put his arm around my waist. He turned to Olly and said "Hey Ols, let me know if you want me to break in any more of your girlfriends for you, it's always a pleasure". Then he gave me a huge wet kiss on the lips and turned to go – that's when Olly pulled him back and thumped him. I know Charles was horribly drunk but that still doesn't excuse his behaviour. In fact I think Olly was pretty cool, all things considered.

I know you might have guessed this, but Olly came home with me after the party and this time he didn't say goodbye on the doorstep.

Clara, he's been in love with me since he met me. It wasn't Caris, it was me. He was biding his time, convinced that things would just fizzle out with Aeron and me. When this didn't happen as soon as he hoped, he turned to Caris for her opinion on the matter. He thought he would subtly find out if he was the only one who thought Aeron and I weren't an ideal match. Caris immediately understood that Olly's interest wasn't just idle curiosity, and jumped into action to try and get me out of what she also considered a completely unsuitable match, into a far better pairing with her best friend. Caris didn't give a damn that this might not be to her brother's best advantage, she was far more concerned that Olly should be with the love of his life, no matter what the cost. I feel so bad that I never appreciated what Caris was trying to do. Apparently she was the one who kept making up reasons for Aeron to go into Cardiff for the day or sometimes even back to London in the middle of the weekend. I always thought she was trying to get Aeron away from me because she didn't want me in her family.

In the meantime, Olly was trying to get into MIT's very competitive post-graduate degree program for architecture. It was a three-year course and he kept delaying the application in the hopes that we would get together and he could persuade me to come with him. He knew my career was important, but hoped that maybe I could get a job with one of Nail Corp's US-based nail bar operations.

Four months before I fell pregnant, Caris convinced him to stop putting his life on hold and to send off the application form. They hatched a plan that if he got accepted he would tell me that he was in love with me and leave it up to me to decide whether I wanted to drop everything and come with him to America. Caris was wildly excited about the whole idea, especially as she was planning her own little bombshell in the form of her secret wedding to Keith.

The night I called Olly to tell him I was pregnant was the night he was boarding a plane from Tokyo. He had received the acceptance letter from MIT and had called Caris. She was thrilled and told him to get on a plane immediately. My call got through to him on his mobile while he was in the airport lounge waiting to board!

The only reason Olly came down to Aeron's parents' house two weekends later was because he wanted to see me one more time before he left for three years. He nearly told me everything that night we stayed up in the garden. He knew Aeron wouldn't stand by me if I had the baby and he wanted to tell me, but he was worried that I would be devastated and it wouldn't be good for me to be so upset when I was pregnant. In the sober light of the next morning he realized how close he'd come to causing a massive emotional upheaval, so took off to London without staying to say goodbye. A few days later he boarded a plane for Michigan and was gone, leaving me none the wiser.

Clara, I can't bear how much time we've lost and now he's leaving England again. Olly says that he's pretty sure he won't need to be in Hong Kong more than two years and we can easily handle that. He said he'd wait for me forever if he had to and that he will travel back and forth to England regularly.

I love him, I really do. I've found the person I want to grow old with and I'm never going to let him go. Loads of people make long-distance relationships work. Think about our grandparents in the Second World War. They spent years apart without being able to SMS, Skype or anything and they made it work. Anyway, I'm going to focus on the present. Olly's going to delay moving until February so I'm not even going to start worrying 'til at least November, which is a good 27 days away.

From: **Clara Harris 4.10.11 9:20**
To: Rebecca Harris
Subject: Re: next bit of the novel!

Bex, I'm so happy for you. Olly is wonderful and I can't think of anyone I'd rather you were with. You're right not to worry just yet about him moving to Hong Kong. Anything could happen in the next month. I know you guys will find a way to make it work.

I thought the party was great and I'm so glad the food was a success. Very annoyingly I missed the black eye and Charles being thrown out by Jeremy. I love a good bar brawl but I was deep in conversation with a strange-looking Czechoslovakian girl whose name I can't remember – she works for you? Fascinating story about her childhood, you should ask her about it sometime.

Got my first set of exams tomorrow morning – terrified, wish me luck. C

From: **Rebecca Harris 4.10.11 9:23**
To: Clara Harris
Subject: Good luck!

Good luck, good luck and good luck ☺

I think you might be talking about Katya, but that seems strange as she doesn't speak any English?

From: **Clara Harris 4.10.11 9:25**
To: Rebecca Harris
Subject: Katya

Yes, Katya, that's it, the one with all the piercings. I promise you, she speaks perfect English!

From: **Rebecca Harris 4.10.11 9:29**
To: Phoebe Combes
Subject: fantastic job!!

Phoebe, you are a Super Star of the first degree. I cannot believe Kylie Minogue came to our party!!!!! Everyone was blown away and even Barbara looked delighted, an emotion that I believe she is extremely unfamiliar with. I took her for more of a Celine Dion fan, but obviously not. The paparazzi went crazy when she posed beside the Hand for photos, it couldn't have been better. Did you get a chance to speak to her? We had a quick chat and she seemed really normal and nice and she was so enthusiastic about The Nail Bar. I saw her and Jeremy chatting until Suki came over looking like thunder and pulled him away.

All the party bags looked so good, and you were right about people turning up on the night. It was packed.

Thank you for all your hard work.

Don't forget Barbara is coming to the meeting and everyone must be on time. Rebecca

From: **Phoebe Combes 4.10.11 9:34**
To: Rebecca Harris
Subject: Re: fantastic job!!

I thought it went great too, and I really got on well with your sister, she's so lovely. Lucky you to have such a grounded, level-headed sibling, someone you can really confide in and get advice from. I adore my brothers and sisters but they're all slightly crazy, not in a bad way, they're just not entirely sane. But still, it would be nice to have someone in my family who I could really talk to and discuss important stuff with. I'm glad you liked the party bags, and of course I will be on time for the meeting. I really hope it all goes well and Barbara isn't too cross.

From: **Rebecca Harris 4.10.11 9:40**
To: Felicity Jones
Subject: we're all gonna be fine

Fi, thanks so much for all your help last night, everyone seemed to have a great time, don't you think? Please thank Brian for me, he was a brilliant waiter and very professional. I think Barbara really enjoyed herself too, the fact that she stayed so long has to be a good sign, right? I know we are facing a bollocking from her at the meeting today, but the success of last night has got to have worked in our favour, so I am feeling quietly confident.

PS I have it from a very reliable source that Katya is in perfect command of the English language?

From: Felicity Jones 4.10.11 9:44
To: Rebecca Harris
Subject: Re: we're all gonna be fine

Hi, I am so hung over I can hardly see. I think the problem was that the only thing I ate yesterday was that sandwich from Charlie's, and then I went quite aggressively into the champagne as soon as I arrived and was plastered within an hour. When Kylie arrived I thought I was hallucinating. I think we chatted for ages but I can't remember what about, except I invited her to my birthday next month and I'm pretty sure she said she would try to come. Shame Jackie Chan didn't turn up.

Not sure I can cope with Barbara this morning. If she starts shouting I might cry.

Re your PS: Apparently Katya only feels comfortable speaking English when she's drunk – that's what she told me.

From: Rebecca Harris 4.10.11 9:47
To: Felicity Jones
Subject: Katya

That's a bit inconvenient. Does that mean she was pissed when she gave my friend Kat a manicure? Apparently they had quite a good conversation!

From: Felicity Jones 4.10.11 9:48
To: Rebecca Harris
Subject: Re: Katya

I'd better look into that.

From: Rebecca Harris 4.10.11 9:50
To: Felicity Jones
Subject: non compos mentis?

I think that might be wise.

BTW, Jackie Chan did come to the party. It was him you were talking to all evening and him you invited to your birthday, not Kylie. Do you really not remember?

338

From: Felicity Jones 4.10.11 9:51
To: Rebecca Harris
Subject: Re: non compos mentis?

Really? No. Bloody hell, that's weird.

From: Rebecca Harris 4.10.11 9:53
To: Felicity Jones
Subject: Top Tips

By the way, I just got an email from Diane Shaker who is beyond furious at losing her manager and three staff to us. She tried to intimidate me into sending them back but I was having none of it. Quite frankly, I think she has done us more wrong than the other way around, and I told her so.

From: Felicity Jones 4.10.11 9:54
To: Rebecca Harris
Subject: Re: Tops Tips Bitch woman

That doesn't surprise me, she's a total shit. Good for you not backing down. I remember her when she came into Marylebone for a manicure. She was being such a cow to that sweet girl Lily who used to work for us. I was there doing an interview and I couldn't believe the way she was talking to her. Poor Lily was shaking like a leaf and could hardly put the nail polish on. Anyway, hopefully this loss of staff will put an end to Top Tips and destroy twatface Shaker. I thought the party was great too, and you looked amazing in that dress. I met your Oliver and he's gorgeous, definitely one not to let go of.

I saw Barbara at the party laughing away with David Tang, and later chatting with Kylie, so she must have had a good time. I'm still feeling pretty nervypants about the meeting. I know Barbara will come down hard on me as I was the most senior person present and I should have had the staff under control. I went up to her at the party to say hi and she totally blanked me, so I'm pretty sure I'm going to get it today.

Who was the guy being thrown out by Jeremy and some other dude? Friend of yours?

From: Rebecca Harris 4.10.11 9:57
To: Felicity Jones
Subject: no need for nervypants

Was a friend, but isn't anymore.

I think you'll be alright with Barbara – remember, Helen actually wrote reasonably positive things about you. It was Suki who really got a slating and the company as a whole, which obviously comes under my responsibility, so try not to worry.

From:	**Adam Green 4.10.11 10:07**
To:	Rebecca Harris
Subject:	Janine Azame

Dear Ms Harris,

I would like to inform you of the situation to date regarding the case brought against you by your employee Ms Janine Azame:

I have been in regular contact with Stratford, Errington & Bond who are the lawyers representing Ms Azame. After a great deal of mediation they have proposed an out of court settlement in the sum of £4,000.00 to be awarded to Ms Azame. I responded in the negative to this and they have just come back with a second and final proposal of £2,000.00. At this stage you have two options; either we accept these terms and pay out the £2,000.00 or we reject the offer and begin preparations for a court case. It would be in our favour to respond to F, E&B today, if possible.

Yours sincerely,

Adam Green

Bernstein & Associates.

From:	**Oliver Barker 4.10.11 10:13**
To:	Rebecca Harris
Subject:	☺ ☺

Morning, Beautiful Girl.

Can I just say again, what a triumphant evening you pulled off. Your boss has to love you for that. No one would ever guess the chaos and drama that preceded such a well put together event. Well done, Sexy Bexy, you were brilliant . . . the after-party was pretty damn great too. X X

PS Have dinner with me tonight?

From:	**Rebecca Harris 4.10.11 10:15**
To:	Oliver Barker
Subject:	Re: ☺ ☺ ☺

I thought the after-party was pretty damn great too. XX Definitely on for dinner tonight as long as Barbara doesn't kill me in the meeting this morning. Bex xxx

From: **Oliver Barker 4.10.11 10:16**
To: Rebecca Harris
Subject: Re: ☺ ☺ ☺ ☺

She won't, and besides, if she did dare lay a finger on my girl, she'll have signed her own death warrant!

From: **Rebecca Harris 4.10.11 10:17**
To: Oliver Barker
Subject: your girl?

From: **Oliver Barker 4.10.11 10:18**
To: Rebecca Harris
Subject: Yes, you little minx, you are my girl.

From: **Rebecca Harris 4.10.11 10:19**
To: Oliver Barker
Subject: I like being your girl.

From: **Oliver Barker 4.10.11 10:20**
To: Rebecca Harris
Subject: well, thank god for that!

From: **Suki Leung 4.10.11 10:24**
To: Rebecca Harris
Subject: good party

Rebecca, very nice party, food bit shit but that ok, English people not know better. Next time I ask Auntie Po make dim sum and crispy spring roll, much better. Uncle Chan have good time, he see Jeremy throw waste of space ex-boyfriend of Rebecca out door. He say Jeremy could have good film career in Kung Fu movies.
Coming for meeting now. Suki

From: **Rebecca Harris 4.10.11 10:26**
To: Adam Green
Subject: Re: Janine Azame

Dear Adam
Thank you for negotiating the price down on paying off Janine. Although it feels so wrong to be paying her anything, I think in the long run avoiding a court case is probably the best move,

especially as we might well have another one pending from a competitive nail bar. Therefore I agree to the £2,000.00 as long as Janine abides by the terms of her contract that fall under the conditions relating to when a member of staff is fired i.e. She is not allowed near any of The Nail Bar premises and she is not permitted to work for a competitor within a one-mile radius of any of our establishments for a period of six months.

Thank you for all your work on this.

Yours sincerely,

Rebecca Harris

The Nail Bar Ltd

From:	**Adam Green 4.10.11 10:29**
To:	Rebecca Harris
Subject:	Re: Janine Azame

Dear Rebecca,

I will inform S, E&B of your decision which, I might add, I think is the right one, and hopefully this will be the end of the matter.

I am delighted to have been of service to you and please do not hesitate to contact me should you need advice or assistance in the future.

Warm regards,

Adam Green

Bernstein & Associates

From:	**Tania Cutter 4.10.11 10:30**
To:	Rebecca Harris
Cc:	Phoebe Combes; Suki Leung; Felicity Jones
Subject:	Reminder:

Meeting will begin in exactly 30 minutes and Ms Barbara Foreman will be attending. Please be sure to arrive on time.

Tania Cutter PA

The Nail Bar Ltd

From:	**Felicity Jones 4.10.11 10:34**
To:	Rebecca Harris
Subject:	Re: Reminder:

Bex, is that Tania getting ahead of herself again or did you ask her to send that out?

From: **Rebecca Harris 4.10.11 10:36**
To: Felicity Jones
Subject: Re: Reminder:

That is Tania getting way ahead of herself.

From: **Felicity Jones 4.10.11 10:38**
To: Rebecca Harris
Subject: Little Turtle

I think our friend Little Turtle might have got it into her head that as she is the only one completely exempt from Helen Carmichael's slating, she might actually fare quite well in the meeting. By the tone of her email I think she might have over-stretched her imagination a bit and is probably right now practising her acceptance speech for taking over your job.

From: **Rebecca Harris 4.10.11 10:40**
To: Felicity Jones
Subject: Re: Little Turtle

She may not be far off. Barbara was pretty impressed by her report. Oh god, if Tania is promoted in any way we are in serious trouble. I wasn't looking forward to this meeting before but now I'm really dreading it. Bex

From: **Felicity Jones 4.10.11 10:42**
To: Rebecca Harris
Subject: slightly overcast with a chance of chunder

Tell me about it. Just to warn you, I'm going to sit as far away from Barbara as possible, not because I'm a coward but because there is a very strong chance that I might need to puke in the next hour and I tend to be quite projectile when I hurl.

From: **Rebecca Harris 4.10.11 10:43**
To: Felicity Jones
Subject: Re: slightly overcast with a chance of chunder

I look forward to it.

From: **Katherine Lease 4.10.11 10:45**
To: Rebecca Harris
Subject: loved everything

Hi Bex, just staggered to work with head from hell and breath of Beelzebub. Thank god I have absolutely nothing to do today.

Loved the party, loved Kylie, loved your dress, looooved the gold hand, loved everything.

Marcus definitely got a kick out of helping Olly and Jeremy chuck Charles out on the street. I always thought my man was a bit of a pacifist but he's obviously got a bit more Jean-Claude Van-Dame in him than I realized, which is quite exciting.

Please can we go to Burger King for lunch? I know we said never again after last time, but I really think my body needs a Whopper – 12.30?

From: **Rebecca Harris 4.10.11 10:48**
To: Katherine Lease
Subject: BK is a go

Marcus was a real hero last night, please thank him for me.

I'm on for Burger King but make it 1pm as we have a meeting about to start and I'm not sure what time it will end.

I have lots of exciting news to tell you.

From: **Bettina Harris 4.10.11 10:53**
To: Rebecca Harris
Subject: hug success!

Beccy darling   what a super evening,, well done yooou. Thrilling to meeet Jackie Chan in ttthe flesh – what a a dish! Thought the canapés were rather good didn't you???   ? you ....looked absolutely marvelous in that dress, reminded me of the Chris de burg song Lady in Red.

What happened to your special friend Richard, I saw him beeeing thrown out of the   party/? Did the two of you have afight?

Loots oflove

mummy

Message sent via BlackBerry ®

From: **Rebecca Harris 4.10.11 10:57**
To: Bettina Harris
Subject: Re: huge success

Hi Mum, thank you so much for doing all the food last night. It was so great and loads of people commented on it.

I'm running to a meeting but just so you know, my special friend's name is Charles not Richard and he isn't my special friend any more. Actually I have a new *much more* special friend, but I will tell you all about him later. Gotta go. Beccy

From: **Tania Cutter 4.10.11 14:44**
To: Rebecca Harris
Subject: Minutes
Attach: Minutes of Meeting 4th October 2011

Rebecca,

You are obviously not back from lunch yet so I have left a hard copy of the Minutes on your desk.

MINUTES OF MEETING 4.10.2011

Meeting proposed by Ms Barbara Foreman, Vice-President of Nail Corp Nail Bars Ltd to discuss strategy for expansion of The Nail Bar Ltd.

In Attendance:

Ms Barbara Foreman
Ms Rebecca Harris
Ms Suki Leung
Mrs Felicity Jones
Ms Phoebe Combes
Ms Tania Cutter

Minutes taken by Ms Tania Cutter

Time of meeting: 11:06

1. Ms. Foreman congratulates all present for hard work on Kensington opening party. Special mention of celebrity guests and gold hand statue at entrance. Positive comments made on design of new nail bar.

2. Ms Foreman gives overview of Nail Corp's plans for future expansion on an international level. Focus for 2011 will be "Global Brand Awareness" with a particular concentration on the Asian market.

3. Hilary Shellwood, VP of International Branding at Nail Corp will be coming in this week to brief staff on new products being manufactured in China for The Nail Bar UK.

4. Foreman and Shellwood plan to open new nail bars in Asia starting with Hong Kong in 2011.

5. Ms Foreman proposes re-deployment of UK Nail Bar staff:

Tania Cutter:
Promoted to in-house Company Accountant. Responsible for monthly reports, managing cash flow of individual nail bars and monitoring competition. Presentation of bi-annual accounts to be made to Parson Majors, Accountants.
Ms Cutter queries remuneration package. Ms Foreman agrees this can be discussed at a later date. Ms Cutter agrees to assist in recruitment of new PA.

Phoebe Combes:
To be responsible for Public Relations and brand building. Ms Combes to work closely with Mrs Shellwood on all future branding projects.
Ms Jones excuses herself to go to the bathroom as not feeling well.

Suki Leung:
To maintain current position as Manager of Marylebone Nail Bar together with additional responsibilities for all-round training for new and existing managers.
Ms Leung responds in a mixture of Mandarin and English but response deemed positive. Further discussion might be needed.

Ms Jones returns from bathroom.

Rebecca Harris:
Offered opportunity to move to Hong Kong and help set up and run new chain of Asian Nail Bars. Move suggested for March 2011. Ms Foreman generously adds that schooling and childcare would be taken care of by the company
Ms Harris accepts with enthusiastic clapping and jumping up and down.

Felicity Jones:
To replace Rebecca Harris as Director of UK Nail Bars. Responsible for overseeing all aspects of the company. Ms Foreman suggests employing a full-time agency to handle recruitment and a new member of staff for Head of Personnel.
Mrs Jones voices initial shock at promotion but readily accepts new position.

6. No mention of *The Mail on Sunday* article

Meeting concludes 12:17pm
Tania Cutter
Company Accountant
The Nail Bar Ltd

From: **Joe Doyle 4.10.11 14:49**
To: Rebecca Harris
Subject: Testimonial

Rebecca luv, I've just driven past The Kensington Nail Bar and I have to say I gave myself a pat on the back, the place looks really great. That's definitely one that Doyle Brothers can be proud of and I hope you are too. Thought I might even treat the missus to a manicure, she could do with a bit of a buff and polish. A woman shouldn't let herself go just because she's managed to get a ring on her finger. Quite the opposite in fact. Take it from me, married women are what is known in the business as a Diminishing Asset. Their looks fade, they cost their husbands increasing amounts of money, and the chances of them contributing to the pot get less and less as time goes by. If a woman doesn't at least make an effort at slowing down the decline, then naturally any man with a good head for business will look for a new investment which promises greater returns – just a bit of free advice for you.

Rebecca, Doyle Brothers is pitching for a bit of business over in Islington. It's a big job and we're pretty confident that we will get it, but the client wants a reference from our most recent job, which is obviously The Nail Bar. If you could knock out a half pager just stating the obvious facts about the work we did for you i.e. quality craftsmanship, innovative design, efficiency etc etc, that would be fine. There's a bit of a rush on because the deadline is tomorrow, so if you could email it over this afternoon, that would work well.

Warmest regards,

Joe Doyle

From: **Rebecca Harris 4.10.11 15:03**
To: Joe Doyle
Subject: Re: Testimonial

Automated response: Rebecca Harris is out of the office.